THE LUZERN PHOTOGRAPH

William Bayer

This first world edition published 2015
in Great Britain and the USA by
SEVERN HOUSE PUBLISHERS LTD of
19 Cedar Road, Sutton, Surrey, England, SM2 5DA.
Trade paperback edition first published
in Great Britain and the USA 2016 by
SEVERN HOUSE PUBLISHERS LTD.

British Library Cataloguing in Publication Data

Bayer, William author.
  The Luzern photograph
  1. Murder–Investigation–California–Oakland–Fiction.
  2. Andreas-Salome, Lou, 1861–1937–Fiction. 3. Nietzsche,
  Friedrich Wilhelm, 1844–1900–Fiction. 4. Detective and mystery stories.
  I. Title
  813.5'4-dc23

ISBN-13: 978-07278-8546-3 (cased)
ISBN-13: 978-1-84751-654-1 (trade paper)
ISBN-13: 978-1-78010-708-0 (e-book)

All Severn House titles are printed on acid-free paper.

Severn House Publishers support The Forest Stewardship Council™ [FSC™],
the leading international forest certification organisation. All our titles that
are printed on FSC certified paper carry the FSC logo.

Typeset by Palimpsest Book Production Ltd.,
Falkirk, Stirlingshire, Scotland.
Printed and bound in Great Britain by
TJ International, Padstow, Cornwall.

'Without an element of cruelty at the root of every spectacle,
the theater is not possible.'

—Antonin Artaud

THE PHOTOGRAPH

On May 16, 1882, two men in their thirties and a woman barely twenty-one years old entered a photography studio at No. 50, Zurcherstrasse in Luzern, Switzerland. The proprietor-photographer, Jules Bonnet, smiled broadly when the trio informed him that they wished to pose for a photograph in the form of a tableau vivant to commemorate a very happy personal arrangement they had just made.

Bonnet suggested various poses, but the older man, Fritz, insisted on setting up the shot. Fritz rummaged through the studio, assembled various props, improvised others, and finally set the scene in front of a large backdrop, a diorama depicting the mountain known as Die Jungfrau. When all was ready, the three posed and Bonnet, beneath the black hood of his view camera, made the exposure.

The picture that was taken that afternoon would become famous, indeed infamous, and on account of its enigmatic aspects it is still discussed and argued about more than one hundred thirty years after it was taken.

ONE

Vienna, Austria. December 1912. A wintry Sunday afternoon of glittering sunlight and frosty air. Crowds mingle on the Ringstrasse, well-dressed men and women wearing fur hats and long winter coats. Cafés with art-nouveau window treatments line the boulevards. Gray stone statues of famous Austrian composers peer down from pedestals. Groups of soldiers in military greatcoats eye young women walking in pairs. A student violinist plays a virtuoso piece by Paganini, while further down the street a gypsy player garners coins with showy interpretations of Strauss. There is a hum, people talking, laughing, the sound too of the hoof beats of horse-drawn carriages and backfires from passing automobiles.

Two women are briskly walking on the Franzensring, passing the Volksgarten, striding toward the Hofburg Theater. Of different ages, they stroll arm-in-arm like a mother and daughter out for a promenade.

The older woman is fifty-one, stout, draped in a heavy unfashionably cut Russian fur jacket. Her name is Lou Andreas-Salomé, the author of ten books and over fifty articles. She is one of the most famous female intellectuals in Europe on account of her writing, her early romance with the philosopher Friedrich Nietzsche, and her long-term love affair with the poet Rainer Maria Rilke. She is also notorious for her role as femme fatale in a photograph taken when she was twenty-one years old in which she holds a whip while sitting in a cart pulled by a pair of men in harness, Nietzsche and his best friend at the time, Paul Rée. She has recently come to Vienna to study psychoanalysis with Dr Sigmund Freud, after which she intends to return to Göttingen, Germany, to start her own psychoanalytic practice.

Her companion, nearly thirty years younger, is a former child actress and would-be writer named Ellen Delp. She wears a stylish set of furs, has a slim figure, sharp Nordic features, and an exquisite mane of dark blonde hair. Although she and Lou are unrelated, Lou regards her companion with great affection, often introducing her to friends as 'my adopted daughter.'

Suddenly Ellen draws Lou close to whisper in her ear.

'There's that man!'

'What man?'

'The one I told you about. The one who's been following us and hanging around our hotel.'

'Oh, that one! Let's find out what he's up to.'

'You're not going to speak to him!'

Lou nods. 'I've been followed before. I don't like it. If someone has business with me, he must approach in a proper manner.'

Lou turns to eye their follower, a young man, barely into his twenties, who, realizing that the women have become aware of him, stops in his tracks and gapes back.

Lou starts toward him. Ellen tries to restrain her.

'You're not going to—'

'Oh, I am!' Lou confirms.

She gently breaks free, then strides forward with confidence, a stern expression on her face. The grand way she moves signals she's not to be trifled with. She has, her manner implies, dealt with fools like this before. Intimidation, she knows, will usually turn a stalker back. She is not afraid of this man or of anyone . . . and never has been.

Approaching the young man, Lou notices a certain shabbiness about him. Though he appeared presentable at a distance, up close his suit is revealed to be threadbare and his shoes are coming apart at the seams. Still, he is decently groomed, cheeks shaven, a mustache curling slightly upwards at the corners of his mouth. His most prominent features are his eyes, which burn with an intensity Lou has encountered before in strangers who, for reasons of their own, become obsessed with her.

It does not occur to her that the young man is infatuated with young and beautiful Ellen Delp. She knows that it is herself, Lou von Salomé, who is his focus. She is certain of that and she is right.

'You're following us.' She addresses the young man without rancor or warmth. 'I don't like that. Be so kind as to state your business, then be off.'

The young man starts to stutter. 'I kn-kn-know who you are.'

'That's nice. I know who I am too. What do you want?'

'My name—'

'I don't care what your name is. Why are you stalking us?'

'I just—'

'What?' And when he cannot manage to respond: 'I see. You're speechless. My presence so bedazzles you, you've lost the ability to explain yourself.'

'Please. I'm sorry. I apologize.'

'You should be very sorry. A stalker must apologize then desist.'

'I promise—'

'What?'

'I don't mean you any harm. I just wanted to . . . talk a bit. If you'd just allow me to introduce . . .'

She cuts him off. 'Not here and not like this. Following us on the street – that's intolerable. My friend tells me she's seen you hanging around our hotel. If you have something you wish to say to me, I suggest you address me in a proper letter, then leave it at the hotel desk. If I decide to allow further contact, you will be informed. Do you understand?'

'Yes! Perfectly. Thank you. I'm so sorry I . . .'

'If you're truly sorry, be so kind as to put your apology in writing. That's all I have to say to you.' She shows him a tight smile. 'Now go! Disappear!'

The young man nods, then walks off rapidly in the opposite direction.

Lou turns back to Ellen, who has been lingering behind throughout the encounter. 'I doubt we'll be seeing him again.' She rubs her gloved hands together. 'Brrr, it's cold. Shall we go to a café? I could use some coffee, and we could share a warm strudel.'

TWO

I have always been attracted by decadence and perversity, and have made them the subject of my art. Which is why from the moment I walk into this loft I know I want to live here. There are plenty of reasons: great views, high ceilings, skylights, it's filled with brilliant sunlight, and is on the top floor of a wonderful spooky eight-story art-deco office building in downtown Oakland. But it's certain items, left behind by the previous tenant, that clinch the matter for me.

The building manager, a young, lanky, beaming Chinese-American, Clarence Chen, gestures toward these left-behinds.

'They belonged to Ms Chantal Desforges, a professional dominatrix.' He pronounces the word with gusto followed by a quick raising of his eyebrows. Clarence, I can see, is flirting with me . . . a good thing since I desperately want to rent the place.

'Just before Chantal moved out,' he continues, 'she held a tag sale and sold off most of her . . . er . . . equipment. What a hoot! You should have seen the characters that showed up! All these pro dommes with their hunky slaves to help them haul the stuff away. Anyway, what she couldn't sell she left behind.' He gestures at an eight-foot-wide steel grill that converts an alcove into a prison cell. Its barred door hangs precariously. Then he points to a seven-foot-high wooden X-frame embedded in the opposite wall.

'She called that her St. Andrews Cross,' Clarence tells me.

I turn back to the cell. 'What happened to the door?'

'Maybe one of her "prisoners" busted out,' he says, clearly delighted by the notion. He winks at me. 'If you *do* decide to take the place and want me to get rid of this stuff, I'll bring in welders to cut up the grillwork and a plasterer to patch the wall. But I'm thinking, hey, why go to all that trouble if the new tenant wants to keep it?' He shoots me a lascivious grin. 'I can kinda tell by your expression that you like it.'

He's right. I'm much intrigued by the perversity of these artifacts and tantalized by thoughts of what it will feel like to live among them. I tell Clarence I find them amusing and if I take the place he can leave them just as they are.

'All right!' he says, pleased he's read me so well.

He shows me the galley kitchen ('top of the line appliances'), the bedroom ('how 'bout that skylight – you can look up at the stars!'), and the huge walk-in closet.

'You say you're an artist, Ms Berenson?' he asks.

'Performance artist, yes.'

'I like artists. Got several in the building. You guys make good tenants and you're a lot more interesting than the accountants.' He chuckles. 'Chantal was an artist. At least so she said, though I never saw any of her artwork.' He shrugs, turns businesslike. 'This loft'll run you seventeen-fifty including utilities. Think that might work for you?'

I hold my breath. 'Actually I think it will.'

'You're saying you'll take it?'

'I definitely am,' I tell him.

Due to the crummy economy the downtown Oakland office-rental market is in a slump, inspiring smart landlords to convert unoccupied office space into live/work lofts. Having just been awarded a Hollis Grant I'm now in a position to rent one.

The Hollis, called the 'mini-genius' to differentiate it from the more famous and lucrative MacArthur Fellowship, provides a female artist (writer, painter, choreographer, performer) with a living of fifty thousand dollars a year for five years. In return the grantee has no obligation other than to devote herself entirely to creative work. Because Hollises are awarded only to women, there's an expectation that the supported work will reflect a feminist perspective. This didn't perturb me as all my performance pieces are about women. I was thrilled and grateful to receive a Hollis for it promised to be a life-altering event. Over the past few years I've gotten by working various boring day-jobs: hotdog-stand vendor outside the Oakland Coliseum; midnight-to-six a.m. night watchperson for a tire company. The Hollis had now relieved me of that, allowing me time and freedom to work up new pieces and now to lease this magnificent space in which to do so.

It doesn't occur to me to try to bargain with Clarence. I want the loft too much. I also know he's offering a fabulous deal. A penthouse this nice would cost three times more in San Francisco.

Heading back to the creaky elevator, Clarence points to a line of cursive lettering over the archway between the foyer and the main room. He recites it aloud: '"If you have no more happiness to give, give me your pain!" – Lou Andreas-Salomé. Chantal had that inscribed,' he tells me. 'She told me Lou Salomé was a famous woman.'

'True, and it's a famous line. Later Nietzsche set it to music. Quite appropriate for a dominatrix.'

'Hey, you're smart!' Clarence says. 'Chantal was also intellectual.' He gestures toward empty built-in bookcases in the foyer. 'She had a ton of books.' He peers at me. 'Cal grad?' I nod. 'Major?'

'Theater, Dance, and Performance.'

He nods approvingly. 'I majored in Viticulture and Enology at UC Davis. Wanted to work in the wine industry.' He spreads his arms. 'So here I am . . . a building manager.'

On our way down I notice the lighting in the elevator dims then brightens between floors, and that the cab moves slowly then speeds up just before it stops abruptly at the lobby.

As we cross it Clarence points out period details.

'How 'bout those sconces! That brass-work! I love the moldings and the coffered ceiling. They tell me this lobby's worth a fortune.'

As we descend to his basement office, he explains that the Buckley, as the building's called, is owned by his great-aunt Esther, an elderly Chinese lady resident in Vancouver.

'She bought it as an investment property. Put me in charge. Which means I get to decide who lives here.' He glances at me. 'I only rent to people I like.'

'That's a really nice thing to say, Clarence . . . especially as we only just met.'

'Well, I hope you'll come around to accepting that I like you,' he says quietly.

In his office, he prints out a lease. We sign papers, I write out a check, then we shake hands.

'If for any reason you're not happy here, give me a month's notice and I'll release you,' Clarence tells me. 'I did that for Chantal.' He turns solemn. 'She was only here a year. Then, don't know why, she told me she had to leave. It was sudden. Couple days later she held the tag sale and cleared out. Didn't leave a forwarding address. Told me if anyone came around asking for her, I should tell them she left town on account of an illness in the family.' He shakes his head. 'I'll miss her. Beautiful. Elegant. Calm and low-key on the outside, but I had a feeling there was a lot going on underneath. She called the loft her "aerie", placed her business card, EAGLE'S NEST PRODUCTIONS, beside her bell downstairs.' He smiles. 'Guess she did that so her clients would know what was in store for them. She told me she liked to get her claws into people . . . then not let go.'

Eagle's Nest – as I'm pondering that, thinking it sounds a little Hitlerian, Clarence flashes his best smile. 'Anything you need, Tess, give me a call day or night.'

Such a reasonable building manager! I can't believe my luck. Clarence nods sweetly as I inform him I'll start moving in the following day and will take up residence by the end of the week.

It's late April, the rains have stopped, and spring is very much in the air. The sun shines full each day, and there's a fresh aroma here in the East Bay, the smell of wild flowers popping up along the fringes of vacant lots, and of fruit trees in the neighborhoods coming into bloom. It could be my imagination, but it seems that even the troubled street people who hang out in front of the marijuana dispensaries are displaying glimmers of contentment.

The next few days are busy. I purchase new furniture – bed, black-leather couch and two matching chairs, a free-form Noguchi knock-off coffee table with ebony base, and a black-and-white checkerboard area rug.

I have in mind an austere living-room arrangement at one end of the loft, with my desk, mike stand, and video equipment at the other, leaving an expanse of dark parquet flooring upon which to rehearse.

I hire a student moving service to haul my boxes of books, kitchen equipment, files, and costumes from my storage unit in Berkeley. After they dump everything in the middle of the main room, I retrieve my four huge rolled-up Rorschach-style inkblots and take them to an art store to be framed. I made them one night ten years ago in a deserted second-floor life-drawing studio at the San Francisco Art Institute. After my then-art-school-boyfriend and I finished making love on the filthy sitter's couch, we smoked, got high, then he inked my naked body. I lay down on folded-in-half sheets of canvas, assumed various positions, then extricated myself after which we carefully folded over the pristine halves creating symmetrical blots.

On my way in and out of the Buckley, I occasionally run into other tenants as well as office employees who work on the lower floors. I notice a number of Chinese men in business suits all sporting slicked-back black hair. I introduce myself to an elderly woman who tells me she's a jewelry fabricator, and to a couple who own a leather store where they sell garments of their own design. Everyone is friendly.

Twice in the elevator I encounter a guy in paint-spattered coveralls. He looks about forty, has dark eyes, and wears a close-fitting black-wool watch cap from which protrudes a tail of dark hair secured by a soiled ribbon. The second time I see him I ask if he's a painter. When he nods I ask if he'd be available to do some touch-up work in my loft.

He gives me an ironic look. 'I *am* a painter,' he confirms, 'but not that kind.'

'Oh, you're an artist! Sorry!'

He laughs. 'Hey, no problem. I've done plenty of house painting, hung wallpaper, made electrical and plumbing repairs, and I know how to weld. Truth is I'd rather think of myself as a modest Jack-of-all-trades than an Artist-with-a-capital-A.' He peers closely at me. 'New?'

I tell him I've taken over the penthouse.

'Nice,' he says. 'Been up there a couple times. Great views. Knew the lady used to live there. Man, she left quick! Didn't

even bother to say goodbye.' He shrugs as the elevator stops
on five. 'Here's where I get off. Name's Josh.'

'I'm Tess.'

'Welcome to the Buckley, Tess.'

As the elevator door rolls shut, I catch a glimpse of the
words BAD ART SUCKS stenciled on the back of his
coveralls.

On Wednesday morning I head over to Berkeley to see Dr
Maude for my regular weekly psychotherapy session. Today I
need more than therapy, I need some serious counseling. It's
getting time to tell my soon-to-be-ex boyfriend that I've rented
the Oakland studio not just as a rehearsal space but as my new
home. Although we've more or less agreed to separate, he
doesn't know my departure is imminent. Dreading his reaction,
I've postponed giving him the news. I'm hoping Dr Maude
will advise me on how to handle what I fear will be a nasty
confrontation.

Maude Jacobs sees her patients in a second-floor suite above
a crafts gallery on San Pablo just two blocks from the martial-
arts academy where I take kickboxing class. I like my
Wednesday morning routine: expunging demons then exuding
sweat, a cerebral hour with my shrink followed by an hour of
vigorous cardio at the gym.

Her office isn't one of those sleek sterile environments
inhabited by movie shrinks. The walls of her therapy room
are crowded with stuff – 60s era rock-concert posters, drawings by her grandchildren, Mexican masks. Impossible to peer
around without one's eyes falling upon some outré object to
which one can free associate. She's told me these artifacts
make her feel at home and that her hero, Freud, had a collection of antiquities displayed on his desk and shelves. A short
plump woman with a direct manner, Dr Maude presents herself
as a former hippie turned neo-Freudian psychoanalyst. It's rare
to find a Freudian in Berkeley. The town's overrun with
Jungians. But when I chose her I wasn't concerned about her
method. It was her earthiness and warmth that drew me.

'So Jerry doesn't know you're about to move out?' she asks.
As always her tone is sympathetic. She sits back in her worn

leather recliner, soft hazel eyes focused on mine. Her neat gray-streaked pageboy speaks of a lack of personal vanity, as do the casual dresses she wears, garments which, if commented upon, she'll dismiss as 'just some schmatte I threw on.'

'Oh, he knows I want to leave,' I tell her. 'Brings it up all the time. But I don't think he believes I'll go through with it.'

'Pretty obtuse since he knows you leased the loft.'

'For all his brilliance, Jerry can be pretty obtuse at times.'

'Tell me, if you can, what you particularly dislike about him?'

I pause to consider. 'I think it's his spitefulness,' I say finally. 'His mean-spirited irony. That British manner he picked up when he got his doctorate at Oxford – debate-club sarcasm, joy in puncturing the other guy's balloon. Sometimes when he talks to me it's like he's peeling a lemon . . . and I'm the lemon. That's what I fucking can't stand!'

Dr Maude smiles. 'I like your anger, Tess. You need to express that when you have things out with him.'

'But, see, I can never win in a confrontation. He's too smart, too verbal. He'll cut me to shreds.'

'A break-up isn't a debate. You win when you leave. He wins if he convinces you to stay.'

I assure her I have every intention of leaving. 'We've stopped loving each other, and I don't enjoy sleeping with him anymore.'

Dr Maude's heard a lot from me about our sex life, the initial attraction, how in the days just after we met we couldn't keep our hands off one another. She's heard plenty too the last few months about the waning of this attraction.

'He's a good-looking guy, but I don't feel attracted anymore. Lately I can't understand how I ever was.'

'Before you were reacting to his looks and love-making. Now you're reacting to his character. Considering the way he speaks to you, seems to me, aside from the bruise to his ego, he'll be relieved you're moving out.' She exhales. 'You know I don't like to give advice, Tess. That isn't what we do here. But today I'll make an exception. I think you should have it out with him, this afternoon if possible. And you should be prepared to move out right afterwards.'

Just the kind of advice I needed. Out on San Pablo I feel

elated. Dr Maude often has that effect on me. If there're times when I question her interpretations, I never doubt her ability to give me a lift. Though she's a fully-trained psychoanalyst, not a life coach, she has a gift for imbuing me with optimism, inspiring me to vanquish my inner demons and take on the world.

Over at San Pablo Martial Arts, I change into gym clothes, jump some rope, shadow-box, then put on gloves and go to work on the heavy bag. I started coming here for the aerobic classes. Friends told me kickboxing was a great way to do cardio. Kicks, knee strikes, and punch combinations make for a terrific workout. But lately watching other women spar, I've gotten interested in developing combat skills. I'm still fairly new at it, not ready yet for full-contact fighting. But sparring invigorates me. I've discovered I enjoy hitting, and, surprisingly, that I don't mind getting hit. Something exciting about the give-and-take, striving to outmaneuver an opponent. But today I concentrate on punching and kicking the heavy bag. Does the heavy bag represent Jerry? I think today it probably does. Finally, after an hour, drenched in sweat, knees, feet and knuckles sore, I shower, get dressed, and head home to have things out with him.

Unlike most UC professors, Jerry Hunsecker is rich. He inherited a wad from his father, who made a fortune in the Oklahoma oil patch, enabling him to purchase his modernist masterpiece house high up in the Berkeley Hills. Constructed of stone, redwood, and glass, it's well positioned on its steep lot. Ceilings soar, floor tiles gleam, the living room is dominated by a magnificent granite fireplace, and every window is positioned to frame a perfect view.

When Jerry invited me to move in, it didn't occur to me I'd ever want to leave. But entering today, after my session with Dr Maude, I know I won't miss living here. It speaks too clearly of Jerry's cruel elegance.

Better my new loft in downtown Oakland with its leavings of a dominatrix, than this compulsively arranged shrine to Jerry's ego.

I'm surprised at how few possessions I keep here. In an hour I'm ready to leave with three suitcases filled with clothing and four cardboard boxes containing my books and papers. I stack everything by the front door so Jerry will be forewarned when he comes home. Then I lie down on the living-room couch, close my eyes, and wait for his arrival.

I must have dozed off. His voice booms to me from the entrance hall.

'So you're finally leaving me, are you, lover? All packed up, ready to make a clean break.'

I sit up. 'Hey, Jerry!'

'Yeah, hey!' He's looming over me, eyes bristling with hurt, the shock of gray hair that crosses half his forehead hanging loose as he stares down at me nodding scornfully at my loss for words. He's dressed in one of his bespoke sports jackets. His bench-made English shoes glow in the late afternoon light.

'Yes, I'm leaving,' I confirm, wanting not to show weakness as he stands menacingly above me. 'Thought the least you deserved was to hear it from me face to face.'

'Brave girl!' *His annoying irony again!* But then I feel for him, watching him struggle to maintain composure. When he sits down opposite and lowers his eyes, I detect a tremor in his voice. 'I've been expecting this, Tess. Every afternoon, on the drive home, I ask myself, "Is today going to be The Day?" And . . . well . . . seems today The Day has come.'

'It wasn't an easy decision,' I assure him.

'Sure. But better to be the dumper than the dumpee, right?'

Hearing him turn edgy, I stiffen, waiting for the follow-up. It comes at me like a jab, hard and fast.

'Funny how that Hollis grant of yours backfired on me,' he says. 'Guess I should've expected it.'

'I'd have left anyway. Things have gone sour for us.'

'And yet . . .'

'*What?*'

He smiles. 'It's not like I didn't have anything to do with your getting it. The Hollis, I mean.'

'Oh, really! You put in the fix for me – that's what you're hinting?'

He raises his eyebrows. 'I *did* tell certain people, whom I *knew* were Hollis scouts, that they should take a good long look at your work. They did and you got the grant. Of course I'm not trying to take anything away from you. I don't mean to diminish your achievements.'

I want to scream then, point out how maliciously he *is* trying to diminish me, and what this says about his character. I want to tell him how I find him nearly unbearable on account of his put-downs, verbal jabs, uppercuts and care-fully aimed knock-'em-out punches. I want to tell him how little respect I have for his take-down book reviews and sterile academic studies of mid-century French *nouveau roman* writers whom nobody reads or cares about anymore. And how I wish I'd never gotten involved with a man twenty years older because, in truth, he makes me feel old, more so every day . . .

Oh, *yes*! I *could* rant on. And what good would that do? It would only raise my blood pressure. Then he'd scream insults ('silly bitch,' 'stupid cunt' – he's called me those things before), maybe even slap me (the one time he did, I warned him never to do it again; but why would that matter to him now?), we'd have a vicious fight and part on ugly terms, which he'd then use to feed his already withering bitterness. And so I decide to leave things as they are, stay quiet and make the break with as much dignity as I can summon.

Let him try to rattle me, shake my sense of self. He only does that to provoke me into lashing back. Ignore him. Go to the phone and call a taxi, then wait outside until it comes. Then go with just a simple understated goodbye, leaving him alone here in his magnificent house to eke out a bitter tear or two and maybe even a stingy drop of remorse . . .

Having made that decision, that's exactly what I do.

I experience a new clarity of mind over the next several days, savoring my freedom, reveling in feelings of relief.

I'm free, I think. And the best part is that I did it cleanly and at just the right time.

I'm eager now to get back to work, to prove I earned my Hollis on my merits and not because Jerry knew people who knew some other people who maybe recommended me. Understanding that his intent was to sow self-doubt, I vow not to let him define me.

This morning I call my friend and regular accompanist Luis Soeiro, inviting him to come over to discuss the music for the new performance piece I'm working on.

'You'll be my first guest,' I tell him. 'Please bring your cello. I want us to try some things out.'

Later I run into Clarence in the ornate lobby.

'You mentioned welders,' I remind him. 'Can you give me a name?'

'You want to take out the grillwork?'

'No. I like it. I want to have the cell door repaired.'

'There's a guy here in the building can handle that.'

'Josh on five?'

'Oh, you've met him?'

'Briefly. Do you think he'd fix it for me?'

'Don't see why not. He built it.' Clarence grins. 'Chantal commissioned it from him. Least that's what she told me. For all I know he built it for her for free. Seemed like they were pretty tight there for a while.'

Interesting! Josh told me he'd been up to the penthouse 'a couple of times,' which, in view of Clarence's revelation, seems something of an understatement. Josh also shrugged off Chantal's sudden departure without a goodbye as if that were merely a breach of courtesy. All of which suggests a lack of candor. But then I realize that having met by chance in the elevator, we don't owe one another our personal details.

I go to the building register just inside the front door and inspect the names. There's a J. Garske in 5-C.

I leave a note under his door asking if he'd be willing to take on the job.

The title for my new piece is *Recital*, inspired by photos I've seen in *The San Francisco Chronicle* of wealthy women who support the city's many fine cultural organizations. It will be a one-off, performed a single time before an audience of imaginary 'wealthy friends' whom I, in the guise of a certain

Mrs Z, will 'host' at an exclusive 'musical evening' in a grand private home. Luis will play something classical, then I'll stand and address the gathering, praising Luis, thanking everyone for coming, then launching into some improvised remarks that will at first seem coherent, but which will become increasingly self-pitying and disorganized, lurching finally toward a meltdown accompanied by tears. I have lots of ideas about the things I'll say and how I'll say them, ideas too about makeup and clothes. Perhaps the hardest part, I think, will be finding a proper venue.

I set to work making calls, checking in with friends I've neglected because Jerry didn't like them. I inform them of the breakup, tell them I've received a Hollis grant and am working on something new.

'I need a performance space,' I tell them. 'A grand apartment, say, on Russian Hill, or maybe one of those great houses in Sea Cliff. Perhaps you know someone who'll let me use her place for an evening. I can't pay much, but she can invite her friends and have the fun of co-hosting a premiere. Please put out the word . . .'

Luis Soeiro arrives at the loft with his weird electric cello that looks like a weapon, a long thin stick of a keyboard with a scroll at one end and a spike at the other. This is the instrument he usually plays when he accompanies me, but soon as I see it I realize it won't work for *Recital*. If the musicale is to come off, Luis has to play his acoustic cello.

'You'll be portraying a musical prodigy,' I tell him.

In fact he is a former prodigy who can play almost anything: classical, rock, tango, jazz. Tall, slim, with shaved head and finely chiseled features, he shuts his eyes and sways as he bows, projecting intense commitment to whatever he happens to be playing.

I explain the backstory. 'I'll be Mrs Z, this oh-so-grand and very rich sixty-seven-year-old widow who's had considerable work done on her face. She fancies herself an important patroness of the arts. She's invited some friends over for a musical evening to hear her brilliant young cellist protégé whose career she's about to launch.'

'So it's a real recital. You want me to play acoustic so they can hear the wood.'

'Exactly! You'll play music for unaccompanied cello, then I'll take over. When I break down in tears, you'll try to cover up the situation.'

'Like the way they play at an awards ceremony when the actress goes on too long? The orchestra sneaks in with a few notes, and if she doesn't shut up, they play her off the stage.'

'Then when I can't compose myself and run off in shame, you launch into something unnerving and crazed. Mental break-down music.' I hug him. 'I love working with you, Luis. I don't know how much we'll earn with this, but like always we'll split it fifty-fifty.'

Today out of nowhere I receive a call from a freshman-year college dorm-mate, Grace Wei, now wife of a venture capitalist who's made several killings investing in internet startups. She and her husband, Grace tells me, have recently purchased an early twentieth-century mansion in Presidio Heights. She's heard I'm looking for a venue and wonders if her place might work for me.

Listening to her description, I realize it could be perfect. The clincher: a large first-floor ballroom.

'Would you really let me use it?' I ask.

'Of course!' Grace says. 'That's why I called.'

After I describe my project, she tells me she's particularly taken with the ending: Mrs Z breaking down.

'I know just those kind of women,' Grace says. 'We have a box at the opera, so we see them all the time, people who get their pictures in *The Nob Hill Gazette* and their names on the *Chronicle* society page.'

'Yeah, that's the type. Do you suppose they cry much?'

'Not nearly as much as they should.' She pauses. 'I may be able to scrounge some audience members for you from the same social set. They probably won't get it's about them. They look down on Silas and me as *parvenus*, but they'll come if I invite them, pay admission too. They want us to serve on their boards.' She giggles. 'They may not think much of our social credentials, but they like our money just fine.'

We make a date for lunch to catch up, and so I can check out her house.

Tonight Josh Garske shows up with tools and welding equipment to fix my cell door. He's wearing the same tight black-wool knit watch cap. I greet him warmly. His responses are monosyllabic. He gives the loft a quick once-over, but when his eyes fall on my inkblots he walks up to them and studies them a while. Then, having taken them in, he nods, moves to the grill, drops to his knees, and sets to work repairing the broken hinge.

I study him. 'I understand you built the cell.' He nods. 'Clarence told me.'

'Sure, Clarence – he's got his nose in everybody's business.'

'He seems nice.'

'Why shouldn't he be?'

'No reason I guess.' I watch him a while, then ask how he thinks the hinge got broken.

'Way I hear it, it happened at Chantal's tag sale. One of her friends wanted this door to convert a closet into a cell. They tried using a car jack to pry it off. When that didn't work, they left it busted.'

'You weren't here?'

'I was in LA visiting my kids. When I got back, Chantal was gone.'

'What's she like, Josh?' He turns to me, quizzical. 'I figured since you built this for her, you got to know her pretty well.'

'She isn't the sort of person you get to know well. It's hard to figure her out.'

'How do you mean?'

'Curious, aren't you?' I nod. 'Well, for one thing, that name, Chantal Desforges – it's probably made up. So what's her real name?' He shrugs. 'I've no idea, and I doubt any of her friends do either.'

'That's weird.'

'She *is* weird. Had to be considering the stuff she did in here.' He snickers. 'She told me she enjoyed it.'

Ever since I moved in, I've caught myself wondering about

what went on in the loft. I've imagined many things: moans of ecstasy and screams of pain rebounding off the walls; the bite of Chantal's stiletto heels as she paced the floor; the whimpers of her naked slaves as they groveled at her feet; coils of rope and an array of canes and whips laid out neatly/ threateningly on a table; the clink of handcuffs; aromas of leather and sweat. There's something repugnant about these imaginings, and, I find, enticing. I like to play around with deviance. My Weimar piece, in which I tell a convoluted story of prostitute murders interspersed with songs from the Weimar era, made my name as a performance artist. It's this same attraction to perversity and decadence that was behind my decision to keep Chantal's cell and X-frame in the loft.

'I wouldn't think a woman would become a dominatrix unless she enjoyed it.'

Josh finishes his weld and turns off his blowtorch. He faces me.

'According to Chantal, some enjoy it, some don't. And some go into it just for the money.' He pauses. 'Want to know what she's like? She's beautiful, educated, well spoken. She chose professional dominance, refers to herself as a sex worker who doesn't engage in sex. Don't know what she's doing now, but whatever it is I'm sure she's doing fine. Selling off all her stuff, then running off – seems like she decided to shake up her life.'

As I have recently shaken up mine.

'It's fixed,' Josh tells me, standing, then swinging the cell door back and forth to show me he has it working. 'Try it.'

I move to the grill, swing the door.

'Heavy,' I tell him.

'Solid steel.' He turns the key. I hear the bolt click into place. 'Put some guy in there and lock the door – he'll be your prisoner till you set him loose.'

When I hand him a check, he reads my name aloud.

'Tess Berenson,' he says. 'I'd like to catch one of your performances.'

At the loft door, he pauses. 'I wouldn't fool around too much with that cell unless you know what you're doing and who you're doing it with. Getting locked up tends to make people nervous. But if you're into games like that . . . well, enjoy!'

He says it like a waiter setting down platters of food, shows me a little smirk, then turns to the elevator.

Dr Maude is attentive as I recount my breakup scene with Jerry.

'You did the right thing,' she says when I'm finished. 'I think a year ago you'd have blown up at him. You certainly had cause. I'm impressed by the mature way you handled yourself.'

I tell Dr Maude I don't feel the Jerry business really is out of the way. On the contrary, the initial elation I felt has given way the last few days to depression. The breakup now feels like a personal failure, as much my fault as his.

'What's going on with you now, Tess, is you're mourning the relationship. In time you'll come to see it more clearly, and then maybe the two of you can give up your anger and become friends. Meantime, you're doing the right thing throwing yourself into work.'

Dr Maude listens carefully as I describe *Recital*.

'Sounds good,' she says when I'm finished. 'Serious and satirical. But I think you need to take care not to make Mrs Z too mean. Make her three-dimensional. When she breaks down, your audience should feel pity for her, not just contempt for her narcissism and delusional world view. If you do that, you'll really have something, a portrait of a lady in distress with the potential to evoke pity and terror.'

THREE

*V**ienna, Austria. January 1913. A snowy day.* The scene: Café Ronacher, one of the famous *gemütlichkeit* Viennese coffeehouses of the era much favored by members of Freud's circle.

Mid-afternoon, an off-hour. Most of the small marble tables are empty. The vaulted ceiling supports a dusty crystal chandelier. The air carries the mixed aromas of coffee, chocolate, and cigar smoke. Newspapers attached to sticks are neatly aligned on a rack. A battered billiards table fills an alcove. A black and white cat roams the room foraging for scraps.

The intense young man from Lou Salomé's encounter on the Franzenring sits at a table dabbing with a brush at a small piece of cardboard. A portfolio of his watercolors is set against his chair out of sight. He wears the same shabby suit, necktie, and rotting pair of shoes. Whenever he hears the door open, he looks up to see who has entered. Each time, disappointed, he returns to his painting.

Finally Lou shows up. She wears the same heavy Russian fur jacket. As soon as the young man spots her, he covers up his watercolor, rises attentively, then fastens his eyes upon her in a manner she finds disquieting.

He greets her. 'Hello, Frau Salomé. Thank you very much for coming. I am so grateful. And a little surprised, I admit.'

She eyes him warily. 'You didn't think I'd show up?'

'No! I mean – of course I knew you would. It's just . . .'

'You sent me a well-mannered note along with a sincere apology. So here I am. Isn't it better to behave with good manners than to stalk a middle-aged married lady on the street?'

'Again I'm so sorry about that. I . . . I don't know if I can explain it.'

She waves her hand to indicate he needn't bother, then summons the waiter and orders a Viennese coffee. The waiter, who wears a formal black cut-away, bows to her, recognizing her as a regular.

She turns back to the young man. 'Now tell me – what can I do for you?'

'I'd hoped we might chat a bit.'

'You have a topic in mind?'

'Many. So many.'

'You asked for this meeting, so you must state your purpose. Or, as they say in certain circles, place your cards on the table.'

'My cards?' He looks down at his watercolor, then at the portfolio resting by his feet. He's tempted to open it and show her its contents. He takes hold of it, places it on the table so she can see it, then decides to talk with her a while before revealing his artwork.

'You probably don't remember,' he tells her, 'but our eyes met briefly at the Westbahnhof. I believe it was the day you arrived. You had lots of luggage. I wanted to offer help carrying your bags but you'd already engaged a porter. I tried to offer you one of my watercolors.' He taps his portfolio. 'Your friend, the woman you were traveling with – she stopped for a moment to look at them, but you swept right by.'

'I was distracted.'

'Still, I thought I detected a bit of scorn . . .'

'Nonsense! I never behave with scorn, certainly not toward a stranger. We were anxious to get to our hotel and unpack.'

'Do you like it there at the Zita?'

Lou smiles. 'What an odd question. The hotel's pleasant and convenient in that it's close to what brought me here.'

'Which is?'

'I don't think that's any of your business. But since you've been following me around, I suspect you already know.'

'You're studying with the man who writes about sex.'

Lou laughs. 'I suppose that's one way to describe him.' She exhales. 'You asked for this meeting, so please say what's on your mind. I'll try to help you. If I can't I'll tell you that too.'

He nods. 'I hoped we might discuss my paintings. Are you willing to look at them?'

She gestures for him to pass over his portfolio. He hands it to her tentatively. She takes it, looks through it quickly, then hurriedly shuts it and hands it back.

'You want a critique?'

He nods again, this time eagerly. Sensing his vulnerability, she employs a gentler tone.

'One doesn't wish to be unkind. But I believe it's always best to tell the truth.'

He nods, then steadies himself as if expecting a blow.

'I have to tell you honestly that your paintings don't speak to me. They're pretty enough. You make nice pictures of famous buildings on tranquil unpopulated squares and streets. I imagine these sketches might be of interest to tourists. But they don't tell me anything new about these places, or, more important, about the person who painted them.' She stares at him. 'I see you're distressed. I didn't intend to hurt your feelings. Clearly you worked hard on these and they're meaningful to you. If your sketches don't speak to me, they're as likely to speak to someone else. Shall we leave it at that?'

'Whew! I'd like to explain what I was trying—'

'Art should speak for itself. I don't mean to be harsh, but yours is simply not the kind of art I'm able to discuss. I think now I've probably said enough.'

He bows his head. 'I appreciate your taking the time to look.'

Lou is relieved. The young man, well-mannered despite his shabby attire, has taken her criticism better than expected. 'Merely an opinion. I should add that I admire people who make art and have the courage to put it out for judgment.'

He perks up at the word 'courage.' Observing him closely Lou understands that courage is a virtue he values in himself.

'I don't suppose there's anything I could do that would make you like them more?'

She smiles kindly. 'To interest me you'd have to paint in an entirely different way. I doubt you'd be willing to do that.'

'Can you explain?'

'I can. But first I must ask why my opinion matters to you?'

'It matters a great deal, Frau Salomé. I recognized you right away. The moment I saw you at the station I knew who you were. That's why I started following you. Not at first. But then at the Imperial Opera House, I caught your eye . . . or, rather, the eye of your friend. It was the night they performed *Parsifal*.

I was in the standing-room area. You'll find me there often. The two of you passed by on the way to your seats. I believe the other lady recalled seeing me at the station.'

'She didn't mention it.'

Actually there were three of us that night, Lou recalls. Ellen, herself, and the psychiatrist Dr Victor Tausk, another student of Freud, with whom she's struck up a friendship and with whom she expects soon to begin an affair. She notes that the young man has neglected to mention she was part of a three-some. *Did he actually not notice Victor, or is he leaving him out because he thinks he's of no significance?*

The young man continues describing the encounter. 'It was very quick. You passed right by. I decided to wait outside after the performance then follow you. I saw you summon a hansom cab and overheard you give an address. That's how I learned where you were staying.'

Lou stares at him. 'I find this upsetting. No one likes being stalked. It makes one wonder what the stalker has in mind.'

'I assure you I would never wish to bother you in any way.'

'But you see, you have. Which is why I confronted you the other day. Ellen said: "There's that man who's been hanging around our hotel." I didn't like the sound of that, so I went straight up to you to express my annoyance.' Lou pauses. 'I must say, you didn't make a good first impression.'

'You were right to admonish me. I felt terrible.'

'For being found out?'

'For that, and even more for displeasing you. And yet I thank you for your admonishment. I learned a good lesson.' He brightens. 'And so here we are . . .'

Again she peers at him. She wonders whether he really thought she and Ellen wouldn't notice him or whether he hoped they would so they would engage, an engagement he was too shy to initiate.

'Yes,' she tells him, 'you achieved your aim. Now please tell me – what's the point?'

'The p-p-p-point? I wanted to meet you, speak with you, hear your voice.'

Oh dear, he's stuttering again. She exhales. 'I believe you simply wanted my attention. That was your motive, wasn't it?'

'You're famous, Frau Salomé. I've seen people walk toward
you, then turn and stare after you pass. I wager many would
like to sit down with you and chat as we are now.'

She neither acknowledges this, nor laughs it off. She is
becoming bored and a bit uneasy. Time, she thinks, to cut the
encounter short.

'My time here in Vienna is precious,' she tells him. 'I'm
very busy. I spend nearly all my hours reading and studying
with . . . the one who writes about sex, as you so amusingly
put it. Is that really all you've heard about Professor Freud?'

'I've heard he entices people to tell him their dreams. Then
like a fortune-teller he reads their futures.'

'You don't have an inkling, do you? That's fine. Sex is not
everybody's favorite subject.' She peers at the wall clock. 'I
really must be off. There's a seminar starting soon.'

She rises. He rises as well.

'May I accompany you?'

'Certainly not! Stay, have another coffee. I'll take care of
the bill.'

'You're very kind. I feel badly about not paying, but I'm
short of funds these days.' He looks at her longingly. 'Will I
see you again?'

She's amused. 'You haven't had enough of me?'

'There are many matters I'd like to discuss.'

Oh, I'm sure there are. 'I'd be willing to have another
coffee with you in six or seven weeks. We can discuss art
then, and perhaps other topics. But before we meet I insist
you spend some time looking at work by important contemporary artists. I'm thinking particularly of Klimt, Schiele, and
Kokoschka. I have one other condition.' She speaks strictly
to him. 'You are absolutely forbidden to follow me or Ellen
again. I'm going to be very angry if I learn you've been
lingering about with the pathetic beseeching expression you're
wearing now.'

The young man nods meekly. She notes that he responds
well to severity.

'If you meet my two conditions, which I think are reasonable, we shall meet again. You have my permission to wait
six weeks, then write a letter reminding me.'

'Thank you very much. I shall meet your conditions just as you've set them.'

'So, goodbye then.'

She shakes his hand, then strides off.

FOUR

This morning I find a hand-written note thrust under my door: 'You asked what Chantal is like. Come by my studio at 4:00 and I'll show you. J.'

On my way downstairs at the appointed time I ask myself why I bothered to have Josh fix the cell door. Was it because half-hanging there it made the loft look messy? Or was it a way to get to know him and through him to learn more about Chantal? There's something mysterious about him and his relationship with Chantal that arouses my curiosity.

Standing before his door, I can smell the aroma of oil paint. Is Chantal inside waiting to meet me and reveal herself? Or, more likely, has Josh invited me down because he finds me interesting and wants us to be friends?

It's clear, soon as I enter, there isn't anyone else in the studio. I'm confronted by a huge nearly finished canvas in the style of Fernand Léger, not one of his impersonal machine paintings, but a stylized cubistic vision of a woman reflected in a wardrobe mirror.

'Wow!' I say, taking it in. 'I had no idea you did work like this.'

'My bread and butter,' Josh explains. He's wearing his black-wool knit watch cap and is dressed in the same pair of paint-spattered BAD ART SUCKS coveralls. 'This'll be the centerpiece for a new Mission District coffeehouse, Café Léger. Couple more days I'll have it done.'

'It's strong,' I tell him. 'It'll dominate the place.'

It's then for the first time that I see Josh smile, not just grin or smirk.

'Is this what you do – make copies?'

'I think of them as appropriations. I take bits and pieces from famous artists' work, then put them together my own way. So there's no mistaking them for originals, I alter the size and sign my name on the back. I've done a Matisse, a Braque,

couple of Arps, and a series of Fragonards for a downtown
hotel restaurant. Most are for bars and cafés. Word's gotten
around, and now I'm considered a specialist. Word's also
gotten out I won't do Picasso.'

'Is there some reason?'

'I've nothing against the guy. But I think saying that makes
me sound interesting. Like: "There's this guy who'll paint
most anything you need, but he refuses to paint like Picasso."
"Oh, really? What's with him anyway?" If someone asks me
why, I smile enigmatically. Makes people think they're
dealing with a character.'

I laugh. I enjoyed his riff. I'm starting to find him likeable.

'But this isn't your real work?'

He shrugs. 'I do it to get by. Reason I asked you down is
to show you my portrait of Chantal. She didn't commission
it. It was something I did for myself.'

He leads me to the far end of his studio, past the residential
section to an area set aside for storage. On our way I notice
an unmade bed, a galley kitchen with dishes piled in the sink,
and a dining table and chairs that look like discards picked
off the street.

Josh gestures toward a rack filled with canvases. 'Personal
work,' he explains. He pulls a canvas from the rack, then sets
it against the wall facing his windows.

Standing before it, I see a large full-length frontal portrait
of a very beautiful young woman with pale skin and long dark
hair cascading upon her bare shoulders. She's standing in what
appears to be a Roman-style chariot, the kind with two large
wheels and a curved shielded front. The only covering on her
upper body is an elegant black-leather bustier. She engages
the viewer directly with her eyes and with a slight smile curling
her lips. One hand rests on the top of the chariot while the
other holds up a crusader's sword as if poised to strike down
an enemy.

I study her face. There's something familiar about it. It
takes me several moments to realize I know her. We met at
the gym a couple months ago when Kurt, my Muay Thai
trainer, paired us up. After we sparred lightly (she was a far
more advanced student), we had coffee together at the gym

café. She told me she recognized me, had seen my Weimar piece and liked it. She was friendly, exhibiting the inner calm I associate with experienced martial artists. She answered all my questions about what to expect if I decided to get serious about developing combat skills. We talked for maybe half an hour. She called me Tess and I called her Marie, the name Kurt used when he introduced us. When we parted she smiled and said, 'See you around.' We ran into one another a couple more times, always greeting one another with a friendly 'Hey!' Thinking back, I realize I haven't seen her in a while.

Josh, I notice, is peering at me, trying to decipher my reaction to his painting. I tell him I find it compelling.

'I painted her as an archetype,' he explains.

'A face card from the tarot deck?'

'Hey, you get it! She's my Queen of Swords.'

It was a lucky guess. I wasn't trying to impress him. Turning to him, seeing admiration in his eyes, I'm glad I have.

'I'm pretty sure I've met her,' I tell him. 'A woman who looks just like her works out at my gym.'

'You do martial arts?'

'Kickboxing. But the woman I met didn't use the name Chantal.'

He stares at me, amazed. 'Chantal's a kickboxer, a good one. What name did she use?'

'The trainer called her Marie. Does Chantal have a sister?'

He shakes his head. 'Had to be her. Maybe Marie's her real name.' He stands back from the painting. 'You wanted to know what she's like. Now turns out you met her. How weird is that?'

'Very weird,' I concede. 'That sword she's holding – is it real?'

'It's a prop. So is the chariot. She bought them at a movie-studio prop auction. She used to keep the chariot in a corner of the loft.'

'She looks so beautiful. Did you—?'

'Idealize her? A little. She was too impatient to pose live, so I did most of the painting from photos, then had her sit while I finished work on her face. The posture is archetypal, but I wanted to make a recognizable portrait.'

'Did she like it?'

'Very much. Wanted to buy it from me. Maybe later, I told her. I've been working on a tarot series. When I finish the four queens I want to exhibit them together.'

'It's an excellent painting, Josh. It gives me a sense of how you feel about her too.'

'Tell me?'

'Admiration. Awe.'

'True. But probably not the way you're thinking. I wasn't into her scene.'

'She looks so dominant here. And defiant. I remember she looked that way when we sparred. She was like: "Hey, try and hit me, then see what happens when you do." But later when we sat down and talked we were just like, you know, a couple girls eager to be friends.'

'She's low-key. I don't mean in session. When she does a scene, I imagine she's quite a terror. But in normal situations, like the two of us sitting around here sipping wine, she was always soft-spoken, secure about who she was and what she felt and thought. Like I told you the other night, she's complex.'

'It shows in the portrait. Is this your personal style?'

'Does it represent who I am as a painter?' He shrugs. 'I don't know how to answer that. I don't even know what it means.'

Turning back to the portrait, I see something tender in Chantal's face that belies the aggression in her stance. *This is a very interesting woman*, I think.

I thank Josh for inviting me into his studio and for showing me his amazing work.

I can see he's pleased. 'I think we may end up becoming friends,' he says.

'I think I might like that. So tell me, what's with the watch cap? Wear it all the time?'

He grins. 'Think of it as an affectation,' he says.

Back upstairs, I ponder the coincidence that the woman I sparred with at San Pablo Martial Arts was a professional dominatrix and that I now inhabit her 'Eagle's Nest'.

I remember how Kurt put us together. He said: 'Marie, show

Tess how to block. Go easy on her. She's just getting into combat.' She did go easy. She looked fierce but when she hit me it felt more like being slapped than punched. She coached me a little, issued a few no-nonsense instructions. After we broke she said: 'I hope I didn't hurt you.' When I assured her she hadn't she smiled and asked if I had time for coffee.

At the café she flattered me a little, telling me how much she loved my Weimar piece. 'I adore that period,' she said. 'So off-beat and decadent.' When I asked how she got into Muay Thai, she told me she took it up for self-defense. She said most women who take up kickboxing do it for exercise, then a few get interested in learning how to fight. But, she said, after they get hit a few times most give it up. 'Sure, it stings,' she told me, 'and it can really hurt, but if you enjoy fighting you understand that's the deal. The trick is not minding that it hurts.' Then she paused. 'Actually the trick,' she advised, 'is to concentrate on out-pointing your opponent even when that costs you some pain.'

Two weeks after I move into the Buckley, I welcome my second guest, my friend, old acting coach, and mentor, Rex Baxter. He works as a freelance director at theaters around the Bay Area, but the role he wants to discuss tonight will be for his private fantasy fulfillment service, Vertigo Illusions, a company he founded and named for the dreamy late 1950s Hitchcock film set in San Francisco.

He's smiling when I open the door. 'Great lobby downstairs,' he says, 'and that elevator's a trip. Weird the way the light brightens just as it jerks to a stop.'

Curious to see his reaction to my new place, I watch him closely as he checks out the Salomé quote over the archway then peers around. He's wearing his usual uniform, khaki safari jacket, black T-shirt, faded jeans. His trimmed reddish beard and mop hair glow as he passes beneath one of the skylights.

'Wow! Some loft!'

The cell-cage immediately catches his attention. As Rex steps into it, I explain that the previous tenant, a pro domina-trix, left it behind, a woman who, by sheer coincidence, I met and chatted with briefly at kickboxing class.

'So this used to be a dungeon.' Rex ogles me lasciviously through the bars. Then, noticing the St. Andrew's Cross, he strides across the room, backs up against the X, and spread-eagles himself.

'Feels good,' he says. 'Fits with the line over the archway. I could put on an interesting little one-act in here. Maybe even a three-act. To paraphrase Chekhov: If your set includes a cell in Act I, somebody's gotta be locked up in it in Act III.'

Amused, I gesture him to the couch, then pour him a glass of Sauvignon blanc.

He continues to study the cage. 'Very theatrical,' he says. 'Actors and dominatrices – basically we're in the same racket. We deal in illusion, use costumes, props, sets. But of course when we hit we fake it. When they hit they really hit.'

While he continues to peer around, taking in my huge framed inkblots, I consider what he said about dominatrices being performers. Or perhaps, I think, they are a special subset of performance artist. When people find out my mother was a jazz singer, they assume it was her example that got me interested in performing. I nod as if to say, 'Yeah, she was my inspiration,' even though I'm sure the impulse came from my father, a con-man who, convicted of fraud, went to prison when I was ten. I remember as a child being enter-tained by him, the numerous roles he could play at will by just sticking a different hat on his head, then moving in a different way and speaking with a different accent. To my brother and me, Dad with his mutable voice and plastic face was the proverbial Man of a Thousand Faces, a performance artist par excellence.

Rex is commenting on my furnishings. 'I like your décor. Everything black and white. Beautiful and also a little scary. Do you see the world that way?'

'You know better. It's a design choice.'

'Well, I like it – very "Tess Berenson".' He takes a sip of wine. 'I envy you having a grand space like this. I'm still living in my Mission District hovel.'

'You have a perfectly decent apartment, Rex. Best of all it's in San Francisco.'

'Big deal! The city's getting like Manhattan, affordable only to the rich and the high-tech crowd. Meantime Oakland's turning into Brooklyn West, the must-live city for writers, artists, and actors. Poor me, living on the wrong side of the bay.' He pauses. 'I'm putting together a new Vertigo. Now that you have the grant I know you don't need to take on little jobs, but I'm hoping you'll be up for this one. I could really use you.'

'Let me guess – femme fatale?'

He laughs. 'How'd you know?'

I knew because that's the kind of role he always wants me to play in the private little dramas he sets up for his Vertigo Illusions clients. Vertigo is an expensive private service for people seeking a dramatic San Francisco adventure. The client provides Rex with assorted story components ('nasty dwarf,' 'purse-snatching incident,' 'woman dressed as a priest,' etc.), which Rex then pulls together into a coherent drama, casts with his actor friends, then plays out with the client in iconic San Francisco locales.

The client doesn't get to see the script in advance, so he/she doesn't know exactly what'll happen, only that the components will be woven into an adventure fantasy the playing-out of which will be safe even when it seems most dangerous. The client is subtly guided through the drama by Rex's actors, who also surreptitiously record the adventure using tiny video cameras attached to their clothing. Minimum cost for a Vertigo is ten thousand dollars. Several have cost clients twice as much. In exchange the client gets to undergo an intense experience, which he can later relive by screening the video.

It's a specialty business catering to the desires of wealthy people who seek dramatic out-of-the-ordinary adventures as breaks from the routine of high-powered corporate lives. Rex gives good value. His Vertigos are expertly produced works of performance art. Nearly all his clients have been from out of town, several from Europe, people for whom the San Francisco setting, due to movies like *Vertigo*, *Zodiac*, and *The Conversation*, holds a special fascination.

'This time the client's a nerdy multi-millionaire computer whiz,' Rex tells me. 'His colleagues are giving him a Vertigo for his birthday. He knows he's going to have an adventure, but has no idea what it'll be about. His friends told me he loves film noir so we're going to work with that.'

'And I'm to be an elusive noirish female?'

Rex smiles. 'At the start the client'll be told to meet a gorgeous thirty-something woman in the Redwood Lounge at the Clift. You'll be wearing a sexy red dress. Got one?'

'Funny enough I do, the one I wear when I perform my Weimar piece. But it might be a little slutty for the Clift.'

'Let's have a look.'

Rex is clever at pulling me into his schemes. He knows that if I model the dress for him I'll be that much closer to accepting the role.

I go to my closet, change into the dress, then do a back-and-forth across the loft.

'Looks great!' Rex says. 'You're right, it is a tad slutty, but we can trick it out with some expensive-looking jewelry and really good shoes. What's the kind with red soles?'

'Louboutins. But never mind, I've got plenty of heels.'

He explains the Vertigo. 'It's a three-acter. Act One: you flirt with the client in the lounge, then two strong-arm guys show up and haul you away. Act Two: after further strange encounters he's taken to a house where there's a weird party in progress with an orgy going on in the back room.'

'In which I'm an eager participant?'

Rex shakes his head. 'Actually, not so eager. He'll spot you there, see someone give you an injection, then the door'll close and he'll lose track of you. Act Three: a stranger will escort him to a seedy strip joint in North Beach where the client will see you a final time. You'll be wearing cheap makeup, pole-dancing, face blank like you've been drugged.'

I pretend to be appalled. 'Pole dancing like in my *Black Mirrors* piece? Will I have to strip?'

'You'll be topless, but you can wear a thong.'

'Oh, you're so merciful!'

'So . . . will you do it?' he asks, pretending to be on tenterhooks. 'Five hundred bucks, a chance to exercise your formidable talent, and a couple of drinks when we meet afterwards to cool off at the Buena Vista.'

'I *will* do it,' I tell him, 'but not for five hundred. I prefer a barter deal. I'll be your femme fatale, I'll shoot up and pole dance. Anything you want. In return I want you to direct me in my new piece, *Recital*.'

He clicks his glass against mine. 'Done!'

I go into San Francisco to see Grace Wei. We meet for lunch at a quiet restaurant on upper Sacramento, one Grace believes is just the sort of upscale place a society lady would lunch with friends to discuss an upcoming charity event. Indeed, it does have the feel of an older woman's place, with damask tablecloths and diet-conscious luncheon specialties, watercress sandwiches and egg-white-only omelets.

I didn't know Grace well at college, but always liked her. Now, meeting her again after a dozen years, I'm surprised at the vehemence of her dislike for what she calls 'the ruling class in this town' – the wealthy women who control the cultural organizations that make San Francisco a world-class city.

'I so identify with what you're doing,' she tells me. 'I want to help you any way I can.'

After lunch we walk over to her house. It has the kind of facade I imagined, one that proclaims its owners' importance.

'Sometimes I look at it and feel ashamed,' Grace tells me as we stand outside the mansion. It has a semi-circular drive-up, a grand entrance, and symmetrical wings. There's even a generic escutcheon mounted above the front door.

'Silas loves it. Makes him feel like he fits with the group of rich young guys who live around here. They all collect art and hang out and tell each other how brilliant and successful they are, and how living so close together in their little cluster of mansions makes this neighborhood the center of the universe.' Grace shakes her head. 'I tried to talk him out of it but he said, "When you make a killing in venture capital and move up here from the Valley, you need to show San Francisco who you are. Live on the best block. Buddy up with the movers and shakers."' She shrugs. 'I see his point, but still . . .'

When she shows me the ballroom, I feel like falling to

my knees. The ceiling's a good fourteen feet high, the flooring's composed of herringbone parquet, there're elaborate
moldings and off-white walls sectioned off by soft gray-
painted frames.

'Oh my God, this is perfect!' I tell her. 'And you have
chairs!'

There're over a hundred cushioned wooden chairs, painted
crackle-white with gold trim, arranged against the walls, just
the kind I'd expect to be seated on at a private musicale.

'They came with the house,' Grace explains. 'Since we're
not going to throw any grand balls, we're thinking about
converting this room into a gym. I'd like you to put it to use
while it's still in this lovely state.'

'You said something about scrounging an audience?'

'I think I can get a hundred people once word gets out. I
thought we'd send out engraved invitations, something like:
"Mrs Z cordially invites you to attend a musical evening
followed by remarks."' She glances at me. 'What do you
usually charge for a ticket?'

'Fifty dollars,' I tell her.

'How 'bout two-fifty? The people I have in mind regularly
pay that for an opera seat. The more they pay for something
the more they value it.'

Two hundred fifty dollars! Way too much for my regular
fans. But then I think: *Why not? This will be a one-off, a one-
time performance in this ballroom. Plus it would be terrific
to have an audience filled out with Mrs Z's real-life peers.*

I turn to Grace. 'Sure, let's go for two-fifty.'

She's delighted. 'I'll cover everything – invitations, valet
parking, champagne, and waiters. I want to turn this into an
occasion. I think we should schedule it for a Thursday evening
– you know, traditional maid's night out.'

'Maybe you should think about this, Grace,' I warn her. 'I
wouldn't want this to hurt your social life.'

'Way I see it, it'll cut one of two ways. These folks'll never
speak to me again and Silas and I'll be blackballed from here
to Nob Hill . . . or we'll be the toast of San Francisco, that
"clever young couple with the big house and the great FY
attitude, just the kind we need to put on our stodgy old boards".

Believe me, Tess, I'll be happy whichever way it cuts. Pariah or society's darling – it's all the same to me.'

Entering the Buckley, I observe Clarence talking with two men in the lobby. The men appear very serious and there's a solemnity about Clarence that doesn't match his normally cheerful manner. I wonder if these men are officials, maybe building inspectors warning him about a violation. I'm still waiting for the eccentric elevator when they leave. Turning I see Clarence standing in the center of the lobby looking stunned.

'Something wrong?'

He peers at me as if lost in thought.

'Hi, Tess. Didn't see you come in.'

'You look upset.'

'The guys just left – they're detectives. They were asking about Chantal, said she was murdered.'

I bring my hand to my mouth.

'Seems three weeks ago they found her body in the trunk of a stolen car parked at Oakland Airport. She was naked and badly decayed. They couldn't ID her until yesterday when someone spotted a wrecked motorcycle submerged near the port. They pulled it out and found Chantal's license hidden inside. They matched her license photo to their victim. That's how they got this address.' Clarence shakes his head. 'They asked me lots of questions about what she did, who were her friends, stuff like that. When I told them she was a dominatrix they wanted to know who her clients were. Fuck! I didn't know her clients! People come and go here all the time. We don't have camera surveillance. I try to stay out of my tenants' business.'

Deeply shaken, I go to him. Our eyes meet and we embrace. 'Oh my God, this is awful. Turns out I met her at my martial-arts school. Didn't really get to know her but liked her a lot. I just can't believe . . . I mean Josh and I were talking about her just the other day. He showed me his portrait of her. She looks so alive in it, like she's ready to step out of the canvas.'

'Those cops think it may have been a client. Someone who sessioned with her. That's what they were asking about.'

'Do you think?' He shakes his head, shrugs. 'Is there anything I can do, Clarence?'

'Nothing anyone can do. She left five weeks ago. Haven't seen or heard from her since. She was always nice with me, always smiled, said "Hi, good morning." Jesus! Who could have done this? How did it happen? *Why?*'

As he wails on I see tears in his eyes then feel them forming in mine. I knew her enough to have a feeling about her, that she was a decent person. Marie, the dark-haired girl from kickboxing class; Chantal, Josh's Queen of Swords; Chantal Desforges, dominatrix, who lived where I now live, called it her aerie, her Eagle's Nest, who spoke so casually to me about pain, and, evidently, inflicted it on others, who practiced her art such as it was in the very space where I now practice mine . . .

FIVE

Vienna, Austria. Late February 1913. The streets are icy but the air is clear. Again, the young man is waiting at the same table in the Café Ronacher, eagerly watching the door. When Lou enters, he stands attentively as if prepared to click his heels.

'Hello again, Frau Salomé! Thank you for coming.'

'You may call me Frau Lou. Everybody does.'

'I'm so grateful.'

Lou sits down. 'You said that last time. I'd appreciate it if you weren't so obsequious.' The young man accepts her criticism with a nod. 'I received your letter and was pleased to learn you took my advice and visited several galleries.'

'Certainly, I obeyed.'

'Why put it that way? I simply made a suggestion.'

'You presented it as a condition. It was either obey or be denied another meeting.'

'Yes, yes – I'd forgotten how tiresome you can be. So . . . what did you think of it?'

'The art?'

'Please don't act stupid.'

'My true opinion?'

'Nothing less.'

He meets her eyes then smiles slightly as he readies himself to meet her challenge. He has decided that on the issue of art he will stand up to her, not with the ferocity he often employs while proclaiming an opinion, but just enough to show her he has some spine.

'In truth,' he tells her, 'I didn't like what I saw. In fact, I was repulsed by it.'

'I find that comment entertaining. What repulsed you?'

'The decadence. The impropriety. The sensualization of everything. Above all, the sheer ugliness of the painting.

Particularly Kokoschka's. The man has no conception of what art should be about.'

'And that would be—?'

'Well . . . I mean . . .' He starts to stutter. 'I d-don't understand your question. Why would you ask me, an artist, such a thing?'

'I believe it's clarifying to get down to fundamentals. What is art? What should be its purpose? How may we differentiate among works and the artists who create them? You're fond of Wagner?'

'I revere him!'

'Surely you've asked yourself why you feel this way?'

'I feel a transcendence when I hear his music. But I don't see the connection. Are you comparing Kokoschka to Wagner?'

Lou shakes her head. 'Of course not. But there's something special in his work. Like all important artists he expresses himself in a unique way. Just as Wagner's music doesn't sound like the music of any other composer, so Kokoschka's paintings don't resemble those of any other artist. The same for the paintings of Schiele and Klimt.'

'At least they can draw! Though I detest what they depict.'

'Can't you explain yourself without using words like "detest" and "repulsed"?'

'Perhaps I don't express myself well. I found their work decadent. Even when they try to pretty things up, their pictures are ugly because of the subject matter. Writhing nude bodies! Twisted limbs! I did as you asked. I went to their exhibitions. Then afterwards I went to the Imperial Art-History Museum to calm myself and cleanse my eyes. By comparison what I saw at those "progressive" galleries was garbage.'

'You certainly have strong opinions. As do I. I looked at your watercolors and what I saw was an artist depicting the surface of things. Churches, houses, pavements. All of which have been depicted many times. There's no harm in painting what you see, but there is far more than the surface of things to be explored. Artists are doing that now. Photography has forced them to look behind surfaces. This, I believe, is what the important art of the twentieth century will be about. Artists will show us new ways of seeing the world filtered through the prisms of their unconscious minds. The subject I'm studying, psychoanalysis, is an attempt to look deeper, to understand and reveal the drives that make us who we are, the meanings behind the fantasies we harbor, the conflicts that rage within us . . . and which, sometimes, we enact to our detriment. This is what I believe the great artists of our time are exploring too.'

The young man smiles broadly.

'You're enjoying our discussion?'

'Very much! I love to discuss ideas.'

'As do I!'

'So may I suggest that though we disagree about the value of the work of particular artists, we at least have this in common?'

Lou makes a face to suggest she doesn't think they have much in common at all.

'You knew Nietzsche,' the young man states. Lou, apprehensive, nods slightly, wondering why he's brought this up and where he intends to go with it. 'No offense, but everyone knows you knew him. And there's the photograph.'

Lou recoils. 'Please, let's not discuss that! I've heard more than enough about it the past thirty years. What it means. How scandalous it is. Especially in view of some things Fritz later wrote: "When you go to a woman, do not forget the whip."' She exhales with disgust.

'This is a personal matter for you – I understand. But, you see, I worship Nietzsche nearly as much as Wagner. I know they had a serious falling out. I read about that in your book about Nietzsche.' The young man meets her eyes. 'I borrowed a copy. Since our meeting I've read through it twice and I'm sure I shall read it several times more. For though ostensibly about Nietzsche, it tells me a great deal about its author.'

Just as at their last meeting, Lou begins to feel uneasy. *This is turning into a one-way street wherein he knows a great deal about me and I know nothing about him.*

The young man, oblivious to her unease, continues to declare his hero-worship.

'Wagner, Nietzsche – for me they were great men, the greatest of the last century.'

'I would describe Wagner as a great composer and Nietzsche as a great thinker. But I would never call them "great men". On a human level both were deeply flawed.'

'I don't believe geniuses should be judged by ordinary standards. They're entitled to live as they like, make their own laws.'

Lou finds herself feeling annoyed. One side of her finds the young man repellent, while another side is attracted by his intensity.

'That's a view I happen not to share,' she tells him. 'You're even sounding like Nietzsche now. Believe me, at times he could be quite obnoxious.' She chuckles. 'You go to a Wagner opera and you think: "Wouldn't it be wonderful to meet this great composer? Speak with him? See him up close?" And, believe me, because I have known quite a few famous men like that, you are likely to find him uncouth, his breath bad, his table manners atrocious. He'll interrupt you, and if the conversation veers for an instant from the subject of himself and his achievements, he'll grow bored and turn away, or throw a tantrum. You have no idea!'

The young man has lowered his eyes. 'I apologize. I shouldn't have brought Nietzsche into our discussion. I look up to these men so greatly that I'm indifferent to whatever personal flaws they may have had. You knew Nietzsche well. You suffered him. So of course your personal feelings take precedence over my youthful infatuation.'

'Please, let us not discuss how I may or may not have suffered another person. As you said earlier, that's a personal matter. In fact, I met Richard Wagner the final year of his life when I visited Bayreuth for the premiere of *Parsifal*.' Lou smiles. 'You gasp! As well you should! It was amazing to be there and hear that glorious music for the first time. I met both the Wagners at Wahnfried. I can't claim I spent much time with them, but we did get on. I gained an impression of a self-centered man very much aware of his own genius. So, you see, the characterization "great man" tends to set my teeth on edge. In my younger days I was much impressed by them. Now a good deal less. By the way, there're quite a few of that species living here now, men whose work and ideas will likely change the way people think. There's one in particular who impresses me beyond all others.'

The young man nods. 'You're speaking of Professor Freud.'

Lou fixes him with her eyes. 'I told him about you, the stalking. I mentioned it then asked his advice as to whether I should take the time to meet with you.' She peers even more sharply at him. 'Are you curious to hear what he said?'

'Very.'

'He encouraged me to talk to you. He said it was clear you felt some sort of connection with me, one-sided to be sure, and that it would be helpful for me to explore this since such one-sided connections will arise frequently when I begin to practice psychoanalysis.'

The young man peers back, confused.

Lou continues: 'It's what Professor Freud calls "transference" – the relationship that inevitably develops between a psycho-analyst and his patient, a relationship in which the analysand reenacts intimate relationships from his early life. He reminded me that I was far from ready to practice psychoanalysis, but he thought a few meetings with you might be useful if I were to think about them in psychoanalytic terms.'

The young man appears unnerved. 'I can't say I follow much of that. Do you view our meetings as some sort of training exercise?'

'I see you're offended.'

'For a moment I thought we were having a conversation about ideas.'

'What I have presented to you just now *is* an idea.' She settles back. 'You had your own motives for stalking me. You knew who I was, you knew about some people I knew years ago, people you admire, and you hoped you might gain from engaging me in conversation. But life, you see, is a two-way street. Did it occur to you to ask what I might have to gain? Or are you so self-centered as to be indifferent to my side of the equation? Do you see yourself as an attractive man, a man of great charm and poise, who would interest a middle-aged married woman such as myself?'

The young man lowers his eyes. 'Again I feel put in my place.'

'You must immediately stop this whipped-dog fawning! It doesn't become you! I've treated you with respect. I'm sitting with you now in a very pleasant coffeehouse, when I could be seeing friends I've known for many years. I don't think you have a right to feel offended, nor do I take your servile attitude as anything but a cover-up for a misguided belief that because you know certain things about my past, there exists some level of intimacy between us. In fact you're a blank slate to me. Your watercolors, as I've said, tell me nothing. This is not an attack on your character. I've known many like you. And I admit I have difficulty with such people. Not that I expect people to wear their hearts on their sleeves. That too can be annoying. But it's the give-and-take in relationships that makes them profitable to both parties. And so I say this to you: if you wish to meet with me again, I would ask that you reveal yourself far more fully than you have. Open yourself up to me, and then, at least from my point of view, another meeting or two may be of value. Otherwise we're just two people of different ages sitting in a café pretending to have a conversation.' She rises. 'Hopefully I've given you something to think about. In any case, I must be off. Please order another coffee while I take care of the bill. And please, before contacting me again, think hard about what I've said.'

After she's gone the young man sits at the table, dejected. After a while his expression changes into a smile. He thinks: *This famous powerful woman has paid me attention. Next time I shall make sure she understands whom she's been speaking with!*

SIX

Tonight, when Josh finally responds to my message, he tells me the detectives just finished interviewing him.

'Clarence steered them to me,' he says. 'I wish he hadn't.'

He accepts my invitation to come upstairs. When he arrives I pour him a glass of Cabernet. He slumps down on my couch. I sit close beside him.

'Those cops,' he speaks bitterly, 'they're just going through the motions. I could see it in their faces. There're gang killings in Oakland every week. To them Chantal's just another case, probably one that'll never get solved.'

'Clarence says they found her license hidden somewhere in her motorcycle.'

'Under a rubber mat at the bottom of her top box. If they hadn't found it she'd still be a Jane Doe, another body found in the trunk of a stolen car. She loved that bike, a BMW F-800. Cost her a mint. Detectives told me it was totally wrecked.' He pauses. 'The young one, Ramos, said something really stupid – "A girl does that kind of work, stuff happens. It's a risky business she was in." I felt like slugging the guy.'

'Good thing you didn't.' I gently touch his arm. 'Did Chantal *think* she was in a risky business?'

'Never said so. Told me she liked being a domme because that way she was always in control. Said she could never take a job in the corporate world. The detectives asked about her family. I told them she rarely mentioned them.'

I ask him if he showed them Queen of Swords.

'Fuck no! After what Ramos said I figured they didn't have a right to see it!'

'Did she ever mention a client who scared her?'

'They asked about that.' Josh shakes his head. 'The way she left so suddenly, sold off all her stuff then fled – I believe something must have scared her. Maybe it had something to do with a client. But like I told the detectives, I don't know anything about the guys she saw or what she did with them.'

I talk through my feelings with Dr Maude.

'At first I was just intrigued by Chantal. Even more so when I realized I'd met her. Now I feel haunted by her, like our lives are somehow connected.' I look at her. 'I was totally wowed by Josh's Queen of Swords. Despite the power stance, I could feel her vulnerability. Then there's the whole woman-with-the-whip thing. You saw my Weimar piece, how I slash at my boots with a crop. I was playing off the same archetype.'

Dr Maude studies me. 'See, what bothers me, Tess, is why you decided to keep the cell and X-frame when the landlord offered to take them out?'

'A pro domme's abandoned apparatus – I was fascinated. I thought it would be cool to live around those things. I had no idea they'd belonged to my friend Marie.'

'I think there's more, something you haven't come to grips with.'

'Like what?'

'Why don't you think about it . . . then tell me.'

I ponder her question a while. 'A dominatrix is an archetype, the cruel woman. And Josh painted her as the Queen of Swords archetype from the tarot deck. I work with archetypes. My Weimar singer. The sex-kitten character in my *Black Mirrors* piece. My rich society lady, Mrs Z. This femme-fatale character Rex keeps asking me to play. It's all of a piece, isn't it?' I smile at Dr Maude. 'I guess we're going Jungian today.'

'Even though I'm not a Jungian analyst, I've always liked his ideas about archetypes. But that isn't what I was getting at. I'm pressing you on this because I believe you *can* account for feeling haunted by this woman. And I don't think it's just because of an improbable coincidence. It's something within you, Tess. You create your performances out of material from your life. I think when you saw the apparatus Chantal left behind you decided to keep it because on some level you thought you could use it in a performance piece.'

'I'm that exploitive?'

'It's not exploitive to use what comes your way. Anyway, I don't make value judgments. It's psychological truth we're after here. I like the way you take material from your life then transform it. I think you may end up using Chantal in a piece once you sort out your feelings about her.'

After session I rush over to San Pablo Martial Arts and attack the heavy bag – kicks, punches, knee strikes.

On my way out of the locker room I run into Kurt Vogel, gym owner and head trainer, a former Muay Thai tournament champion whose natural charisma is heightened by his German accent, gleaming shaved head, and watery green eyes.

I ask if he heard about Marie.

He nods solemnly. 'Read about it in the paper. Terrible thing. She was a warrior so whoever did that to her must have taken her by surprise. If he came at her straight she'd have put up a tremendous fight.'

I peer at him. *Why*, I wonder, *must he frame everything in terms of combat?*

He peers back, eyes unblinking. 'I want you to train harder, Tess. Work on your fighting skills. From now on, whenever you come in report to me. I'll set you up with a sparring partner and if no one's available I'll spar with you myself.'

Later, back in the loft, I think about my session with Dr Maude. She was correct about my process. I am a scavenger. I take bits and pieces, shards of my own and other people's lives, combine them and reassemble them into stories I then declaim as monologues. It's my way of coping, working through my fantasies and making sense of the world.

I rejected her notion that when I saw the cross and the cell in the loft I immediately thought about creating a performance piece. But now I admit to the possibility that on an unconscious level I was considering how those artifacts could be used.

I believe the reason I'm now feeling so haunted by Chantal is because, though she played the role of an archetype in her work, she was a real person whom I happened to meet who suddenly started to act strangely and then met a very bad and cruel end. There's an unfinished story there, questions to be answered, a quest to be pursued, a mystery to be solved.

Josh calls, asks me if I'd like to join him for an evening stroll.

'It's first Friday of the month, *Art Murmur* night,' he reminds me. 'Tonight the streets of downtown Oakland come alive.'

We meet in the lobby, Josh wearing his watch cap, jeans and a faded blue and white OAKLANDISH T-shirt, I in black tank top and shorts. We move up Broadway with the crowds, angle off on Telegraph Avenue, then stop in at a funky bar for Stoli Greyhounds made with freshly squeezed grapefruit juice.

I like the scene here, a cross-section of Oakland, people of all ages talking, laughing, drinking in a long narrow room. The walls are festooned with weird inscriptions, shriveled stuffed reptiles and layers of unrelated bric-a-brac which give the place a suffocating quality I find appealing, perhaps because it's the opposite of my own minimalist aesthetic.

'I love these voodoo walls,' I tell Josh. And when he signs he can't hear me due to the music and noise, I shout it again into his ear.

'Yeah, it's like a three-dimensional piece of outsider art,' he shouts back. 'Whoever assembled this stuff had a bad case of *horror vacui.*'

Surprised by his use of the art-history term, I realize I know little about him. He presents himself as a rough-around-the-edges type. I think he's a lot more sophisticated than he lets on.

Emerging again on Telegraph, he turns to me.

'I saw the way you peered at me in there.'

'Peered? Really?'

'When I said *horror vacui*. You wondered where I picked that up.'

'For all I know you have a PhD.'

He laughs. 'Put in two years as a grad student at CalArts, then quit. Didn't want to be an art teacher so didn't see the point sticking around for the fucking MFA. At heart I'm an autodidact. Something interests me, I delve into it. Chantal was also like that. Told me she was at San Francisco State, double majoring in psychology and German. Then when her parents died she decided to take a leave. She went to Vienna where she met this old domme, apprenticed with her a couple years, then came back to the Bay Area and set up shop.'

We're working our way toward the cluster of galleries above Twenty-First Street. The sidewalks are less crowded here, but the restaurants and cafés lining the avenue are filled with young people eating, drinking, yacking away. Due to *Art Murmur*, downtown Oakland, usually deserted and ominous after dark, is teeming with life.

Josh points out a grouping of large blue-gray birds resting on the limb of a tree. 'Black-crowned night herons. They say the gulls chased them out of the port. They like lampposts, buildings, and people so they settled downtown. They roost in the yucca trees. I happen to like them, but a lot of folks don't. They leave an inordinate amount of shit.'

'Guano.'

He laughs. 'Yeah, whatever—.'

Since we're getting along so well, I decide to try and find out more about Chantal.

'Those built-in bookcases in my loft – did she put them in?'

I feel him stiffen. 'Funny you should ask,' he says. 'I built them for her. She had a helluva lot of books.'

'Were they sold at the tag sale?'

'I heard her fetish-book collection was. But she had plenty more, serious non-fiction. I believe she sold them in bulk to a local used bookstore.'

We work our way through a mob clustered outside a trio of galleries. The pub and gallery crawl is now at full throttle. Two rival street bands playing on opposite sides of the avenue create a weird cacophony. A rapper is holding forth in tortured rhymes from the flatbed of a pickup truck, and a tall anorectic stoned-out girl with long stringy blond hair stands in the entranceway of a boarded up shop plucking aimlessly at a double bass.

We enter a gallery. There're so many people inside it's difficult to see the art. Josh offers his hand, I take it, then let him lead me to the wall. I observe him as he scrutinizes the artwork. I can tell by his expression he doesn't think much of it, but I'm impressed at the respect he shows each piece, pausing before it, devouring it with his eyes before moving on to the next.

'See anything you like?' I ask back out on the street.

'Yeah. The triptych. Reasonably priced too. Not that I'd buy it. I've got tons of my own work and nowhere near enough wall space to hang it.'

He's right about the triptych. It was the only decent piece in the exhibition. *He has a good eye*, I think.

We make our way through a dozen more galleries, viewing hundreds of paintings, sculptures, mixed-media pieces. In a garage on Twenty-Fifth we come upon an in-progress performance. A group of young people, dressed in black sweatshirts that identify them as members of THE FUCK-ALL COMMUNE, are seated at a round table feasting on asparagus spears while mock-seriously spouting anarchist slogans. It's funny and ridiculous, but I'm more intrigued by the attention of the onlookers than the performance.

'It's crap like this gives what I do a bad name,' I whisper to Josh.

Engrossed in the scene, he doesn't react.

Are these his politics? I wonder.

Emerging again, turning toward Broadway, I ask if he took part in Occupy Oakland.

He shakes his head. 'I like what they stood for. But their encampment was overrun by druggies and pickpockets. Since I live in the neighborhood I didn't feel like fouling my nest.' He turns to me, grins. 'But, yeah, at heart I'm an anarchist.'

He seems to have an uncanny ability to read my mind.

We find a free sidewalk café table, sit down, order coffee.

'Enjoying yourself?' he asks.

'It's a fun scene.'

'But the art mostly sucks, right?'

'Oh, does it ever!'

'Hey, don't look now,' he says, 'but Clarence is across the street. If he sees us he might come over. We wouldn't want that, would we?'

'Sometimes when I go out for a run I see him walking around the neighborhood, but outside the building he doesn't seem to recognize me. He kinda slinks when he walks. And he rarely blinks.'

'Yeah, I've noticed that too.'

'When he talks to me he giggles a lot. Does he do that with you?'

'Yeah and I've no idea why. Mornings he stands in the lobby behind the concierge's podium greeting everybody with a big smile, then couple hours later I see him dumpster diving out in the alley. One time I went out early and caught him going through trash barrels. So I yell, "Hey, good morning, Clarence." He looks up, gives me this shit-eating grin. "Yeah, hi, Josh." It's like there's this happy-go-lucky side and this weird side that's into other people's garbage.'

'He's always nice to me.'

'To me too. But "Who know what evil lurks in the hearts of men?"'

'"The Shadow knows." Right?'

'Yeah, *The Shadow*,' Josh says, seemingly delighted I recognize the line from the old radio show.

We laugh, then Josh turns serious. 'I'm surprised you're not attached.'

'Does it show? I recently got detached. Feels good too.' I meet his stare, then decide to change the subject in case he's thinking of coming on to me. 'Something I want to ask you about Chantal?' I continue even as I feel him tighten up again at the mention of her name. 'You said something like "none of her friends knew her real name either".'

'I probably said that, yeah.'

'So that tells me you met some of her friends?'

He nods. I peer closely at him. He's going cagey on me the way he did when I first encountered him in the elevator. Which is odd since a few minutes ago he offered information about Chantal's college career and apprenticeship in Vienna. But rather than take his cageyness as a signal to drop my questions, I decide to see how far I can press before he cuts me off.

'I'd like to meet her friends,' I tell him.

'And you're asking me – what?'

'Would you introduce me, or give me a name or two?'

'And where might that lead?'

'Wherever. Look, I see you're reluctant. You're protective of her. But you did show me Queen of Swords . . . and that spoke to me, Josh. It *did*. I'm intrigued by her, maybe because

I met her and now I live and work where she lived and worked. Who was she, Marie or Chantal? I'd like to find out all I can, get a sense of what she was really like. Your portrait tells me a lot, but I know there's more. So, yeah, I'd like to meet some of her friends and hear their impressions. If that annoys you please tell me and I'll drop it.'

He studies me a while as if assessing my sincerity. 'You could try Lynx,' he says. 'Another pro domme. They were partners for a while, then Chantal took the penthouse and set up on her own. Still they stayed friends. You want to find out about Chantal, Lynx would be a good place to start.'

'So how do I find this Lynx?'

He smiles. 'Shouldn't be too hard, not for a smart girl like you.'

He pulls out his wallet, places a ten on the table, stands. 'On *Art Murmur* nights the free shuttle runs till midnight. It'll take you within a block of the Buckley.'

'You're not going to walk back with me?'

'No offense, Tess, but I think I'll walk alone for a while.' He gives me a quick hug. 'See you around.'

I watch him as he saunters back into the gallery district.

What's with him? I wonder. First he tells me stuff about Chantal, then he stiffens and goes monosyllabic when I ask about her. I decide not to worry about it. He coughed up Lynx's name, and perhaps inadvertently gave me another lead: that a local bookstore bought up Chantal's library.

Shouldn't be too hard to find out which one . . . least not for a 'smart girl' like me.

Early the next morning Jerry calls.

'This murdered pro dominatrix I'm reading about – she the one used to live in your loft?'

'Good morning, Jerry. Is this really why you called?'

'Yeah, good morning, Tess. Sorry. Saw an item in the paper. Wondered if it was the same woman.'

'It was.' I pause. 'I didn't know we were speaking, actually.'

'I don't see why we shouldn't be.'

'When I left you said some hostile things. I'm still reeling from that.'

'People often say things when they're stressed, things they don't necessarily mean.'

'Thing is I think you *did* mean them, Jerry. So if there's nothing else on your mind, I'd like to get back to work.'

'Sure,' he says. 'Sorry to bother you.' And then in an unfamiliarly feeble tone: 'Be well, Tess. I mean that, I really do.'

I wait two days before searching out Lynx. Doesn't take me long to find her. I start with a BDSM internet board that provides links to Bay Area pro domme websites. Chantal Desforges is on the list. When I click on her link I get a blank screen. A note in tiny letters informs me the site's been taken down at its owner's request.

Next I click on the link for Mistress Lynx, gaining entry by agreeing I'm over eighteen and not in law enforcement. An image comes up of a pretty light-skinned black girl wearing a seductive smile. There's a caption: DON'T MISTAKE ME FOR NICE. I CAN BE *VERY* CRUEL!

The ABOUT section describes attendance at an exclusive Swiss boarding school. 'I was even dominant back then,' the commentary reads. 'I enslaved my roommate and enjoyed disciplining a groom when I caught him mistreating my horse.'

Under SPECIALTIES Lynx provides a lengthy list that includes every form of BDSM behavior I've heard of . . . and several I haven't. At the end she adds: 'Plus anything else your twisted little mind can think up!'

There's also a statement in bold capitals:

**DOMINATION IS NOT PROSTITUTION.
REQUESTS FOR SEXUAL FAVORS WILL
RESULT IN INSTANT DISMISSAL!**

The GALLERY section shows Lynx in various dominant poses and a CONTACT page gives precise instructions for arranging an appointment. Applicants are required to fill out a detailed questionnaire with information regarding their fetishes, experience, and a reference from at least one other dominatrix.

The final paragraph is explicit:

'PLEASE BE ADVISED: it is a PRIVILEGE to session with MISTRESS LYNX. If I find your response of interest, I will email my phone number so that we may discuss your needs and schedule your session. If you don't hear back from me after a reasonable time, you may assume I have no interest.'

I click on the questionnaire, fill in my full name, address, and phone number, then skip to the section marked 'Anything else I should know?' I write:

'Hi! I have your name from Josh Garske. As should be clear I'm not contacting you regarding a session, and please be assured I'm not a journalist nor do I work in law enforcement. I'm a performance artist (please check out my website: www.tessperformances.net) interested in learning all I can about your late friend Chantal, whom I knew slightly under the name Marie. I now occupy her old loft in the Buckley. I'm sure this is a sensitive time for you, and I hope this message doesn't come as an intrusion. Please let me know if you're willing to meet for coffee or a drink? Sincerely, Tess Berenson.'

Pressing SEND, I figure there's probably a one in three chance she'll respond.

I take the BART to San Francisco to meet with Rex. He's invited me to his place to go over my part in his new Vertigo. When I enter and see the pole he's erected in the center of his living room, I figure he wants me to demonstrate my pole-dancing skills.

Fine! I think. *He needs a charge, I'll give it to him.*

But then when I start to strip, he surprises me.

'What the hell are you doing?'

'You want to see me work the pole, right?'

'No need. I saw you work it in *Black Mirrors.*'

'So what's it doing here?'

'I use it for exercise.'

'*Really?*'

'Yeah, *really.*' He looks embarrassed. 'Show me your moves later if you want. But first let's go over your role.'

We sit down. His apartment, no kind of hovel, is roomy and flooded with sunlight. The living-room walls are covered with theater posters, the shelves filled with stage-set models interspersed with books on acting and theater history.

'You want to come off as this very classy escort,' he explains, 'say in the fifteen hundred a night range. Mike, our client, will recognize you from a photograph and your red dress. He'll come over, you'll signal him to sit, then you two will have the kind of conversation you'd typically have on a blind date, during which you'll feign serious interest in his background and achievements. You'll both be playing out a classic getting-to-know-you scene. Play it like a call girl pretending to be fascinated by a john when they both know she's really interested in getting his money, getting him off, and getting away.'

'So I act classy in Act I. How 'bout Act II?'

'Less so. At the party you'll look cheaper and a lot more stressed out. You'll recognize Mike, but shake your head to warn him off. Then you'll slip away. Later he'll catch a glimpse of you in the orgy room. You'll be in your underwear, your makeup'll be messed, and he'll see you get an injection administered by one of the goons, presumably heroin.'

'Act III?'

'You're hitting bottom, totally drugged. The classy escort he met at the Clift now behaves like a cheap hooker. From the pole you'll come on to him, beckoning him by making cock-sucking motions with your mouth. By overdoing it you'll be telling him you're putting on an act. He'll see track marks on your arms and be repulsed, but he won't be able to take his eyes off you because something about you continues to fascinate him. Then you'll collapse like you've OD'd and the thugs who abducted you will drag your limp body off stage.'

'So . . . a tragedy. I can do all that.'

'Of course you can! Acts II and III will be fun for you. But the bar scene's crucial. You need to be really seductive there . . . as only a very pricey top-of-the-line escort can. The illusion depends on getting the hook in his mouth. Otherwise he won't care about your downfall.'

'Suppose I play it like a spoiled-rotten rich girl fallen on hard times? Like in that old Bob Dylan song – "You've gone to the finest school all right, Miss Lonely . . ."'

Rex nods. 'Yeah, that's it!'

'Suggestion. This'll mean hiring another actor, but I think it'll enhance the story. A tough-looking gangster type, fat, ugly, and powerful. And, to keep it noirish, with an unlit cigar clenched between his teeth. The thugs work for him. He owns me. He pimps me out. He likes to degrade me. He's waiting in the back of a limo outside the Clift. The client'll catch a glimpse of him as the thugs shove me into his car. At the strip joint he'll be standing there getting off seeing me humiliate myself. The client'll notice him because he'll have seen him two times before, so he'll figure it's a master/slave relationship. The client'll be disgusted by my performance on the pole, but he'll be fascinated too because for all his decency there's also a side of him that likes seeing me degraded.'

'Love it! And I know just the actor. We'll call this character Fat Man. As always, Tess, you know how to take an idea for a sketch, add a level, and deepen it.'

And as always I'm a sucker for his flattery. 'So – want to see me pole-dance?'

'Sure, if you want.'

I nod, strip to my underwear, then do a few turns. The pole's the portable kind, spring-loaded, but firm enough for me to work it.

'I've forgotten some of the routines – allegra, batman, flying ballerina. Want me to study up?'

He shakes his head. 'What I want you to do is make love to it. Treat it like a gigantic dick. Try much too hard to act sexy – so hard you come off as sloppy. Act like pole-dancing's not your thing. Fat Man's making you do it.'

I try a routine, stumble, pull myself up, make myself dizzy swinging through four or five fast loops, finally collapse into a heap.

Rex is pleased. 'You're nailing it, babe! Put your clothes back on and let's get something to eat. I want to hear about *Recital*, where you want to go with it, and how I can help you take it there.'

Back home in Oakland I find a voicemail message from Lynx. She thanks me for writing and says she'd definitely like to meet. I call her back. We agree to meet up tomorrow morning. I suggest Downtown Café, but Lynx has another idea.

'There's this fetish shoe store, Madame deRouge, on Harrison and 18th. I've got shopping to do so let's meet there. Then if we both decide to continue the conversation, there's a coffee place around the corner.'

I understand: she wants to check me out.

'Sure. Meet you at eleven at deRouge,' I tell her.

I spend the early part of the morning working on *Recital* in front of my camera, rehearsing then stopping to critique the video. I try to keep Dr Maude's advice in mind – don't over-satirize, grant Mrs Z a full measure of humanity. My object is to evoke pity and terror – pity for the woman's pathetic sense of entitlement, and terror on account of her blatant moral corruption. As Rex told me yesterday at lunch, 'Satire's fun and easy to do, but, as a great showman once put it, satire closes on Saturday night.'

I spot Lynx right away. She's the only one in the store. She looks just like her website photo, but without the lascivious smirk. I catch her glancing at me as we browse the merchandise. She picks up a shoe with an exaggerated stiletto heel.

'What'd you think?' she asks.

'Nice piece of sculpture, but I couldn't walk in it.'

She smiles, then leads me over to a glass case near the cash register filled with fetishistic black-leather head-encasement helmets and hoods.

'What'd you think of these?' she asks.

The cashier, a busty freckled redhead, gazes at me amused.

I get it. I'm being tested. If I blink, blush, blanch, or act uneasy, I'll fail and Lynx'll blow me off. So to make sure I pass I run my tongue subtly across my upper lip.

'I like them,' I tell her. 'Something to wear to church. Or maybe the Easter Parade.'

Lynx and the redhead guffaw.

'Let's go get coffee,' Lynx says.

She leads me to a café two doors down. We settle in at a sidewalk table. After we order she studies me as she quizzes me about my interest in Chantal.

'You wrote that you knew her slightly?'

I tell her about meeting her at kickboxing class.

Lynx nods. 'She had a barter deal there. Twelve BDSM sessions with the sensei in exchange for Muay Thai training.'

Well, there's a revelation! I never would have imagined Kurt being submissive.

'You wrote she used the name Marie?' I nod. 'That was her middle name. She used it sometimes in her, you know, vanilla life . . . such as it was.'

Lynx turns serious. She admits she's extremely upset about what happened to her friend and is still trying to work it out in her head.

'I'm not the only one,' she tells me. 'The whole East Bay domme community's in pain over this. Everyone liked Chantal. She didn't have any enemies in the business I know about. Now everyone's scared there's a woman-hating killer on the loose. No one wants to take on anyone new.' She sips her coffee. 'There was a San Jose domme killed last year. Shot twice. And, the weird part – whoever did it went to a lot of trouble. After he killed her he dug out the bullets. That's the story going around. What'd you think?'

I tell her that suggests the killer was worried the bullet markings could be traced.

'Like maybe a cop?' she asks.

'Are there cop clients?'

'We don't ask people what they do. Cops session just like everybody else. If you're wondering why I wanted to check you out it's 'cause I wanted to make sure you weren't a cop.'

I tell her I understand even though I don't. Seems to me that other women in the business, feeling threatened, would bend over backwards to help the police.

But Lynx is on to other things. She tells me the last time she saw Chantal was at her tag sale.

'Practically all the East Bay dommes came,' she says. 'Her decision to sell off her stuff – that seemed weird to me, coming so sudden, but most of the girls figured it for another case of domme-burnout. Happens in our business. People quit cold turkey, sell off their stuff, and move on. Some go back to school, others get a straight job, others might marry a client, settle

down, and start popping out kids. But I knew Chantal well
enough to see this wasn't just burnout, that she was seriously
disturbed. When I asked what was going on, she whispered,
"Something's gone horribly wrong here." When I asked what
she signaled she didn't want to talk about it. She was usually
open with me so I figured whatever it was was cutting her pretty
deep. Anyway, it helps me to talk about her. She was a terrific
kid. I'm going to miss her a lot.'

I'm pleased at her willingness to talk. I also find myself
liking her.

'Josh told me you two used to work together.'

'We shared space for a year. Saw our clients separately.
Occasionally we'd do a double. Not often. Our styles were
too different.'

'How do you mean?'

'I'm more a physical type. I specialize in corporal punishment.' She grins. 'The masochists love me. I wield a mean
whip.'

'And Chantal?'

'She liked working the psychological side – what she called
"therapeutic dominance". She knew how to punish a slave.
She wouldn't hesitate to slap one across the face. But she
wouldn't take on masochists, only submissives. She thought
of herself as a healer and her work as a form of therapy.
Chantal wasn't into inflicting pain. She used to say her greatest
pleasure was to burrow way deep into someone's head and
take up residence there. Or as she liked to put it, "pull a demon
out of a guy's closet and give it a kiss". Basically she got off
on mind-fucks.'

Hearing this, I can't decide which form of BDSM strikes
me as more caustic: Lynx's sadism applied to the flesh or
Chantal's psychological dominance inflicted upon the brain.

'Still,' I say, 'she had the cell and the St. Andrew's Cross.'

'Sure, she had that . . . and a lot more. But, see, a major
part of a mind-fuck is to create a mood. My place, the one
we used to share, is in a cellar. It looks like a dungeon. Chantal
wanted something elegant with lots of light. Soon as she saw
that loft she knew it was perfect.'

As did I!

'The building manager told me she called it The Eagle's Nest.'

'That's how she thought of it – high up, aloof, a place where, if you went there, you were likely to get clawed.'

'Weird name to use, don't you think?'

'Because of the Hitler connection?' She smiles. 'Tess loved stuff like that. Anyway, to answer your question, she had hundreds of tools, most just for show. That's what she sold off – whips, canes, bondage devices, hoods, manacles, and her collection of fetish wear. For her those things were props, rarely used, which was why all her stuff was in great condition.' Lynx crinkles her eyes. 'I bought her Australian single-tail, the one she called Blackspur. She knew how to crack it, but I doubt she ever used it on a client. It's a gorgeous instrument. It's going to be fun breaking it in.'

I wince.

'Hey, am I making you uncomfortable?'

'It's OK,' I tell her. 'My monologues are about making people uncomfortable. The other night my old acting coach came up to the loft. He saw the cell and cross, and when I told him a domme used to live there, he pointed out that you guys are performers too.'

Lynx giggles. 'It's all about the performance. I'll raise welts on a guy's butt, but even when we're engaged like that we both know we're play-acting. Chantal was fascinated by the combination of real and artificial. Also by the fact that it's a transaction, that we're fee-for-service providers.'

I ask her if she knows Chantal's real name.

'Chantal Marie Marceau. I know that sounds made-up. Most of our work names are. Believe me, my parents didn't name me Lynx! Her background was French Canadian. Both her parents were teachers. When they died in a car accident, she quit college and went to Vienna. That's where she met this high-end domme, Gräfin Eva. Eva took a liking to her and invited her to be her assistant. That's how Chantal learned the trade . . . the old-fashioned way by apprenticeship. She spoke often of this woman. Gräfin means countess in German. She was in her fifties, and, according to Chantal, greatly influenced by Freud. She liked to do mock-psychoanalytic sessions with her clients, ordering them to lie naked on a couch, then reveal their secret fantasies. If Eva felt they were withholding or fabricating, she'd punish them for lying, then, at end of session, hold them close and comfort them. It was Eva who got Chantal into thinking of herself as a healer. She came out here once to visit so I got a chance to meet her. Amazing woman! She radiated dominance. She also had this mantra: "We use pain to defeat pain." Chantal loved that! It became her mantra too.'

I'm impressed by Lynx. She's smart and articulate. I can understand why she and Chantal were friends.

'Did Chantal have siblings?'

'There's a brother, a ski instructor in Vermont. I'm sure he's been informed. You said Josh talked to the cops. He probably told them how to contact him.'

'I'm not sure about that. Josh says he didn't know much about her.'

Lynx shakes her head. 'He knows plenty. Don't believe a thing he says. He's a forger. He forges paintings then sells them to dumb-ass collectors.'

'You're sure?'

'That's what Chantal told me.' She pauses. 'I don't mean to trash your friend.'

'He's not really my friend. I barely know him.'

'Well . . . like I was saying, Chantal had this brother, but they weren't close. Still I hope somebody got in touch with him. Considering the way she was found the least she deserves is a decent burial.'

I decide to steer the conversation back to performance. Like Chantal I'm fascinated by the combination of real and artificial in my own work.

'I'm preparing a new piece,' I tell her. 'It involves convincing my audience I'm sixty-seven years old, filthy rich, elegant on the surface but full of resentment and repressed rage beneath.'

Lynx snorts. 'Sounds like a hoot!'

'I was rehearsing this morning, then running back the video to check whether my monologue was convincing.'

'Good method! We do that too, video recording. We don't talk about it because our clients are ultra-concerned about confidentiality. But Chantal and I always recorded our sessions in case someone claimed something wasn't consensual, and also, like you, to make sure we were bringing off our scenes. We'd check out each other's videos then make suggestions.'

I'd love to see a video of Chantal in action, but hesitate to ask Lynx for fear she'll be turned off.

'In acting class we call that critiquing,' I tell her.

Lynx nods. 'Our clients would kill us if they ever found out.'

At the word 'kill' we stare at one another, then Lynx brings her hand up to her mouth.

'Jesus! Sorry! I didn't mean that the way it came out.'

'Makes me wonder, though . . .'

'Yeah. What if someone *did* find out? Still, like I said, we only did it for professional reasons. We weren't into the so-called "consensual blackmail" scene, a fetish of guys who want to be forced into obedience under threat of being exposed to their loved ones and employers. We prided ourselves on treating our clients with honesty and respect. We always trashed the videos after we ran them.'

'Did Chantal record sessions up in the loft?' I ask casually.

'She recorded everything. She was fanatical about it.'

'Where was the camera?'

'She had two actually, hidden in the moldings high up, one in the corner where the cell grill meets the wall, the other in the corner opposite. You'd never notice them. When you get back take a look. You'll see where they were.' Lynx smiles. 'Hey, for all I know they're still there!'

I find this revelation unnerving. *Why would the cameras still be there? Wouldn't Chantal have taken them down before she left?*

Lynx, noticing I'm upset, continues to explain the reasoning behind making videos. 'There's also a security concern. Say a guy comes to you for a session, then freaks out. You do your best to calm him, ease him out, but it's safer for you if someone's monitoring the session in real time. If your monitor, usually a male friend, sees things aren't going well, he can come in and help. Now if you're with a regular, you'll probably turn the camera off. But with a new client, someone you don't know, you want somebody nearby to watch and make sure everything's OK. The old way was to leave the room, make a quick call to your friend who was maybe waiting downstairs in his car, then say a code word like "green light" so he knows you feel safe. But a live feed from a camera's better, assuming there's someone you trust monitoring at the other end.'

'So who was watching Chantal's feed?' Even as I ask the question, I have a queasy feeling I know the answer.

'Josh. She told me he loved watching her sessions, got off on it. According to Chantal, watching was his thing. Great trait in a bodyguard. And there he was just three floors down, ready to run upstairs if she needed him. Wish I had someone like that in my building.'

Jesus!

Walking back to the Buckley, I wonder whether to confront Josh about why he hasn't been straight with me. Lynx told me not to believe anything he says. *Now*, I think, *I won't.*

Back in the loft I check the corners. The cameras are still there, well concealed. I wouldn't have spotted them if Lynx hadn't told me where to look. Not knowing whether they're hard-wired, I'm reluctant to yank them out. Instead I snip off the tiny microphones and cover the lenses with black tape.

I'm spooked. Could they still be live? Could Josh have been spying on me all these weeks? Suddenly I'm feeling paranoid. Even though I've deactivated them, I wonder whether there might be other hidden cameras and microphones Lynx didn't know about.

Josh lied to me about not knowing anything about Chantal's clients or the scenes she played out with them. So why did he steer me to Lynx? He had to know there was a good chance she'd tell me about his role as Chantal's security guy. Could his tip to contact her be part of some devious game he's been playing . . . such as *wanting* me to discover he's been watching me?

Whatever his motive, it's now clear he can't be trusted. But rather than confront him, I decide to play it cool, let him wonder what I think, whether in fact I *like* being watched.

Which, I admit to myself, on a certain level I do. But not surreptitiously, not without my consent. A good issue, I decide, to raise with Dr Maude: whether there's a side of me that actually likes the idea that a voyeur has been secretly spying on me from the day I moved in.

I go out for a run to think things through, why Josh lied, and something else Lynx mentioned – that a dominatrix can be a healer who uses corporal pain to defeat the inner psychic pain of her clients.

I also ask myself again why I care so much about a deceased woman I barely knew. Dr Maude suggested I want to understand Chantal in order to portray her character in a performance piece, that this is the subconscious reason I chose to keep her SM gear when I leased the loft. But I feel something else is going on, something deeper, a strange but real feeling of kinship with Chantal, a feeling that our lives are not just tangentially connected, but are closely and perhaps even mystically linked.

I'm musing about this, not paying much attention where I'm heading, when suddenly I realize I just ran by a used bookstore on the block behind. Stopping to catch my breath, I consider whether to backtrack and check it out. It would be too weird if it turns out to be the store where Chantal sold her books. But then, I tell myself, perhaps not so weird. It's fairly close to the Buckley and therefore the most likely place to which Chantal would turn to sell her library to raise cash for her escape.

My T-shirt's soaked. I feel the sun beating down, feel it strongly on my forehead. It's the brilliant hot sun of a sparkling spring afternoon in Oakland, so brilliant it makes the storefront windows and building walls seem to shimmer in the heated air. I look up at the sky. The sun blinds me. I close my eyes and allow the heat to play upon my face. Then I make up my mind, pivot, and stride back to the bookstore.

A bell tinkles when I enter. It's cool inside. There's a special smell too, a library stacks smell, the aroma of dusty old books. At a desk near the door an elderly man with a trimmed white beard is working at a computer. I catch an aroma of whisky as I pass. *Ah, a lover of books and fine Scotch.* I smile at him, but he doesn't bother to look up.

A little further in, a woman in her sixties, white hair compacted into a bun, sits at another desk cataloging books. When I pass near, she looks me up and down taking in my running garb. Then smiling she displays a questing expression.

'Just browsing,' I tell her.

She nods and turns back to her work.

I make my way down a long center aisle lined with bookshelves. In typical used bookstore fashion, the books are organized into sections: ART, MYSTERIES, LITERARY FICTION, GAY STUDIES, RUSSIA, BASEBALL, WORLD WAR II. There are five main aisles. Near the rear it's necessary to step around shopping bags and boxes filled with books as yet unshelved. Some of the back aisles are nearly blocked. The deeper I penetrate the more chaos I find, including books stacked into precariously balanced piles, some reaching up to the ceiling. There're corridors back here so narrow I can barely squeeze through. These lead in turn to a rabbit warren of backrooms (JUVENILES, FOREIGN LANGUAGES, TRAVEL, EROTICA), some so stuffed it's impossible to do anything except stand in the doorways and gaze inside, imagining what treasures lie hidden beneath the literary rubble.

I make my way back to the front of the shop. White Bun looks up at me with the same questing expression.

'I don't know if this is the right store,' I tell her. 'A friend recently sold her books, and I'm wondering if she sold them here.'

'Can you describe your friend?' White Bun's words come out in a whisper.

'She was very beautiful. She had very pale skin and long dark hair. She lived in the Buckley Building.'

'I know the one,' White Beard breaks in. 'We bought her library.' He studies me. 'You say she *was* beautiful. Something happen to her?'

I think a moment how best to put it. 'She recently passed away,' I tell him.

Silence, then White Beard speaks again. 'Sorry to hear that. She was a very nice young lady. Didn't haggle. Invited me up to her loft. I looked over her library, offered her a price, and she accepted it. I paid her and sent two of my boys to pack her books and haul them here.'

'Still have them?'

He laughs. 'Oh, sure! Haven't unpacked them. Probably won't get to them 'til sometime next year.'

'Could I look at them?'

'You interested in buying?'

'I might be. I took over her loft. I remember she had some very interesting books,' I lie. 'I thought if I could see them, I might want to buy some back.'

White Beard and White Bun exchange a look.

Another crazy – is that what they're thinking?

'It's not possible to pull those books out of boxes and spread them out for you. But if you're serious my wife will show you the boxes, and you can take a peek inside. If you see some you want, we can price them for you. But only if you're serious.'

'I'm very serious,' I assure him.

White Beard nods at White Bun. 'Why don't you show the young woman where we put those Buckley Building books.' He looks sternly at me. 'Don't mess them up. They were boxed the way your friend had them organized. Mess them up and I'll never get them properly shelved.'

'I'll be very careful,' I promise.

White Bun leads me back into the dark recesses of the store, then up a narrow staircase I hadn't noticed, which leads in turn to a long narrow room, the length of the shop below. At the far end dust-coated windows overlook the street.

She leads me to a pair of stacks five boxes tall, all marked DESFORGES. 'You can open the top one and take a look. That should give you a general idea.'

I nod, open the top box. The first book I see is a biography of Sigmund Freud. I pull it out, open it, notice that passages are highlighted and that there're marginal notations.

'About half of them are marked up like that. Which is why we couldn't pay much for them,' White Bun explains. 'Our customers don't expect used books to be pristine, but they prefer to do their own highlighting. Your friend's books were well studied.'

I pick up a book from the top box of the second stack, William Shirer's *The Rise and Fall of the Third Reich*. It too is heavily notated. Beneath it I find a biography of Lou Andreas-Salomé, the source of the quote on the archway in my loft. I notice a letter sticking out between pages in the middle.

'Yeah, there's mail inside some of them. It's like she used her library as a filing cabinet. We've bought other libraries like that.' She giggles. 'Once one of our clients found a hundred-dollar bill folded up inside a Bible. He'd paid for the book so he got to keep it.'

I turn to her. 'The letters come with the books?'

'Sure. Why not?'

'How will you price them?'

'My husband does the pricing. You seriously interested?'

'If it's not too expensive I'd like to buy the whole collection,' I tell her.

'Let's go downstairs and talk to him.'

The negotiation goes quickly. I know from what White Beard said that he doesn't like to haggle. I ask what he paid for Chantal's library. Pretending to look it up, he tells me he paid six hundred dollars. I figure he probably paid three, but decide to let it go. Pointing out that I barely glanced at the books, I offer him seven hundred if he'll have the boxes hauled back up to Chantal's old loft.

The old man gives me a quizzical look. 'Off her shelves and down the stairs, then back up the stairs and back onto her shelves. Interesting,' he says. He ponders my offer. 'OK, you can have the lot for seven-fifty including delivery. If you tip my boys they'll shelve them for you too.'

I meet his eyes. He's smiling. I turn to look at White Bun. She brings her hand up to her face to conceal her grin.

I grin back at them. As my father used to say: the best deals are the ones where each side believes he's gotten the better of the other.

SEVEN

ienna, Austria. March 15, 1913. It's pouring with rain. When Lou walks into the Café Ronacher, she's carrying an umbrella. She finds the young man at a larger table than before, sketchbook and pencil set in front of him. The moment she enters he rises swiftly to greet her. This time there's no obsequious fawning. Today he seems a different person, bursting with confidence. She thinks: *If I weren't aware of his insecurities, I'd likely find him repulsive.*

He snaps his finger at the waiter, orders coffees and chocolate tortes for them both.

'You don't bother to ask what I want?'

'I assumed, based on our last meeting . . .' He lowers his eyes. 'I apologize.'

'Never mind. In your letter you spoke of a willingness to reveal yourself. You used the words "full disclosure".' He nods. 'I'm listening?'

'I am prepared to answer all your questions. In return I ask permission to sketch you while we chat.'

'I thought you didn't like drawing people. There were no people in your paintings.'

'Occasionally I'm moved to draw a portrait of someone I admire.' He looks cannily at her. 'May I?'

She nods. As they talk he sketches her, looking up at her from time to time, then back down at his sketchbook. He holds it in so only he can see the drawing as it progresses.

'You seem quite confident today,' she tells him.

'People often say that about me, even when they disagree with what I'm saying. I certainly have my opinions, but I pride myself on being open to a change of mind when someone I respect, such as yourself, offers me a good reason.'

'May I ask you some personal questions?'

'Certainly!' He is, she sees, eager to accommodate her.

'Do you have a girlfriend?'

'I've yet to fall in love, but I do look forward to the experience.'

'Do you think of yourself as bitter or angry?'

'I am well acquainted with those feelings. My application to attend the Academy of Fine Arts was twice rejected. Needless to say that was discouraging.'

'I can imagine.'

He shakes his head as if to say she has no idea. 'There is no work for me here.' He continues to sketch her as he speaks. 'Two years ago I was reduced to carrying suitcases at the station in exchange for tips. I'm currently living in a shelter in the Brigittenau district along with several hundred other unemployed men. So, you see, my daily existence isn't pleasant.' He takes a deep breath. 'In fact, if it weren't for the meager amounts I'm able to scrounge for my paintings and the paltry allowance I receive from my family, I'd be hungry and destitute. Under such circumstances, Frau Lou, it is difficult not to feel some bitterness.'

Lou nods kindly to show she understands. Up until now she's regarded him as an object of curiosity; now for the first time in their acquaintanceship she feels some empathy.

'Do you frequent prostitutes?'

The young man is taken aback. He looks up from his drawing. 'This is something I would never discuss with a lady!'

'Perhaps sexuality, which is a normal part of human existence, frightens you?'

'Is that what your esteemed Professor Freud would say?'

'Do you know anything about his work?'

'You mocked me before for my ignorance. So to educate myself and also to please you, I conducted some research.' He grins. 'Let me put it this way – I feel the same way about this so-called science you are studying as I do about the so-called art work of Mr Egon Schiele.'

'Contempt?'

'I couldn't put it better.'

'Tell me about yourself. How do you spend your time?'

'I'll be happy to. But first may I ask why you're so curious about me, a man of small consequence compared to the many famous people in your exalted circle?'

She ignores his sarcasm. 'Like many writers I like to see

the world through others' eyes. When a young man follows me on the street and then writes me admiring letters, of course I'm curious to know who he is.'

He resumes sketching as he describes his life. 'Most mornings I work on my painting. I go into an old part of the city, sketch scenes, then return to the Mannerheim shelter, where I have a little corner where I can work. Here I refine my sketches and color them in. The other men there leave me alone. I think I frighten them a bit . . . which is fine. I don't like being disturbed.' He pauses. 'I also spend a good deal of time reading, philosophy mostly. The writing of your old friend Friedrich Nietzsche in particular. It doesn't bother me that in person he may have been coarse and disagreeable. It's his ideas I care about. There are many levels in his writing, and even when I believe I grasp what he's saying, I'll reread the passage and understand it in an entirely new way.'

He glances at her to be certain she's listening closely.

'In the evening, I like to walk, explore the city, discover its dark corners. In daylight, scouting scenes for my sketches, I'm struck by architecture and angles of viewing that will result in strong compositions. But at night I search for something else. I'm not sure I can explain it.'

'Please try.'

'I find the city morbid and gloomy at night. I'm attracted to that.'

'Some call Vienna at night a "dream city",' Lou tells him. 'My friend Arthur Schnitzler and other writers see it that way.'

'For me it has been more like a nightmare.' The young man grins. 'At night I follow streets guided only by instinct. "Should I turn here . . . or continue on?" I'll ask myself. And then I'll take the turn or not depending on my mood. Because in the end it doesn't matter which street I take or where I end up so long as it's someplace new and interesting. I like to find my way into unfamiliar neighborhoods. Then I'll gaze at the people on the streets or sitting in cafés and restaurants. I'll peer up into lit windows where I might see a young woman moving about from room to room, a family at dinner, perhaps an elderly man sitting alone smoking a pipe, or a young couple having an argument. Sometimes, when I hear someone practicing a musical instrument, I'll stand still below on the street and strain to listen.'

He pauses, meets her eyes. 'I love music, so sometimes I attend the Imperial Opera, but only when Wagner is being performed. Then I'll purchase a space in the standing-room area beneath the royal box and revel in the music. After the opera is finished, while others, regular box-holders and elegant men and women such as yourself, step into automobiles or carriages and go off to luxurious restaurants, I'll stand in the shadows watching, observing, making up stories about those people, who they are, what they're like, how they talk and think.

'After the audience has dispersed I often linger at the stage door with other opera-lovers waiting for the singers to come out. When the great ones finally emerge (and I'm speaking now of such as Anna von Mildenburg), I never push myself toward them as others do, the ones who hold out their programs begging for autographs. I simply watch them, study them, noting how different they seem from the way they appeared on stage – not so big and powerful, but still rich and sleek, reveling in the triumph of their performances. Sometimes, if a performance has particularly excited me, I might join in the applause outside the stage door. Sometimes one of them, perhaps the orchestra conductor or a great soprano such as Lucy Weidt, will catch my eye, there will be a moment of contact between us, then she will turn and look away. It's always the other person who breaks eye contact first, never me.' He stares hard at Lou. She has the impression he's now sketching her eyes. 'And though the singer will likely forget my face, I will never forget the look in her eyes, the regard, however momentary, that has passed between us, her understanding that I truly grasp the extent of her talent, and her appreciation for that. And sometimes, strangely, I will also see a glimmer of recognition just before her eyes disengage from mine, as if she sees something in me as well, perhaps something momentous . . . or simply disturbing.'

The young man grins. 'I confess I rather like that feeling. It's as if there has been an exchange of energy between us, something electric.'

Lou peers at him. 'I must tell you – you're an excellent talker.'

'And you, Frau Lou, are an excellent listener.' He takes a long deep breath. 'Earlier you asked me about prostitutes. I refuse to discuss what I may or may not do in that regard, but sometimes late at night, after the opera, I will walk over to Spittelberggasse and look at them perched in their windows trying to lure in customers.'

'Do such women appeal to you?'

He vigorously shakes his head. 'They revolt me! And yet I am as curious about human scum as I am about members of all the classes.' He pauses, looks up at her. 'May I speak to you about Schiele now?'

She nods.

'I'll say this for him, his work gave me nightmares.' Lou notices the way his eyes burn as he speaks. 'All those emaciated self-portraits, those strangely twisted malnourished naked bodies – I couldn't push them out of my mind. I felt he was trying to tell me something, but I couldn't grasp what it was. Perhaps some vision of the future, what he thinks the world may someday become. And those naked women, legs spread – I have to admit that standing before them I felt embarrassed. The postures, so strange, other-worldly. The eyes, burning, staring out at me. And those cadaverous men, like meat hanging on hooks in a slaughterhouse. It's a frightening vision. Nothing ennobling in it. As I said, a nightmare.' He peers at her. 'You're smiling.'

'I am, because what you've described is exactly what I believe Schiele intended. That his work gave you nightmares speaks to the power of his art. He is showing you his world, the world of his dreams. He looks deeply inside himself and fearlessly paints what he finds there.'

'It's a dark vision.'

'I believe there is darkness within us all. When we deny the darkness it eats away at us, but when we own up to it, expose it as Schiele does, we feel relieved. The fact that you found his paintings nearly unbearable to look at tells me he has reached you.' She catches his eye. 'How old are you?'

'I'll soon turn twenty-four.'

'I believe Schiele's the same age.'

He scoffs, then resumes sketching her. 'I could never make art that looks like that!'

'I understand you paint scenes to sell to tourists, but I hope that at some point you may decide to really test yourself as an artist, explore your own soul including the dark crevices you deny are there.'

'I must think about that.'

'You should. And if you can't find a way to express your deep feelings in a pictorial way, then perhaps there's some other mode of expression in which you can.'

'Such as?'

'I can't answer that. You must discover it on your own. All you need is a strong idea.'

Taking this in, he sketches in silence for a while, then finally raises his head.

'There is something I must tell you. I promised not to follow you. That was the condition you set for further meetings and I agreed to it. I don't mind telling you how difficult that was.'

'Was it a compulsion?'

'I don't understand . . .'

'Did you feel you *had* to follow me?'

'Perhaps. Yes, I believe I did, as you say, feel compelled.'

'Can you explain why?' She's very attentive to him now, eager to understand why he's attracted to her and by so doing to better understand the concept of transference Freud emphasizes when discussing analytic technique. 'Do I remind you of someone in your life, perhaps someone in your family?'

He shakes his head. 'I suppose I could say it was your connection to Nietzsche that attracted me. But I think it was really that photograph that haunted me, the one you don't like to talk about.'

Hearing this she feels disconcerted, but tries not to show it.

The young man resumes sketching. 'In the picture you harness Nietzsche and the other man together, make them pull your cart like animals.'

'The picture was a joke. It was totally Nietzsche's idea. He conceived it, found some props lying around the studio, put them together then staged the scene. Then he stepped into the frame, and, flash! The photographer took the shot.'

'But why?'

'I have written about this. It was a special occasion. We

were celebrating what we thought would be our life together, the three of us studying, writing, energizing one another's minds. We had made a compact to live like this, in this "scandalous" manner, and Fritz wanted to celebrate the moment. So he dragged us up to that studio to be photographed.'

'That strikes me as bizarre.'

Lou smiles. 'Believe me, you're not the only one who's called it that. I'm asked about that image all the time: "What were we thinking?" "What does it mean?" "What does it say about the relationships between the three of you?" Fritz's sister despises me for many reasons, not the least for that photograph, which she thinks I set up and then showed around so people would think I had her brother in my power. That's so stupid! At the time I was all of twenty-one years old. I may have held a few illusions back then, but nothing so grandiose! The truth is that when I showed it to people it was just to make them smile. "Look at this silly picture," I'd tell them. Then they'd laugh and we'd go on to talk of something else. But later those same people who pretended to be amused would gossip about it and draw nasty conclusions. So please, if you don't mind, explain to me why that silly little picture would have such a powerful effect upon you that it would drive you to follow me around Vienna, if I understand correctly, almost against your will?'

The young man strokes his chin. 'You say the picture was meant as a joke, but for me it possesses a haunting power.' Throughout this exchange he has peered past Lou, but now he meets her eyes. 'I've heard it said that the break-up of your relationship with Nietzsche was the inspiration for *Thus Spake Zarathustra*. Is that true?'

'I have no idea. But if in some small way I inspired Nietzsche to create his masterpiece, then of course I would feel greatly honored.'

He looks down at his sketch, then lays his sketchbook face-down on the table.

'I want to make a full confession. I kept my word about not following you. But you never told me not to follow people you associate with.'

'Did you?' she asks, appalled.

He nods. 'Some nights by chance I find my way to the Alsergrund, the district where you're staying and where I gather you spend much of your time. One night, quite late, I happened to be passing Professor Freud's house on Berggasse. I've passed by there many times. That night I happened to see the two of you emerge together. It must have been after one a.m. To assure your safety, I decided to follow you. Actually *not* you since you had ordered me not to, but the professor who at the time just happened to be *with* you. I followed him as he escorted you back to your hotel, and then continued to follow him as he walked back alone to his residence.'

'So you *did* follow me?' She feels herself becoming angry.

'No! I kept my promise. I was following the professor!'

'You're splitting hairs. I find that devious. Who else have you followed whom you associate with me?'

He looks down. 'Just one other person, the man I've seen you dining with at the Alte Elster. I can see you're angry hearing this, so let me assure you I noticed you there with him before you instructed me to stop following you, and that after that, if I saw you two together, it was completely by chance.' He looks into her eyes. 'I believe his name is Dr Tausk.'

Lou raises her hand. 'Stop! I mean it! That is really unsupportable!'

'I'm sorry you see it that way. But I did keep my promise.'

'You deliberately narrowed the meaning of your promise to suit your convenience. I find that slippery, very slippery.' She rises to leave.

'Please! You're not going? I must finish my sketch.'

'You'll have to finish it without me now.'

'Please don't leave like this, Frau Lou. There're so many things I want to say.'

'You had your chance. I hope our meetings have been helpful to you. This will be the last one. I wish you luck in life. Goodbye.'

And at that she summons the waiter, hands him money, unfurls her umbrella, and walks out into the rain without looking back.

EIGHT

Chantal's books: my first impression is that I've acquired the library of a well-educated person with numerous connected interests. I'm also impressed by the depth of her explorations. She didn't own just a half-dozen books about the Third Reich, admittedly a fascinating period. She had over fifty.

Among them I find numerous biographies of Hitler and other Third Reich personalities; books on the SS; the Gestapo; Nazi occultism, theater, cinema, music, art, architecture, and sculpture; and, oddly, two books devoted to Hitler as artist and watercolorist, illustrated with drawings and paintings he produced in Vienna before World War I.

There're also numerous books about Vienna, understandable since I know from Lynx that Chantal apprenticed there. Some of these are quite old, including a Baedeker's guide published in 1910. Inside I find a folded map of the city with routes highlighted in different colors. It's as if Chantal were tracing walks she'd taken during her residency.

There are books about early twentieth-century Austrian art, particularly the work of Klimt, Schiele, and Kokoschka; biographies of Freud and his circle with a special emphasis on the heroic early days of psychoanalysis; a psycho-biography of Friedrich Nietzsche; and a host of volumes about Lou Andreas-Salomé, the source of the archway quote, biographies as well as translations of her books.

I start looking through the books, searching for letters filed between pages. Most are of little interest: correspondence with rare-book dealers; postcards from vacationing friends; a neatly folded cloth swastika armband. Others are fascinating, such as two rambling letters signed 'X', evidently from one of Chantal's clients. In them he expresses gratitude for 'highly enjoyable and instructive sessions' and makes coded references to fetish interests he hopes to pursue next time they meet.

I also find seven handwritten in German. I don't read the language but am able to make out the scrawled signature, 'Eva', or sometimes just the letter 'E'. These, I decide, were likely from Chantal's mentor, Gräfin Eva, the Vienna-based dominatrix mentioned by Lynx. Alas, Jerry Hunsecker is the only person I know fluent in German. Can I ask him to translate them for me? I'll have to give some thought to that.

There are numerous newspaper clippings stored between pages. One in particular catches my interest: a yellowed article from *The Washington Post*, datelined Montevideo, Uruguay, about the exposure, arrest, and deportation back to Germany of a former SS officer who'd been practicing for years as psychoanalyst with a phony Jewish name and forged diplomas and credentials.

Making a quick inventory of Chantal's marginalia, I find these treasures:

On a page in a book about the relationship between Hitler and Wagner: 'To achieve the proper gravitas, play Wagner during sessions!'

In a biography of Hitler, beside a passage about Martin Bormann's supervision of the construction of Hitler's Alpine teahouse, The Eagle's Nest (*Kehlsteinhaus*), Chantal has written: 'Seems Bormann had a hand in most everything!'

On a page in a book about the Holocaust: 'I keep hearing from Jewish men who want to reenact the humiliation of camp internees. Please send me some fascists who want to play at being slave to a Jewess!'

On a page in the psycho-biography of Nietzsche: 'Pain seemed to fuel him. It flowed like a river through his life!'

On a page in a biography of Lou Andreas-Salomé: 'Wary of intimacy, she arranged her personal life so she was always in a triangle with two men.' And on another page in the same book: 'L keeps telling the men in her life she's not interested in an erotic relationship. So what *was* she interested in?'

One of Chantal's recurring obsessive interests is a striking photograph of Lou Salomé with Nietzsche and another man named Paul Rée. This photo, I learn from accompanying texts, was taken by a studio photographer in 1882 in Luzern, Switzerland. It's reproduced in nearly all the Salomé biographies and in many of Chantal's books about Nietzsche. In it Salomé, holding a vine attached to a stick meant to resemble a whip, is sitting in a cart harnessed to Nietzsche and Rée. Even though the three are dressed in street clothes, there's a mock-sadomasochistic undercurrent which, I learn, caused this image to be considered scandalous when it surfaced early in the twentieth century. Clearly Chantal was fascinated by it. Often when it's reproduced she adds comments in the margins. A quick sampling:

'What were they thinking? The poses are absurd!'

'N looks nerdy, perhaps a bit insane. R appears bored. L grins fiendishly. She has no idea of the ruination to come.'

'Lousy staging! My chariot would have been so much better! And that whip – really! L could have used some domme training with the Gräfin!'

'Trinity? Triad? Troika? Troika is best since L was Russian.'

'If I'd set this up, I'd have had the guys naked!'

'In this frozen moment they pose to celebrate their pact of chastity while unwittingly revealing the seeds of its imminent dissolution!'

'Time bomb. The image foreshadows everything . . . but they had no idea!'

'Project: reenact this picture. Make it more explicit, more theatrical, more powerful!'

Chantal also seems interested in Nietzsche's various opinions of Lou, as recorded in one of the biographies – opinions that swing back and forth from admiration to hatred depending on whether he's in love with her or staggering from the blow of her rejection. Chantal has underlined the following from Nietzsche's letters and diary entries:

'She's as shrewd as an eagle and as brave as a lion . . .'

'She unites in herself all the human qualities I find most repulsive . . .'

'Could Lou be an unrecognized angel? Could I be an unrecognized ass?'

'She treated me like a twenty-year-old student. She told me she had no morality, and yet I thought she had, like myself, a more severe morality than anybody.'

'Lou is by far the shrewdest human being I have known.'

'Those two, Lou and Rée, aren't worthy to lick my

boots. Their behavior toward me was shady, slanderous, mendacious . . .'

I see these books as a passageway into her mind. I have much to do these next few days, prepping for Rex's Vertigo and refining and rehearsing *Recital*, but I know I'll be coming back often to these volumes to mine them for deeper insights.

Dr Maude, I can see, is not happy. 'You're really going to use her name as an alias?'

'It's not an alias,' I correct her. 'It's a character name perfect for a high-priced escort. I'll just be using it in the one skit.'

'But surely, Tess, you understand what you're doing?' From her expression I can see she's appalled. 'You meet this woman casually at your martial-arts class, then coincidentally move into her loft. In a matter of weeks you become obsessed with her and buy up her library. And now for some reason that escapes me you're going to use her name.'

She's edgy today. 'I'm worried about you, Tess. You've always struck me as well grounded. But since you moved into that loft, you've been skewing off-center. It's like you think you're strolling down an ordinary street, when really you're stepping out on a tightrope.'

I search her eyes. 'That bad?'

'It's as if you see Chantal as your mirror image.'

'No,' I correct her, 'I see myself as *her* mirror image. Couple weeks after I move into her old loft, I hear she's been murdered! Of course I'm all wrapped up in her. How can I not be? Especially with all the connections – kickboxing, performance art, a fascination with psychoanalysis, decadence, perversion.' I pause so Dr Maude can feel my annoyance. 'And, frankly, though I appreciate your saying so, I'm not sure I've ever been what anyone would call well grounded. If I were I doubt I'd have chosen the kind of work I do – inhabiting roles, trying, as any artist does, to turn my personal pain into something resembling art.'

She's silent for a time. When she speaks again, I recognize a tone she uses when a session's about to end.

'I want us to explore this professed love you have for the

transgressive, the perverse – where that comes from. I believe when we figure that out, we'll better understand your fascination with Chantal.'

Great idea! Let's definitely explore it. That's why I came to you in the first place, Dr Maude, the core issue behind everything we discuss. It's all connected to my new-found 'obsession' with Chantal. Don't you see that, dear Dr M? Don't you see that it can't be separated out?

The session did not go well, I think as I exit on to San Pablo, then head up the avenue to kickboxing. It was like a tug of war in which she and I were pulling so hard on opposite ends of a rope it burned both our hands.

And the rope? My soul, I suppose, perhaps even my sanity, which, in opposing ways, Dr Maude and I are struggling to save.

But is my sanity really at risk because I purchased Chantal's books and am going to use her name in Rex's Vertigo? Seems to me Dr Maude has exaggerated the harm. Or am I in denial, as she seems to think, and am now precariously poised on a tightrope?

After kickboxing, feeling the time has come to clarify things with Josh, I don't bother to shower but go straight home in my workout clothes, buzz his studio from the street, and, when he answers, announce myself.

'We need to talk,' I tell him, speaking into the intercom.

'I'm painting. Can't this wait?'

'No, it really can't.'

When I step off the elevator on the fifth floor I find his door partially open. I knock anyway.

'Enter,' he yells. 'I'm cleaning up. You sure picked an inconvenient time.'

'Well, *so* sorry!' I yell back. 'Real life isn't always convenient!'

He walks toward me drying his hands. 'You're in a great mood! Slick too. Why so sweaty?'

I ignore his comment. 'You fibbed to me, Josh. I want to know why?'

He blinks. 'That's what's urgent?' Then he asks if I'd like a cool glass of water.

'Fuck that! I came here to get a few things straight. You weren't truthful when you told me you didn't know Chantal very well and that you didn't know anything about her clients or what she did with them. Now I find out you were monitoring her security cameras. You're quite the voyeur, from what I hear. And by the way, I've blocked off the cameras and snipped off the mikes. But you probably already know that, seeing as how you were using them to spy on me.'

'Not true!' he says, angrily.

'How can I believe you,' I demand, 'after you lied to me about everything else?'

'Did we know each other so well that fibbing was off the table? Did we make a compact we'd only tell each other the truth?'

I shrug. 'I like to take people at their word. I suppose that makes me naive. I can't imagine why you'd lie to me about your relationship with Chantal when I was certain to hear about it from Lynx. I don't get it, I don't like deception, and I don't appreciate being punked in whatever devious game you're playing with me.'

'OK,' he says, 'let's take up your issues. One, I'm not playing any kind of game. Two, I had no idea you blocked the cameras and snipped the mikes because the only way they could be monitored was when Chantal relayed the feed to me through her computer. She only did that when she was in session, and not always then. Only when she thought there might be problems.'

'You didn't record any of these sessions?'

'Absolutely not!'

'Why not?'

'Because Chantal forbade it.'

Forbade – that's a strange word to use. Is he saying she gave him orders?

'Are there any more cameras or mikes beside the two in the ceiling?'

'Not that I know of. And I would know since I'm the one who installed them.'

'Why fib about how well you knew her?'

'Because I didn't feel like talking about that to you or to anyone else, including that pair of asshole detectives who came sniffing around. Chantal ran off without telling me, then turned up dead. That was devastating. And there you were, a beautiful stranger, with your insatiable curiosity, prying into our relationship. I barely knew you. Did I owe you full disclosure? Is that what you expect from people on short acquaintance? I didn't think I owed you anything, so I fibbed or side-stepped. Call that lying if you want. I think of it as self-protection.'

'Why show me Queen of Swords? Why suggest I contact Lynx?'

'I showed you the painting because you wanted to know what she looked like. And you're right, I guess I *did* know Lynx would tell you about my relationship with Chantal, and then you'd either confront me about my pathetic fabrications or cut me out of your life.' He smiles. 'I'm actually glad we're discussing this. Feels good to clear the air.' He peers at me. 'Sure you don't want something to drink?'

I stare at him. *Beautiful stranger* – what's that about? Does he think flattery will earn him points? Has he even been *listening*? Does he grasp how I feel about being lied to? Of course not! How could he know that lying was what my charming con man of a father did all the time, that 'Liar', as in Larry 'The Liar' Berenson, could have been his middle name?

'There's other stuff,' I tell him, 'like your bullshit explanation of why you refuse to paint like Picasso. Lynx says you forged paintings then sold them to dumb-ass collectors. She says I shouldn't believe a thing you say.'

'She really said that?'

'Did you forge Picassos?'

He shrugs again. 'Let's just say I don't "do" him anymore.'

I sniff. 'So she was right, you *are* a forger.'

'If you're an artist you do what you must. Getting by is the trick.'

'Depends how you do it. I think the real trick's holding on to one's core integrity in a morally corrupt world.'

'I'm not getting into a discussion with you about the nature of the universe.' He pauses. 'Look, I happen to have a talent for pastiche. Maybe I didn't always put it to good use. Now I do. As for Lynx, sorry to hear she thinks so poorly of me.'

'Did you tell the detectives Chantal has a brother?'

He nods. 'I contacted him myself. He authorized me to arrange her cremation. I took care of it and had the funeral home send him half her ashes.'

'The other half?'

'They're here.' He speaks flatly as if to disguise his feelings.

I study him a while then stand up. 'I'm performing tomorrow night. I need to prep a scene. And I'm sure you want to get back to your easel. So . . . see you around.'

'Yeah,' he says. He escorts me out to the elevator. 'I hope we can still be friends, Tess.'

'Yeah, well, I'll have to think about that, Josh.'

NINE

Vienna, Austria. March 28, 1913. A fine evening in early spring. Lou and the very handsome young blond-haired psychiatrist Dr Victor Tausk emerge from the Urania Cinema. They've just seen an American movie, *Cleopatra*, based on Sardou's play, starring Helen Gardner as the queen and Charles Sindelar as Antony.

Walking amidst the evening crowds along the Donau Canal, they follow Franz-Josefs-Kai to Rotenturmstrasse, reveling in one another's company and the warm air carrying the aroma of early blooming flowers.

After a silence, Lou broaches a subject that has recently concerned her.

'Ellen tells me I was discussed before my arrival. At one of Freud's Wednesday evenings, no less.'

'Does that surprise you, Lou?' Tausk asks. 'A famous woman coming to study with him and join our little group – of course everyone was curious about you.'

'Was this an informal discussion, or . . .?'

'Actually, Hugo Heller presented a paper about your fiction.'

'Really! Heller never mentioned it. He was complimentary, I hope.'

'It was an excellent paper. You'd have been flattered.'

'And after the paper there was discussion?' Tausk nods. 'About the photograph?'

'Yes, yes – the "infamous photograph". Of course that came up. How could it not since it established you as a great femme fatale?'

Lou scoffs at the notion. 'Is that really what they think?'

'Please, Lou, everyone was excited you were joining us, in awe of you and perhaps a little worried too that you'd try to dominate discussions. An unnecessary worry as it turned out. You've been wonderful, an excellent listener. It's clear to all that Freud holds you in high regard. Everyone agrees it's nice to have a woman in our circle, moreover one who's built a reputation outside the profession and who, by the way, doesn't happen to be Jewish. None of us wants psychoanalysis to be viewed as an exclusively Jewish field.'

'So like Jung I was especially welcome.'

'The Jung issue is something else. I hear Freud's about to break with him.'

'You say the photo came up, Victor. Do you mean mentioned in passing, or analyzed?'

Tausk laughs. 'There was some analysis, as you'd expect from our group.'

'Such as?'

'You want me to tell you what was said?' Lou nods. 'As I recall, basically two questions were raised. The first was whether it really was Nietzsche who instigated the whole thing.'

'It was!'

'I believe you. The second question was whether as a key participant you understood what the poses seemed to signify, or whether you took part in the naïve belief that it was all just fun and games?'

Lou exhales: she's answered this query many times. 'It was a joyful moment commemorating a serious plan – my plan that we three would live together chastely in a kind of intellectual commune.' She looks at Tausk. 'What was Freud's reaction?'

'He didn't say much, just listened and smiled slightly the way he often does.' Tausk chuckles. 'That, as you know, can carry more meaning than a lengthy speech by anybody else.' He stops walking, turns to Lou so they're facing one another, then peers into her eyes. 'Didn't you suspect your plan couldn't possibly work, that if two men, rivals competing for a woman's love, were forced to live together the end could only be explosive?'

'Yes, a time bomb! I've heard that. Call me naïve, but at the time my plan seemed worthy and on the day that picture was taken I was certain great things would come of it.'

'As apparently they did.'

'You're speaking of *Zarathustra*. But, you see, I've never

believed that book was a reaction to our failed plan. Fritz was deeply troubled even then. As I wrote . . .'

'I know the line, Lou. "The depths of his misery became the glowing furnace in which his will to knowledge was forged." Do I have it right?'

Lou nods.

'I still have a question regarding the symbolism. Did Nietzsche want to suggest that, harnessed along with Paul Rée, the two of them would transport you to some undefined but exemplary future destiny, or was he suggesting that under your discipline he and Paul would fulfill the promise of their greatness?'

'That's a truly wonderful question, Victor, the best one, I think, that's been raised about the picture. Knowing Nietzsche, I believe the former – that he saw himself and to a lesser extent Paul as mentors who would pull me along.' She laughs. 'Who knows? Maybe it was all just harmless fun and these deep hidden meanings, so dear to those of us in the profession, are simply, as Freud so often points out, unprovable interpretations superimposed upon a perfectly innocent joyous shared experience.'

Tausk stops to light a cigarette. 'Actually Freud did say something about the photo. He said it seemed staged like a frozen moment in a dream, and the only way to interpret a dream is to put the dreamer under analysis. As a result, he added, anything more he might say about it would be speculative. But he did make one observation. He told us he recognized the Alpine peak in the background, that it was the mountain known as Die Jungfrau, The Virgin. Then he reminded us that in a dream every little detail is important, his way of telling us that choosing the Jungfrau as the background would be an important clue to decoding the dream.'

Hearing this, Lou smiles knowingly. Tausk, catching her smile, asks her if she agrees.

Lou shrugs, signaling she'll have nothing to say about the then-state of her virginity. Then she laughs and takes Victor's arm.

'Let's go to that Italian place we like, grab something to eat, then go back to the Zita. My little friend Ellen's out for the evening, doubtless seducing another of her numerous admirers.' She stops, turns to Tausk, looks him in the eye. 'Her interest in you hasn't escaped me, Victor. I noticed it when I returned to the room the other day and found you two reading *Faust*. She makes a fine Gretchen, doesn't she? So young and devilishly pretty. You've been tempted too, haven't you? I understand. She's a seductive little creature. But let's hope she doesn't take her Gretchen role too seriously and try to poison her old mama.'

Tausk seems a little unnerved by this. 'Believe me, Lou – nothing could be further from her mind. She adores you. As do I. Please don't think such things.'

Lou giggles. 'I love her too, so never mind. It's good she's out tonight. We'll be able to fully express ourselves without worrying the little vixen will tiptoe in and interrupt us in our passion.'

TEN

I'm sitting on a red leather couch in the Redwood Lounge sipping from a thirty-dollar glass of champagne. The room is large, the lighting soft. The redwood paneled walls glow like copper. Above the long bar, made from a single plank of redwood, bottles of spirits, arranged in tiers, are silhouetted against yellow light. Paintings, slowly dissolving one into the other, are displayed on plasma screens. A warm buzz issues from the couches, chairs, and tables all around.

Rex, I think, has chosen a perfect setting for this rendezvous. This is just where a high-end escort would meet a john. I feel glamorous in my red dress, the one I usually wear when performing my Weimar piece. A tiny video camera, disguised as a button, has been subtly concealed in the front of it. My high-heeled shoes show off the shapeliness of my legs. The faux black-pearl necklace Rex draped about my neck glows against my bare tanned skin.

I may be playing an escort, but I don't feel slutty. On the contrary, I feel secure, confident, in command. I will myself into the proper mindset. Taking another sip from my glass, I think: *Now where oh where is my needy date?*

I recognize him immediately as he lopes toward me. With his awkward gait and mop of bed-hair, he looks like a prototypical Silicon Valley nerd, one who likely feels comfortable in a worn T-shirt facing a computer screen but clumsy in a suit and tie in this elegant hotel bar.

'Chantal?'

I enjoy being addressed by my alias. I show him a feline smile. 'Mike.'

'*C'est moi!*'

'Sit,' I order after shaking his hand. 'Very nice to meet you. I've heard awesome things about you. I've heard you're a *very* interesting guy.'

He lowers himself onto the couch so we're sitting side by

side, but, observing first-date etiquette, not *too* close. He tries
to act suave, but I can see he's embarrassed. I peer into his
eyes, again offering a smile. He's neither handsome nor unat-
tractive. Watery brown eyes, slightly scruffy cheeks; he looks
the single-minded internet entrepreneur – late twenties, pale,
socially maladroit, unaccustomed to meeting a beautiful and
expensively-put-together older woman, the type of woman
who excites him even as he fears she'll eat him alive.

To relax him, I get him talking about himself. I feign interest
as he mentions people at work, people I don't know and
couldn't possibly care about, colleagues with names like Dan,
Rich, Art, Herb, who set up this 'date' and the 'noir adventure'
he's been promised will follow, and I think (the way I imagine
my character would): *Like who gives a flying fuck what their
stupid names are!*

Finally, when he becomes too tiresome, I interrupt.

'So what turns you on, Mike . . . aside from algorithms and
cool software?'

'Turns me on? Gee, lots of stuff. Cool movies. Comics.
Great food. Wine.'

'A man after my own heart. But what turns you on in a
woman?'

'You mean sexually?'

I shrug. 'Sure, since *you* bring it up, what turns you on
sexually in a woman?'

'Gee, just normal stuff, I guess. You know . . .'

'Whatever "normal" means, right?'

'Yeah, right!' He giggles.

'Wanna know what turns *me* on, Mike?'

'I would definitely like to know that,' he says, trying his
best to keep his cool.

Oh, I bet you would! I peer into his eyes. 'An interesting
man, accomplished. A man who knows who he is. A guy
secure in his maleness . . . as you so clearly are.' I lean into
him so my mouth is practically against his ear. 'A guy who's
good in the sack. That's the *real* turn-on for me.' I pull back,
giggle, resume my speaking voice. 'Now how 'bout that?' I
ask bewitchingly.

'Like wow!'

Mike giggles, embarrassed and also dazzled by my effrontery. *Like who would talk that way in the first ten minutes of a first date?* He isn't used to a woman so brazen and seductive.

'So, Mike . . .' I draw out his name, tasting it, rolling it around in my mouth like I'm savoring a delicious chocolate. 'Has anyone ever read your palm?' He shakes his head. I take hold of his hand, run my finger lightly across it. 'Good strong lifeline,' I tell him. I stroke it again, tracing the crease. 'And this—' I run the tip of my forefinger up the length of his, then down his thumb, taking special care to massage the loose flesh between. 'This,' I tell him, stroking his thumb again, 'tells me you're . . . how shall I put it?' I lean in again to whisper. 'On the well-hung side, shall we say?'

At this I grin and daringly enlarge my eyes, exhibiting some serious lewdness. I can tell he likes what I've said by the way he wets his upper lip. But then how could he not?

'I get this feeling you and I are going to have an awesome time,' I tell him.

He doesn't have a response for that and I don't expect him to. He's totally attentive to me, can't tear his eyes from mine. *Got him now!* I think.

I lower my voice and speak directly into his ear. 'I'm going to do things with you I suspect no one's ever done before. For starters I'm going to coax you into confessing your deepest longings, the ones you never dared confide to anyone. And then, no matter how kinky, you and I are going to bring them to life. We're going to awesome mind-blowing sex. Now I'm sure you've been told this will be a one-time adventure. After tonight we'll never see each other again . . . which is good because that allows us to be totally shameless. So let's make the most of it, shall we? No one will ever know what we did. Not Dan or Rich or Art or Herb. It will be strictly private, our secret night of ecstasy. And because it'll be a one-off, I'm going to do everything in my power to make it unforgettable for you. And oh yes, for me too! I want to leave you with terrific memories. Now how does that strike you? Perhaps a wee bit excited, are we?'

'Oh, yeah!' he agrees.

'Good! Because I'm excited. *Very* excited.' I run my hand very lightly across his lap, allowing my fingertips to graze and linger momentarily upon his hardness.

'Oh, we *are* excited now, aren't we! Feeling you down there – I can't tell you what a huge turn-on that is for me, Mike.'

Oh, I have him going! He isn't looking much like the computer genius with the PhD from Cal Tech; now he's leering at me like a horny adolescent. And just in time too, because I catch a glimpse out of the corner of my eye of the pair of goons who've come to snatch me away. They stand together by the door of the lounge, a well-matched pair of husky thuggish guys in identical shiny black suits. Their appearance tells me I've got just a few more seconds to lock Mike in. I lean in again to whisper into his ear: 'You know I want to suck it, don't you? Of course you do.' I pause, then lower my voice to a throaty whisper. 'You have no idea how much!'

The goons are moving toward me now. I tighten as they approach. Mike, picking up on my change of mood, asks if something's wrong.

I motion with my head toward the approaching men. 'I may have to leave you for a while.' I whisper: 'Can you remember this address, 2700 Locust – can you remember that?'

'Sure. But who're those guys? Why d'you have to go?'

'Can't talk about it now. Meet me in an hour at that address. We'll reconnect and I'll explain. I don't want to lose you, Mike. But now I gotta—'

The goons are standing in front of us, ignoring Mike, staring down hard at me.

'Boss wants you, Chantal,' the first one says. 'He's waiting in the car.'

'That means *now,* Chantal!' the other one orders. 'Off your butt!'

I nod, obey. Rising from the couch, I turn to Mike: 'Excuse me. Something work-related.' I narrow my eyes to show him a glimmer of fear. 'Hope to see you later on.'

'Fat chance of that,' the first goon mutters, grabbing hold of my arm.

He grasps it so hard I'm forced to wince, to which I add a little cry of pain to show Mike the goon's hurting me. I shush him when he starts to protest, shake my head vigorously to warn him these aren't the kind of guys you mess with. After that I give in, allow the goons, one on each side, to march me toward the entrance. Pausing there I turn, look directly at Mike to again show him my distress – enough, I hope, to encourage him to follow me outside. When I see him rise, I turn and again yield to my escorts, knowing Mike will soon catch up.

Out on Geary, I see the limo – long, black, ominous. I catch a glimpse of Fat Man in the rear compartment, cigar between his teeth, watching menacingly as I approach. I glance back at the hotel door. Mike's standing there confused. The goons shove me roughly into the limo. Fat Man stares at me. With the limo door still open so Mike can see, Fat Man smacks me hard across the face. I cry out, Fat Man leers, then the goons slam the door and get in front. Mike approaches. He's just a few feet away as the goon-driver starts up the engine. I peer out the window at him. I mouth HELP through the soundproof glass. Then the limo lurches forward leaving Mike standing dumbfounded at the curb.

I meet up with Rex at the Locust Street house, borrowed for the evening from one of his friends. Rex's troupe is sitting around talking theater – who's working, who's not, what parts are coming up. They're all well turned out, the women in evening dresses, the men in dark suits and ties. Soon as I enter they cluster around, eager to hear how the bar scene went.

'Good first act,' I tell them. 'Mike's OK. Not what I'd call a horndog, but horny enough.' Everyone laughs. 'Actually it was fun. I had a good time. There's a certain pathos in being a call girl.'

'If you say so, Tess!' one of the women says. More laughter.

Rex motions me to a pair of chairs. He wants to confer in private.

'Seriously, did it work for you?'

'It did. I kept thinking of Jane Fonda in *Klute*, used her trick, rolling Mike's name around in my mouth like I was tasting it. I had him going just as your goons showed up.'

The actors playing the goons come over. 'Arm OK?' one asks.

I nod. 'You guys were great. Had me scared.'

They laugh and move away.

I turn back to Rex. 'Fat Man's nasty.' I point him out, glaring at me from across the room. 'Smacked me hard. Refused to speak in the car. What's with that guy?'

'He likes to stay in role, keep the intimidation going.' I wince when Rex strokes my cheek. 'Don't worry, kid. No more hurting. Acts II and III are mind games.'

Yeah, mind-fucks, I think, dreading what's ahead. I gesture toward a door. 'Orgy room?'

Rex nods. 'My horny crew of orgyists are deep into rehearsal.'

'Uh oh . . .!'

He smiles. 'Just simulated sex.'

'Want to ask you something about *Vertigo*, Rex. Been years since I saw it. Way I remember, the Kim Novak character becomes obsessed with this dead woman from the past.'

'Yeah, but, see, she's not really obsessed with her. She's been hired to *pretend* to be obsessed in order to draw the Jimmy Stewart character into the murder plot.'

'So is Novak playing a professional actress?'

'Not really. That's one of the flaws in the story.' He studies me. 'Why so interested?'

'It's a great San Francisco movie, but for me that's a really big flaw.'

I excuse myself to use the restroom. Inside I stare at my image in the mirror above the sink.

'Hello, Chantal,' I whisper to my reflection.

When I come back, Rex fills me in on what's been going down: after the limo pulled away, a homeless guy approached Mike, told him the car belongs to a vicious pimp and that I, Chantal, am just one of several girls on his string. He tells Mike that Fat Man abuses his girls, that most of them expect it, and some actually like it. 'All except Chantal,' he tells Mike. 'She resists, tries to set up dates on her own. Tonight she got caught. Now she's in trouble!"

The homeless guy tells Mike he's seen me walking around marked up pretty bad after one of Fat Man's beatings. He also tells him how nice I am, not snobby like the others, how I always ask how he's doing and give him a few bucks to help him out.

'Idea is to keep Mike liking you and worrying about you,' Rex explains.

'Then what?'

Rex looks at his watch. 'In a couple minutes Homeless will get rousted by a uniformed security guy. Homeless'll call out to Mike for help as Security Guy starts to drag him away. When Mike tries to intervene, Security Guy'll warn him off, tell him Homeless is a pest, that he makes up stories to soften up passersby before he robs them. He'll tell him Homeless is a fake, lives in a nice apartment, and that now he's going to take him to an alley behind the hotel and teach him to mind his own business. Just then Homeless'll break loose, pull a knife, and stab Security Guy. This is taking place about now. Then as Security Guy lies bleeding on the sidewalk, Homeless'll start shouting at Mike: "*You* stabbed him. I saw you! *You* did it, you son of a bitch!" That's to put a big scare into Mike.'

'Wow! He's getting the full treatment.'

'That's what his buddies are paying for.'

'Then?'

'Our taxi'll pull up. The cabbie'll beckon Mike in, ask him where he wants to go. Soon as Mike gives this address, the cab'll take off.' Rex checks his watch again. 'He'll be here soon. Got to start blocking the party.'

He stands and calls everyone together. 'OK, people, it's party time. Grab your drinks and take your places. Tess, I want you to stand against the far wall. Goons, on either side of her. Tess, make nice with the guests, but don't hide your fear. When Mike comes in we want him to see you're still afraid. Fat Man's ordered his goons to teach you a lesson. You know it's coming. You just don't know how harsh.'

Things go as planned. I've got to hand it to Rex: his cast does a great job giving the party an undercurrent of menace. People move in strange over-attenuated ways and make extravagant stylized gestures as they converse. The women are gothed-up with weird eyeshadow, deeply colored lipstick, and overdrawn eyebrows. The men look feral and leer like rodents. People light up cigarettes and deeply exhale. Others slosh glasses of ice and amber-colored liquid. Faces grow hard, expressions brittle. The room rebounds with whispers broken by inappropriate cascades of laughter. Sinister electronic music pulses in the background.

Mike enters, disoriented. He doesn't know why the party scene disturbs him. *Something off here*, he thinks. He peers around, spots me, and starts to approach. I shake my head to warn him off, but he comes up to me anyway. I tell him I can't talk to him, then glance furtively at Fat Man sitting in a throne-like chair nearby.

Fat Man beckons Mike over. He tells Mike he's welcome to stick around and enjoy himself, but that I'm out of bounds.

'You don't want to play with her,' Fat Man instructs Mike. 'She puts on airs but she's just a cheap junkie whore.'

Mike, taken aback, starts to protest. Fat Man shuts him down with a sneer. 'Look at her,' Fat Man tells him. 'She's shaking. She needs a fix. My boys'll give it to her. Then you can watch her give head in the backroom. I got clients in there waiting to be serviced. They paid good money. Time for Chantal to earn her keep.'

The goons frog-march me into the orgy room. Through the open doorway Mike can see a foursome of swingers frolicking naked on a huge bed. He watches as the goons roughly strip me to my underwear. Then they bend me over and hold me down as an older woman with heavy black eyeshadow and a haughty manner approaches with a stage-syringe. I scream, struggle, try to fight loose, but the goons hold me tight as she injects me. Then the goons rip off my bra, shove me toward the bed, and force me onto my knees.

Fat Man appears in the doorway. 'Get to work!' he commands. Fat Man turns to Mike, laughs then slams the door shut.

At this point, Rex, playing a new character, Friendly Guest, approaches Mike, beckons him aside, explains that Fat Man doesn't like it when a girl 'tries to go into business for herself.' He tells Mike I'm out of bounds, but there're other girls available who'll give him as good a time. All he has to do is point and pay. Meantime, as guests enter and exit the orgy room, each time slamming the door behind them, Mike catches quick glimpses of me being used.

'Forget her!' Friendly Guest urges Mike. 'Fat Man runs a tight ship.'

When, finally, thankfully, the glimpses-of-the-orgy sequence is done, I get up from the bed and retreat again to the restroom to calm myself. Again I regard my face in the mirror.

'You think you're a pricey escort,' I instruct my reflection, 'but you're just a cheap whore on Fat Man's string.'

Having put myself in a mind-set appropriate for the ordeal to come, I mess up my makeup then rejoin the goons in the orgy room. The woman with the needle uses a lipstick to write SLUT in big red letters across my back and PIG across my bare chest. She ties my hands in front of me, buckles a dog collar around my neck, attaches a leash, and hands the leash to one of the goons while the other opens the door and pushes me out into the party room.

I'm poised now to make my drugged-up, stumbling way through the party. This 'Walk Of Shame,' Rex has warned me, will be the most difficult portion of my role. I close my eyes and repeat the mantra I always murmur to myself before I go on stage: *You're a warrior-actress. Now go out there and kill it!*

I start forward. The guests part to make way for me. All eyes are upon me. There's catcalling and hooting as they delight in my degradation. I steel myself: *Don't cry! Don't show them your hurt!* And so I force myself to face their hard brittle smiles, my head held high, face expressionless. But even as I do their eyes drill me. They want to unmask me, pierce me, rend my soul. Safe in their cruel communal schaden-freude, they want more than anything to see me break. It takes all my will to deny them.

Halfway through the ordeal one of the goons pushes me hard. I stumble, fall to the floor. The other goon yanks me back up by my leash. The crowd reacts with smirks. I hear someone say: 'She got outa line. She's being punished.' A ghoulish woman brings her head close to mine, blows cigarette smoke into my face. Then I catch a quick glimpse of Mike. He's watching, unable to resist feasting on the sight of me.

Our eyes lock. I see compassion in his. I'm grateful for that. I'm really feeling the humiliation now. I want to blot out the hoots of the crowd by withdrawing into myself. The sounds of mob cruelty blur together, becoming a low-volume hiss. Mike's eyes and mine are still locked, the moment between us prolonged. Finally my eyes are torn from his when the woman who blew the smoke grasps hold of my collar, yanks my head toward her, stares ferociously at me, then spits into my face.

Isn't Mike supposed to join the mob, join in the derision? That he does not, that he cares, that he's appalled by what I'm being put through – that gives me strength.

Perhaps there is some kernel of decency in this cruel world . . .

Then it's out the front door and into a waiting limo that transports me to the private strip club, where, in the final act, I will further humiliate myself by pole-dancing topless in front of panicked Mike and leering Fat Man for the delectation of an audience of grinning voyeurs.

On the pole, twirling and lewdly working my mouth, I see tears of compassion forming in Mike's eyes. Seeing him moved by my agony, I let loose myself. I hadn't planned on bawling, but the tears come and then I can't help myself, they stream down my cheeks. But even as they cloud my vision, I continue to work my body robotically against the pole, thrusting my pelvis at it again and again, reveling in the degradation, enjoying it . . . then twirling and twirling and thrusting and thrusting until finally I collapse in a heap.

As the goons drag me off-stage I think: *Thank God it's over . . .*

There's a small after-party for the cast at Buena Vista Café. Here, sipping Irish coffees, we watch raw video of our performances. Rex congratulates us, tells us we all did a terrific job. He orders another round, then raises his glass to me: 'To Tess, our fab femme fatale!'

Everyone applauds.

The goons are warm, solicitous. Fat Man and the woman

who wielded the syringe and wrote with lipstick on my body turn out to be husband and wife. They kindly confess to being great fans of my performance work.

At one a.m., as I'm about to step into the rented limo that will take me home, Rex tells me that on their way out of the strip club Mike asked for my real name and number.

'He got pissed when I refused. I had to remind him you were a professional actress giving a one-time performance. He said he understood that but insisted I give you his card.' Rex hands it to me. 'He said to tell you he hopes you'll call him. Said he liked you a lot and would very much like to ask you out.'

I shake my head. 'It's Chantal he wants to date. Not Tess.'

'He seemed nice. A lot nicer than Jerry Hunsecker.'

We laugh, then set up a time for Rex to meet me at Grace's house for a first full rehearsal of *Recital.*

'Looking forward to getting your take,' I tell him.

'Looking forward to giving it to you. I like your script and I got a few ideas.' Rex hugs me. 'Listen, I know tonight was rough. It was a tough role to play. You were brave, Tess – damn brave to take it on.'

'I enjoyed the slovenliness of it,' I tell him. 'It was definitely an adventure. At the end there I got carried away. Those tears were real.'

'I know.' He strokes my cheek. 'You did great, babe. Don't know anyone else could've killed it the way you did.'

'Thanks,' I tell him. 'But please, Rex, next time cast me as the dominatrix.'

Riding back to Oakland, I realize that when Mike and I shed tears as I worked the pole, we did so for different reasons. Mike teared up with pity for Chantal. I wept because, emotionally overwrought, I needed to purge my pain.

Traffic is light on the Bay Bridge. As we leave Yerba Buena Island and start across the suspension span, I'm moved by the profile of downtown Oakland, dark city towers limned by the light of the three-quarter moon.

Since moving into the loft I've often wondered why people went to Chantal Desforges, what she offered them, what needs she fulfilled. Tonight's ordeal gives me insight: if they can survive the kind of degradation I just went through, go through it and come out safe on the other side, then perhaps they feel, as I do now, steeled and empowered.

Yes, that could be it: Chantal gave her clients a safe way to enact the humiliations we all endure, then transform those painful feelings into erotic pleasure and release. She provided the pain that can obliterate pain. No wonder they went to her, paid her handsomely, and later were grateful for her artful abuse. She gave them one of the most valuable things one person can give another: strength to carry on.

ELEVEN

Vienna, Austria. Sunday, April 6, 1913. A glorious spring day. The air is balmy, yet there's a dour mood in the city, an intimation of war.

The young man, sitting on a bench in the park opposite the Votiv Church, waits nervously. Beside him, a small portfolio made of marbled black-and-white cardboard tied shut with a gray ribbon.

Lou, wearing a loose-fitting cloak, arrives looking rushed . . . as indeed she is for this will be her last day in Vienna. She is due in an hour at Freud's home on Berggasse for a farewell drink.

As soon as she spots the young man, she strides toward him. He rises, gestures for her to join him on the bench. Noting his new shoes and new green Loden forester's jacket, she nods and sits.

'Please understand,' she tells him, 'I have only a few minutes. Though I resolved not to meet you again, I was sufficiently moved by your latest letter to change my mind. You begged for this meeting, said you had something important to tell me. Please say what it is, and make it short as I'm soon expected somewhere else.'

The young man nods. He addresses her gallantly. 'First, thank you for coming. I am grateful for that. I asked to meet with you because I heard you were leaving Vienna and I wanted to see you once more before you left. In fact, I'll be leaving myself next month. Since I last saw you my situation has changed. My father's estate was finally settled. I received my share and am now better off than I've been in years. I'll be heading soon to Munich with the intention of seeking entrance to the Art Academy. And if war should come, as most people believe, I prefer to serve in the German rather than the Austrian army.'

Lou nods, wondering where this is leading.

'Meeting you,' he continues, 'has been important to me. Although we only met three times, those occasions were memorable and I shall not forget them. Nor shall I forget your kindness, willingness to listen and advise. I asked to meet with you because I wanted to give you a farewell gift, a small token of my appreciation.'

'That's not necessary. Whatever I gave you was given freely without expectation.'

'I understand. Let me just say that though my gift is small it is also heart-felt.' He holds up the portfolio. 'A single drawing which I believe may interest you. I would prefer that you not open this until after I leave.'

He pauses. Studying him, she sees him harden up his eyes the way people do when they're trying to conceal strong feelings.

'That's really all I have to say,' he tells her. 'I understand you're pressed so I won't take any more of your time. Please believe me when I tell you that I respect you greatly and apologize for anything I've done that may have distressed you.'

He rises, takes her hand. 'Goodbye, Frau Lou. I wish you a safe journey.'

And with that he clicks his heels, bows formally, then turns and walks away, leaving her sitting alone on the bench.

She watches him as he crosses the park, then heads up Alserstrasse. When he is out of sight, and she is certain he's not lingering in order to follow her, she stands, then starts walking swiftly toward Berggasse for her farewell meeting with Freud.

A few minutes later, arriving at Freud's residence, Lou is greeted by Freud, his wife, Martha, and eighteen-year-old daughter Anna, with whom she's recently struck up a friendship. After a celebratory drink with the family, she joins Freud in his study where they discuss several of his latest ideas as well as her plan to open a psychoanalytic practice in Göttingen.

At one point in the conversation she asks if he remembers counseling her to accede to entreaties for a meeting by a young man who'd been stalking her.

'Yes, the street artist. You told me you met with him several times.'

'The meetings were useful to a point, but when he became too familiar I had to cut him off. Just before coming here I met with him briefly in Votivpark. He wanted to say goodbye, thank me for my advice, and present me with a gift.' She shows Freud the portfolio. 'He's off to Munich himself next month. He believes there will be a war, and he prefers to serve in the German army.'

Freud nods. 'I feel certain a great war is coming and that it will be extremely brutal, perhaps a breaking point in history. It will grind up many young men, and those who fight and survive will be changed for ever. I'm worried for my sons.' He glances at the portfolio. 'Have you opened it?'

'Not yet.'

'Well, let's have a look,' he says.

She nods, unfastens the ribbon, opens the portfolio and extracts a drawing. She examines it then hands it to Freud.

'I can't believe he drew this. I'm shocked!'

'Ah, I see.' Freud nods. 'He parodies the famous photograph!'

As Freud studies it, Lou is tempted to bring up the Wednesday evening meeting described to her by Tausk at which she and the photo were discussed. She decides to restrain herself. *After all*, she thinks, *this is my last day, and I have no wish to embarrass my teacher.*

Freud is still peering at the drawing. 'It seems he's reproduced the photograph then redrawn it. Redrawn you more or less as you are today, no longer the grinning twenty-one-year-old but the fine middle-aged woman you've become. And the furs! They're certainly yours. And he's replaced that silly whip made from a vine with a very serious whip indeed.' Freud shakes his head. 'This is straight out of Krafft-Ebing. Your young artist has turned you into Sacher-Masoch's *Venus in Furs*. Or perhaps some sort of powerful Wagnerian woman to show how greatly he venerates you. I see this as a seduction picture. He believes this is the kind of relationship you would enjoy having with him and so he draws it to seduce you, or, at the very least, to make himself memorable.'

'But that's not all,' Lou tells him, still recovering from the impact of the drawing. 'He's stripped Nietzsche of his frockcoat and shirt, then placed his own head on Nietzsche's half-naked body.'

'He sees himself as Nietzsche! Astounding! Especially considering your well-known role in his life.'

'I'm stunned,' Lou tells him. 'I urged him to express himself, to stop painting the surfaces of things and expose his deepest fantasies. But this is impossible! He's gone too far! The nerve of him! I'm insulted!'

'You mustn't be.' Freud speaks kindly to her. 'He took your advice to heart. Clearly he sees you as an archetype of female power and himself as a beast of burden pulling you about in a cart, half-naked and cowering under the threat of your lash. That he's drawn a parody of the famous photograph of you, Nietzsche, and Rée – I find that quite interesting. He's revealing himself shamelessly here.' Freud turns the drawing over. 'Look, he's written on the back: "This Is The Dream I Have Of Us", then his initials and the date. I would take this as a kind of love letter, Lou, an expression of passion. In analytic terms it's an almost perfect visual expression of a transference relationship. This tells me you reached this young artist on a very deep level.' Freud smiles warmly. 'I always believed you'd make an excellent analyst. Now, seeing this, I'm certain of it!'

Lou takes the drawing, turns it over, observes the inscription, then turns it again to study the image closely.

'I very much appreciate what you're saying. But don't you agree this is pathological?'

'He's a troubled young man with a rich fantasy life originally fueled by that old photograph then reenergized when he met you in person. I sense a good deal of pain here and a great reluctance to express it. The drawing strikes me as something willed, not something that came easily to him. And there's something else in it I find interesting.'

'His treatment of Paul Rée?'

'Precisely. He blacks out Rée, turning him into a silhouette. Thus he transforms his rival into a shadow figure.' Freud nods. 'There's much to interpret here. If he were my patient I'd devote several sessions to probing the many levels he's trying to express.'

Lou replaces the drawing in the portfolio, shuts it, reties the ribbon, then lays it on the floor. She and Freud go on to speak of other matters, particularly the differences between incurable abnormalities and treatable neuroses, how the two cannot be approached the same way, that the best one can do for a patient suffering from a deep-seated perversion such as sadomasochism is to assist him to find a way to live peacefully with his abnormality, while a neurotic patient, in the hands of a first-rate analyst, can be restored to a near-unconflicted state, then go on to lead a fulfilled productive life.

Lou listens closely to her mentor, taking notes on the many ideas he throws out at her, and, at the end of their meeting, happily accepting his warm embrace and gift of a bouquet of roses.

'Studying with you,' she tells him at the door, 'has been a turning point in my life.'

'Coming to know you,' he tells her, 'has been a high point in mine.'

Walking back to Hotel Zita, the portfolio under her arm, Lou thinks back upon her meetings with the young man and the extraordinary gift he has bestowed upon her. In many ways she is repulsed by his drawing. It makes her uncomfortable that she has played a role in his fantasies, and she resents the fact that he has parodied and perverted a key image from her early life.

It's as if he's implicated me in his personal pathology, she thinks.

Then she remembers Freud instructing her and others in his seminars that an analyst must not take such things personally but simply use them as tools to help a suffering patient.

She thinks: *I asked him to look deeply into himself and then to draw what he saw. By his gift he shows me he has done just that.*

TWELVE

It takes me two days to recover from Vertigo. The walk through the party of sneering guests seems more like a nightmare than a lived experience. I doubt it lasted three minutes, but in my memory it seems to go on and on. It was everything I dread and fear and thus I welcome it into the mental space where I store extreme experiences for later use in performance.

Searching out Clarence in his office, I find him at his desk wearing a tank top. The walls are covered with his collection of California wine labels. I gather he lives in an adjoining windowless basement apartment.

He looks up at me with a grin. 'Hey, Tess, how's it goin'?' And before I can answer: 'Come in, sit down. What's your gripe?' This is what he always asks, his way of saying he'll be happy to fix whatever needs fixing.

I ask him about the detectives who brought the news about Chantal. I tell him I've heard they weren't nice.

'Ramos, the Hispanic one, seemed like a hardass. But Scarpaci, the one with the sad eyes, struck me as sweet. They play the old good cop/bad cop routine, like anyone still falls for that.'

He passes me their business cards. I can copy down the info, then go back upstairs, phone Scarpaci, and introduce myself.

'You're a what?' he asks.

'Performance artist.'

'Call me stupid, but what's that?' As I start to explain, he interrupts. 'So you perform monologues?'

'Yeah.'

'Tell stories?'

'Yep.'

'So you're a storyteller.'

'There's a French word for it: *diseuse*.'

'I like that! Why not just say so instead of spouting this performance artist jive?'

'*Excuse me?*'

He guffaws. 'Sorry. Don't mean to give you a hard time. Just seems like everyone's called an artist these days. Robbers are rip-off artists. Pickpockets practice the art of the lift. Bottom line – are you a femdom? I ask because I hear they call themselves artists too.'

'I told you, I'm an actress.'

'And they're *not* actresses?'

'All I'm saying—'

'Yeah, I get it, you're a real actress, a thespian.' He pronounces the word carefully. 'OK, we got that settled, what can I do for you, Ms Berenson?'

I tell him I'm now living in Chantal Desforges's old loft and as a result I've gotten interested in her lifestyle and very sad end.

'You're a journalist?'

'No.'

'Did you know her?'

'Slightly.'

'Kinda monosyllabic, aren't we?' He pauses. 'Why so interested?'

'I'm thinking I might construct a piece about her. Haven't decided yet.'

'So what can I do for you?'

'I'm hoping you'll give me an update on your investigation.'

'Why would I wanna do a dumb thing like that?'

An excellent question which I decide to answer with a dare.

'Because you want to solve this murder, and I might know a few things that could help.'

'Do I understand you're proposing some kind of trade?'

'Maybe.'

'Hmm. Interesting.'

'So, you won't mind updating me?'

He laughs. 'You're a clever one!'

I tell him that if he wants to see just how clever, he'll meet me for coffee. 'We're both curious so let's meet and see if we can satisfy all this free-floating curiosity.'

'Sounds good. I'll check with my partner and get back to you.'

'I'd rather meet you alone.'

'Got a problem with Detective Ramos?'

'I hear he was kinda cold about Chantal, like he thought she brought what happened upon herself.'

'Don't recall him saying that, but, yeah, he can be an asshole.'

We set up a meet at Downtown Café, just three blocks from the Buckley.

As we sit down and engage in pleasantries, it's clear each of us is trying to psych out the other.

'You can call me Leo,' Scarpaci says. 'May I call you Tess?' I nod. 'OK, we interviewed some of Chantal's domme friends, picked up a few crumbs, but most of 'em wouldn't tell us squat. So I was kinda hoping you *were* a domme. A cooperative one. Hope that doesn't offend you.'

I shake my head. Actually I'm pleased. 'The idea you might take me for a domme gives me a little tingle.'

He laughs. 'What's your angle here, Tess? You mentioned something about working up a monologue.' He searches my eyes. 'That strikes me as, well, a pretext.'

Peering back at him, I find myself agreeing with Clarence's assessment. I see sadness in Scarpaci's eyes, a sadness I connect with numerous middle-aged, world-weary detectives I've seen in movies, a type I've always found attractive. He has a long face, sunken cheeks, prominent cheekbones, and there're circles under his I've-seen-it-all eyes. He doesn't wear the typical cop mustache or have a cop's typical husky build. He's tall, gaunt, and slightly bent over. I have a feeling he eats sparingly and there's more sinew than muscle beneath his baggy suit.

I decide to come clean with him. As I tell him about meeting Chantal at kickboxing class, he raises his eyebrows as if in mock appreciation of my prowess. But he gets interested when I describe my decision to keep the artifacts Chantal left behind in the loft.

'Like I said, I might work up a piece about her, or someone like her. Living where she lived, I've become fascinated by her. My shrink's worried about me. She thinks I'm getting obsessed. She says I'm overidentifying with Chantal. She could be right.'

Scarpaci nods. 'I used to see a shrink. Police contract shrink, actually. I was involved in a shooting couple years back. Drug case. There was an exchange of gunfire and the other guy, a mid-level dealer, got killed. When that happens they assume you're suffering PTSD, so they send you to this lady doc and she decides whether you get your gun back and go back on the street, or get assigned a desk job in the Cold Case Division collating stuff stowed in smelly old evidence cartons. Some of my buddies who'd been through it told me how to game her – admit to stress, then describe how hard you're struggling to deal with it. I told her my priest was helping me cope.' He grins. 'Truth is I didn't have a priest, but a cousin of mine, who became one, backed me up. So here I am, working OPD Homicide. Pretty sorrowful gig, you wanna know. Times I think I'd be better off behind a desk.'

I like him. He's open, and, best of all, seems real. I have a feeling he likes me too.

'I hear Chantal had a brother in Vermont.'

Scarpaci nods. 'I talked to him. He said all the right stuff, but didn't seem like he was grieving much. Most folks ask questions – how was she killed? do you have any leads? who could have done such a terrible thing? He didn't ask any of that. Seemed like he couldn't wait to get off the phone. He said if I faxed him documents he'd sign authorization to release her body to a funeral home where a friend of hers would arrange for cremation. I faxed him the forms, he signed them, and we released her. The friend was the same one ID'd her body. Lives in your building. Maybe you know him. Some kind of commercial artist.' Scarpaci shakes his head. 'He wasn't much help. Worse than her domme friends in a way. I can understand why they didn't want to talk. They're in a sketchy situation. But her friend – what's he worried about?'

Josh ID'd Chantal! He never mentioned that, another of his omissions. I shouldn't be surprised. Josh, it seems, has but the barest acquaintanceship with full disclosure.

Scarpaci peers at me like now it's my turn to confide, so I mention I've been in contact with Lynx, one of Chantal's close domme friends, who told me Chantal had a barter arrangement with the owner-sensei at San Pablo Martial Arts. I suggest that might be a lead worth following. I also offer to try and persuade Josh Garske to cooperate.

'If you're interested, that is.'

'Oh, I'm interested. I have a heavy case load. Gang shootings mostly. A few domestic killings. But this case . . . something haunting about it. We talked to Lynx. She didn't tell us much.'

'She doesn't like cops. She told me there was a domme murdered in San Jose last year. She heard rumors the killer dug out the bullets. To her that spells cop.'

'I wonder where she heard that. That's not the kind of info that gets released.'

'She told me dommes have cop clients. Maybe one of them mentioned it.'

'Maybe. Anyway, thanks for the tip on the kickboxing coach. I'll look into it.'

He grins at me. I like the way his expression shifts from dour to cheerful in a second.

'Generally speaking, we don't like civilians playing cop. But if you were to become a confidential informant . . . that'd be another story.'

Confidential informant – I like the sound of that.

'Sure, why not,' I tell him.

'So, game on!' He raises his coffee mug, gestures for me to raise mine, then we click. 'To my new CI,' he toasts.

I like his style. Like a good actor he knows how to play on people's sympathies. I called him today thinking he might help me. Now I feel like I want to help him.

'If I talk to Lynx again what in particular do you want me to find out?'

'Anything about Chantal's slaves, clients, whatever she called them. From what we hear, most guys into that scene don't give real names and the dommes don't ask questions for fear the client'll be scared off.' He pauses. 'But one thing we did find out about Chantal. She had a specialty that attracted a particular type most dommes aren't comfortable dealing with. So if Lynx knows anything that could identify these guys, that could be helpful.'

'What type're you talking about?' I ask, thinking he means

psychological domination. But then Scarpaci says something that catches me off guard.

'We heard she dabbled in Nazi role-play.'

'*Huh?*'

'Yeah, "Huh?". That's what I wanted to know. So I asked around. Seems there's this subset of pervs who want to submit to women who dress up in SS uniforms – boots, insignia, swastika armbands, all that, then prance around with a riding crop and give them a hard time. Sometimes a *very* hard time. They use a German accent and play old Nazi songs in the background. The more elaborate the props, the more convincing the scene. Or so I'm led to believe.'

German accent! I use one in my Weimar piece. Again, I'm struck by the parallels in our lives.

'Chantal did *that*?' But even as I express disbelief, I realize that what he's described fits perfectly with many of her books and the swastika armband I found folded inside one.

'Two sources told me so. Said when they had clients who expressed an interest in that kind of play, they passed them on to Chantal. In return Chantal paid them referral fees.' Scarpaci scratches one of his sunken cheeks. 'Seems it's a specialty most dommes won't touch. Too inflammatory, too much chance the guy'll freak out.' He peers at me. 'You're Jewish, right?' I nod. 'I figured that from your name. I ask because I don't want to make you uncomfortable.'

'You won't,' I assure him. 'One of my monologues involves a proto-Nazi sex serial murder case. I'm kinda inured to German anti-Semitism, if that's what you're worried about.'

He searches my face. 'I hesitated because there's a really weird aspect to this. At least I thought so at first. Seems the guys these two women sent to Chantal were both Jewish. The men insisted that abuse by a Nazi female was an essential ingredient in their fantasies.' He shakes his head. 'As I said, this struck me as pretty sick, but after I thought about it, it started making sense. Like you're going to be transgressive, why not go all the way? Say a Jewish guy wants to be abused. A domme acting the part of a sadistic female concentration-camp guard . . . well, I could see how that might work for him.'

I study Scarpaci. His expression's thoughtful. He strikes me as a man who worked very hard to comprehend something totally foreign to his experience. I'm impressed by that. It's probably that quality, I decide, that makes him a good detective.

What he says next confirms this. He looks up at me. '"Nothing human is alien to me" – the Roman playwright Terence wrote that.'

He quotes from Terence! This is one erudite cop!

'Now my partner, Ramos – if I quoted that to him he wouldn't know what I was talking about. Hector believes in pure evil. To him everything's black and white. Me – I look for the grays. So if some Jewish guy wants to hire a woman to dress up like an SS guard and abuse him, it's my job to understand where he's coming from. Because maybe . . . just maybe . . . he's the guy I'm looking for, the guy who did this woman in.'

'Why would he turn on her if she was giving him what he wanted?'

'Maybe because she *was* giving him what he wanted, *too much* of it. Maybe the scene they created was so shameful he couldn't bear the thought he'd exposed his darkest desires to her. She'd have witnessed the most secret side of him, something his rational side believed was evil. So he did what some people do when there's a witness who can really damage them, chilled her so no one else would ever find out.'

'You see this as a psychological crime?'

'I do. But of course there's a problem with that, something Ramos keeps pointing out. Her body was in the trunk of a stolen car. That's like a scene you see in a movie, an old-fashioned gang-style killing. My gut feeling is that this was a psychological crime, a crime of passion, and stashing her in the car trunk was an attempt to throw us off.'

There's something so disturbing about what he's telling me that I have trouble coming to grips with it. While we sit there talking calmly and sipping coffee, I work hard to stay composed. But soon as we part on the street, I begin to shake. For me being Jewish has never been an issue. My family's been secular for three generations. I had little experience with the anti-Semitism prevalent in my grandparents' time. But still the notion of Jewish men paying to be humiliated by a domme decked out as an SS guard – on a rational level, there's something appalling about that. And yet on the dark counter-intuitive level of psycho-erotic excitement, it makes a certain amount of sense. Thinking about it I'm repelled . . . and also, I admit, fascinated.

I stride swiftly back to the Buckley. Soon as I'm home I go straight to the shelves where I've arranged Chantal's books. Gazing at them anew, I view them as a research collection assembled by Chantal in order to learn how to effectively enact Nazi role play.

My reaction to this verges on revulsion. A side of me wants to be done with Chantal. But I know that's impossible. I've gone too far, probed too deep; she's become part of me now. I recognize too that Dr Maude may be right – my obsession with her could be pathological.

And yet as repelled as I am by what I learned from Scarpaci, I feel compelled to learn even more. Surely Josh knew about Chantal's specialty. How could he not, since he monitored her sessions? And I don't doubt that Lynx knew too. I decide to call her and put it to her straight.

'Sure, I knew!' Lynx tells me. 'Everyone in the scene did. It wasn't a secret. Chantal wanted other dommes to know so we'd send over clients who had that fetish.'

'Is there some reason you didn't tell me about this?'

'For one thing, you didn't ask.' Lynx pauses. 'I also figured you'd find it disturbing.'

'I do, but never mind. The cops think it could be relevant.'

'Then they should look into it.' She pauses. 'Actually, I didn't mention it because it's something of a sore point with me, part of the reason Chantal and I decided to go separate ways. I don't like racial humiliation. I get requests for it – white guys who want to be enslaved by a black woman. Reverse plantation-slave treatment. Some black dommes get off on that, but for me race play cuts too close. Chantal was fascinated by what she called Nazi/Jewish dynamics. And that always struck me as deeply weird because Chantal's mother was Jewish.'

There it is again, more mirroring!

'Did she try and cover it up?'

'No way! She was proud of it. She identified as Jewish. Summer of her freshman year at SF State she signed on for some kind of birth-right tour of Israel. She told me she got a lot out of it.'

I know about those free cultural enrichment visits. At one time I considered applying for one myself, but in the end opted for a summer theater workshop in the Berkshires. My secular background was typical for a participant, but I didn't like the Israel-right-or-wrong orientation and I was turned off by rumors that the intention behind the tours was to groom future pro-Israel supporters.

'I don't get how she could play a sadistic Nazi if she really felt Jewish,' I tell Lynx.

'But, see, that's *not* what she did. When clients said they wanted that, Chantal would act like she was willing to go along. Then she'd flip the script on them, put them through what she called a "denazification drill". Say a Jewish guy wanted her to wear a swastika armband. Instead she'd dress up in one of her tailored Israeli paratrooper uniforms, inter-rogate him, then inscribe a Star of David on him, sometimes by dribbling hot wax. This was her way to work them through their fetish and instill Jewish pride. It was tough but in the end the guys loved her for it. They'd come to her for ethnic humiliation. Instead she'd give them an ethnic boost. I doubt anyone who played that game with her would ever want to harm her. I think he'd be too grateful.'

'What if the guy wasn't Jewish?'

'Then she'd do some real denazification. Then she'd use the whip.'

Lynx tells me that this denazification ritual was something Chantal learned during her apprenticeship with Gräfin Eva.

'She said there were these real neo-Nazi types in Vienna. Eva taught her how to handle them. As for working with Jewish guys, she liked doing that. She felt like she was taking a sick desire and turning it into a healing experience.'

Denazification – that at least is something I can relate to.

Lynx goes on: 'We had a number of conversations about this. You have to understand how Chantal viewed herself. "I'm a healer, Lynx," she'd tell me. She told me that if she didn't feel that way, didn't feel she was helping people, she would never be able to do domme work. Not just the denazification stuff, but any of it.'

Before ending our call, I ask Lynx if she knows what happened to Chantal's chariot, the one she posed in for Josh's Queen of Swords painting.

'That old thing. I remember seeing it at her tag sale, but I don't think anyone bought it. A couple of the ladies were intrigued, but it was too big and heavy. You'd need a van to haul it off. So maybe she just left it in the loft and the landlord kept it, or maybe put it out on the street.'

I decide to give in and call Jerry. Now that Gräfin Eva's name has come up again, I think it's important to discover what's in her letters, filed between the pages of a book about the traditional coffee houses of Vienna.

Jerry's cool at first, but he warms up when I explain why I'm calling.

'It would take me too long to write out full translations,' he says, 'but I can read through the letters, summarize them, then orally translate the parts that interest you.'

I'm so pleased by his willingness to help I decide to offer him a reward. Wealthy as he is, I remember how much he likes getting stuff free.

'I'll be performing in San Francisco fairly soon in the ballroom of a mansion in Presidio Heights. Tickets'll run two hundred fifty, but if you want to come I can get you comped.'

'Thanks. That'd be great!' he says.

Dr Maude, I can see, is restraining herself. I know her well enough to feel the degree of her revulsion even as she tries to conceal it.

'Chantal was half-Jewish yet she played these scenes with her Jewish submissives because she thought they could be healing experiences! What do you really think about that, Tess?'

'I find her denazification concept extremely fascinating. Maybe doing it was also healing for her.'

William Bayer

'I think what she did was extremely dangerous. She was opening up serious wounds. Like the detective told you, something like that can spark a violent response.'

'You think he could be on to something?'

'I think it's something he should investigate. But what concerns me is *your* reaction. If I understand you, you're saying that when you first heard about this you were repulsed, but when you learned she "flipped the script" you saw some merit in it.'

'Don't know about seeing merit. What Chantal did was definitely perverse.'

She nods. 'It was. And as you've told me many times you've always been attracted to the perverse. What I'd like us to consider is where this fascination of yours comes from. I believe the more deeply we examine that, the more profitable our sessions will be. Please think about it.'

I nod. Then I decide to engage with her.

'OK,' I tell her, 'you're Jewish, I'm Jewish. The Nazis are our worst nightmare. And here we have a half-Jewish woman who played around with that, reversed it, eroticized it. Troubled people paid her to play this game with them because by playing it they found some degree of peace. Detective Scarpaci quotes to me from Terence: "Nothing human is alien to me." I'd think that as a humanist and an experienced shrink you'd be open to understanding my fascination.'

'Oh I *am*, Tess. More than open to it. My hope would be to use this fascination you feel as a key to unlock an attic room in your mind. There are powerful unconscious feelings in you that drive your creativity. Let's explore those feelings and everything that surrounds them. Much as I like and respect your performance work, I think with such an understanding you'll be able to create even more powerful performances.'

So, I think, getting up to leave, *now the hunt is on. A double hunt actually: Scarpaci's hunt for Chantal's killer, in which I'm to participate as his confidential informant, and Dr Maude's hunt for what drives my art.*

There's a thunderstorm tonight. It comes suddenly, waking me up. Even though we're entering the dry season, I know from years of living in the Bay Area how fierce these late-spring showers can be.

I check my bedside clock: 1:20 a.m. I turn onto my back, look up at the skylight high above my bed. It's not the bubble type you find on new structures, but the old-fashioned kind built like a little house with glass walls and a pitched glass roof. No leaks; the old panes are well grouted or I wouldn't sleep beneath them. It's exciting to stare up as sheets of rain splash across the glass like wild rivers in the night.

Flashes of distant lightning are followed seconds later by thunder, the intervals narrowing as the storm moves toward downtown. In one sustained burst, a bolt of blinding light seems to crack the sky. My skylight goes all white. Then, perhaps a second later, as the light starts to fade and the roar unleashes a torrent of rain, I see a figure in a hood looming up there, lying flat spread-eagled across the skylight, hands grasping its edges, face pushed hard against the glass as if peering down at me lying twelve feet beneath.

My reaction: sheer terror, followed by the thought that no one would go up on a roof in weather like this. So, an apparition, optical illusion, ghost? The image fades as quickly as it came. It can't have been visible for more than a second, but an after-image burns my eyes: like an etching, a black silhouette in human form set against the roiling bleached-out sky. I didn't see his face (if it is a 'he'), just the outline of his splayed form. And then after the wind drives another wave of water across the skylight, the next crack of lightning reveals emptiness. If there was someone up there, he's gone now or been blown away.

Terrified, I phone Rex. His voice is groggy. I realize I've woken him up.

'It's Tess. I think I saw someone on the skylight above my bed.'

'Come on! You're spooked by the storm. Go back to sleep.'

'I'm afraid.'

'Who was it? Did you recognize him?'

'I think it was a man wearing a dark hooded slicker. He was clinging to the skylight, then he was gone.'

'Want me to come over? I can be there in half an hour.'

I thank him, tell him that isn't necessary, that I'll move my bedding to the living-room couch and call the building manager in the morning.

'Sorry to bother you, Rex. Don't know why I called you, really.'

'I know why – we're close and you know I'll always be there for you.'

In the morning I phone Clarence, tell him what I think I saw.

'No, Tess, that couldn't be. I keep the staircase door locked and the roof door bolted. But, really, I can't imagine anyone climbing around on the roof in a lightning storm like that, let alone managing to get up there.' He pauses. 'I wish you'd called me last night. I'd have gone up there and checked. Like I keep telling everybody, I'm on call for my tenants day and night. You know that, right?'

'I do. Thank you, Clarence.'

'I'll come up now and we'll go look together.'

Our expedition to the roof yields one clue: I'm able to open the door to the roof staircase which Clarence assured me he keeps locked. All I have to do is turn the knob. The door that opens to the roof isn't bolted either.

Clarence admits he's embarrassed. I think he's a lot more upset than he lets on. He sputters something about how the last person to whom he gave roof access was a TV dish installer, and that was two weeks before.

'After workmen leave I usually check to make sure the roof's locked up. I thought I'd done that, but maybe this last time I forgot. I apologize.' He peers at me. 'But that doesn't explain why anyone would come up here during a storm. I mean, that's totally crazy. And then to stay up here in the wind and the rain – why would anyone do that?'

The roof, I note, is now barely wet, the May morning sun having already burned off most of the rainwater. Clarence escorts me on a tour. There are layers of dried guano from the night herons that perch in the neighborhood. I'm surprised the rain didn't rinse the stuff away. We check out both my skylights. No sign of anyone having clung to the one over my bed – if the intruder did leave traces the storm would have washed them off.

'You keep calling him an intruder,' Clarence says. 'But he didn't really intrude. He stayed outside.'

'If he came in through the building then he's an intruder, Clarence. Unless you think he got up here by jumping from another roof.'

We check the edges of the Buckley. The gap between it and the building to the east would be too dangerous for a leap. But the roof of the building to our west, the McCormick, is just a foot lower and separated by less than a yard.

'Maybe he climbed up from there,' Clarence says.

'Pretty dangerous during a storm. He could have slipped.'

'Yeah . . .' Clarence has a far-away look in his eyes. He's trying to figure the thing out. 'You're sure you saw somebody, Tess?'

I tell him I'm pretty sure, but not one hundred percent. The vision was too quick, too shocking, and I was too frightened by it.

'Might have been something like a newspaper blown onto the glass,' he suggests. 'Or a big bird. Maybe somebody's old coat. Lots of stuff blowing around in a storm. Could have stuck onto the glass, then a second later got blown off.'

'Yeah, maybe that's what it was,' I tell him. But the fact that both doors were unlocked making the roof accessible causes me to wonder if the rather creepy Josh Garske could have been up here last night.

On our way back down the stairs, I ask Clarence if he knows anything about Chantal's Roman chariot. He says he does, that she abandoned it when she moved out. When I ask him why he didn't leave it in the loft like the jail cell and the X-frame, he says the chariot had wheels and was mobile while the other two apparatuses were built in.

'I still have it stored in the basement.' He giggles. 'You know, in case I ever want to play Ben-Hur.'

'Can I buy it from you?'

'Are you serious?' And when I nod: 'Hey, you can have it. I'll bring it up and leave it by your door.'

THIRTEEN

Extract from the Unpublished Memoirs of Major Ernst Fleckstein

(AKA Dr Samuel Foigel)

. . . at this point in my life, after my work on the Geli Raubal affair,[1] and most particularly in the matter of the termination of Bernhard Stempfle[2] (for which I still feel considerable regret), I was regarded by Hess[3] and most particularly Bormann[4] as a fixer of the first order. Both were aware of my background as a private detective in Munich specializing in matrimonial investigations, and after the Führer came to power I was the person they relied upon in circumstances when special work was required that ordinary operatives could not perform.

My detractors called me a 'hatchet-man'. I find that description

---

[1] Angela 'Geli' Raubal (1908–1931), Hitler's niece, who died under highly suspicious/mysterious circumstances (by suicide? murdered?) in Hitler's Munich apartment.

[2] Father Bernhard Stempfle, an anti-Semitic priest, former editor of *Mein Kampf*, found murdered in the forest near Harlaching with a broken neck and three bullets in his heart on June 30, 1934, the 'Night of the Long Knives,' when Ernst Roehm and the SA leadership were slaughtered in Bad Wiesee and Munich on Hitler's orders. It is believed that Stempfle tried to blackmail Hitler by threatening to release a letter Geli Raubal had written describing Hitler's sadomasochistic demands upon her.

[3] Rudolf Hess (1894–1987), second in command of the Nazi Party, sometimes referred to as 'Fräulein Anna' on account of his suspected homoerotic activities. He committed suicide in Spandau Prison while serving a life sentence for crimes against humanity.

[4] Martin Bormann (1900–1945), Hess's private secretary, and in 1941, after Hess flew to Scotland, head of the Party Chancellery, in effect Hitler's private secretary, and thus one of the most powerful leaders of the Third Reich.

offensive. I have always prided myself on being able to undertake difficult assignments with the required level of subtlety or severity depending on the requirements of the mission.

In September 1934, shortly after I took care of the Stempfle matter, Bormann summoned me to his office in the Braunes Haus.[5]

'You did a fine job resolving a difficult situation,' he told me. 'I can assure you the Führer is extremely pleased. As for party leader Hess, I believe he's a bit concerned as Stempfle's corpse was found not far from his residence.' Bormann chuckled. 'No matter! I have another assignment for you, one requiring considerable delicacy. It will take all your wit and guile to properly carry it out.'

Bormann explained that officers working in the Party Archive were actively tracking down and collecting as many of Hitler's early paintings as possible in order to collate them, document them, and more importantly, take them off the market. People buying and selling these pictures were making unconscionable profits and there were several forgers at work creating new 'Hitler paintings'. The Führer found this extremely annoying and wanted it stopped. Furthermore (and Bormann lowered his voice when he said this) people in certain circles were speaking mockingly of the Führer's youthful artistic aspirations. This was causing the Führer considerable personal hurt. My job would be to take possession of a particular drawing the Führer had made prior to the World War, which he had presented as a gift to a rather famous lady with whom he'd been slightly acquainted at the time, a certain Frau Lou Andreas-Salomé, now a practicing psychoanalyst in Göttingen.

'Is this woman Jewish?' I asked.

'She is not,' Bormann replied, 'though in Göttingen there are people who refer to her as a Finnish Jewess, probably because she practices what we call "the Jewish Science". Others do so following the lead of Elizabeth Förster, who

---

[5] The NSDAP (Nazi Party) continued to be headquartered in the Braunes Haus (Brown House) in Munich even after Hitler became Chancellor and moved permanently to Berlin.

makes no secret of the fact that she despises her.[6] No matter, she is Aryan, from a fine Russian-German family, the daughter of a distinguished general. She is now seventy-three years old. The Führer is most particular that she not be harmed or threatened in any way. She is to be treated with the greatest respect. It's possible that she no longer possesses this drawing, or that she doesn't recall having received it. That's for you to find out. If she does have it, you are to purchase it back from her on the Führer's behalf. As for price, the sky's the limit. You will judge her circumstances, then offer her whatever it takes. As I said, Fleckstein, this is a delicate mission. Of all my operatives, you're the only one to whom I'd entrust it.'

I asked him what it was about this particular drawing that made it so special. He told me he didn't know and that he could tell by the Führer's manner that the Führer did not wish to say, only that it was something of a highly personal nature and that if I were able to retrieve it I could expect a significant bonus and a double promotion in party rank.

Needless to say I readily accepted the mission.

My first task was to research the woman. Doing so I discovered some interesting things, among them that at a young age she had been a love interest of Nietzsche's, that she'd later been the muse of the poet Rainer Maria Rilke, and that at age fifty-one she'd gone to Vienna to study psychoanalysis with Sigmund Freud. I tried to read several of her books but found them tough going and soon gave them up. I also attempted to read articles she'd written for psychoanalytic journals about deviant sexuality. I found these dense and difficult to comprehend.

My first decision was how best to present myself. A little research among party officials in Göttingen revealed that lately the lady had been quite ill, and, since her husband's death (Carl Andreas had been a distinguished professor of Oriental languages at the local university), had become reclusive. I considered approaching her as a prospective patient, but gave up that idea

---

[6] Friedrich Nietzsche's sister (1846–1935), wife of Bernhard Förster. Together they founded the *Nueva Germania* colony in Paraguay. Creator of the Nietzsche Archive, she was famous for her anti-Semitism, pro-Nazi sympathies, and lifelong hatred of Lou Salomé.

when I learned she was phasing out her practice. Then, because she was nearing her seventy-fifth year, I decided to present myself as a Munich journalist who wished to interview her at the approach of this important birthday regarding her memories of the many famous men and women she had known.

I wrote her a flattering letter in which I thickly laid on the manure regarding my boundless admiration and respect. A week later I received a positive reply. I was summoned for tea and conversation to her residence, Loufried, a fine old house situated among linden trees on a forested slope north of the city.

Arriving at the appointed time, I was received by the house-keeper, then shown to a large sunny study. A faint aroma of boiled beef and potatoes seeped in from the kitchen. The walls there, covered with blue-gray fabric, were embellished with colorful Russian peasant embroideries, and there was a pair of bearskin rugs on the floor. Waiting, I scanned the book-shelves. There were a good thousand volumes, many of them obscure. After several minutes the famous Frau Lou appeared, greeted me graciously, and gestured me to a seat.

My first impression when she entered was of a rather sickly elderly woman. But when she sat down and peered at me, I felt myself devoured by a pair of brilliant searching pale-blue eyes.

So this is the famous seductress! I thought.

The housekeeper soon appeared with a teapot and cups. Frau Lou poured, we sipped while engaging in a few minutes of small talk about the weather, the view from the house and so forth, then she brought her hands together in her lap and sat silent, a signal she was ready to be interviewed. At this point, having determined she was in full command of her faculties, I decided to drop the charade.

'I must confess, Frau Lou, that in truth I am not a journalist.'

She showed no surprise.

'As soon as I saw you I figured as much,' she said. 'Is your real name Ernst Fleckstein?' And when I nodded: 'You're a government official?'

When I asked her why she thought that, she smiled slightly. 'Something officious in your manner.'

I explained to her that in fact I held no official position, that I was a freelance private investigator who from time to time took on special assignments for the NSDAP, and it was in that capacity that I had come to speak to her.

'You're a party member?' she asked.

'No,' I lied. 'I'm non-political. But I'm here today on the party's behalf.'

Again she nodded. 'For some time I've been expecting such a visit. When I received your letter I assumed it was a subterfuge. I could have ignored your request. Despite the fact that we are now in precarious times I didn't believe I had anything to fear. Because, you see, like yourself I am apolitical.'

I assured her that indeed she had nothing to fear. I had simply come regarding a private matter and that as soon as it was cleared up I would be on my way. Then to put her further at ease I assured her that I had it from the highest authority in the NSDAP that she was not to be bothered or provoked in any way, that I had come to ask her for a small favor which I hoped very much she would be willing to grant, but which like any citizen she had every right to accommodate or not as she saw fit.

'And what favor might that be?' she asked, adding that she couldn't imagine what a little old lady such as herself could do on behalf of Germany's ruling political party.

At this point I received the impression she was toying with me, that she knew perfectly well why I had come and now was trying to force me to come straight out with it. I was also impressed by her allure. This woman may be old and ill, I thought, but her face is alive and her mind razor-sharp. I decided then to postpone stating my business, preferring, as they say, to 'beat around the bush' for a while, because, to tell the truth, I found the lady intriguing, and I thought it might be amusing to engage her in a bit of cat-and-mouse before getting to the point.

'Well,' I told her, 'I believe you know why I've come.'

She shook her head. 'I have no idea.'

'Earlier you said you were expecting such a visit.'

'Yes, but without knowing what it would be about. For example, perhaps an official wishes to purchase my house for a paltry sum. Or the Nietzsche Archive wishes to take possession of my Nietzsche letters. Or perhaps the government would like to close me down, as it does not sanction the practice of psychoanalysis. Or perhaps simply confiscate my library,' at this she gestured at the bookshelves, 'because many of my books are considered decadent, morally corrupting, vile. I'm referring to the writings of Heinrich Mann, Bertolt Brecht, Heinrich Heine, Sigmund Freud, Robert Musil, Erich Maria Remarque, Arthur Schnitzler, Ernst Toller, Franz Werfel, and others . . . many of whom have been close friends. I'm sorry to say there was a celebratory burning of books by these authors and others last year by students at several of our finest universities. So perhaps such a confiscation would be the purpose of such a visit?' She shrugged. 'There are many possibilities.'

'You say you're apolitical, Frau Lou, but in your words I detect a strong undercurrent of political opinion.'

'I don't consider my views to be political. I am but a humble old lady with a great fondness for German literary culture.'

At that she smiled rather kittenishly. *And so*, I thought, *the game is on!*

'Do you have views concerning our Führer?' I asked.

'I have listened to his broadcasts. I think he is an amazingly compelling public speaker.'

'And the content of what he says?'

'I don't pay much attention to content,' she said. 'I'm far more interested in presentation.'

'I understand you were in Vienna in 1912 and 1913?' She nodded. 'Our Führer was living there then. In *Mein Kampf* he wrote about that period. He wrote that those were the years that made him "hard".'

'So I am told,' she said. 'Perhaps he was influenced by something Friedrich Nietzsche wrote in *Thus Spake Zarathustra*.'

'What was that?'

'The last line of "The Other Dancing Song". Nietzsche wrote: "Become hard!"'

Ah ha! It was now clear there would be no admission she'd ever known Hitler. My tea was getting cold, Frau Lou seemed to be tiring and had not offered to refill my cup. Time, I decided, to get down to business.

'All right,' I told her, 'a certain gentleman, whose name we won't mention, made your acquaintance back then. Even today, after his meteoric rise, he remembers you with fondness and has no wish to cause you any difficulty. I have been so instructed. It seems that some years back, in the spring of 1913 to be precise, he presented you with a drawing as a personal gift. He does not expect you to return it to him, but he would like to purchase it from you at a very generous price.'

'Theoretically speaking, just how generous a price are we talking about?' she asked.

Theoretically speaking indeed! I took her question as a promising sign. The drawing, I believed, was now in play.

I gestured to show her that I meant a very high price indeed, adding that the amount would be many times more than anyone else would ever be willing to pay.

'And why,' she asked, 'would the gentleman be so generous? What could possibly make such a drawing so valuable?'

I told her that truthfully I had no idea, that my instructions were simply to pay whatever amount she asked in exchange for the drawing, and if there happened to be some special value to it I assumed she would understand what that was.

She smiled again, the same kittenish smile she'd been showing me all along. At that moment I realized I'd overplayed my hand, that Frau Lou had drawn me out to find out how much I knew. I'd been out-gamed. She had no intention of selling back the drawing at any price.

'Well,' she said, 'this has been very interesting. I wish I could assist you, but I cannot.'

'You're saying you won't sell me the drawing even though I'm prepared to offer you an enormous sum?'

'I'm saying that I have no such drawing in my possession, that I never had such a drawing, and that I have no idea of whom you are speaking or what you are speaking about.'

She sighed. 'Forgive me. I'm tired. The years have taken their toll. These days my memory is poor.' She rose. 'It's time for my nap. As charming as you are and amusing as this has been, I think it's time now for you to leave. Unless there's something else?'

Not waiting for me to respond, she snatched up a little bell. 'I'll ring for Marie. She'll show you out.'

We stood in silence. I could feel her measuring my disappointment.

'Well,' I shrugged, 'in my business you win some, lose some. That's how it goes.'

'You seem a nice young man. I hope this loss won't get you into any trouble.'

'They won't kill me for failing, but they won't pay me either. I work on commission.'

'You're a species of salesman, then?'

'Yes, I suppose,' I agreed. 'Please, Frau Lou, if your memory should improve and you should happen to come across the drawing, don't hesitate to contact me. May I leave my card?'

'Certainly.'

I laid my business card on a side table, then gestured toward a chaise longue covered in fine needlepoint. It was, I observed, set in a prominent position in the room.

Noticing my gesture, she peered at me curiously.

'Is that where it's done?' I asked.

'You mean psychoanalysis?'

I nodded. 'It seems so mysterious what you people do, all that talk about sex.'

'It's not all about sex,' she corrected me. 'That's a common misconception. And it's really not all that mysterious. The chaise longue, or analytic couch as we call it, is not a kind of confessional, as some believe. It is simply a comfortable place for the patient to relax, open up his heart and soul, and reveal what is troubling him. I sit in the chair behind. That way he cannot see my reactions. The most important aspect of my job is to listen very carefully and in a very particular way, to pick up on clues much as you likely do in your work as an investigator. So you see the analytic couch is but a tool, an important one, some might say a powerful one, but in the end it is neutral. It is simply . . . a couch.'

The housekeeper appeared, Frau Lou and I shook hands, then the housekeeper showed me to the door. Just before I stepped into my car, I turned to look back at Loufried. I spotted Frau Lou standing in the window of the room in which we'd met gazing out at me, a smile of triumph curling her lovely lips.

*   *   *

Bormann, needless to say, was not pleased.

'The lady was firm?' he asked, his squinty eyes betraying his annoyance.

'She denied all knowledge,' I told him.

'Did you believe her?'

'Frankly, no. She's old and ill, but mentally very alert. You could almost say steel-willed. She's also crafty, devious, and very sure of herself. But there were certain things she did – shifts in the eyes, tension in the hands – that made me think she has the drawing, or at the very least remembers receiving it. She is not, I should tell you, much of a fan of our new order. She made it clear she's offended by it. Of course it's possible she may decide she needs the money and reconsider. But, to be honest with you, I doubt she will.'

I exhaled. I felt I needed to give Bormann something to chew on, something he could take back to Hess and Hitler.

'I have a hunch she hasn't long to live,' I told him. 'I shall keep a close eye on her, and if it appears she's about to die, I'll let you know. Meantime I suggest we prepare to raid the house as soon as she passes, go in there, turn everything upside down, make a thorough search. If she has the drawing we'll find it. And if she doesn't then we'll know that too.'

Bormann grinned. 'Excellent idea! I like the way your mind works, Fleckstein. Even though you've come back empty-handed, I'm going to authorize half payment. Consider it an advance against the full amount when and if your post-mortem search succeeds.'

I should mention here that my 1934 visit with Frau Lou was highly memorable. In fact it would be years before I fully understood the impact of our interview and the ways it would affect my life. Even after so many decades I clearly recall her words and expressions.

I should also mention that the sight of her analytic couch and what she had to say about it were etched firmly in my mind, incubating a fascination with this strange science called psychoanalysis, a fascination that crystallized some years later when I devised my personal escape plan and created my alternate identity.

FOURTEEN

Soon as we arrive at Grace Wei's, Luis walks around the ballroom gazing at the walls and floor. Then he pulls a chair to the front of the room, tunes up, and starts playing Bach. His smile tells me he loves the acoustics. Grace's ballroom is a perfect sound-box.

Rex shows up, oohs and ahs over the venue, then I introduce him to Grace. We chat a bit, then when she withdraws he asks us to run through our performance. When we're done he'll offer notes and 'a few ideas.'

Up to now Luis and I have been rehearsing apart. It's now time to integrate our performances. And though Rex constitutes but an audience of one, his presence changes the dynamic.

When we finish, I slump down against a wall. My breakdown scene took even more out of me than my performance at Vertigo. Luis is tired too. His playing was magnificent. The energy he put into the final mad Morton Feldman solo was enormous.

'Your piece is called *Recital*,' Rex tells us, 'a musical performance followed by remarks. But what's it really about?'

'It's a portrait of a lady,' I tell him.

'Right! But the way it's structured now the music seems like a pretext to get people into a room so they can watch a middle-aged lady experience a melt-down. *Recital* shouldn't just be a piece about a gifted cellist and his older woman patron, it should be about their relationship. That's what you've got to work on. Your characters need a shared secret.'

Rex wants us to be involved in a smoldering affair. 'For Mrs Z (and she must know this) it's most likely her last amorous adventure. For Luis it's perhaps the first in a series of affairs as he moves toward musical stardom. Each of you needs and uses the other. Each also knows that this recital, in which Mrs Z introduces Luis to the elite of San Francisco, will mark the end of the affair. *Recital* is an emotional turning point for you both. Your roles in each other's lives are about to change.

'Playing her off the stage is too cruel,' Rex tells Luis. 'I'd like it better if you go to her after she cracks, comfort her, and then, when she grasps your arm, gently lead her off. The way you touch her,' Rex turns to me, 'and the way you react to his touching, should say it all. Some in the audience will get it, others won't. All the better – they can discuss it on the way home.'

Rex shows me how he wants me to sit during the music: at the end of the first row with my chair angled so the audience can see how moved I am as I listen.

Both Luis and I are excited by Rex's notes. We agree to meet here again in ten days for a full-dress run-through. I'll wear my evening gown and makeup. Luis will wear a black suit with open-neck black silk shirt. If the next rehearsal goes well, Grace will set a date and send out invitations.

A knock on my door. It's Clarence, wearing jeans and a tank top, standing beside Chantal's movie-prop chariot.

'I thought it'd be nicer to deliver it in person,' he says. 'Dusty in the cellar so I cleaned it up.' He looks around. 'Where do you want it?'

I ask him to roll it into the main room. He positions himself between the traces, grabs them, and with rippling biceps pulls the chariot to a corner of the loft.

'Hey, cool!' He points at my framed inkblots. 'You're into psychology?' I nod. 'Chantal majored in German and psych. Told me she combined them when she became a domme. She was into what she called "ceremonies of penance and absolution".' He pats the chariot. 'She used this in her games, said it was great for obedience training. She was special,' he adds wistfully. 'I really miss her.' He looks at me, brightens. 'I'm thrilled you're living here, Tess. As I told Aunt Esther, having a famous performance artist in house classes up the joint.'

When I try to tip him for bringing up the chariot, he politely shakes his head.

'Not necessary. Always a pleasure.'

Chantal's chariot looks good in the corner of my loft. Squatting there it reminds me of a big cat poised to leap. It's perfect for a swords-and-sandals epic, the front elaborately carved, the letters

SPQR set beneath an imperial eagle. It's the kind of superb prop movie-studio craftsmen made in the heyday of Hollywood.

I wonder why Chantal bought it. Did she see herself as a Roman empress, legion commander, gladiator? Did she pose in it, as she had for Josh, to impress her clients by her militancy? Did she ever actually hitch a client to the front extension, as Clarence says, then have him play beast of burden as he pulled her around the loft?

I keep hoping I'll run into Josh. I want to sit down with him, find out why he didn't tell me he ID'd Chantal's body, ask him too about her denazification scenes. Since it's a week since I've seen him I think maybe he's avoiding me.

Jerry calls. He's read through Gräfin Eva's letters to Chantal.

'They're love letters,' he tells me. 'This Eva seems to have been very much in love with Chantal. She writes that she misses her terribly, urges her to come back to Vienna so they can take up where they left off. In one letter she describes coming to Oakland to see her, and what fun they had, "just like old times". "I understand you have a new life there," she writes. "You're young, I'm old. You don't think it could work for us again. But I will always be here for you. You will always have a place in my heart." She addresses Chantal as "*Liebste Schatz Liebling*", which roughly translates as "dearest sweetheart darling". The letters are filled with sweet nothings and the kind of shorthand people use when they have a shared past.'

'Thanks for reading them for me. You're on *my* list for *Recital*. You'll get an invitation soon as we set a date. I can put you down for two if you want.'

'One seat'll be fine. I wouldn't want to throw you off by bringing a date,' he says.

So Chantal was bisexual or lesbian . . . something no one who knew her bothered to tell me. I'm not surprised. She was a complicated woman. But I'd have thought it worth a mention.

*   *   *

Luis comes over twice so we can rehearse playing out our secret relationship. His tenderness tells me he understands Mrs Z's crisis.

'She has given me a great gift,' he says. 'Sure, there'll be an audience out there, but it is only for her ears that I'll play.'

I start reading one of Chantal's psycho-biographies of Lou Andreas-Salomé, referred to in most books as Frau Lou or just plain Lou. I pick the one that shows the most wear and bears the most marginalia. In it I read about how, just after Lou died, the Gestapo came to her house and carted off all her books.

In the margin I find this enigmatic note scribbled by Chantal: *What were they looking for? Letters from Nietzsche? Rilke? Freud? Books inscribed by her author friends? Books by Jewish authors to be burned? Or something else that no one except E and I know anything about?!*

I find extensive underlining in the chapter concerning the year Lou spent studying with Freud. Clearly Chantal was fascinated by that. When the author quotes from Lou's journal that she was staying at the Hotel Zita, Chantal writes in the margin 'Room 28'. And then scrawls the hotel address: 'Pelikangasse 14'.

I put the biography down, pick up the English translation of *The Freud Journal of Lou Andreas-Salomé*. In the third entry, dated October 26, 1912, Lou writes of having arrived in Vienna the day before accompanied by a certain Ellen Delp, described in an editor's footnote as a young actress she met in Berlin through the famous director Max Reinhardt. In this same paragraph Lou describes taking up residence in the Hotel Zita 'only a few steps from the Alte Elster restaurant where the Freud group gathers after lectures'.

On a hunch I retrieve the folded-up map of Vienna I found in the Baedeker Guide. Chantal drew a little black square to mark the hotel at Pelikangasse 14. In the margin she's written 'Zita (building now destroyed)'. A red highlighted line shows the route from that address to another not far away. Beside it Chantal has written 'Freud's house, Berggasse 19'.

The highlighting on the map now makes sense. It seems that Chantal, obsessed by Lou Salomé, traced routes taken by Lou to various locations in Vienna. I learn from the *Freud Journal* that Lou visited Freud at his home several times, usually late at night.

What to make of Chantal's fascination with this extraordinary woman, a line of whose poetry is inscribed over the arched entrance to my loft? What was it about Lou Salomé that so greatly interested Chantal to the extent she marked places she stayed and visited over a hundred years ago and routes she may have followed in between?

When I'm not working on *Recital*, rehearsing my remarks, playing back the videos and subjecting them to self-critiques, I feast my eyes on the 'infamous photograph' that so intrigued Chantal. The more I look at it the more I see.

It strikes me that the expressions on the faces of the three 'actors' (for they were performing for the camera if I'm to believe Lou's account) belie the passions that roiled beneath. Paul Rée appears composed, even bored. According to Lou he hated being photographed. The great Friedrich Nietzsche, on the other hand, looks to be in distress, perhaps even a bit crazed. Yet, according to Lou, it was he who set up this *tableau vivant*, choosing the props and positioning the players. And Lou herself, wearing a mischievous half-grin, appears oblivious to the underlying dynamics.

I understand from studying the photograph, and from Chantal's notes surrounding it, that it's regarded as a crystallization of the network of relationships between these three exceptionally brilliant people, and a foreshadowing of the embroilments and betrayals that will soon reduce their communal dream to ash. Reading about the moment and its aftermath in a half-dozen books in Chantal's library, I gain a kaleidoscopic view of the story behind this striking image and the emotional undercurrents that converged within it.

Lou meets Rée who, much taken with her, introduces her to Nietzsche, his best friend at the time. They both fall hard for the twenty-year-old young woman, so handsome of feature, so brilliant of mind. Both propose marriage to her. She

proposes instead that they live together as a triad in chaste
intellectual companionship. The photo is Nietzsche's idea, a
memento, he tells the other two, to celebrate their pact of
chastity and study.

But within weeks the whole thing falls apart. After Nietzsche
is eased out of the triad, he nearly goes mad with envy and
despair. Rée and Nietzsche, formerly best friends, will never
speak again. Lou and Rée will go on to live together in Berlin
for several years in what was probably a chaste ménage-à-
deux. Then the scholar Dr Friedrich Carl Andreas will come
along, court Lou, win her away from Rée, and marry her, after
which the two of them will live in a deeply loving yet sexless
marriage until Andreas's death.

Rée, after his dismissal, will devote the rest of his life to
the practice of medicine. Nietzsche, on the other hand, fueled
by Lou's rejection, will go on to write *Thus Spake Zarathustra*.
Perhaps pushed on by Elizabeth Förster-Nietzsche, his controlling sister who carried on a decades-long verbal war against
Lou, he too will later turn against the former object of his
passion, writing to her: 'You have the predatory pleasure lust
of a cat . . . a brain with only a rudiment of soul!'

In 1889 Nietzsche will suffer a complete mental collapse.
In 1900 he will die in Weimar, finally recognized as one of
the great poet-thinkers of his time. Lou, in turn, although
married to Andreas, will engage in a long affair with Rainer
Maria Rilke, and, at the age of fifty-one, will go to Vienna to
study psychoanalysis with Freud.

For all the sexual energy implicit in the Luzern photograph,
it would seem (though none of the biographers are certain)
that renunciation of sex by the men may have been the divi-
sive issue. Lou insisted on chaste relationships with two men
who burnt with lust for her. She controlled them by refusing
all requests for intimacy. Most biographers believe she only
began to lead a full sex-life years later when she fell in love
with Rilke. Others point to a pattern, neurotically repeated
throughout her life, of positioning herself in triangular
relationships.

Such a complicated woman! 'Complex,' I remember, was
the word Josh used to describe Chantal. Was it their shared

complexity and deviant sexuality that caused Chantal to so thoroughly identify with Lou?

I take the problem to Dr Maude along with a copy of the Luzern photograph. She studies it as I explain the background.

'Yes, it's fascinating,' she agrees. 'There's much to analyze. If we're to believe the accounts, the entire set up was Nietzsche's. Yet in the photograph he appears out of it.'

'You see why I'm intrigued?'

'Yes, because Chantal was intrigued. She's possessed you now, hasn't she, Tess?'

'I wouldn't put it that way. But, yes, her obsessions have become mine. That's how I hope to understand her.'

'But toward what end? Do you see yourself collaborating with this detective you've met, helping him solve her murder?'

'I want to help him, but I think the end, as you put it, is to create a performance piece about Chantal and her obsessions.'

Dr Maude agrees that Chantal's story, if I do figure it out, could make for a great dramatic piece. But she wants to turn the discussion back to me.

'Remember, Tess, when you brought in those photographs of your dad, how you tried to "read" them for me.'

It was six months ago. I was thinking a lot about Dad then, had dug up a box of old family pictures and was trying to puzzle them out. I wanted to get a fix on this man who was so elusive, conned everybody including his family, and was so protective of whatever inner life he had that he never showed us his core.

'You've become very perceptive about photographs. And I think that's carried over to this one. But back to your father: do you remember the one that affected you most?'

How could I forget? It was a snapshot I took of Dad the morning after he came home from prison. He'd served four years for fraud. He arrived at the house after dark, greeted us warmly, wrapped me in his arms then kissed me on my forehead and many times on my hair. The next morning when I entered his room with my camera hoping to surprise him, I caught him sitting hunched over on the side of my parents' bed. He wore a gray sleeveless undershirt frayed at the neckline and was staring down at the floor as if depressed. I don't know why I took a picture of him then. I believe I did it without thinking. Even today that photograph brings tears to my eyes on account of the sadness in it, the way it captures him so beaten down.

Dr Maude nods as I recall the photo and my reaction to it.

'It *is* a sad picture,' she says, 'but maybe not just for the reason you think. It's possible he woke up just before you came in and was sitting there trying to clear his head. Or he was thinking how good it was to be home again. But for you that image shows him unmasked, unaware he's seen and thus not wearing his con man's smile. There's no bonhomie in it, none of his false charm. It's a photo of a loser who spent four years in prison. That's what brings tears to your eyes. When you look at it you feel the old emotion. Such is the power of an image.'

Dr Maude picks up the Luzern photograph again.

'You've told me about all the tortured interpretations of this image, what this scholar and that scholar thinks. Whether it's about Lou controlling the men, or the men leading her into the future. Whether it was meant as a joke or demonstrates the instability of their triangular relationship, a portent of the mess they'll soon make of it. And so on. Well, like Lou I'm a Freudian so I'll give you a Freudian-style interpretation. The three went to the photo studio to have their picture taken in order to celebrate their newly formed chastity/study pact. By allowing themselves to be harnessed in tandem to Lou's cart the men are saying they've placed their libidos in her hands. The silly whip she holds is symbolic: she will enforce her vision of chastity upon them, mobilize their phallic power on behalf of finer, nobler, intellectual goals.' Dr Maude nods to herself. 'That's what I think the picture says.'

'Wow!' I tell her. 'That's brilliant. I never read that anywhere.'

'Maybe I'm right, maybe not. We can argue endlessly over the meaning of an image, but what's important is its meaning to a particular beholder. Just as that snapshot you took of your dad has a special meaning for you, so the Luzern photograph had a special meaning for Chantal. It doesn't matter what I or anyone else thinks it means. It's what it meant to *Chantal* that should be important to you. If you're going to create a strong piece about her that's what you need to figure out.'

Arriving at San Pablo Martial Arts, I report as instructed to Kurt.

'Skip rope, work the bags, take five, then prepare to spar in the ring. I'm setting you up today with Rosita. She'll give you a good workout.' He smiles. 'What're you waiting for?'

'I've seen Rosita fight. I don't think I'm ready for her yet.'

'Your instructor says you're ready, you're ready.' His voice turns gentle. 'You say you want to learn to fight. The only way to learn is to do it. Sparring with Rosita will give you a taste. Then you can decide if you still want to learn, or go back to taking class for cardio.'

He says I'm ready then I'm ready, I tell myself as I work up a sweat in the gym. I take a five minute rest, then go to the mirror, put in my mouthguard, pick a head guard from the pile, put it on, and approach the ring.

Rosita's waiting for me. She's shorter than me and a lot more muscular. Her biceps bulge in her tank top. She has unshaved armpits and the kind of triangular face you often see on Mexicans with lots of Indian blood. She's also got an attitude on her. Kurt's whispering to her as I approach. I can't hear what he's saying but I figure it's about me. Listening and nodding, she watches me as I climb into the ring. Her stare says it all: *Today you're going to get it, bitch!*

We circle each other. Her eyes lock into mine. I glance at Kurt. He's watching us closely. Just then Rosita snaps out a punch. I reel back. She grins. Then she unloads a flurry of elbow strikes and kicks.

I try my best to block them, but several get through. The ones that land really hurt. I reel back. I feel my skin's reddening from the blows. Remembering what Chantal told me, that pain is part of the process, I try to ignore it and counterattack. Rosita laughs as I try to fight my way through her blocks. She's quick, and every time I come close to landing a strike, she snaps out one of her own.

'Get in there, Tess!' Kurt yells. 'Kick–punch! Kick–punch! Kick–jab–cross!'

I try to do what he says but nothing lands. Or if it does, Rosita scornfully laughs it off. She ducks and slips, backs off a couple inches so she's just out of reach, then puts herself forward as if to taunt me: *Come on, bitch! Try again!*

When I do she lands a kick in the center of my stomach. I reel back in pain.

Kurt yells: 'OK, girls – that's it. Break!'

Rosita immediately drops her fists and steps back. For the first time her smile turns friendly. 'Nice round,' she tells me. We bump gloves. Then she shrugs, turns her back, and ducks out of the ring.

'You need blocking practice,' Kurt tells me. 'Next time just defend.'

After I change and shower, I go up to him.

'That was rough. Why'd you put me with her?'

'It's good to be over-matched. Toughens you up.'

He stares at me. I stare back. *I know your secret, Sensei. You want everyone here to think you're alpha, but I know you were submissive to Chantal. Maybe you didn't want that to get out. Maybe . . .*

'Why'd you put me with Marie?' I ask.

'Oh,' he says, surprised by my question, 'that was her idea.'

'Marie asked to spar with me? You're sure? This was over two months ago?'

'She said she recognized you. She'd seen you in something. Wanted to get to know you.' He sniffs. 'Said you looked hot.'

'Hot! You're saying she was attracted to me?'

He shrugs. Clearly he prefers not to talk about her. I decide to mention this to Scarpaci and that maybe he should give Kurt another look.

'You did good today, Tess,' he says. 'You didn't pull back and quit like a lot of them. You took the hits like you didn't care. You have fighting spirit. I like that in a girl. But you're going to have to work a lot harder if you want to compete. Next time I'll run you through a set of blocking drills. If you don't learn to block and counterpunch you won't last a round.' And with that he turns away.

FIFTEEN

Unpublished Exchange of Letters Between Lou Andreas-Salomé and Sigmund Freud, December 1935—February 1936

Loufried, Göttingen

December 9, 1935

Dear Professor:

I am writing you briefly today as I am concerned about a number of matters, first among them my health. Old age, it seems, is rapidly catching up with me. I have recently endured the surgical removal of my left breast, a thoroughly unpleasant operation, which I hope will stop the spread of the cancer.

I am of course very concerned about your future in Vienna. You know that I like to hold myself aloof from politics, but these days that's increasingly difficult. We keep hearing rumors of *Anschluss*. How much longer, I wonder, will our saner countrymen be able to withstand the pressure for annexation building by the day?

In regard to the 'young man' whose drawing we analyzed my last day in Vienna, I marvel daily at the mystery of fate, this great reversal of fortune. Twenty years ago he groveled before me. Now all of Germany grovels before him!

I recall describing to you his obsession with the operas of Richard Wagner, his love of Wagner's *gesamtkunstwerk*. The other evening I went to the cinema to see a movie everyone is speaking of, *Triumph of the Will*, directed by that pretty actress, Fräulein Leni Riefenstahl. Afterwards, quite shaken by her vision, I understood that our young man is set upon transforming an entire nation into a Wagnerian spectacle. Horrifying thought!

In this regard, do you remember my describing the visit of a rather oily fellow named Fleckstein who claimed he was prepared to offer me an enormous sum in return for the drawing just mentioned? Now I learn that Fleckstein has been making regular inquiries about my health, going so far as to ask the hospital where I had my surgery to keep him closely advised regarding my condition. They are, you see, eagerly awaiting my death, after which I believe they intend to descend upon my little fortress to retrieve that 'precious' item! However I do not believe that they will find it. I have secreted it well.

These are difficult times, dear Professor, times that truly try us. I hope you and Anna are well. With all affectionate wishes to you and your family for a fine holiday season.

In deep gratitude,

Lou

Vienna IX, Berggasse 19
January 11, 1936

My Dear Lou,

I have been thinking of you today, and, I admit, worried for you. Anna has spoken to me with great concern about your recent medical issues. We both hope for the very best outcome. This kind of thing happens to us all, an inevitable consequence of age. As you know, my cancer of the jaw has become more serious of late. As my eightieth birthday approaches, I more clearly foresee the end. As you yourself put it so well, we have both long since 'passed through the portal of old age.'

In regard to Anna, I am concerned about rumors floating about that she was the actual subject of my 1919 paper *A Child Is Being Beaten*, and of her own first published paper, *Beating Fantasies and Daydreams*

(1922), on which you provided her with such generous assistance as acknowledged in her footnote on the title page. Certain people are saying that both our papers are actually about Anna's own masochistic dreams cleverly disguised as being those of an unnamed patient.

Of course only you, Anna and I know the full truth of the matter. Meantime these rumors, fanned by cowards who, afraid to attack me directly, choose to get at me by undermining the substantial achievements of my daughter, are a matter, I have told Anna, to be waved aside and ignored. Such attacks are the small price one pays for advancing the study of human psychology. Let me just say that I am immensely proud of Anna's paper and pleased that it won her membership in the Vienna Psychoanalytic Society.

Yet as I think of these two papers, mine and hers, I am haunted by the sadomasochistic drawing of our young friend, the one he presented to you in a public park on your last day in Vienna, 1913. Listening to his rant on the radio last evening, I could not help but associate that drawing with the way he currently presents himself. It's as if he has turned his erotic inclinations inside-out, concealing the submissive desires imparted in that image within intoxicating fantasies of domination. Of course such inversions are common and well known to those of us who practice analysis. But I am troubled by the notion that I too cavalierly dismissed the potential for inversion implicit in his drawing, never dreaming, of course, that one of so little account could ever rise to a position where he would have the ability to realize such fantasies on a massive public scale. One hopes that cooler heads will soon prevail and he will be dethroned. The German people are, I hope and must believe, too wise to place their destiny in such unstable hands.

Wishing you the best for 1936. Most faithfully,
Freud

Loufried, Göttingen
February 3, 1936

Dear Professor,

Thank you for your recent letter and your generous financial gift for my seventy-fifth birthday. Your kindness toward me through the decades has been indispensable to my survival. For this I am forever in your debt.

In regard to our young friend, I also listen to him on the radio. It would seem that he has now adapted a compensatory pose – the Great Man puffed up by delusions of grandeur. The excess in his rhetoric, the pontification, the rise and fall that stirs people even as they ignore the content of his speeches, strike me as thoroughly Wagnerian. It's as if the obsequious and troubled failed artist whom I once knew has been subsumed by an ogre, one who writhes as he speaks, whose voice trembles, and whose hypnotic oratory arouses dark atavistic notions buried deep within the ids of his obedient followers. Listening to him I wonder: *What force is pulling the strings of this marionette?*

One of my patients (and I have only four now, since, as you know, I have been winding down my practice) reports seeing him in a dream, in which the ferocity he expresses is greatly amplified and his features become transformed into those of a wolf. Such is the power of his Wagnerian rhetoric.

I don't believe I mentioned to you that at one of our meetings he told me he found the paintings of his contemporary, Egon Schiele, frightening and nightmarish on account of the contortions of the under-nourished bodies of Schiele's subjects. Now watching him in newsreels I'm struck by *his* contortions. It's as if he has internalized some of the poses of Schiele's personae. He also, as best I recall, wondered whether those drawings might be prophetic, suggesting a future of emaciated souls wandering a world reduced to ruins. Could that be the future he envisions as he leads Germany upon a course that must strike the sane as total madness?

I probably shouldn't put down such thoughts in a letter

that might be opened and read, but at my age I see no profit in pretense.

In regard to the rumors circulating about Anna and who may or may not have been the actual patient whose fantasies she elucidated in her brilliant paper, I have written her that, just as you advised, such gossip must be ignored. To respond to the chatterers is to give them credence. Her analytic work speaks for itself and will be regarded as important long after her detractors are forgotten. Let me add that I think it was singularly brave of you to turn Anna over to me for analysis. I took that as a strong vote of confidence and worked my very best with her. But I must tell you that she herself did the hard work required for true self-exploration and for that I commend *her* bravery. For this and the real affection I feel for her, I shall always think of her as the daughter I wish I'd had.

Yours devotedly and in renewed gratitude,

Lou

SIXTEEN

*C*hantal asked to spar with me because she thought I
looked hot!

Fueled by that revelation I suffer a restless night in
which Chantal/Marie weaves in and out of my dreams. At
times she whispers to me. As I struggle to make out her words,
I feel her mouth graze my ear. 'You are *so* hot,' she tells me,
'I want you *so* much . . .'

I wake up in the middle of the night sweating and trembling.
Peering up at the skylight, I check to make sure no one's
watching me.

It's then that I realize I have just dreamt of making love
with Chantal, the two of us together naked in my bed, kissing,
moaning, stroking and orally pleasuring one another, then
moving together toward a shattering climax.

Did this dream carry me over the top? Seems it did. I
enjoy the notion. I also find it frightening that I have drawn
so close to this woman who allegedly found me hot that she
now has entered my dreams and in them ravished me with
her love.

Dr Maude wants to know how I felt when Kurt told me what
Chantal said.

'Strange,' I tell her, 'and also moved because that means
she related to me in a way that now seems intimate. We weren't
matched up casually. She asked to spar with me. I played a
role in her fantasies just as she now plays a role in mine.'

'And your erotic dream about her – what does that tell you?'

'That there's something about her that draws me. Something
more than just a fascination with her life and obsessions.
Something corporeal. Her body.'

'You sparred with her, made physical contact.'

'That came back to me in the dream. The sweat on her
forehead. The way her sports bra fit her bust. The attractive

way she moved. And I knew from Eva's letters that she was gay.'

'Your lovemaking – was it sadomasochistic?'

'No, we made love tenderly.'

'You look troubled, Tess,' Dr Maude says. 'How does this erotic dream make you feel about your Chantal project?'

I think about that, then blurt it out. 'Like I'm caught in a spiderweb,' I tell her.

This morning, a little after eleven, my intercom sounds. A male voice inquires: 'Chantal?'

'No,' I tell him, 'she doesn't live here anymore.'

'Oh . . . well, sorry to bother you. Her website's down and her phone's been disconnected. I came by to see if she's still around. When I saw the new name by the buzzer I figured she'd left, but decided to give it a shot.' He pauses. 'Any idea how to reach her?'

'I really don't,' I tell him.

'I'm from New York. Used to see her whenever I came to the Bay Area. Drove over from San Francisco this morning hoping she'd still be here.' He pauses again. 'You wouldn't be in the same line of work?'

My first instinct is to blow him off. I hesitate. He's polite and I don't detect anything creepy. That he came by suggests he was one of her regulars. If he's willing to share, this could be a chance to get a client's perspective. So instead of telling him I'm not in the same line of work, I ask if he has time for coffee.

'Sure.'

I direct him to Downtown Café, tell him I'll meet him there in fifteen minutes, ask him to describe himself.

'Dark hair, gray business suit, blue shirt, red and gray striped tie.'

Sounds like an old-fashioned gent.

I tell him I'll be carrying a copy of *The New Yorker*.

Since he's in business attire, I change from black T-shirt and jeans to blouse and skirt, and forgo wearing my black moto jacket. I slip on a pair of medium-heel pumps, grab my *New Yorker*, snatch up a pair of blue tinted shades to complete the ensemble, and check myself in the mirror.

Be sincere, I tell myself. *Don't wait too long to tell him Chantal's dead. If he thinks you're playing him, he'll shut down.*

I spot him right away. He's sitting facing the door. Soon as I walk in, he smiles and rises.

I introduce myself as Tess. He tells me his name's Carl. There's a moment when I'm tempted to repeat his name the way I repeated Mike's in the Redwood Lounge.

We check each other out. He's younger than he sounded, about forty, appears prosperous, perhaps an internet company exec. No wedding band, but if he's married he probably slipped it off.

'So what brings you to the Bay Area?' I ask.

'I'm an architect. We're setting up a branch office. I'm looking for an industrial loft with lots of light, preferably in San Francisco.'

'Not Oakland?'

He shakes his head. 'Oakland's got a bad rep. Our clients would be scared off.' He peers at me. 'You're very attractive.' I peer back, noncommittal. 'And,' he adds, 'you've taken over The Eagle's Nest, my favorite Bay Area playroom.'

Time, I decide, to set him straight.

'Yes, I've taken over Chantal's old place, but I'm not in the same line of work. You're wondering why I asked to meet. There's something about her I felt you should know, something I didn't want to say over the intercom.'

He peers at me, concerned.

'Chantal passed away a few weeks back. The police say she was murdered.'

'Is this true?' When I nod he shakes his head. 'Wow! That's awful! I can hardly believe it.'

'It's a weird story. She moved out suddenly like she was scared, disappeared, then turned up dead. I've been talking to some of her friends. Seems she was a fascinating woman. I'm thinking of writing something about her.'

'You're a journalist?'

'Dramatist. I write stories then perform them as monologues. Look, you don't have to talk to me. But if you feel like talking about Chantal, you have my word I'll never use your name, not that I know it anyway.'

'It's Carl Draper.' He fishes a business card from his wallet, hands it to me: DRAPER & ASSOCIATES ARCHITECTS. There's a phone number bearing the San Francisco area code and a PO box address.

Stirred by this act of trust, I reciprocate by handing him one of mine.

He reads it aloud: 'Tess Berenson, monologist. Have I heard of you?'

'That you ask tells me you haven't.'

'Sorry. Dumb question. My mind isn't working too well. I'm still in shock.'

'Everyone who knew Chantal was shocked. None of her friends can figure it out. And neither can the police . . . though they're working on it.'

He studies me. 'You seem very nice. I'll be glad to talk to you about Chantal.' Again he lowers his eyes. 'I guess you've figured out I was one of her clients.'

I nod. 'I'm trying to get a sense of what she was like. You're the first person I've met who sessioned with her.'

'Suppose I take you to lunch? Chantal and I would some- times grab a bite at the Cambodian place around the corner. Good food and there's a quiet table in back.'

I know the place. The food is good. I tell him I'll go with him if we can split the check.

We walk to the restaurant. The streets of downtown are filled with office workers on their lunch hour, some strolling, others sitting on park benches munching sandwiches, still others lying on concrete piers taking in the sun.

After we sit and order, he leans forward.

'This may surprise you but I'd like to describe some of what we did. Not the details, but the parameters. I'm not ashamed of my sexuality.'

I tell him I appreciate his openness and promise again not to betray his confidence.

'I enjoy sessioning with pro dommes, so whenever I travel I check out the local websites. About a year ago, when I started coming out here, I found something interesting and unusual on Chantal's site. Most of the pros list the same specialties. She offered what she called "Psychological Sessions", "BDSM Oriented Life-Coaching", and "discussions of BDSM Theory and Aesthetics". She also listed "Confessionals". That struck a nerve. I called her to discuss what she meant by it. We met at a café down the street. That's why, when you suggested coffee, I thought you might be a pro checking me out. Anyway, she quickly put me at ease. She seemed genuinely interested in my needs. We set up a session. Two days later I drove back over here and we got into it. My scene . . . well, this is kinda embarrassing, but I've told you this much so why not tell it all? My scene was to be in a kind of mock church confession combined with a parody of a session with a psychotherapist.'

If I was attentive before, I'm doubly so now. 'Did she use the word "psychotherapist"?'

He shakes his head. 'She told me in California you have to be licensed to call yourself that. She used the term life coach.'

'How did the scene resemble a psychotherapy session?'

'I think it would be better to tell you how it *didn't*. For one thing, I was naked. For another, I was bound face up on a gurney. Actually it was less like therapy than an interrogation with a very strict priestess-interrogator. She began slowly, then picked up the questioning. She wanted to know *everything*, wanted me to expose my entire private life – dreams, fantasies, sexual history. The more I told her the more she demanded. It felt liberating to be stripped so bare. She intended, she told me, not only to explore my conscious mind, but to probe my unconscious, the "animal core of you", as she put it, "the deepest part of you that defines who you really are".'

Our food arrives. The waitress sets down our platters and moves away.

'You're probably wondering where the BDSM comes in. I won't go into that except to say that when she didn't feel I was being forthright or thought I was lying, she punished me by binding me into painful stress positions, and then applying pain to sensitive areas.'

'Sounds like an inquisition.'

'Oh, she was a grand inquisitor all right! I found it impossible to resist her.' He looks up at me. 'Hey, let's eat before the food gets cold.'

As we dive in to our respective dishes, I consider the liberation effect he described. It reminds me how I often feel when I leave Dr Maude's.

'This fetish of yours for confession – did Chantal ask where that came from?'

'I told her upfront. I was brought up Catholic. Like other Catholic kids you've heard about, I was abused by a priest. I went through years of psychotherapy trying to resolve it. Nothing seemed to work. Then I found I could obliterate the pain by eroticizing it. Somehow the abuse by my childhood confessor and my sessions with various shrinks got combined into a fantasy of submitting to a dominant priestess. Chantal seemed to understand exactly what I needed, and best of all was able to deliver it.'

'Sounds like she really helped you.'

'Though we only sessioned a dozen times, I view those experiences as life-altering. I always left her place with a sense of clarity, a feeling that the muddle in my mind had been wiped clean.' He pauses. 'Of course that only lasted a while, and then I'd need another fix. I became addicted to her.' He shakes his head. 'I'm really going to miss her.'

'Did she reveal anything about her personal life?'

'Only after session. We'd go out, grab a bite, often here. Then we'd talk as equals. She was strict in session, but nice outside.' He pauses. 'What I liked about her was that she wasn't big on therapeutic mumbo-jumbo. "We're doing this together," she'd remind me. "It's not the why that's important. It's the reality, the action, the emotional work-out."'

After we split the check, Carl walks me back to the Buckley. On the way I ask how he'd characterize Chantal's style of domination.

His answer comes quickly. 'Commitment and presence. Total commitment to me as her client, and, when we sessioned, being totally present in the scene.'

Just like a really good actress, I think.

I glance at him. He's been candid with me, perhaps a little

too candid, I think. Why reveal so much to a stranger? One side of me likes him; another side is suspicious.

'I'm very glad to have met you,' he tells me at the door. He pauses. 'I have fond memories of the loft. I'd love to come up and see it again. You know . . . for old times' sake.'

I tell him I'm sorry but that's not possible.

He nods. 'I understand. Anyway, thanks for giving me the opportunity to spill my guts.'

I thank him for sharing, let myself in, pause on the other side of the glass door. I turn, our eyes meet. He looks distraught. I smile. He smiles back then walks away.

This afternoon, after hours of solo rehearsing, I decide to go out for a walk. I check out a new pop-up gallery on Telegraph, try on a beautiful handmade necklace, decide not to buy it, then walk past the bookstore where I discovered Chantal's library. A block later I spot Josh sitting in a café a couple doors down from the Fox Theater.

He spots me at the same time, calls out.

'Hey, Tess! Where you been? Haven't seen you in a while.'

I walk over to him. He motions me to sit.

'I've been here,' I tell him. 'What about you?'

'Down in LA for a week visiting with my kids. Now I'm trying to finish my tarot queens. Got Queen of Coins done. Finishing up Queen of Cups. What a bitch!' He chuckles. 'But then she would be, wouldn't she?' He peers into my eyes. 'So . . . have you decided yet?'

'What?'

'Are we going back to being friends?'

'I didn't know we ever were.'

He laughs. 'That's a haughty response.'

'I'm a haughty girl. Think of me as Queen of Cups. You know, a bitch.'

'Would you pose for her?'

'The Queen? Thought you were almost finished.'

'Everything but the face. Left it blank. But now, running into you, I'm thinking—'

'If you use my face, Josh, you just might end up in one of my monologues. Be warned – it might not be a pretty picture.'

He laughs again. 'I like the way we get on. Always fun talking with you.'

'Actually, I'm glad I spotted you. Got a couple questions.'

I tell him I've spoken with Detective Scarpaci, who told me he'd ID'd Chantal's body. 'That's something you neglected to mention.'

'I'm sure there's plenty I neglected to mention. Let's make a list. Then I can apologize for everything at once.' He eyes me carefully. 'What else did Scarpaci say?'

'I think you should talk to him.'

'I've got nothing to tell him.'

'Seems to me you have a hell of a lot, seeing you monitored Chantal's sessions.'

'Some, not all.'

'Including her denazification scenes?'

'Who told you about that?'

'Scarpaci found out a lot. But not enough to ID her killer. Not yet anyway.'

'Chantal was very sensitive about those scenes. She was afraid they'd be misunderstood.'

'Tell the truth, I was pretty offended when I heard about them. But Scarpaci seems to understand them. He thinks the murder may be connected to them.'

'Did you tell him I watched her?'

'Not yet.'

He shakes his head. 'Seems like you want to drag me into this.'

'You *are* in it, Josh! As much as anyone. If she was killed by one of her clients, you could be a real help.'

'Like I told you, I didn't see everything she did. Just the sessions she wanted monitored. Her denazification game – she kept that private. I only saw her doing it once wearing her snazzy Israeli uniform. That was a fluke. She forgot to turn off the feed.' He shakes his head. 'What makes Scarpaci think it was a client?'

'Strikes me as a reasonable theory. Contrary to what you thought, he's serious about tracking down her killer. I'd think you'd want to help with that.'

'I'll consider it.' He pulls out his cell phone. 'Mind if I take your picture?'

'For Queen of Cups?' He nods. I shake my head. 'Here's
the deal – open up to Scarpaci, tell him everything you know,
and not only will I let you put my face on Queen of Cups,
I'll come down to your studio and pose for you. And, to put
a little frosting on the cake, I'll slip you into the premiere of
my new performance piece. Oh, one other thing: will you loan
me Queen of Swords?'

'You don't want much, do you?'

'It's a brilliant portrait. I'd love to feast my eyes on it.'

'Suppose I say yes? Can I use your likeness any way I
want?'

'Sure, make me a bitch. I've played that role lots of times.'

He smiles, raises his phone. 'Pretty for the picture!' *Click!*
'Got it!'

We walk together to the Buckley. On the way, I tell him
about seeing a guy clinging to my bedroom skylight.

'It was during the big storm. There was this huge thunder-
clap, I woke up, there's lightning, and suddenly I see this guy
in a hooded slicker spread out face down on the skylight above
my bed. Next lightning strike, he's gone.'

'I don't believe it. How'd he get up there? There're locked
doors between your floor and the roof. And why would anyone
go up there on a night like that?'

'The next morning I went up to the roof with Clarence.
Both doors were unlocked. Plus there's a way to get there
from the next building.'

'So what happened to him when he disappeared?'

'There're corners where someone could wait a storm out.'

'So some perv voyeur was up there peering down at you?'

'I think so. And maybe not just once. Maybe many times
in the middle of the night when I'm asleep. The whole thing
creeped me out so much I moved my bed into the main loft.'
I look at him. 'Could you rig up a way to screen off my
skylights, drapes I can open and close?'

'Sure, but won't be cheap. Cost you eight-fifty including
fabric.'

We're at the front door now. 'Worth it. When can you speak
to Scarpaci?'

'Why don't you set it up for the three of us – he can

come over and interview me, and I'll sketch you at the same time.'

'That's a lot going on at once.'

'That's how I'd like to do it.'

I phone Scarpaci, tell him I've persuaded Josh to spill.

'It's going to be a little weird,' I tell him. 'He wants to sketch me while you two talk.'

'Sounds like he wants a witness. Any idea why he was such a hardass?'

'He was disgusted by Ramos and thought you were just going through the motions. Also I think he's wary of cops. He may have forged some paintings, Picassos. He makes his living doing Légers and Matisses for restaurants and cafés. He calls them appropriations, but I think he may have done some outright forging in the past.'

I tell him then about Kurt at San Pablo Martial Arts, the odd way he acted when I brought up Marie's name. 'Like he's afraid I know about their barter arrangement. I know you talked to him but you might want to check him out some more.'

'You did good, Tess. I appreciate it. Hope we can get together soon, maybe go out for a drink.'

The *Recital* run-through goes well. Rex makes minor corrections. I confer with Grace. We set a date: Thursday June 10, 8 p.m. Engraved invitations will go out, champagne and canapés ordered, valet car service arranged.

I'm excited and a little nervous. I phone Dr Maude, invite her. 'Jerry will be there, so you can have a look at him. Also Rex the director, Josh the forger, Scarpaci the detective, and a couple old friends.'

'Sure you want to include Maude the shrink?'

'Absolutely. I want everybody to check out everybody else.'

Josh appears at my door with a ladder and Queen of Swords.

'Here to measure the skylights,' he says. 'And I brought The Queen.'

Soon as he enters the main room, he stops cold. 'You got her chariot!'

'Clarence was storing it. He gave it to me. Pretty great, huh?'

Josh shakes his head. 'You're turning this place into a museum of . . . what would you call it? Chantalania?'

He carries Queen of Swords over to the St. Andrew's Cross, positions it, then stands back so we can admire it together.

'Looks cool beside the chariot,' he says. 'If I'd known Clarence had it I'd have tried to wangle it for myself. Wonder what else he's got of hers. Couple times when we ran into him I'd catch him looking at her a certain way. Like he found her drop-dead gorgeous. Which of course she was.'

He sets the ladder under the main room skylight, takes measurements, then does the same in my bedroom. As he works, he describes how the draping will work: lightweight black velour will be threaded with drawstrings, then gathered at the sides of the skylights into neatly drooping folds. When the strings are pulled, the velour will unfurl across the bottom of the skylight wells blacking out the glass above.

'The way Chantal had this place fixed up it was like a theater.' He shows me where she kept her gurney, and an ob-gyn table with stirrups for intimate examinations.

'She had one of those!'

'She believed good props were essential. She hated the dark dungeon she'd shared with Lynx. She wanted what she called "a clean, well-lighted place".'

'The more I learn about her, the more interesting she becomes.'

'She had something going on in her head, a story she didn't want to share. She was focused when we talked, but I had the feeling there was a private movie playing in her brain.'

Josh says it'll take him a week to get the drapes set up. He pauses at the door.

'I went up on the roof. Clarence took me. He admitted he was upset the doors were unlocked when you two checked it out. You're right, there're places up there where someone could ride out a storm. And it wouldn't be that hard to cross over from the next building. But if there was someone there, my bet is he came up through the Buckley. I told Clarence he ought to put in a security system, cameras in the lobby and on the landings. He said his aunt doesn't want that, thinks it'll mess up the priceless period decor. Said he'll pitch the idea to her again, but I have a feeling he won't.'

'Why?'

'I think maybe there's something sleazy going on here like with those Chinese guys in black suits I keep running into in the lobby. Ever notice how they barely nod if you say hello? They look like folks who wouldn't want video surveillance.'

'You think they're into something illegal?'

He shrugs. 'You don't think it was Clarence up there that night?'

'God, I hope not!' I tell him. But the possibility did cross my mind.

Often when I go out for a run around Lake Merritt, I pass a homeless guy camped on the corner of 14th and Alice. People call him Jake, he's black, looks to be in his sixties, and always greets me with a big 'Hi, Toots' and a toothless smile. Today he's pushing along his grocery cart, piled high with empty soda cans. I wave to him as I approach, but he doesn't respond. Then just as I pass he whispers: 'Watch out for the green man, Toots.'

I invite Scarpaci up to the loft. The jail cell stuns him. 'Chantal put that in?' I nod, then gesture toward Queen of Swords. 'That's her portrait. Josh painted it.'

Scarpaci stands in front of the painting gazing at it the way a museum-goer might gaze at a Matisse. 'Strange how alive she looks. Lot different than at the morgue.'

He peers around. 'I see why you like it here.' He glances at my over-size inkblots. 'The shrink who checked me out showed me a set like that. I saw a lot of weird stuff but since I wanted back on the street I kept it to myself.'

To prepare him for his interview I tell him about the concealed cameras and microphones Josh installed so he could monitor Chantal's sessions when she had security concerns.

'So he saw her sessioning with her clients. How long have you known this?'

I tell him I've known it for a while.

'Please in future don't hold anything back. From now on we share everything, OK?'

When I mention the skylight incident, he looks concerned. 'Cameras in the ceiling that may have been live and maybe someone on the roof staring down at you in bed – I want to bring in my technician, have her do an electronic sweep.'

'Is that really necessary?'

'It's for your protection. If someone's snooping on you, it's best to find out.'

He phones his technician then suggests we continue our conversation on the street until she shows up. 'You know, in case your place is bugged.'

On our way toward the Oakland Museum, he fills me in on the San Jose killing.

'I spoke to the detective who worked the case. Lynx was right. The bullets were dug out. Which suggests the killer used a gun with a registered ballistic signature, or a gun he liked so much he didn't want to dump it.'

'So it could be a cop?'

'Maybe. But the victim, aside from being a pro domme, had nothing in common with Chantal. She was British, middle-aged, worked the low end of the trade. She was found in her dungeon . . . if you could call it that, a shabby basement room in East San Jose. The door was unlocked and there were no signs of a struggle. The detective thinks it was probably a client. And yes, some cops do go to pro dommes.'

'So it doesn't fit.'

'Doesn't seem to. It would be interesting if there was a pattern, a guy who sees dommes and then gets enraged and kills them. But here you've got a shooting and a strangling, one body left in place and the other stuffed into the trunk of a car, a middle-aged low-end domme and a young beautiful high-end one. Feels like unconnected homicides.'

Shortly after we return to the Buckley, my buzzer sounds. A female voice at the other end tells me she's come to meet Detective Scarpaci. I buzz her in. She turns out to be a small Eurasian woman carrying a backpack filled with electronic gear, earphones, probes, and meters.

Scarpaci introduces her. 'This is Nadia, my *fortochnitsa*.'

'Great! What's a *fortochnitsa*?'

'It's a derivative of *fortochka*,' Nadia tells me. She speaks with a Russian accent. 'That's a kind of very narrow kitchen window you find in Moscow apartments. A *fortochnitsa*'s a small wiry girl like me who can wriggle through a window like that.'

'So are you a cat burglar?' I ask.

'Used to be.' She smiles. 'Until Detective Scarpaci caught me one night rappelling down from a roof with my pockets full of gems.'

'She was a first-class thief,' Scarpaci explains, 'expert at getting into places she didn't belong and excellent safe-cracker when she did. I was working robbery. There'd been a slew of break-ins at wholesale jewelers' offices, the kind you find on the upper floors of buildings like this. I got a tip and staked the place out. I caught Nadia just as she hit the ground. After I collared her we worked out a deal. She'd plead guilty and give up her boss, a Russian who had a crew of *fortochnitsas*. In return the DA went light.'

'Not all that light,' Nadia says. 'A year in Chowcilla. But it wasn't a total loss. Got my cosmetology license. Now I'm legal to cut hair.' She grins. 'When I got out I looked up my old friend Scarpaci here. He got me into a security training program. Now I work on contract for the Oakland, Hayward, and Berkeley PDs.'

'She's one of the best. Do a full sweep, Little One. Then I want you to check for access.'

'I can tell you right now if I was on the roof I wouldn't have any trouble getting in. Penthouses are easy.'

As she hooks up her gear she points to the ceiling cameras. 'You know about those?'

I turn to Scarpaci. 'Did you tell her?'

He shakes his head.

'Easy to spot,' Nadia says. 'I saw them soon as I came in. When I finish the sweep I'll take them down.'

While Nadia starts work, Scarpaci peers again at my inkblots.

'Tell me about these?'

I describe how I made them and how everyone who visits

comments on them. 'Maybe they think they reveal something
. . . you know, my secret inner life.' He laughs.

I tell him more about Josh while Nadia moves about the
loft, running her probe across the floor, then up the walls,
listening to her scanner through heavy earphones.

Scarpaci tells me he's skeptical about Josh's role as Chantal's
security guy.

'I don't doubt she had him do that, but I'm sure he got off
watching. Sounds like he was pretty obsessed with her.' He
gestures toward Queen of Swords. 'I'd say that portrait proves
it.'

I don't admit to the degree to which I too have become
obsessed.

'I think on some level Josh was smitten by her,' I tell him.
'After the cremation he kept back half her ashes. I believe he
truly wanted to protect her. I think that's the main reason he
wouldn't talk to you guys – he wanted to protect her memory.'

Nadia comes out of my bedroom. 'So far no bugs,' she says,
'but I'm getting a reading from the closet floor. Could be an
old pipe, but I don't think so.'

'Let's take a look,' Scarpaci says.

Nadia leads us to my closet, points to an area beneath the
clothes rack, crouches, runs her hands along the flooring, then
pulls gently on the baseboard. A section comes loose. She
pulls it out and peers into a cavity behind. 'There's a safe in
here,' she says. She pulls out a shallow metal strongbox with
a keyhole in the top.

'Typical small business strongbox,' Scarpaci says. He tests
the top. 'Locked.'

Nadia smiles. 'Give it to me.' It takes her five seconds to
get it open. She hands it back to Scarpaci. 'I'll finish the sweep
then take down the cameras.'

Scarpaci carries the strongbox back into the main loft.

'Not much here,' he says, pulling out the contents then
laying them one at a time on my coffee table.

Looking at the array I'm amused at first, and then amazed:
another swastika armband like the one I found inside the book
on Third Reich uniforms; a pair of ordinary domino masks
(why keep them in a strongbox?); a well-worn Aleister Crowley

tarot deck; a joke-store rubber pig's snout with band so it can be attached to someone's face (humiliation device?); a bunch of military pins, rank insignia and medals, some bearing swastikas and SS symbols (for use in denazification scenes?), others bearing Hebrew lettering (fittings for Chantal's Israel Defense Forces uniform?); and a black-and-white photograph which, soon as I see it, gives me the shakes.

The photo shows Chantal standing in her chariot wearing a smartly tailored business suit. She holds a black single-tail whip in one hand and a double set of reins in the other. But the aspect that causes me to tremble is the pair of men to whom the reins are attached. They're equally tall, equally muscular, and totally naked, a matched pair of human beasts of burden. Though both face the camera, their heads are encased in identical full black leather buckle-on hoods with eye and ear holes and mouth openings zippered shut, the kind I saw in the glass case at the fetish shoe store where I first met Lynx.

It's a bizarre compelling image. In it Chantal appears incredibly glamorous, even more than in Josh's Queen of Swords. But what fills me with awe is the clear reference to the photograph of Lou Salomé, Friedrich Nietzsche, and Paul Rée that so obsessed her.

I can't help but wonder what was in Chantal's mind. Was this photo taken to memorialize her reenactment of that famously 'infamous' image? Was she trying to reproduce it or parody it? And did the male participants have any notion of the reference?

It takes me a while to explain all this to Scarpaci. I bring out books in which the Luzern photo is reproduced while explaining the backstory and Chantal's obsessive interest in it. When I'm finished, Scarpaci shakes his head.

'Weird disconnect,' he says. 'We find a hidden locked strongbox filled with odds and ends along with a photograph you think could be important. I gotta ask myself – why store trinkets in a hiding place, and if the photo really was important why'd she leave it behind?'

I wonder about that too. *Might she have forgotten it?*

Seems unlikely since she was so thorough about cleaning

out her loft and selling off her stuff. But as I gaze at the items laid out on my coffee table, I realize they tell a tale about Chantal, who she was and what she did.

Could she have left these things behind for someone like me, someone who'd find them and think about them and perhaps use them as a way to unravel her story and the final drama of her life?

SEVENTEEN

Extract from the Unpublished Memoirs of Major Ernst Fleckstein

(AKA Dr Samuel Foigel)

Returning to the case of Frau Lou Andreas-Salomé, I was well prepared when in early 1937 I received news that she was close to death. In preparation I secured a large room in the cellar of the Göttingen city hall for the inspection of her books and files. In addition on Bormann's orders I was assigned a highly trained unit of Gestapo assault troops under the command of a young lieutenant named Hans Beckendorf.

Young Beckendorf, with his short-cut blond hair, piercing blue eyes, and lean athletic physique, met all the physical requirements of a cliché Aryan warrior. In fact some years later, watching a newsreel in Berlin, I saw him decorated for leadership and valor with a Knight's Cross of the Iron Cross. Back in '37, Beckendorf struck me as an intelligent and efficient young officer who was annoyingly curious about my mission. As we awaited Frau Lou's death, he irked me by his insistence that I tell him precisely what his men would be looking for when we raided her house.

I had prepared a cover story hinted at by Frau Lou during our 1934 interview, namely that her library included a great number of inflammatory and dangerous communist tracts and 'Jew-books' that must be confiscated.

I clearly recall the unbelieving expression on Beckendorf's face.

'You're tying up twenty of my men trained in assault tactics to pack up and transport books! Ridiculous!'

At this I felt the need to remind the callow lieutenant that he had been temporarily assigned to me on direct orders from Reichsleiter Bormann. Thus it would behoove him to obey all my instructions lest I find it necessary to report him for insubordination. I added that the rationale for this confiscation of Frau Lou's books and papers had to do with matters far beyond his purview. Then to further quiet him I whispered that there was a good likelihood we would uncover some valuable Nietzsche material, including personal letters, that would be of great interest to the Führer. Young Beckendorf assured me that, as an avid reader of *Zarathustra*, this was something he fully understood. Then, in what was clearly meant as a friendly gesture, he invited me to join him on his rigorous morning exercise regime by which he kept himself in top-notch fighting condition. I noticed a little sneer when I declined, but by employing the Nietzsche gambit I was able to shut him down during the final days of our deathwatch.

Finally, on February 10, 1937, a cold rainy morning, I received word that Frau Lou had passed in the night. I immediately ordered Beckendorf to assemble his men, then proceed to Loufried and retrieve everything we could find there that resembled documentation. We sped out of town, through the mist and rain and into the forested hills north of Göttingen, arriving at Loufried in the manner of a raiding party prepared to bust down doors and arrest communists and Jews.

The housekeeper, Marie, the woman I'd met back in 1934, expressed outrage at our intrusion. She shouted at me: 'The poor woman is dead but a few hours and already you and a gang of thugs come to pick through her bones.' Beckendorf, furious, wanted to arrest her but I instructed him to leave her alone. Meantime, while his Gestapo troops were busy packing up Frau Lou's library, I asked Marie if there were any safes or strongboxes in the house. She solemnly shook her head. As we spoke I noticed a teenage girl peeking out from behind the kitchen door. This, I knew from my research, was Marie's daughter, named Mariechen, sired by Frau Lou's late husband, Friedrich Carl Andreas, who, denied the pleasures of congress with his wife, had with Lou's permission turned to their loyal housekeeper for satisfaction.

After everything had been packed up and carried out to the trucks, I made a final search of the premises, tapping on walls, seeking out possible hiding places, all under the close scrutiny of Marie. Something in her manner, the amused expression on her face, led me to believe she'd been told a thorough search was to be expected and was fully confident that whatever it was her late mistress had concealed would not easily be found.

Back at City Hall, I spent several days going through everything, examining every document, glancing through Frau Lou's many notebooks and diaries, even holding every one of her books upside down then vigorously shaking it to see if the drawing, concealed between pages, might just happen to fall out . . . but to no avail. I found letters, photographs, postcards, cancelled checks, even ticket stubs, pressed flowers, and old receipts, but not a single drawing.

Her body, on her instructions, had been cremated, and although she requested that her ashes be spread upon the grounds at Loufried, the town authorities would not allow it.

Depressed by my failure to find the drawing, I attended the burial of her ashes in the town cemetery. It was a cold rainy day. Marie was there, of course, and the love-child, Mariechen. Again I noticed a mocking supercilious grin, this time on both their faces. Annoyed by this and certain I had missed something important, I hired a taxi to transport me back up to Loufried.

Beckendorf, on my instructions, had ordered his men to seal the place up. I used my penknife to cut the red wax, then entered and went straight to the study-consulting room where Frau Lou had received me in '34.

Memories of her flooded back, her quick wit and engaging eyes. As I had reported to Bormann, I'd found her highly intelligent and crafty, and although I knew she'd spoken falsely to me, I'd still found her greatly likeable.

I walked over to a pair of armchairs, sat in the chair she'd used that day, then tried to imagine what she'd thought of me as, gazing at one another, our eyes met. My eyes then fell upon the solitary chair positioned behind the tilted back of her analytic couch, where she'd sat while her patients, lying down, willingly spewed out their most intimate fantasies and dreams.

During my time as an investigator I had heard quite a few

confessions proffered during moments of personal stress. Later, after joining the party, I had heard others coerced by beatings and torture. The willingness of a patient to confide in an unseen analyst was something I found difficult to grasp. But perhaps, I thought, the end result would be the same: the feeling of relief that comes after one has spilled one's guts. I began to muse upon the possibility that under the guise of psychoanalysis a targeted individual might be induced to reveal matters that could later be used for purposes of extortion and blackmail. What a wonderful methodology, I thought: under the pretense of compassion the most dangerous secrets could be extracted and exposed. How much cleaner than the crude methods of torturers. And the only device needed would be a simple chaise longue. As Frau Lou had told me, the couch was merely a tool, so much more soothing than a red-hot needle, set of electrodes, or pair of pliers, and in all likelihood a good deal more efficient. This is definitely something to ponder, I thought.

Setting that aside, my thoughts turned back to the matter at hand: where might Frau Lou have hidden the Führer's drawing? I stood again and paced the room. While doing so I noticed that I was actually circling the prominently positioned couch. Recalling how my eyes had been drawn to it at the end of our interview in '34, I recalled something that had escaped my attention at the time, what poker players call a 'tell.' A 'tell', I'd been taught, could be something as simple as a tightening around the eyes, a fidgeting foot, a turning away, or just a slight change in position. And I remembered how, as Frau Lou and I briefly discussed the efficacy of the psycho-analytic couch, she had seemed to grow tense in a way that in retrospect was inappropriate since our interview was over and I was about to be shown the door.

I asked myself: *Could it have been hidden the entire time we spoke not two meters from where we sat, even as she claimed she had no idea what I was asking about?*

Maybe, I thought, that was the trick that brought a smile to the housekeeper's lips. I have described Frau Lou as crafty. Could she have been *that* crafty? Could she have been inwardly laughing at me the entire time we'd talked?

I went over to the couch, ran my hand over the tilted portion where a patient would rest his upper body and head. The cushion there was covered for hygienic reasons with a removable rectangle of white cloth. But the long cushion upon which the patient would stretch out was decorated with fine needlework. I pulled the head cushion off the frame of the chaise longue. There was nothing beneath it, not surprising since this cushion often would have been removed, recovered, and then replaced. But the long cushion was another matter. It was, I saw, lightly sewn to the thin box spring beneath. Again I brought out my penknife and used it to slice through the thread. Then, heart beating rapidly, I pulled the long cushion off the chaise and set it on the floor.

Eureka! There it was! A cardboard portfolio with a faux-marble black and white cover bound with a gray ribbon, a perfect container for a drawing.

I took it to Frau Lou's desk then carefully opened it with shaking hands. Inside I found the Führer's drawing. An inscription on the back made it clear this was a vision he had dreamt up concerning himself and Frau Lou in what I can only describe as a highly compromising positional relationship. Further, due to my earlier research into Frau Lou's past, I immediately recognized this positioning as identical to the way figures were posed in a comedic photograph taken in the late nineteenth century of Frau Lou with Nietzsche and another gentleman. The difference was that due to the inscription and expressions on the faces of the parties, it was clear that Hitler's drawing was intended as a dead serious homage.

I will not claim that I was shocked. By that time I was well aware of some of the Führer's, shall we say, personal proclivities. The Geli Raubal case was replete with accusations of sadomasochism. In fact it was a letter from Geli about this aspect of her uncle's personality which Stempfle had been threatening to make public that made it necessary to arrange for the good priest's termination. Thus it was not a matter of my being shocked, but of becoming aware of how inflammatory the release of this drawing would be if it fell into the wrong hands, and why the Führer had been so anxious to pay a grand sum to buy it back.

With this awareness there came a further realization: if I were to bring this drawing back to Bormann I would certainly win for myself considerable gratitude. At the same time, I would make myself vulnerable to the sort of unpleasant endings that seemed to befall people such as Fräulein Raubal, Father Stempfle, and others in possession of embarrassing information regarding the Führer's intimate behavior. Thus, I reasoned, I must decide whether it was worth the risk to deliver the drawing to Bormann only later to face some sort of terminal consequence. My decision, I knew, had to be made quickly for I was expected to report back to Bormann the following day.

To better describe what I'm speaking about, let me add that there was a well-known streak of ruthlessness in the NSDAP, a fondness for violent resolutions to unpleasant situations, that manifested itself in events such as late-night automobile 'accidents' in remote heavily forested areas, house 'break-ins' by thuggish thieves who, finding a robbery victim at home, don't hesitate to slit his throat, as well as a propensity for setting up otherwise inexplicable 'suicides.' I knew a great deal about this kind of behavior for I had myself been party to it. And though I derived no personal pleasure from handling matters in this fashion, I knew many operatives who did. How ironic, I thought, if I, Bormann's personal fixer and hatchet-man, should be struck down by the very sword by which I'd lived!

It took me but moments to make my decision. No, I would not deliver the Führer's drawing to Bormann! The risk would be too great. I would tell him that I could guarantee one hundred percent that at the time of her death Frau Lou was *not* in possession of any of the Führer's artworks, and if she ever did possess such artwork it had long since been discarded. Meantime, I would keep the drawing safely hidden so that if ever I needed a bargaining chip to get myself out of a serious jam, I could quickly retrieve it and use it as payment for, perhaps, my very life.

Before leaving Göttingen I returned to the basement of City Hall to arrange for the return of Frau Lou's library and papers. Looking through the books, I picked up a copy of Freud's *The Interpretation of Dreams*, a rare first edition dated 1900 bearing a lavish inscription:

'For Lou with special thanks for all your fine insights and

contributions to our field. May you always have magnificent and fruitful dreams! Devotedly, Freud.'

Very nice, I thought, deciding to keep it as a memento of my encounter with that extraordinary woman.

Again as in 1934, Bormann was not pleased. Knowing how much he disliked reporting a failure to Hitler, I was prepared to be thoroughly chewed out. In fact, he was less abusive than usual, and seemed to accept at face value my conclusions regarding Frau Lou and the missing drawing.

'Good!' he said. 'I'm glad that's settled.' He made the kind of gesture one makes when washing one's hands. 'I have a new assignment for you, Fleckstein. It is a highly sensitive matter requiring urgent attention. I think you will enjoy this one,' he added, rubbing his hands with glee.

Then, with what I can only describe as a high degree of relish, he asked me if I'd ever heard of the film actress Renate Müller.

EIGHTEEN

I gaze out at my audience seated on beautiful chairs in Grace's ballroom. Careful to avoid eye contact with my personal friends in the back row, I engage the attendee friends of my fictional Mrs Z.

Slowly I scan their attentive faces. I smile as I meet the eyes of several women as if I regard them as especially close. I am so *very* pleased to see them all, my smile says – these friends of many years, with whom I've served on committees and boards, whose Christmas gatherings and children's weddings I've attended, who have come so exquisitely clothed and bejeweled to attend my evening musicale, *Recital.*

I have much to say to them tonight. First a few niceties:

'Oh, thank you so very much!' I say turning to Luis, expressing gratitude to him for filling the ballroom of my home with glorious sound, also acknowledging by gesture my thanks for his attendance to an elderly lady's personal needs . . . such as they are.

'The arts are everything to us, are they not?' I ask rhetorically. 'I think of something my dear late Sam used to say: "The arts add luster to our lives."' I pause. 'Now isn't that true?'

Most nod. I turn again to Luis, sitting coolly on his stool, cello secure between his legs. 'Oh, dear Luis – your *portamenti*! And your wondrous bowing. Bravo! Bravo!'

I turn back to my audience. 'The arts heal us. Without them we'd be lost. I'm sure *I* would be. They give us solace and quiet our souls, so important in this hectic world we live in. And so we give much of our time and fortunes to support them.

'Now that I have you here . . . again thank you all so much for coming . . . allow me, if you'll permit, to, as they say, get a few things off my chest.' I pause, glance down at my rack, give a little shudder, then face them again. 'Yes, a few things, several of which you may find a bit indelicate. But that, as they say, is "hostess privilege".'

Some tittering, shuffling of feet, repositioning of chairs. I wait until they settle down. As a grande dame, I insist on full attention. I'm ready now to expose some of the injustices I've suffered through the years, little hurtful lapses of respect and expressions of ingratitude.

I speak of the mean-spirited reviews that greeted my son Kevin's painting exhibition, how the critics assailed his artwork as 'derivative' and 'amateurish', how they said he'd never have been exhibited at all if it hadn't been for the money I'd thrown at the museum.

'*Thrown!*'

I emphasize the word, slowly twisting it in my mouth to show how deeply it cut. 'Then the public gloating when my other son, Justin, was convicted of running a Ponzi scheme.

'There are some, perhaps a few here tonight, pleased that he's incarcerated. You invested money with him, lost it, and now you're pleased to know he's suffering.' I take a short bitter breath. 'Schadenfreude – that's the new blood-sport in town these days, *isn't it*? You all know what I mean.' I take a long pause as if trying to remember what to say next.

'And now,' I tell them, 'we come to the matter of Madame's parking permits. They say I have too many.' I titter, amused. 'How much time and money do you have to give around here before they leave you alone? It isn't enough, evidently, to collect old fur coats for the homeless. That was my idea, by the way – collect them from you when it was no longer politically correct to wear them, cut off the sleeves and turn them into blankets for those sorrowful unfortunates who live on our streets. Thanks to me your old fur coats and stoles, some reeking of your veddy expensive perfumes, now protect the homeless from the cold. As for those silly parking permits, this is, as you all can see,' I gesture broadly, 'a not incommodious residence. It requires a sizeable staff. My employees need to park. Thus I purchased permits for them. Yes, I needed quite a few more than your average citizen. But is that so evil? *Really?*' I wipe my eyes. 'Oh my God, what do they want of me? How much more must I give?'

I tell them I feel disrespected by the rumors going around, such as the one that Sam was gay and kept a pied-à-terre in Japantown where he met little Asian boys for romps in the hay.

'For God's sakes, the man's dead! His philanthropies . . . we're talking about tens of millions. But never mind that and never mind that the poor guy's in his grave. Let's roast him now that he can't defend himself, mock him for his little peccadilloes! The point I'm making is it's quite *quite* unfair. But then what do they want of us? Are we to give and give only to be reviled? Is that what it all comes to these sorrowful days?'

I pull myself up into a regal stance. 'In this regard let me say that *we* are not amused. I believe Queen Victoria said that once. Yes, I've made my full share of (to put it kindly!) *faux-pas*. When the Modigliani exhibition came to the DeYoung and I held a reception in this very room, and the *directrice* of the Musée d'Art Moderne in Paris, who loaned most of the works, asked to see *my* Modig . . . well, I said something rather shall we say . . . inopportune. At least so I've been told. I don't truly recall, as I was a bit tipsy at the time.'

I give out with a little snort of amusement. 'I believe I told the lady I kept my Modig upstairs in a room my granddaughter uses on those rare occasions when the little brat deigns to sleep over. Because, I told the lady, I don't really *like* old Amedeo. Oh, the *shock*! The glances of *derision*! What a rude philistine was *I*!' I puff out my bust. 'You'd think I'd vomited on the poor woman's borrowed second-hand Valentino! I simply spoke my mind, spoke truth to power . . . though we could certainly debate who actually held the power in that particular social context, she the lender or yours truly the benefactor? But never mind! Point is I was mocked for it, *severely* mocked.'

I tell them how one spends forty years contributing, giving, kissing (if I may be crude about it) butt, and still they want more. And how, God knows, one must *always* be *politically correct*. God forbid one give offense to anyone! Because then they all look askance at you and whisper (but plenty loud enough so you can hear!) that your late husband was queer and your younger son's a poseur, and the other one's in the pokey because he made some inadvertent business errors.

'Were all fair game, all of us. You *and* me! Our crime – well, we all know what it is. All of us here are guilty of it. Being, to put it bluntly, *rich!* Some of us *bloody damn rich!* And how very sweet it is to make the rich pay for being so! How they love to see social nobles such as ourselves rolling in the dust of disgrace. If I've learned one thing in my sixty-seven odd years it's that no matter what I do, how much I give, it will *never ever* be enough.'

I peer around, careful to avoid the eyes of my real friends, concentrating on the eyes of the paying audience.

'Luis here, who is of Brazilian heritage, told me about a Mexican soap opera that's very popular in Latin America.' I turn to Luis. He smiles at me and nods. 'The title's quite expressive, *Los Ricos También Lloran*. "The Rich Also Cry". I could tell you a lot about that. I'm sure some of you can as well.'

At this I observe some knowing nodding in the audience.

'I have found myself in tears quite often lately, about what things have come to in this world I thought I knew and understood. Aging is difficult too. Our beauty fades. People show less respect. And the new people, as Sam used to call them, the up-and-comers – they don't seem to know who we are. Or were. How we built the great cultural institutions here – symphony, opera, ballet, museums. Supported them through thick and thin. And then . . . *what?* Who are we *really?* Who am *I?* Just some dumpy old dyed-hair society broad who passes out smelly old fur coats to the homeless. Oh, and the politics these days! The crude way people dress on the streets! Please don't get me started!' I take a long pause. 'But there's a sadness to it, isn't there? A sense of time passing one by, an era ending. The world that we all knew and loved, the world we created and nurtured here, all passing now. Gone, as they say, with the wind . . .'

Another long pause.

'I look in the mirror some mornings and don't recognize myself. "Who am I?" I ask the glass. "Has all I've done in my life been for naught? Has it all been meaningless?" All that giving and organizing, the luncheons and charity balls, the planning and pleading – what, I wonder, did it mean? Will time vindicate us? Who knows? There's an old expression: "'Not I,'" said the walrus!"

'Forgive me now,' I beg. 'I know I'm ranting. I can see it in your faces, how embarrassed you all are on my behalf. Are you sorry you came? Sorry even to have received the gift of Luis's beautiful playing? The way he makes his gorgeous old cello moan with pleasure the way a woman moans in the arms of a skillful lover. Or perhaps I should say as a woman *would* moan if the man . . . well, never mind! As I was saying, the arts feed us, heal us, give a special sheen and luster to our lives. And yet, it seems, not always, and, well, perhaps not even tonight. For me tonight is bittersweet. I also choose not to go into that. Let it simply be said that soon an extremely talented and very handsome young man will be off to New York to build what I am certain will be a brilliant career. And I am very, *very* proud of him. An old lady, this withered old windbag of a thing who stands before you now, with her lines and wrinkles and sagging boobs . . . she'll still be here soaking up the abuse. The abuse which never seems to stop . . . the mockery, the lies and the vicious, ever-so-vicious schaden-freude . . . which, and I say this quite merrily too, makes our cruel world go 'round and 'round . . .'

As I break down into sobs, I see my audience turn away. Luis comes to me, holds me, supports me, leads me from the ballroom. I cling to him, a sobbing old lady broken on the wheel of age. Even out of their sight I continue to sob. I hear some shuffling. Are they standing to applaud? *Of course not! How could they?* Finally I straighten myself, take Luis' hand and we go out to stand before them again. I refuse to bow. My eyes remain watery and aloof as I stare stone-faced at the far wall of the ballroom.

Finally the applause begins. Jerry, my ex, leads it. I want to acknowledge him, thank him for doing so, but I don't want to break character, and so I grimace, act embarrassed, then even more distraught. The applause turns thunderous, or so it seems. And the ones who paid so dearly to come – they love my piece for the way it mirrors them and yet allows them to remain aloof. For a few moments listening to me they forgot it was a performance. Now they remember that's all it was. And so they yell, 'Bravo! Bravo!' and still I refuse to beam or in any way acknowledge their praise. I start sobbing again. I can't help myself. I cling to Luis as once again he escorts me off stage.

I do not attend the after-show reception. I told Grace that it would be part of my performance that I not do so. I told her I want to leave the audience perplexed about what they've seen, wondering whether I identified something as yet unrecognized in their lives.

After I wash off my makeup, shower, and change upstairs, Rex, Luis, and I slip out silently through a back entrance. A taxi is waiting to take us to Zuni Café. En route Rex turns to me.

'You totally slayed it, Tess! Good as you were in rehearsal, performing it for an audience brought out something special. You electrified those people. They were in thrall to you, awed by your anguish. There were waves of pity and terror in that room. I've seen most everything you've done, but I've never seen you give so much of yourself.' He turns to Luis. 'You were great too. Your powerful playing made it work. And you performed the backstory with subtlety and finesse.'

When we arrive at the restaurant I'm so drained I barely find the energy to speak. But half an hour later, in the midst of our late dinner of oysters and roast chicken accompanied by champagne, I catch a second wind.

Luis turns to me. 'Are you OK, Tess?'

I assure them both I am. 'I just need a good night's sleep. Mrs Z has been in my head too long. Time to expel her and go on to something new.'

Did I really 'slay it' tonight? I hope so. Good or bad, I'm glad it's over and that I'll never have to perform it again. I'm excited now only about what lies ahead: a major piece about Chantal, the murdered Oakland dominatrix obsessed with Lou Andreas-Salomé, and the young woman (me!) who takes over her loft and in turn becomes obsessed with them both.

*   *   *

I sleep in. When I wake it's nearly eleven. I find a slew of congratulatory messages on my voicemail.

Grace is ecstatic. She says most of the audience hung around for hours talking about what they kept calling 'the show.'

'They wouldn't shut up about it,' she says. Best of all, she adds, no one complained about the price. 'They felt they'd really seen *something*! I'm proud to have hosted *Recital*, Tess. Let me know if you decide to perform it again. My ballroom will always be available.'

Jerry is not nearly as effusive, but his message does contain a line that washes away some of the bitterness between us: 'Your Mrs Z was a perfect *monstre sacré*. There've always been people like that going back to ancient Rome and before. Proust knew them well. Yours was the twenty-first-century century model. *Quel cri de cœur!* If I ever had doubts about your talent, tonight you put them to rest.'

To have your ex admit he may have underrated you – not a bad outcome!

Dr Maude says my performance left her with tears in her eyes, 'on behalf of the person you created and then stripped bare before us, and perhaps even more for all you put into her.' We will, she promises, discuss this more extensively next session.

I think the most unexpected reaction comes from Leo Scarpaci. He calls around noon. Seeing it's him, I pick up.

'Is bedazzled a word?' he asks.

'It is. But I'll settle for dazzled . . . if that's how you felt.'

'It was. Don't know anyone like Mrs Z. Don't hang out with her kind of folks. You took me into a world I knew nothing about and made me believe it could exist.' He pauses. 'Is it OK for me to tell you this, Tess?'

I assure him I can't imagine a finer compliment.

He pauses. 'I want to get to know you better, Tess. We'll be seeing each other tomorrow when I interview Josh. But I was thinking . . . would you . . .?'

'Go out with you? If that's what you're asking the answer's yes.'

'Thanks. You make it easy. If Saturday night's OK, I'll pick you up, we'll have dinner and then I want to take you to see something I doubt you've seen before. Not elegant like last night. But it's decadent and I remember you told me you like decadent stuff.'

Late in the afternoon Josh arrives to drape my skylights.

'Loved your show, Tess. Thanks for inviting me. Was kinda surprised to see the detective there. I'm still not crazy about talking to him.'

'It's about Chantal, Josh. You'll be doing it for her.'

'Sure,' he says, 'but cops have a way of sweet-talking you, then getting you to admit to something.'

'Stop worrying. I'll be there for most of it. You'll be sketching. By the way, Scarpaci's not too happy about that. He likes to look a witness in the eye. So you'll have a little advantage there. My suggestion – get used to him while you're sketching me, then give him your full attention after I leave. All he wants is to bring in Chantal's killer. I know you want that too.'

After he hangs the drapes, he comes down from the ladder and shows me how to work them. They draw beautifully, and once closed block out all light from above. No one can watch me through my skylights now.

From the moment Scarpaci steps into Josh's loft he makes an effort to put Josh at ease. He pauses in front of the unfinished Queen of Cups in whose face Josh has already roughed out my features.

The painting isn't what I expected: a lean lone female figure in jeans and black tank top, bare arms toned, standing casually in a desert amidst dunes. There's no one else around and nothing man-made in the background. One of the Queen's hands rests on her hip. The other holds out a white porcelain cup. Though the painting is frontal and hieratic like Queen of Swords, there's something attractively casual about this Queen, loose and contemporary, that defies the tarot norm. She's confident but not haughty, and definitely *not* a bitch.

Scarpaci squints at it. 'She already looks like Tess.'

'She'll look a lot more like her when I'm done,' Josh says. We settle down, Scarpaci beside me on Josh's couch, Josh in a chair across from us, a low table in between. As soon as he's seated Josh picks up his sketch pad and begins to draw. Scarpaci sets up his recording device on the table, watches Josh a while, then starts the interview.

Josh, to my surprise, doesn't obfuscate as he has so often with me. He describes Chantal's security system, and admits he watched many of her sessions.

'I never saw anything go wrong,' he tells Scarpaci. 'I don't think she had real security concerns. She was very careful about taking on new clients. She'd always meet them first at one of the neighborhood cafés.'

'So why have you monitor her sessions?'

'*Selected* sessions,' Josh corrects him, 'only when she activated the feed. Frankly, I think there was an element of exhibitionism involved. She liked having me watching her.'

'Think she was trying to turn you on?'

'She told me one time that she liked having an audience, that she believed that being aware I was watching improved her performances.' He turns to me. 'You and she are alike in many ways, Tess. I think she'd have admired what you did the other night.'

Scarpaci leans forward. 'So she was an exhibitionist and you were her voyeur – that's what you're saying?'

'Something like that.'

'And you never saw a client step out of line or give her any cause to be afraid?'

'If I had I'd have told you. I've no idea what she was frightened of. Chantal was not a fearful person.'

'What about a threat?'

'I believe she could have handled that. And if she couldn't she'd have taken it to someone who could. Maybe even the cops.'

Scarpaci responds with a grin. 'You never recorded any of her sessions?' Josh shakes his head. 'Sure?'

'I'm sure.'

Scarpaci nods, then pulls out the chariot photo and places it on the coffee table. Josh puts down his sketch pad and picks it up, allowing me a quick look at his drawing. I like it. He's caught something in me – the long steady stare I employ sometimes, similar to the way I peered past the audience at *Recital* when I came out unsmiling at the end.

'What can you tell me about this?' Scarpaci asks.

Josh gazes at the photo. 'I can tell you plenty. The guy on the right – that's me. The other guy – I've no idea. But I'm certain he was one of her regulars.'

'*You?*' I ask. 'You're kidding, Josh.'

He laughs. 'Want me to strip so you can compare our bods?'

'OK, OK.' Scarpaci squints. 'She's in this chariot wielding a whip over two naked guys wearing fetish hoods pulling her around.'

'We didn't pull her. We posed in place. She wanted it to look staged. That was the point of it, she said. She told me she wanted an image that would be a work of art, something powerful that would make a statement about who she was and what she did. She showed me an old photo in a book. The guys in it were dressed in frock coats, there was a cart instead of a chariot, and the girl holding the whip grinned like she thought the whole thing was a joke. Chantal told me that was her inspiration. She wanted to use it as a model, recycle the imagery, and by remaking it turn it into something rawer and more intense. But despite the changes she was adamant it be in black-and-white and that the content and angle of vision be exactly the same. When I asked her why this was so important she said she was haunted by the original, and that people who knew of it would instantly recognize the source.'

'Who operated the camera?'

'She did by remote. It was her concept, her camera, her lights. Once it starting clicking, we had to stay still and pose.' He sits back. 'There were some problems. For the first set of shots she had us wear black fabric hoods. But when she checked the images she saw that the lights burned through the fabric and exposed our features. She didn't like that. She wanted her slaves to be anonymous. I told her she could easily black out our faces on the computer, but again she was adamant, our faces *had* to be masked even before she manipulated the image. So she brought out this pair of matching black-leather fetish hoods she used in sessions, had us buckle them on, then did a reshoot. She chose this image to put up on her website.' He shakes his head. 'I wish I'd copied it. Her website's gone now. Seems she took it down when she decided to leave.'

'This picture was taken . . . when?'

'About two months ago. It's pretty damn great I think, powerful, bizarre, and disconcerting like she wanted it to be.'

'Let's go back to the posing part. You say you didn't know the other guy. That seems kind of odd.'

'We weren't introduced. He was just, you know, this guy who'd agreed to pose for her. He got hard at one point, which made me think posing for her turned him on.'

'And you – did it turn *you* on, Josh?'

Josh smiles. 'She'd posed for me, so I posed for her. Did I enjoy it? Sure. I'd never been naked in front of her before. She kidded me: "Anytime you want to explore your submissive side just let me know." We used to joke around a lot like that.'

Scarpaci asks Josh to describe the other man. Josh shrugs. 'Well-spoken, educated, someone who's probably an alpha type in everyday life.'

'And you'd never seen him before in any of Chantal's security camera feeds?'

Josh shakes his head.

At this point I decide to excuse myself. I don't know where Scarpaci is going with this, why he's so interested in the second man, but since Josh has stopped sketching me it seems like a good time to leave. When I tell them I'm going to slip out, Josh looks unhappy. When I rise he sees me to the door.

'Going well, don't you think?' I whisper.

'Not how I'd have chosen to spend the afternoon,' he whispers back, 'but, yeah, it's going OK.'

Back up in the loft, I stare at Chantal's chariot and think about all the things I've discovered about her. Matching fetish hoods. A whip she called 'Blackspur'. Denazification scenes wearing an Israeli uniform. A rubber pig's snout in a strongbox. *What was she up to?* Did she see herself merely as a fee-for-service-provider fulfilling her clients' fantasies, or did she get something from these bizarre performances that fulfilled her own needs too?

One thing's clear: Chantal's commitment to her work. She threw herself totally into the roles she played, as I throw myself into mine.

On my run this morning on my way to Lake Merritt, I intersect with Jake on 14th Street. He's standing by his grocery cart filled with detritus. He grins as I approach.

'Hi, Toots!' he says, and then in a rasping whisper as I pass: 'Beware the man in the green hoodie.'

I stop, trot back to him.

'Hey, Jake – you said something like that the other day. What're you talking about?'

He averts his eyes. 'Watch out for the green man,' he mutters, then turns away.

Dr Maude receives me with a big hug.

'You look so *young*, Tess! Last time I saw you, you looked even older than me!'

Again she praises my performance. She tells me she hung around for almost an hour feasting at Grace's buffet and listening in on audience comments.

'I think a lot of people were confused. I overheard one woman say she found bits and pieces of "half a dozen of the bitches who run this town". An elderly man said he found Mrs Z pathetic.'

I ask her if she noticed a tall lean guy with hawkish features wearing a black suit, sitting near her in back.

She nods. 'He was on the edge of his seat. Couldn't take his eyes off you.'

'His name's Leo Scarpaci. He's the Oakland detective working the Chantal homicide. He asked me out this weekend. Says he wants to show me something I've never seen before.'

'Attracted to him?'

I admit I am.

'Good. He struck me as real, a little out of his element but very attentive to you. Jerry was there too, wasn't he?' I nod. 'I was pretty sure I recognized him. He looked nicer than I expected. He and this Scarpaci guy – different types.'

She pauses. 'I hope someday you'll consider creating a

piece inspired by your dad. I think your monologues are a healthy way to disempower your demons.'

She gives me her usual hug at end of session. When she pulls back I notice a glint of amusement. 'Good luck on the date. Hope it goes well for you. And for him too, of course.'

At San Pedro Martial Arts, Kurt tells me to warm up then report to him for blocking drills. He demonstrates various moves, has me make them in slow motion, then use them to block his strikes: catching, hooking, cupping, parrying. He also coaches me on evasive moves – ducking, slipping, stepping in, stepping back. He works me till I'm tired, then has me strike at him so he can show me how he does it. When we're done I ask him if he knew that Marie also used the name Chantal.

He says he didn't know that until he heard about the murder on local TV news. 'In here she was always just Marie.'

It's then that I give him the kind of close look that says, 'I don't believe you and I may know more than I've let on.' He peers back at me annoyed.

'Next time you'll train with Rosita,' he tells me. 'We'll see if you can block her strikes.'

'If I can't?'

'We'll keep training you till you can.'

That feels like a threat. Is it punishment for asking him about Chantal? Now I'm annoyed.

'I know you went to her,' I tell him. 'I know you exchanged training for sessions.'

He sniffs. 'Whatever you think you know about that, Tess, you still have a lot to learn about Muay Thai.'

Scarpaci has told me to dress up or down, but not, he advised, in between.

'Where we're going,' he said, 'the ladies go fine or funky.'

I don't own anything particularly fine, so it's down and funky for me: black tank top, black jeans, black leather moto jacket, short black boots.

'Wow, you look just like Queen of Cups!' he says, when I meet him in the lobby.

He drives us to the Ramen Shop, a small sit-at-the-counter Japanese noodle joint in Rockridge. The cooks here produce great ramen concoctions and the mixologist makes terrific cocktails. Since they have a no-reservations policy and the counter is occupied, we wait our turn in the bar. A good opportunity, I think, to find out what Scarpaci thought of Josh.

'Less resistance than I expected,' he says, 'and plenty of subterfuge.'

'But you've ruled him out, right?'

He shakes his head. 'I wanna take another shot, see if I can crack him.'

'Do you really think in terms of cracking people?'

'Appalled?'

'A little surprised. You're so soft-spoken.'

'It's not my style to yell, Tess, or even bear down hard. But homicide's a rough business. It's rare someone lays himself bare. You got to work 'em a while to open 'em up. Cracking's just my crude way of putting it.'

I like that he doesn't apologize.

'As for Josh,' he continues, 'he's going to sketch the other guy in the photograph. He laughed when I offered to put him with a police sketch artist. "I'll do the damn sketch," he said.'

'Why so interested in this other guy?'

'Like I said before, I think this was a crime of passion. I see passion in that picture, so I'm interested in both men hitched to the chariot.'

Scarpaci, as it turns out, would much rather talk about *Recital*.

'I felt I was in one of those toney movies, the kind where you're supposed to feel sorry for privileged folks on account of how hard it is for them to be so privileged. But the longer you went on, the more I got into it. By the end I was totally hooked.'

'My shrink was sitting near you. She says you were on the edge of your seat.'

'The middle-aged lady wearing tribal jewelry and the shape-less purple dress?'

'She calls her dresses shmattas, Jewish for old housedress.'

Scarpaci laughs. 'Some folks there didn't seem to know whether to laugh or cry.' He pauses. 'What about the snooty looking guy with the hair flap, the one who led the applause?'

'My ex.'

'I'm surprised you'd be involved with a guy like that.'

I peer at him. 'You're a perceptive man, Detective Scarpaci.'

'You can call me Leo if you want.'

'I kinda like calling you Scarpaci. Do you mind?'

'Coming from you I like it.'

Later, sitting caddy-corner at the counter, slurping our soup and noodles, we fill each other in on our respective backgrounds, as well as the usual punch list: books, movies, TV shows, what moves us, makes us laugh, what we do for exercise. He was married to a school teacher, divorced after five years. Then a series of long-term relationships, the most recent with a chef. That, he wants me to know, ended last year.

He doesn't act surprised when I tell him my dad was a con man who served time for fraud.

'Con men can be very charming,' he says.

'He was a liar through and through. He couldn't tell a straight story. The last time I saw him before he died he said something about that. It was the only time I can remember when he let down his guard.'

'What'd he say?'

'I remember his exact words. I had just told him an obvious fib. He looked into my eyes then spoke very gently: "Try real hard not to lie, Tess. Every time you tell a lie you die a little inside." I never forgot that.'

'You're honest, sometimes brutally so. I think your father's face was a mask he couldn't take off, but you only wear masks when you perform.'

That's so perceptive, I can barely believe he said it.

'And the rest of the time?' I ask.

'I'd say you're complex but figure-out-able.' He grins at me. 'Is there such a word?'

'Probably not. But I get what you mean. Sort of what-you-see-is-what-you-get-if-you-know-where-to-look . . . or something.'

He gazes into my eyes. 'I see a woman who's very nice

but for some strange reason would rather not be seen that way.'

Gazing back at him, I find I'm more touched by his back-handed appraisal than I would have thought.

Hey, careful! I warn myself. *Don't be so quick falling for this guy.*

Scarpaci drives us across the Bay Bridge to a warehouse district in San Francisco's SOMA neighborhood. There're several new buildings here, high-rise condo towers, but most of the structures are early twentieth-century brick warehouses now converted into live-work lofts, galleries, dance clubs, dojos, and cafés. We park then walk to a three-story building with blacked-out windows on the second floor and bricked-in windows on the third. A tough-looking black dude is standing beside the front door, one foot posed hustler-style against the wall.

He examines Scarpaci. 'Yo! I 'member you,' he says, granting us entry with a nod.

The dim first floor is deserted except for a battered vintage Ducati motorcycle parked against a wall. The second level looks like it might once have been an art gallery – white free-standing walls, empty pedestals, gray concrete floor. There's a roped-off staircase far in the back attended by a grim-faced, muscular Asian guy with a shaven head. He's wearing a black T-shirt and black drawstring sweatpants. As we approach the stairs I hear noise coming from above.

Scarpaci mutters something to the guard, who nods, then lifts the rope.

'What's up here?' I ask Scarpaci as we mount the stairs.

'Private fight club. Semi-legal. So far nobody's shut it down. I know you're into fighting so I figured you'd be interested. It's a little different from what you're used to.'

We reach the top of the stairs. The entire space is empty except for an elevated boxing ring set up at the far end. There's a fight in progress, two young guys, both boyish, both extremely cute, one with long hair tied back in a ponytail, the other with the kind of sunken cheeks and high sharp cheek-bones you see on Slavic models. They're stripped down to gym shorts and slugging it out, their lean toned torsos slick with sweat.

An older Eurasian man acts as referee. A young tuxedo-clad guy sporting a trimmed goatee, the time-keeper/promoter, stands beside a gong. One of the boys has an old man in his corner. The other is being coached by a young woman. There's a ring girl dressed in a bikini and high heels who parades between rounds holding the round number card. Scarpaci, gesturing toward an unshaven middle-aged man with a paunch, tells me he's the attending physician.

I peer around. There're a couple hundred onlookers. Most look like affluent educated types – young lawyers, high-tech engineers, fashionistas, maybe sons and daughters of the people who attended *Recital*. I'm struck by their alert attention. Unlike a typical rowdy fight crowd, these people seem mesmerized.

I'm no boxing connoisseur, but I can tell the boys in the ring aren't much good. And they bear no resemblance to the kind of fighters I'd expect to see at an unlicensed fight club: blue-collar cage-fighter types, truckers, construction workers, mixed martial arts specialists.

'Who are these guys?' I ask Scarpaci.

'Pretty boys.'

'Huh?'

'Second Saturday every month is what they call Pretty Boys Beat-Down night, fights between ad and runway models, some local, others from LA. Most took up boxing for exercise, tried light sparring, then got serious and decided to get down and dirty and compete. But see for me it's not the fighting that's interesting, it's the fighters, that they're willing to risk their fifteen-hundred-dollar-a-day pretty faces to prove they're manly. They're looking for a kind of hard reality they don't find in the shallow fashion world.'

Maybe that, I think, explains my interest in fighting. Theater's great but when someone gets slapped in a play it's faked. Maybe what I'm seeking in Muay Thai is the here-and-now hard reality Marie/Chantal described succinctly as 'hitting and getting hit.'

'Lots of heart but not much talent,' Scarpaci whispers into

my ear. 'Hopefully the next few pairs will be better . . . if you're willing to stick around.'

I'm willing. The scene interests me. No question it's decadent. I get a feeling the audience is hoping to see something that will thrill their jaded souls – a spilling of blood, a fighter crumbling, a face badly bashed. I see it in their eyes: fascination with violence combined with an eagerness to see one of these beautiful flailing boys beaten to the floor. It's an excitement, I know, as old as the human race. I think of ancient Greek theater, the audience eagerly waiting for the moment when Oedipus gouges out his eyes, or in Roman times, the mob in the coliseum cheering wildly as their favorite gladiators fight to the death. This crowd radiates that same cruel energy. These people aren't interested in sport. They're here to witness hurt.

I ask Scarpaci if he agrees.

'I do,' he says. 'I get why models want to test themselves, but until you said that I didn't understand what the audience got out of watching these third-rate match-ups.'

We stay for two more pretty-boy fights and then a stylized kickboxing match between two beautiful tall slim female models. The girls fight better than the boys. They move with more grace, dodge and weave with more skill. They seem almost too perfectly matched, as if their moves have been choreographed. In the end the ref, declaring a tie, holds up both their arms, then the girls embrace. The crowd responds with a mix of cheers and boos. They've come for blood, and all they've gotten from this pair is a sparring exercise.

'You were right about decadence,' I tell Scarpaci as we drive back to Oakland. 'But if it's semi-legal how come they let you in?'

'I know the guy owns the building.' He glances at me. 'I wanted to show you something you'd probably never seen before. Hope you weren't offended.'

'Not at all. To paraphrase your favorite Roman playwright: "I am a man, nothing human is alien to me."'

'*Homo sum, humani nihil a me alienum puto.*' Scarpaci enunciates the Latin with the sonority of a priest. 'I love that quote. I once thought of having it tattooed on my arm to remind me not to give in to sorrow on the job.'

We stop at a bar he knows near his apartment in Temescal. As we sip beers, he asks why I identify so strongly with Chantal.

'She was also a performer. She set up scenes, took on roles, put on costumes, and used props. For me that's artmaking.'

'Artmaking's important to you.'

'Without it I'd be lost.'

He studies me. 'I have a feeling you were damaged.'

When I neither confirm nor deny, he tells me then about his love of breaking open cases, finding solutions to puzzling crimes.

'It's the only thing I really enjoy,' he tells me. 'It seems we both like to live with purpose.'

We acknowledge that we share an obsession with Chantal and that we're both eager to unravel her story if for different reasons. I want to understand it so I can turn into something I can dramatize. He wants to understand it so he can bring her killer to justice.

'Seems we're both story tellers,' he says.

I very much like the way Scarpaci makes love to me: slow, easy, solicitous. After the first time, he asks me to share some of my fantasies.

'And if they're a little kinky?'

'Especially then,' he says.

Figuring nothing I can tell him will upset him, I reveal a few special desires, at which revelations he nods and proceeds to gratify.

'You're a very accommodating lover,' I tell him afterwards.

'I try my best.' He peers at me. 'You're special, Tess. I felt that the first time we had coffee. When you described yourself on the phone as a performance artist I wasn't sure what to expect. But when we met I realized how special you were. And I got the feeling you liked me too.'

In the morning, while he makes us breakfast, I look around his apartment. His bookshelves are crammed with classics, and it's clear from the wear on them that he's reread them many times: Melville, Joyce, Dostoyevsky, Hemingway, Graham Greene. Not just the famous titles, but a good half-dozen works spanning each writer's career.

There're books too about ancient Greek and Roman history and best of all from my point of view, plays written by the ancient dramatists: Sophocles, Euripides, Aristophanes, Terence, Plautus, and Seneca. I also notice books by Thomas Merton and a beautiful edition of the poetry of Gerard Manley Hopkins.

Just as Chantal's library told me much about her, so Scarpaci's tells me much about him.

'I went to a Jesuit college,' he says, bringing me a mug of coffee. 'Studied classics. Wanted to be a teacher. How did I get sidetracked and end up a cop? That's a long story.'

A story, I assure him, I'd like to hear one day.

'When I retire I want to try writing crime fiction. Not puzzle mysteries or cases solved by forensics. Real hard-boiled stories, stories of the street.'

'Told in the first person?'

'Haven't decided yet. But the lead character (I won't call him "the hero") will likely have my flaws and virtues, such as they are.'

'What about sensitivity?'

'Not sure how high I rate on that, but kind of you to mention it.'

'Amorous skills?'

'You *are* feeling kindly.'

'Attraction and attractiveness to younger women.'

'Please go on!'

'I'll think of more traits as I get to know you, Scarpaci. But I do think this detective character of yours should have a girlfriend. You don't want him to come off as a loner.'

'That how you see me, Tess?'

'I see you as rueful. I'm not sure where all the regret's coming from.'

He gazes at me. 'I can see we're going to have a lot to talk about,' he says.

NINETEEN

Extract from the Unpublished Memoirs of Major Ernst Fleckstein

(AKA Dr Samuel Foigel)

Bormann's question regarding Renate Müller was facetious. Of course I had heard of her! I doubt there was anyone in Germany at the time who hadn't. She was a huge star, a great beauty, the lead actress in the hit movie *Viktor und Viktoria*,[1] and the equally popular *The English Marriage*. She was endlessly profiled in fan magazines. It was impossible in those days to pick up a newspaper and not find some mention of her.

Well . . . it seemed that this gorgeous blond, blue-eyed quintessential Aryan screen goddess now presented a serious problem. The Führer, it seemed, although ostensibly devoted to Fräulein Eva Braun, had been much taken by the actress, had invited her to his residence, and had there engaged her in a manner that had disgusted and appalled her.

'Or so she claims,' Bormann added with disdain. 'She has, we've heard, made some vicious allegations. Now we can't have some woman, no matter how popular, going around whispering falsehoods about our national leader. Slanders like hers not only impugn the Führer's reputation but undermine the moral authority of the regime.'

Feigning shock, I asked: 'What garbage has the bitch been spreading?'

'That, my dear Fleckstein, is for you to find out. Undertake a full investigation. Find out what she's saying about the alleged episode, and then if what we've heard is true, take care of the

---

[1] Released in 1933, this musical comedy about a female impersonator was filmed the same year in France under the title *Georges et Georgette*, and again in 1982 as *Victor Victoria* starring Julie Andrews.

matter by any means necessary.' At this Bormann stared at me sternly. 'Am I clear?'

'Clear indeed, Reichsleiter,' I assured him.

I don't want to dwell too long here on the Müller affair. Some of the details are unsavory and I'm not particularly proud of my role. But because much that has been written about it is incorrect, I shall take this opportunity to set the record straight. I also want to sketch it out because the unfortunate finale of the business marked a major turning point in my life.

As to Frau Müller, it didn't take me long to assemble a list of unpleasant rumors, not unexpected regarding a celebrity of her magnitude. Among them: she was overly fond of alcohol; she was addicted to morphine; she had a Jewish lover, a certain Georg Deutsch, who had recently fled to Paris to escape persecution; and Reich Minister Joseph Goebbels had taken a special interest in her, offering her major roles in dramatic propaganda films, all of which, to Goebbels' dismay, she'd turned down.

It was also rumored that Goebbels had set up her meeting with Hitler, that she'd gone to see him at the Chancellery Residence, and that there, after only brief conversation, the Führer disrobed and demanded she do the same. Then he flung himself naked upon the floor, proclaimed himself her slave, reviled himself with all sorts of insults, and begged her to beat and kick him to show her contempt. At first she refused, but upon his further insistence, and fearing for her safety, she met his demands, screamed obscenities at him, then savagely beat him with his own whip which lay conveniently on a nearby table. After he masturbated to climax, the Führer stood up, adjusted his clothing, poured them each a nightcap, engaged her in several minutes of small-talk, then thanked her for a pleasant encounter and summoned his personal chauffeur to drive her home.

The specificity of this tale gave it credibility, and it was consistent with what I already knew concerning unsavory aspects of the Führer's personal life. It was clear that Frau Müller had to be the source, as there was no other witness. Moreover, it was said that she'd been badly shaken by the encounter. As an actress she was accustomed to playing roles that differed greatly from her actual persona, but in this instance, in which there was no director, camera, lighting crew, or film set, the reality of what she'd felt forced to do had overwhelmed her. Describing the incident to friends she stated that not only had she been disgusted by Hitler's demands, but she felt she'd been badly used. She told several people she was especially angry at Goebbels and would have nothing further to do with him. She also hinted to friends that she was seriously considering following in the footsteps of Marlene Dietrich, leaving Germany, moving to France to live with Georg Deutsch, and from there denouncing the regime.

As far as I could tell these rumors were being widely discussed in cinema circles in Berlin. At the time Frau Müller's most recent film, *Togger*, had recently opened. I went to a well-attended matinee at the Kino Universum on the Kurfürstendamm. In this fairly ridiculous propagandistic story, Müller played a columnist writing exposés of an evil foreign-owned conglomerate. I found her performance over-done. It was clear she hadn't taken any pleasure in the role, probably because, as I'd heard, she'd been forced to accept it.

How to handle the situation? The rumors of her encounter with Hitler were starting to spread through the upper stratum of Berlin society, and, I assumed, were exaggerated at each retelling. There was no practical way to shut the rumor mill down. The cat, so to speak, was out of the bag. I could think of only three solutions: induce Frau Müller to vehemently denounce the story and all who were spreading it; have her declared insane and confined to a mental institution where she could rave all she liked and no one would care; or make an example of her by arranging the kind of 'accident' Bormann hinted at when he handed me the assignment.

If she'd been an ordinary woman any of these solutions could work. But she was a major movie star who moved in elite artistic circles and hobnobbed with highly placed officials. I decided my best next step would be to have a little chat with her.

I met her at her villa in Berlin-Dahlem on the morning of September 23, 1937. It was not difficult to get in to see her. She'd been under close Gestapo surveillance for weeks.

Bormann's secretary contacted Goebbels' office and arranged my appointment. When I rang the doorbell, I was greeted by a female servant who led me to a small sitting room on the second floor. Here Frau Müller, dressed in a slinky pale-pink silk dressing gown, awaited me.

My first impression was that she was indeed very beautiful, and also that she appeared nervous and shockingly thin. Her eyes were magnetic and yet I saw in them desperation akin to that of a gorgeous bird with a broken wing. It was difficult for me to connect the woman before me to the high-spirited actress who had sung the sprightly *'Ich Bin Ja Heut' So Glücklich,'*[2] and on account of that had become Germany's sweetheart.

I spoke softly to her and her responses were softer still, so much so that I had to lean close to hear her. I told her that, as she no doubt knew, wild tales of an encounter she'd allegedly had with the Führer were currently making the rounds, and these tales were dangerously slanderous. I told her I had no interest in hearing what had happened between them, or indeed whether anything at all had occurred. My point was that the tales, whether true or not, were causing grave concern to certain highly placed people. I then outlined the first two remedies mentioned above, leaving the third to her imagination. I suggested that since it would be understandably difficult for her to denounce people to whom I'd traced back the origin of these tales, people such as her close friends, the actress Gabriele Schwartz and the American-born producer Alfred Zeisler (I wanted to impress upon her that I knew the names of her confidants), perhaps a voluntary commitment to a psychiatric clinic would offer the best solution. A believable cover-story would be circulated regarding exhaustion and ill-health, and in, say, nine months or a year, she could re-emerge and again take up her illustrious career.

I don't believe I'll ever forget the sadness that transfixed her face. 'You're saying I must go to the loony bin for a year?' she whispered, tears forming in her beautiful eyes.

'There are luxurious sanatoria,' I assured her, 'far from anything that could be described as a loony bin.'

---

[2] 'I'm So Happy Today!' sung by Müller in the film *Die Privatsekretärin.*

'How about "nuthouse"?' she asked. 'Or "booby hatch"? Are those better descriptions?'

'I think "rest home" would be the way I'd describe such a place, something akin to a luxury hotel in a restful Alpine environment.'

Suddenly she raised her voice. 'Restful! Ha! I haven't had a good night's rest in weeks. Not since that awful evening—'

'Please, Frau Müller,' I begged. 'I implore you not to speak of that.'

'Why?' she demanded. 'Because you're scared to hear the truth?'

'Because,' I countered, 'it's none of my business.'

'So what exactly is your business, Herr Fleckstein?' she asked combatively.

'I came here to offer you counsel.'

'I see! Earlier you spoke to me of a voluntary commitment. Since these people you mention are so anxious to be rid of me, why don't they just have me bound up in a straitjacket and hauled away to one of their awful dungeons?' She started to cry. 'I did not bring this upon myself, sir. Something terrible was done to me. Did I not have the right to confide my distress to my friends?'

At this point, seeing how upset she'd become, I began to worry I'd overstepped.

'I think it would have been better,' I suggested in the softest tone I could muster, 'if you had taken your story to a psycho-analyst, one bound by an oath of confidentiality.'

'But they're all Jews!' she said, suddenly exploding in hysterical laughter. 'And you think Goebbels wouldn't have found out what I said? That he doesn't have spies everywhere even among the Jews? If you believe that, sir, then, as the Americans like to say, I have a bridge over the Rhine to sell you!'

Addiction, depression, hysteria, and now paranoia – the famous film star was exhibiting a full range of symptoms. Indeed, I thought, a good long rest at an Alpine clinic would do her the world of good. Resolving to suggest this in my report to Bormann, I thanked her for her time, wished her well, and took my leave.

According to the story later bandied about, that same day four Gestapo men went into her house, confronted her, then threw her off her balcony. In another version the four agents pressured her into taking her own life, and, minutes after they left, she jumped from her terrace. The reality is that she jumped just minutes after I left her. I know this because at the time I was sitting in my car in front of her villa writing up my notes when I heard the servants' screams. At this I and the four Gestapo men who'd been watching the house rushed inside.

I was distraught to find the beautiful woman I'd been speaking with just moments before lying in a pool of blood beneath her balcony. There could be no doubt she had voluntarily jumped. I found the sight of her, this time broken not just in spirit but also in body, utterly devastating. Discovering she was still alive, one of the agents called for an ambulance. She was transported to a nearby hospital, lay there in a coma for fourteen days, then passed away. Her death was attributed to an epileptic seizure. She was cremated and buried, and despite the protestations of her family, her jewelry and other possessions were sold at public auction to satisfy her debts.

Over the next few weeks guilt over my role in her death became increasingly corrosive. Why, I asked myself, do I continue to accept these clean-up missions having to do with the Führer's unsavory proclivities? Such missions were highly taxing on a personal level and also extremely risky since the more I learned the more dangerous my position should doubts ever arise as to my loyalty or willingness to stay silent.

It was then, recalling my brief encounter with Frau Lou Salomé and her analytic couch, that I had a vision of a new career for myself. About a month after the death of Renate Müller I went to Bormann to inform him I'd decided to make a major life change.

Fixing me with his hard narrow eyes, Bormann appeared amused. 'And what, dear Fleckstein, do you have in mind?' he asked sarcastically.

'I've decided to take up the study of psychoanalysis,' I told him. 'I think it could be an important tool with which to extract information from our enemies. Because, Reichsleiter, as we both know, generally speaking torture does not get us good results.'

He chuckled, but when I went on to explain my theory, I could see he was intrigued.

'Fleckstein, you may be on to something,' he said.

He then mentioned that Dr Matthias Göring, Reich Minister Hermann Göring's older cousin, now headed the Institute for Psychological Research and Psychotherapy in Berlin.

'He's gotten rid of all the Jews,' Bormann told me, 'and is now developing purely Aryan techniques. If this is truly what you want to do, I can call him and put in a good word.'

'That would be very kind, Reichsleiter.'

He grinned at me. 'I shall miss you, Fleckstein. You're an amusing fellow and you do excellent work. If in future delicate matters require special handling, I know I can count on you.'

I assured him that he could.

And thus, not long after the demise of the great film star Frau Renate Müller, and inspired by the example of the exemplary Frau Lou Salomé, I moved from Munich to Berlin to embark upon the study of and later to become a full-time practitioner of the 'black art,' the one people call therapeutic psychoanalysis . . .

TWENTY

Dr Maude smiles when I tell her I spent the night with Scarpaci.

'It was pretty fucking terrific too if you want to know,' I tell her.

'Glad to hear it. We all need good sex in our lives.' She settles back. 'Two sessions ago you told me you sometimes felt lost. Still feel that way?'

I shrug. 'Internalizing so many characters makes it hard for me to see myself. I do a Vertigo for Rex and suddenly I'm reveling in being submissive. Then I see photos of Chantal wielding a whip and I want to try my hand at dominance.'

'Our minds are theaters, Tess, where we construct dramas out of our conflicts. I think you're suffering from a problem many performers face, confusing the roles you play on stage with your roles in your internal dramas. I think that's why you're asking yourself who you are.'

'Actually I'm asking you.'

'Oh, Tess, only you can figure that out. We grow and change. We take on one persona and then another. Think of Lou Salomé, the many roles she played – muse, author, psychoanalyst. You're an actress. For you these transformations are frequent, intense, and often extreme. But I believe you have a strong core. By playing all these roles – the connoisseur of perversity, the aesthete in pursuit of decadence – you never have to show the world your true self. But someone astute, say an experienced shrink,' she smiles, 'or an experienced detective can see the fine courageous woman behind the mask.'

'So am I a fraud?'

She shakes her head vigorously. 'Not at all! You're a wearer of disguises. Your father was a fraud.'

I'm in the ring at San Pablo Martial Arts. Rosita is coming after me. She's so quick I can't block her strikes. Her blows connect and they hurt. She's not coming on full force, rather toying with me, trying to show me up. I retreat, glance quickly at Kurt. He meets my eyes with a blank stare.

I drop my gloves. 'I'm done.' Rosita nods, drops hers, glances at Kurt, bumps gloves with me, and climbs out of the ring.

I go over to Kurt. 'What're you trying to do? See me get pummeled? You know I'm not ready for her.'

'I wanted to see if you really had fighting spirit. Watching you today I'm not so sure.'

'I'm not so sure either. Overmatching – what kind of training is that?'

'If you're not happy here don't train here. There're plenty of other gyms.'

'You're saying you want me to go?'

'Up to you,' he says.

I stare hard at him. 'Is this because I know about you and Chantal?'

'You know nothing about that. Anyway Chantal's dead.'

'I notice you don't call her Marie anymore.'

'A detective's been around asking questions. Are you his mole?'

'Do you know how absurd that is?' I gaze at him, but he doesn't respond. I shake my head. 'OK, I get it. You don't want me here. Fine. I'll clean out my locker.'

He shrugs and turns away.

Back out on the street, I phone Scarpaci, tell him what just happened and how incredibly pissed I am.

'I never mentioned you,' he tells me. 'But since that's what he thinks, you're probably better off training someplace else. There're lots of martial-arts gyms.'

'Sure, but it hurts to get kicked out. Is Kurt a person of interest?'

'He owned up to having been Chantal's client. Said he liked working out with her at his gym and also at hers. Kinda strange way to define her sessions, but, bottom line, I don't think he frightened or harmed her.'

*   *   *

Inspiration: it came upon me suddenly this afternoon, and now, hours later, I'm still at work, deep into the flow, hitting the computer keys, writing and organizing my notes, thinking up scenes then sketching them out, working out different ways to tell the story of myself and Chantal Desforges, the strange woman whose loft I now occupy and whose personality and obsessions take up so much space in my head.

I photocopy the best of the many images of the Luzern photograph from Chantal's books, place it beside my computer so I can stare at it as I work.

Gazing at it now I ask myself: what did Chantal see in this strange image that would explain her many efforts to decipher it? What was she trying to say when she went to so much trouble to reenact it? Was her obsession with Lou Salomé a form of madness? Was it connected in some way to her own violent death? These are the issues I want to explore.

I'm certain this new piece won't be like any other I've created. I don't envision it as a monologue, rather as a grand theatrical experience, a full-length play with other actors beside myself performing a multitude of roles. It will be about three women whose lives are interwoven: Tess Berenson, seeker/performer; Chantal Desforges, dominatrix/victim; and Lou Salomé, writer/psychoanalyst/role-model.

I work late into the night. Whenever I get stuck I simply gaze at the Luzern photograph and a new stream of ideas cascades through my brain. So many notions, so many scenes – I can barely keep up with them. Some I like; many I reject. My focus narrows. I lose track of time. When the phone rings a little after eleven it jolts me as if from a reverie.

It's Scarpaci. He just got home after a long day. He wouldn't call so late, he says, if I hadn't told him I rarely go to bed before midnight.

'How's the writing going?'

'It's flowing.'

'Good. Listen, Tess, I've been thinking about your little show-down with Kurt. Once he realized you knew about his barter relationship with Chantal, he couldn't bear having you around. He probably thought, knowing about his submissive side, you wouldn't respect him. Isn't respect what martial arts is all about, the disciple's respect for the sensei?'

Scarpaci's probably right. That could explain what happened. But, I tell him, understanding why Kurt dismissed me doesn't make it any easier to forgive him.

'Let it go. He's not that important to you.' He pauses. 'Josh came by this afternoon to give me his drawing of the other guy. He seemed a lot more relaxed than the other day. When I asked him why Chantal matched them up, he said he thought it was because they were the same height and had the same build. He also said he'd never seen her so controlling as she was the afternoon she set up that shot.'

Jerry calls. He wants to take me to lunch at Chez Panisse.

'I want to be clear,' he says. 'I'm not trying to woo you back. You were brave to leave. I got pretty nasty about it and lashed out. You left because you felt over-powered. I get that.'

'More like over-controlled,' I correct him.

'Fine. I'm difficult. I admit it. But seeing you the other night I realized how talented you are. As for those cracks I made about your Hollis grant – that was unforgiveable. Please consider my request that we have lunch a prelude to a sincere apology. I don't want you to despise me.'

I give in. We make a date for Friday. He offers to fetch me, but I tell him I'll meet him at the restaurant. I don't want him asking to see my loft and going pouty on me when I refuse.

Over dinner at a small family-owned Sicilian place in Temescal, Scarpaci proposes that whenever we spend the night together we do so at his place instead of mine.

'It wouldn't be good if Josh spotted us. He's still very much a person of interest. He knew Chantal well. He monitored her sessions. He was conveniently away when she moved out. Beyond all that he's a forger, which tells me he's a habitual liar.'

As the waitress sets down our pasta dishes, Scarpaci accesses an image on his phone then hands it to me: Josh's drawing of the second man in Chantal's strange chariot photograph.

'Hey, I know this guy!' Scarpaci, surprised, puts down his

fork. 'His name's Carl Draper. He rang my buzzer a few weeks ago. I met him for coffee, then we had lunch. He's an architect from New York. Told me he was one of Chantal's regulars. When he found her phone disconnected and her website down, he came over to the Buckley to see if she was still there.'

I describe our meeting and how after lunch he asked to come upstairs.

'Claimed he wanted to see the loft again because he'd had such intense experiences there. "For old times' sake," he said. I was kind of spooked by that. His request didn't make sense. Needless to say I didn't let him in.'

'You wouldn't know how to reach him?'

'He gave me his business card. It's somewhere in the loft.'

Scarpaci digs into his pasta norma. 'If you don't mind, Tess, we'll drive back there after dinner. If you find his card tomorrow I'll track him down.'

Later, at his apartment, Scarpaci shows me photos of his family, parents, brothers, sisters. I notice an old-world formality. There isn't one image in which anyone cracks a smile.

'You all look so grave,' I tell him. 'Like you didn't have much fun.'

'We were a gloomy family. I think there's still some of that gloom in me.'

Later, in bed, after we make love, I tell him again that it was his aura of rue I first found attractive.

'Oh damn, I thought it was my body!' he says.

He turns serious, asks if he can share a dream. 'Don't know where this came from,' he begins. 'We were together in Sicily. Not one of the tourist places like Taormina, but in a hill town in the middle of the island, the kind of town my grandparents came from. We were staying at an inn. It was off season and we were the only guests. We took long hikes in the forest. I could feel the stony ground beneath my feet, could smell the soil and the aroma of wild thyme. The innkeeper hunted game birds. His wife roasted them. We feasted on them after sunset in the deserted dining room accompanied by a dark local wine. Later we made love with moonlight pouring in through the window. It was an idyll, as different from the streets of East

Oakland as any place on earth. Like I said, I don't know where that dream came from but I think it means I'm falling for you, Tess.'

This morning on my way through the lobby, Clarence beckons to me from the concierge's podium.

'There's this guy lingering around. I've spotted him across the street. I think he may be stalking you, Tess.' He describes a tall white guy wearing a green hoodie. 'Like he's trying to conceal his face,' he says.

'Jake the homeless guy on Fourteenth muttered something about "beware the man in green".'

'Must be the same guy. Keep an eye out. There're some weird characters around.'

He's right, most of them potheads hanging around the marijuana dispensaries. But is someone in a green hoodie really stalking me?

I'm annoyed as I climb the stairs to the second-floor café at Chez Panisse, certain Jerry will be late, employing one of the passive-aggressive moves which, I remind myself, I no longer need endure. But when I enter I spot him waiting for me at a small window table overlooking Shattuck Avenue.

He rises as I approach, then acts disappointed when I sit without allowing him to buzz my cheek.

An unpropitious start, I think, as we scan the menu, order, then stare at one another in silence.

I speak first. 'Don't you hate the whole meeting-with-the-ex-over-lunch concept?' I ask. 'Not over drinks or a quick coffee. It's always fucking lunch!'

He raises an eyebrow. 'Lunch works because it's a narrow timeframe. And sometimes when it goes well it can lead to an amorous post-affair matinee.'

'And if it goes poorly, one party or the other can throw in her napkin and walk.' I meet his eyes. 'I'm going to make this easy for you, Jerry. I have no interest in seeing you grovel. Your apology is accepted. Which is not to say that what you said that awful day didn't hurt. If I think about it, it still does. So I don't think about it.'

'I appreciate that, Tess.' He clears his throat. 'I told you how much I loved *Recital*. You left your heart on the field of battle. You totally commanded the room.'

'Thanks. What made you decide to lead the applause?'

'I felt the power of what you'd done and wanted to acknowledge it. I was also afraid some of the ninnies there would start to boo.'

'That would've been OK, another form of acknowledgment.'

'I thought you deserved better.'

When the food comes and we start to eat, he asks me what I'm working on. He smiles as I describe my project.

'Why the grin, Jerry?'

'I brought you something that may help.' He extracts an envelope from his jacket, passes it across the table. 'I translated those letters for you.'

I open the envelope. Each of Eva's letters is stapled to a translation. 'This is great. And I'm surprised. You said you didn't have time to write them out.'

'I figured these letters were important to you or you wouldn't have asked me for help. Think of it as my small way to show good will.'

'Thanks again.'

Our eyes engage. This time he's the first to speak. 'I recognized several of your friends in the back row the other night. Rex and a few others. But there were some I never saw before. The older lady in the sloppy muumuu – was that the famous Dr Maude?' I nod. 'I noticed her checking me out, probably wondering whether I'm as monstrous as described.' I laugh. 'There were also two guys who weren't exactly dressed to kill.' He crinkles his nose. 'One of them was wearing a watch cap.'

'Don't be a snob, Jerry. That was Josh. He's a painter.'

'And the observant one with the lean and hungry look – he was definitely taking you in.'

'He's a cop.'

'I won't ask if you're dating one of them.'

'I wouldn't tell you if you did. And I'm not going to ask about your personal life.'

He looks closely at me as we finish dessert. 'It was so good at first, wasn't it? And the sex was really great. We started out so well then it went bad.' He shakes his head. Do I detect moisture in his eyes?

'Just the way things go, Jerry. Think of it as entropy.'

'Entropy – yeah, kinda the story of my life,' he says as he hands his credit card to the waiter.

The letters from Gräfin Eva to Chantal are more passionate than Jerry led me to believe. I feel a deep longing in them, nostalgia for a shared past. They're filled with memories of extensive explorations on foot in Vienna as she and Chantal sought to retrace the daily routes of famous long-deceased city residents. There are references to L, F, and H. Knowing Chantal's interests I have no trouble identifying these as Lou, Freud, and Hitler.

I bring out the map with marked routes folded into Chantal's old Baedeker guide. The same three letters in different colored inks mark various locations in the city. Clearly these were places where the three characters once lived and worked. Did Chantal and Eva spend their free time roaming Vienna in search of intersecting paths?

There are tasteful references to love-making. Eva writes of missing the warmth of Chantal's body against hers in the night.

There are also references to clients, some of whom, Eva writes, still ask for Chantal:

'Remember that old Nazi from Berlin, the one who loved to scrub the kitchen floor to please his Jewish mistresses? How we made him think he'd fallen into a Mossad honeytrap? And the guy who made a fetish of polishing my Biedermeier daybed, the one I use for "psychoanalysis"?'

Eva, as if trying to evoke nostalgia in Chantal, conjures up images of the changing seasons in Vienna: leaves falling in autumn in the Prater, shrubs budding in spring in the Volksgarten. She remembers the glee with which the two of them played out the famous Ferris wheel scene from the movie *The Third Man*.

'We were the only ones in the compartment. The *Riesenrad* turned. We giggled our way through the dialog, you as Holly Martins, me as Harry Lime. At the bottom you told me I made a fine Orson Welles. I told you your Joseph Cotten imitation could use some work!'

She writes of their visits to famous cemeteries: the Zentralfriedhof, where they placed a single lily on the grave of Hitler's niece, Geli Raubal, and the Hietzinger, where they knelt in awe before the grave of Gustav Klimt.

'I miss you so very much,' Eva writes. 'Will you come back to me one day? I often dream you have.'

I'm moved by Eva's letters and struck by the fact that she chooses to write to Chantal on light blue paper in dark blue ink.

I go to my computer, access her website. The text is in German but there's an English version accessible by clicking on a British flag icon.

On the HOME page she's posted a quote from Nietzsche: 'Without cruelty there is no festival.'

On the BIO page there she is, the Gräfin, a middle-aged woman staring out with a subtle expression of scorn. She looks to be quite the butch with her short iron-gray hair and no-nonsense eyes. There's an alertness about her, a suggestion of serious intelligence.

On the SPECIALTIES page in addition to the usual list I find the following intriguing options: 'Dominant Therapy in the Viennese Tradition'; 'Freudian Fantasies Fulfilled'; 'Nietzschean Psychodrama'; 'German-Jewish Dynamics'; and my favorite: 'Kneel before the Gräfin, confess, take your punishment, and be absolved.'

On the CONTACT page I find an email address. I draft a note to her, then redraft it several times. In case Eva isn't aware Chantal was killed, I phrase this disturbing news with care.

> Dear Gräfin Eva:
> I hope this email doesn't come as an intrusion. I'm an American performance artist who recently took over the loft in downtown Oakland previously occupied by Chantal Desforges. I only knew her slightly, but I have heard a lot about her from her former business partner, Lynx, whom you met when you visited

here last year. Lynx told me you and Chantal were close friends.

I don't know if you've heard the sad news concerning Chantal. In the event you haven't, I am sorry that you are hearing this from a stranger. Chantal died some weeks back after hurriedly vacating her loft. It's still unclear exactly what happened to her or why.

After I took over the loft, I learned a good deal about her from Lynx and also from the artist, Josh Garske, who painted her and who lives in the building. I was even able to find many books that belonged to her, and in several of them I found letters from you. I'd like to return these personal letters and also learn more about Chantal if you're willing to share some of your memories.

This may seem odd coming from a person who didn't know Chantal at all well during her lifetime, but I have become intrigued by her life, her work, and her interest in a number of matters reflected in her notes in books from her rather esoteric library. I have also been in touch with an Oakland police detective who's investigating events surrounding her death. If there's anything you'd care to tell me that might be relevant to his investigation, I would be happy to pass it on or put you into direct contact with him.

Please let me know if you are willing to talk about Chantal. If you are not, I will fully understand. I am hoping we might speak on the phone, or at least exchange emails. In the meantime please accept my condolences on the death of your friend.

Sincerely yours,
Tess Berenson

I send the email with trepidation. I believe that if I were in her position such an email would give me pause. Although I'm hopeful my careful phrasing will inspire confidence, I know it's quite possible the Gräfin won't respond.

'Don't look! Green man's a block behind!' Jake mutters through his teeth as I run past him on Harrison Street.

I continue jogging down to Alice, then, breaking from my routine, cut across a parking lot to Thirteenth, continue down to Jackson, turn right, and head into Chinatown. When I get to Ninth Street I dodge into Madison Park. I feel safe here. There're people around, moms with strollers, old men chatting in Chinese. I stop under a tree, turn, and wait.

Half a minute later I see him loping down Jackson looking both ways wondering where I am. I'm tempted to step out and yell, 'Yoohoo!' but decide I'll do better taking him by surprise.

When he stops out of breath, bends, and places his hands on his knees, I rush up to him and stick my phone video camera in his face.

'Hey you!' I yell. 'Why're you tracking me?'

'Huh?' He pretends to look panicked.

'Pull down the hood and show yourself,' I demand, still shooting him. Then before he can answer: 'Hey, I know you! You're what's-his-name, Dick—'

'Mike,' he corrects.

'Yeah, Mike from the Vertigo.' I gaze hard at him. 'Stalking me? I don't like that.'

'Sorry . . . sorry . . .' he mumbles, trying to turn away from my camera-phone. He's clearly embarrassed, but not, I think, embarrassed enough.

'How'd you find me?'

He lowers his eyes. 'Private detective,' he mutters.

'You didn't get it that my little seduction number was just a paid performance?'

'I just thought . . . if you got to know me a little you might consider . . .'

'Going out with you? No way, Mike! Rex told you that.'

'I know . . . I know . . . I just couldn't get you out of my head.'

'I suppose I should take that as a validation of my acting skills, but frankly I'm damn annoyed. You hired a private detective to find out my name and address, and then started following me. I'd think a high-tech whiz would have better things to do.'

'Please . . . I didn't mean . . .'

'I think you did. So here's the deal. If I see you following me again, I'll introduce you to a real detective I know. Believe me, you won't like that. I'll also file a civil harassment suit. Hearing me, Mike?'

'I'm hearing you,' he says meekly.

'Good! 'Cause this is the last conversation we're going to have.'

I wait till he scurries away, then head back to the Buckley, wondering where I got the nerve to come at him so strong.

Scarpaci calls. 'The box address on the business card's been cancelled,' he says. 'Most likely the name's fake. But the San Francisco phone number's active. I wonder if you'd—'

Even before he explains I know what he wants me to do. 'Sure, I'll call him, see if I can lure him back to the East Bay.'

We plan the lure together. I'll call the number on the card, tell Carl I'd like to see him again. I'll explain I'm working on a performance piece about Chantal (true) and that I'd like his advice on a scene (false). If he hesitates I'll imply I might let him come up to the loft for a look around (not a chance!). We'll meet at the same café. At some point, after I've gotten all I can out of him, I'll tell him the detective working Chantal's murder wants to talk to him too.

'At this point he'll probably be pissed,' Scarpaci says, 'so after introductions you'll excuse yourself. I'll keep it civilized, explain I'm working hard on the case and need his help. If he balks I'll tell him that whoever he is, I doubt he'll want it known he was the client of a murdered dominatrix.'

'You play rough, Scarpaci.'

'Only when I have to,' he says.

In the morning, when I turn on my computer, I find the Gräfin's reply. It's written in perfect English.

> *Dear Tess Berenson:*
> *Thank you for your kind message. Thanks to Chantal's brother, I was aware of what happened, but the details are vague and I'm hopeful you can tell me more.*
> *I am still in shock over this. I'm also hesitant to talk*

*on the phone about my friend. However I will be coming
to New York on business in a couple of weeks. If you
want to meet up that would be the place to do it.*

*Thank you for offering to return my intimate letters.
Please destroy them. My philosophy is never to brood
upon the past, but to process it and move on. That is
what I am trying to do now in regard to the loss of my
dear Chantal. As difficult as this is, I am doing my best.*

With kind regards,
Gräfin Eva

I'm thrilled. A face-to-face meeting in New York would be
perfect. As for her request that I destroy her letters, I can't
bring myself to do it.

I run into Josh in the lobby. We step into the elevator
together.

'Your floor, madame?' he asks, acting the part of elevator
man.

'Isn't it early in the year to be groveling for tips?'

'I'm intrigued by your use of the word groveling,' he says.

'I like that word. In fact, I used it just the other day.'

'What was the occasion?'

'Lunch with my ex.'

He guffaws. The elevator stops at five. He turns to me. 'I
finished Queen of Cups. Want to look?'

I see it the moment we enter his studio. It's prominently
displayed on an easel facing the bank of windows. It's an
excellent painting, I think, as good as and yet very different
from his Queen of Swords. I like the way he's depicted me,
face open, vulnerable, as I stare out of the canvas. His painting
of Chantal holding a sword exuded power and mystery. His
painting of me holding a coffee cup makes Queen of Cups
look friendly and accessible.

He steps into his galley kitchen to prepare tea.

'Talked to that detective friend of yours again. Like I said,
he's quite the character.'

'I wouldn't exactly call him my friend.'

'Really?' He turns to me after he puts his kettle on the fire.

'I got the impression . . . well, never mind. Cozying up to him makes sense.'

'Don't know what you mean by cozying. He's a source. I wish you were as open. You hold your cards pretty close.'

He pours hot water into the teapot, sets it along with cups and saucers on a tray.

'Why don't you ask me outright what you want to know?' he says as I follow him into the living area.

'How can I do that, Josh, when I don't know what to ask about?'

'Give it a shot.'

I thump my forehead. There're too many metaphors in play – cozying up, holding cards, taking shots. Time to stop the nonsense, give Josh a serious push.

We sit on the couch. I turn to him soon as we're settled.

'You monitored her sessions, so you know what she was into. If it wouldn't embarrass you I'd love to hear descriptions.'

He exhales. 'It wouldn't embarrass me. But I think the most interesting things about Chantal didn't have to do with her sessions. They had to do with the weird things that intrigued her. Like that photograph I posed for. What was that all about? And her obsession with Hitler. When I'd ask her about that, she'd show me her guarded smile and change the subject. She had some kind of bug up her butt about him. She showed me pictures of his crappy paintings. She seemed to think he could be understood through his artwork. I told her artists often use their art as a way to conceal rather than reveal, and in my opinion he was more an illustrator than an artist.' He shrugs. 'It was like she had this closely guarded inner life she kept locked away. That's what I think is interesting about her.'

'Do you think this guarded side may have led to her getting killed?'

'I've wondered about that. But since she never revealed what it was . . .' He shrugs again. 'I thought of her as a friend, but I understood our friendship only went so far. She compart-mentalized. She didn't want you to know who she was. She liked being a cipher. She once told me she liked hiding inside the dominatrix archetype. When I painted her I tried to work in the idea that there was a lot more to this Queen than just a mighty lady holding a sword.'

'You did that, Josh,' I tell him. 'Your Queen of Swords is powerful and enigmatic. I love having it on loan. When I get stuck writing I turn to it for inspiration.'

As I work on what I'm now calling the Chantal Project, I remember Rex's admonition that every major character in a drama should possess a secret, something she holds back from the audience and other characters, something that underlies everything she says and does.

What, I ask myself, are the secrets I can assign to my three principals? What drives them toward an intersection? I realize that if I knew that my drama would write itself.

One thing I *do* know: what intrigues me most about Chantal is the hall of mirrors effect – that the more I discover about her the more distant and complex she seems to be.

Often when I'm working, I pause and peer around the loft. I gaze at Queen of Swords and then think of the role-playing that was enacted inside these walls and the strange pleasures that were felt by the role-players.

At other times, when my writing's going well, I feel as if Chantal is guiding my hand.

This is what she wants me to say, I think. *This is how she wants to be seen and understood.*

Today Dr Maude wants to talk about Lou Salomé. She tells me she's been reading up on her. She tells me she wanted to know more about this person I keep talking about, and also because Lou was a serious committed shrink.

'She wasn't a key figure in the history of psychoanalysis,' she tells me, 'but still she was important. From the time she and Freud met they became lifelong friends. Yet for the most part their correspondence is formal. She addresses him as "dear Professor". After a few years he writes her back as "dearest Lou". Once he addresses her as "My dear indomitable friend!" Each held the other in very high regard. Early on she asks him to send her his picture. He agrees on condition that she send him one of herself. When he receives it, he places it on the bookshelf behind his desk. Today if you go to the Freud Museum in Hampstead you'll see it there just where he kept it.'

As always, near the end of session, Dr Maude attempts to link things up.

'I know you identify with Chantal. I think you're wrong when you say you're her mirror image. I believe you see things in her you find lacking in yourself.'

I ponder her analysis. 'I face people and address them. She got down and dirty with her clients. I act things out. She lived them.'

'Do you envy that?'

'No, I'd be afraid to go so far. We still don't know why she was killed, but Scarpaci is certain it had to do with her work.'

'What about her obsession with Lou Salomé? Any new thoughts about that?'

'The whip imagery in the Luzern photograph – I have a feeling Chantal fixated on that, which is why she decided to re-enact it with herself playing the Lou role. I also believe she identified with Lou in the sense that like Lou she recognized she was very neurotic. In Lou's case that recognition led to her becoming a shrink, in Chantal's to becoming a dominatrix. Each, I believe, genuinely wanted to help people, but ultimately each was seeking to understand herself.'

Dr Maude smiles. 'The quest to understand ourselves draws many of us to this profession. But don't undervalue our desire to relieve others of pain.'

I tell her I don't undervalue that, but that understanding this about Lou helps me to understand things about Chantal such as her belief in 'the pain that obliterates pain,' the corporeal pain that can relieve the awful psychic pain deep inside. I tell her I think both women believed that, and that I do too.

'I think that's what drives me to stand up in front of an audience and tell my stories.'

I remind her of my *Black Mirrors* piece, during which I stood by a pole in the center of an octagon constructed of eight panes of one-way glass, then degraded myself by stripping and pole-dancing while talking dirty with the knowledge that behind each dark mirror sat a lustful man jerking off in a private booth.

Dr Maude nods. 'The other day you seemed to doubt knowing who you are. I think you understand yourself very well, Tess, and why you're so intrigued with both these women.'

I leave the session perplexed. Is Dr Maude right? Are Chantal and I more different than I first thought? And, more to the point, can I use our differences in my play to define my quest to know and understand her?

Late today I make a major decision. In this drama I will not present the interactions between Lou, Chantal, and myself in a real-time sequence, but will intercut them, moving back and forth in time, forcing the audience to piece the story together.

But what *is* the story? And what, I ask myself, is my role in it? Prober? Investigator? Snoop? One thing for certain: I can't be an uninvolved bystander. The story, I remind myself, has to be as much about me as about Chantal and Lou.

Again I wake up in the middle of the night sweating and trembling. I have dreamt again of having sex with Chantal, but this time our love-making isn't so tender. This time there's a dominance/submission aspect: Chantal giving me instructions in a throaty whisper as to how she wants to be pleasured, and me, face buried between her legs, obeying her every command. She moans and writhes, pressing me harder between her thighs. When she comes in spasms, I raise my head to peer at her. A smile of contentment curls her lips. 'Good girl,' she whispers.

I wake up, hot and wet, knowing I'm trapped now deeper than ever inside her web.

Responding to Eva, I make no mention of her request that I destroy her letters. I tell her I would like very much to meet her in New York and am prepared to travel there once her plans are set. I also refer her to my website and tell her a little about my work. I mention that although my performance pieces are fiction, they're always based in part on fact, and I admit that the little I've discovered about Chantal has inspired me to develop a piece based on aspects of her life, in particular her fascination with the extraordinary Lou Salomé. I write that I hope this does not seem exploitative. I also promise that when I see her I will fill her in on everything I know about the police investigation . . . my hope, of course, being that this will make her all the more eager to confide in me.

Carl peers at me anxiously waiting for me to explain myself. Does he suspect this summons is a set-up?

We're sitting mid-morning in Downtown Café, sipping from lattes.

'I read about you on *The Chronicle*'s society page,' he tells me. 'You gave some kind of recital in a mansion in Presidio Heights. I gathered some people thought it was pretty mean.'

'Is that why you're looking at me this way?'

'I'm curious why you wanted to see me again.'

I meet his eyes. 'I'm curious about something too. Exactly what was your relationship with Chantal?'

'I told you all about that.'

'*Everything?*' He peers nervously at me. 'Frankly I don't buy the reason you gave for wanting to come up to the loft. You know – "for old times' sake". *Really?*'

He lowers his eyes. 'I was totally obsessed with her,' he whispers.

'Did she know you were?'

'I told her I wanted to be full-time under her control. She didn't take that well. She said it wasn't her I was obsessed with, it was an archetype. She said I had no idea of what she was really like. She reminded me I was a client with whom she had a fee-for-services relationship. She also said she had a strict policy regarding boundaries.'

'How'd that make you feel?' I ask, enjoying my role as amateur shrink.

'Bad. I tried to persuade her, but she was adamant. The more I begged, the sterner she became. Finally she told me we should take a break. I knew what that meant. Banishment. After that she wouldn't take my calls. I was devastated.'

My heart goes out to him even as I realize he'd become

dangerously obsessed with Chantal, and that she was right to cut him off.

'Your name isn't Carl Draper, is it?' He shakes his head. 'You knew Chantal was murdered when you came by last time?' He nods, then looks down at his coffee. 'You weren't honest with me. Fine, we didn't know each other. But what gets me is that you made a big pretense of being open.'

'I'm sorry, Tess. You make me feel ashamed.'

'That's how you should feel. And I hope it's not just because I found you out. It's time to come clean, Carl. The detective who's working the case wants to talk to you. His name's Scarpaci. He's sitting now at a table just outside. I think you should talk to him.'

'That's why you called me, isn't it?' His expression tells me he's resigned.

'Want me to introduce you?'

'Do I have a choice?'

'No, not really,' I tell him.

Scarpaci calls me late this afternoon.

'His real name's Carl Hughes. He's a curator at the San Francisco Fine Arts Museum. He's married, has two kids, owns a house in the Marina. He saw Chantal once a month for nearly two years. He was, in his own words, addicted to her. He was also into a rare fetish, a control game called "consensual blackmail". In this game the sub wants the domme to accumulate embarrassing documentation about him then threaten to expose him as a pervert to his family, friends, colleagues, and employer unless he pays or performs further humiliating acts. Chantal refused to play this with him. She told him it was against everything she stood for. He begged, she continued to refuse, he continued to beg, until finally she told him she couldn't see him anymore.'

'So he wasn't really in thrall to her. He just wanted her to threaten him with ruin.'

'Yeah, but this is where his story takes a strange turn. One day he receives an envelope at his office. There're photos inside, a series of shots taken during the photo session Chantal did with him and Josh. They show him wearing the fabric hood that exposed his features. According to Josh, Chantal trashed those images. But maybe not. Hughes says his features were clear in the pictures and that anyone who knew him would recognize him. He wasn't frightened or upset. On the contrary, he was thrilled. He figured her earlier refusals were part of some devious power play and that now the blackmail game he'd asked her for was on. He was looking forward to the psychological struggle. Now that he'd received the photos he expected her to contact him and make harsh demands. But when he didn't receive any follow-up he started calling and emailing her again. Finally she called him back. According to him they had an angry exchange. She denied she had anything to do with sending him photos. When he described them to her, she reminded him the first set had been destroyed, so he couldn't possibly have received such images. She told him again she regretted having to cut him off, but that his insistence on a blackmail relationship had made further contact impossible. According to Hughes this was their last contact. He also says there was never a follow-up to the mailing.'

'Wow! What do you think?'

'I think he's one sick pup. Or else he's worked up a slick story. I asked if he still has the photos. He swore he destroyed them. No way, of course, to verify that, but in the end I believed him because his story's so detailed and self-harming. He may have wanted Chantal to tighten her control by threatening to expose and embarrass him, but he certainly doesn't want me or anyone else to tell his wife about their sessions or their relationship.'

'So is he a person of interest?'

'For now. But if he's telling the truth, the big question is who sent him those pictures?'

'You're thinking it was Josh?'

'He's at the top of the list.'

This morning I receive a second email from Gräfin Eva.

Dear Tess Berenson:
    Since our last exchange I visited your website and was impressed by your work. Congratulations on receiving

*the Hollis Grant. You appear to be a serious artist. I'm
sure Chantal would be appreciative of your interest, and
would not consider your project exploitative before
hearing more details.*

*I am open to helping you providing you can convince
me of your sincerity and that you have a positive attitude
toward my dear friend. This is not to say that I plan to
ask for any control over what you do, only that I must
be convinced of your good intentions. As I'm sure you
understand, mutual trust is essential. I believe the best
way to build such trust is to meet in person.*

*I will be visiting New York for approximately six days
beginning on July 20. I hope this suits your schedule. I
look forward to meeting you and hearing more details
concerning your project, as well as any progress you can
report on the police investigation.*

With kind regards,
Eva Foigel

TWENTY-ONE

Extract from the Unpublished Memoirs of Major Ernst
Fleckstein

(AKA Dr Samuel Foigel)

I n late 1942 I began to hear rumors in my 'psychoanalytic
practice' of serious trouble on the Eastern Front. Around
this time several of my patients (consisting almost entirely
of the haughty wives of well-born military officers) came to
me with dreams fraught with anxiety. Employing techniques
I'd devised from my studies at the Institute for Psychological
Research and Psychotherapy (supplemented by a few I'd picked
up from various tarot-card readers of my acquaintance), I was
able, while interpreting these dreams, to uncover their underlying cause: huge as yet unreported losses around Stalingrad
and the possibility of a major Wehrmacht defeat.

Around this time I also started hearing from patients of
whispered talk in their respective social circles regarding prepar-
ations in the event Germany lost the war. Several confided
that their husbands had set up secret foreign bank accounts
and had made 'just in case' arrangements for refugee status
in South American countries. It was clear to me that if Germany
did lose, the post-war environment would not be pleasant, and
that because of my role as an undercover agent acting as a
mock-psychoanalyst on behalf of the Abwehr,[1] I could find
myself in some danger.

(I should add that my former patron, Martin Bormann,
having become personal secretary to Hitler after the flight of
Rudolf Hess in 1941, was no longer accessible to me, and that
even if he were, I couldn't possibly discuss such matters with
him.)[2]

---

[1] Germany's Military Intelligence Service.

[2] On May 10, 1941, Deputy Führer Rudolf Hess, having become increasingly

It was then, at the approach of New Year's 1943, that I began to devise my own 'just in case' plan, a secret mission that could get me safely out of Germany with an ingeniously created new identity. As the details began to crystalize, I understood that gaining approval for such an audacious mission would require my achieving a major success in my current role. As it happened, I was on the verge of just such a triumph.

Since the end of the war, the Solf Circle Tea Party Affair[3] has become common knowledge, with most of the credit going to the Swiss physician Paul Reckzeh, working as an undercover agent of the Gestapo. Until now my own role has never been revealed. In fact it was my 'psychoanalytic work' that set the Reckzeh operation into motion.

In late 1942, my patient, the very beautiful and highly neurotic Countess Annelore von T, in session on my analytic couch, expressed great anxiety regarding subversive conversations taking place among her friends. Under the guise of relieving her of stress, I immediately put her under hypnosis and was thereby able to extract every bit of knowledge she possessed about the Solf Circle, including the names of all its principals.

I claim no direct role in the final unmasking of this group and take no responsibility for the subsequent arrests and executions. That was strictly a Gestapo affair. But I did provide the initial tip that led many months later to Reckzeh's successful penetration. Though I found those people (and in fact all the ladies I was treating) snobbish and elitist, I had nothing personal against any of them. Still, since Germany was at war

---

unstable, flew solo to Scotland in a crazed and unauthorized attempt to bargain for peace with the British. He was made a prisoner of war, tried at Nuremberg, and sentenced to life imprisonment. In 1987 at the age of ninety-three he died by his own hand in Spandau Prison.

[3] The Solf Circle was a resistance group of intellectuals and high-ranking German officials secretly plotting against the regime. In September 1943 the group met at a tea party in Berlin hosted by Elisabeth von Thadden. In January 1944, Himmler had seventy-four people (attendees at the party and others associated with them) arrested for treason. Most were tortured and executed.

none could rightfully claim they were unaware of the consequences should their treasonous plot be exposed.

Colonel Heinz Fruehauf, my Abwehr superior, was impressed
by what I'd been able to get out of Countess von T. I had finally
managed, he told me, to justify the elaborate ruse we'd set up,
whereby a group of elite Berlin physicians had been ordered to
refer selected female patients to me for 'psychoanalysis.'

My job was to extract whatever information I could from
these fine ladies concerning anti-NSDAP sentiments. The
set-up had been quite expensive. Appropriate certificates were
created, and my office suite (formerly occupied by a Jewish
internist) in a posh building on Wielandstrasse was fitted out
with luxurious furnishings. These included a fetishistic analytic
couch I had personally selected and then conspicuously placed
in the center of my consulting room, the same couch position
I'd observed during my visits in 1934 and 1937 to the study
of Frau Lou Salomé. Additionally my position as a 'high-
society analyst' required that I be outfitted with a closetful
of expensive hand-tailored suits. In short, mine was a high-
maintenance operation, which had, until my exposure of the
Solf Circle, provided little in the way of results.

Now by identifying this group, I was finally in a position
to propose my own plan: to be infiltrated into the United States
in the guise of a Jewish refugee psychoanalyst seeking asylum
after a daring escape from Nazi Germany. Upon arrival I would
present my credentials and then hopefully be permitted to open
a psychoanalytic practice in Washington, DC similar to the
one I had in Berlin. From there I would act as a liaison with
other Abwehr agents while at the same time eliciting intelligence from female patients whose husbands worked in the
upper levels of the US military and espionage apparatus.

Fruehauf, as anticipated, was skeptical. What made me think
I'd be accepted by an American psychoanalytic community
already flooded with German and Austrian Jewish refugees?
And since war was raging, wasn't it a little late to credibly
claim to have escaped from Germany?

Good questions, which I was prepared to answer. Our documents department, I told him, was fully capable of providing
me with a complete legend. After all, it had done that for me

already. Moreover, I would take the name of an actual Jewish psychoanalyst named Samuel Foigel, to whom I bore a close facial resemblance and who I knew from my research had died at Buchenwald in 1939 after being arrested during a routine round-up.

In addition, my legend would include the following fascinating detail: not only had I *not* been killed but had miraculously survived in plain sight in Berlin using the false identity of the ostensibly Aryan analyst Dr Ernst Fleckstein, whose society practice could easily be verified.

As for my defection, it would take place during a forthcoming psychoanalytic conference in Zurich organized by the Aryan analyst Dr C. J. Jung, rival and ideological enemy of Freud. While there I would slip away to the American consulate where I would request asylum in the US and recognition of my true identity. If rigorously questioned (as I was certain I would be) I would recount in great detail, emphasizing close calls and much derring-do, the saga of my amazing imposture in Berlin. I would also give samples of intimate details I had obtained in my practice regarding high-ranking officials in the Wehrmacht and SS, suggesting possession of a fount of intelligence that would be irresistible to the Americans.

Fruehauf was highly amused. 'You're telling me, dear Fleckstein, that this Foigel character will claim that, pretending to be you, he was able to carry on a practice in the capital of the Third Reich?'

'Precisely!' I told him. 'Foigel transforms himself into Fleckstein to survive the purge of Jewish analysts. When finally he defects to the US, he resumes his original identity as Foigel.'

Fruehauf, I should add, was a mediocre character. Short of stature, round of belly, and slow of wit, he had intimidating hooded eyes. He also sported an absurd mustache in the manner of former President Paul von Hindenburg, for which he was much mocked around our headquarters.

'Foigel-Fleckstein-Foigel,' Fruehauf repeated the sequence several times, smiling as he allowed the names to roll resonantly off his tongue. 'You say you look like him? Hmmm, perhaps you *are* a Jew, eh, Fleckstein? I've long suspected as much!'

'Oh my God, you've found me out! Ha ha ha!' As always I pretended to be dazzled by the little man's riposte.

'Ha! Well, one can't be too careful these days, can one?' Then he turned serious. 'It's so absurd it might actually work. But the orchestration will require much effort.'

'Still,' I told him, 'you have to admit that this is just the kind of operation that will appeal to Canaris.[4] He's always urging us to come up with schemes so audacious that no enemy counter-intelligence officer will suspect them. I believe he'll relish the notion of placing a new agent in the American capital, one bursting with alluring disinformation, an agent in the guise of a Jewish psychoanalyst to whom certain ladies, in the process of confiding their anxieties, may inadvertently reveal their officer husband's closely guarded secrets. It would simply be the reverse of the operation I've been conducting here. Think too of all the blackmail material I'll be able to obtain regarding these ladies' improprieties. And what better place for our agents to drop off material for transmission than the office of a Jewish refugee doctor. What, dear Fruehauf, could possibly be more audacious than that?'

'Write up your proposal and I'll present it,' Fruehauf instructed. 'I'd say the odds of acceptance are slim. But,' he added smugly, 'at the very least this office will gain credit for audacity.' By which, of course, he meant himself.

I will remind readers that my experience at Matthias Göring's Institute for Psychological Research and Psychotherapy had not been pleasant. I was not well received there when in 1937, determined to become an analyst, I presented myself for training. I was not a psychiatrist, not even a doctor of medicine, so how, I was asked, could I presume to study psychoanalysis? But Bormann's good word got me in the door, and once enrolled I was permitted to attend lectures and seminars so long as I kept quiet and showed I knew my place.

---

[4] Admiral Wilhelm Franz Canaris (1887–1945), chief of the Abwehr, dismissed by Hitler in February 1944, arrested for his involvement in various assassination plots against Hitler, and executed by hanging in the last days of the war.

I mention this again to contrast it with my magnificent training once Admiral Canaris approved my plan. My instructors taught me a variety of counter-interrogation and survival techniques in the event my risky operation were compromised. They emphasized that the more absurdities I added to my stories, the more believable and seductive they would be. They told me that the American spy agency, the OSS, was desperate to understand the relationships between our leaders. I could make up most anything and present it as fact so long as I stayed consistent regarding details.

Together we came up with a good excuse for the termination of my practice: I had been transferred on an urgent basis to the Eastern Front to serve as a field psychiatrist. All my patients were so notified and dutifully referred to other analysts. I will admit here that I did miss several of them. As is well known these transference relationships often cut both ways.

I also won't deny that I enjoyed the romantic fantasies that several patients developed toward me, not to mention the erotic dreams about me which they exposed on my analytic couch. Hearing descriptions of the torrid desires of outwardly cool upper-class women was (and continues to be!) among the great pleasures I obtain from therapeutic work. I also won't deny that on several occasions I took advantage of these patients' vulnerabilities, usually after putting them into a hypnotic trance. Since I was not a real doctor and these therapeutic relationships were bogus, there could be no issue of ethical transgression. We were adults engaging in consensual activity. Enough said!

Back to my training. I did well in all my espionage courses while working with the Documents Department on the creation of appropriate diplomas, identity cards, letters, and transcripts, as well as a series of ingeniously doctored photographs that served to enhance my resemblance to the poor deceased Dr Foigel.

I had one trump card which greatly excited my trainers: Frau Salomé's inscribed copy of Freud's seminal book on dream interpretation. What better credential could there be if I were confronted regarding my bona fides? To have been presented with such an object by one of Freud's closest acolytes would establish a direct connection between Foigel and the legendary founding father of psychoanalysis. And lest anyone dare inquire as to how I obtained this treasure, I would show an accompanying letter-of-gift created by an Abwehr master forger which even close friends of Frau Salomé would likely swear had been written in her hand.

Let me add that though I had only one brief personal encounter with this imposing woman, her manner made a great impression upon me. Regarding her as an exemplar, I used her as a model for my therapist persona, for which I owe her a considerable posthumous debt of gratitude.

My reception at the American Consulate in Zurich went as smoothly as anticipated. When the military attaché heard the tales I had to tell about Hitler's sexual deviance (stories which, of course, were true, based on knowledge I'd gained while working as Bormann's fixer) his eyebrows shot up like the ears of an excited rabbit. Within hours he had communicated my resume to the OSS station chief, Allen Dulles,[5] who ordered that I be transported immediately to his HQ[6] in Bern for what proved to be a lengthy, exhausting, and brutally frank credibility debriefing.

I'll say this for Dulles: he was as shrewd a man as I ever encountered. He was soft-spoken and friendly, but beneath his composure I detected an extremely canny card player who knew just how to bluff an opponent (in this case, myself!) seated on the other side of his table.

After listening patiently to my elaborate cover story, he sat back, lit his pipe, gazed at me with unblinking eyes, and got straight to the point.

'I don't know whether your real name is Fleckstein, Foigel, Finkelstein or something else,' he told me, 'and, frankly, I don't

---

[5] Allen Welsh Dulles (1893–1969). Following his exemplary wartime service as OSS chief in Switzerland, Dulles, after a career in law and politics, was named director of the CIA in 1953. In 1961 he was forced to resign this position after the debacle of the Bay of Pigs.

[6] Situated at 23 Herrengasse in a historical mansion known as the von Wattenwyl House.

care. Of one thing I'm certain: you're an Abwehr agent. As to how I know that, let's just say that we have sources within your organization.[7] I knew you were coming and have been anticipating your arrival. Now that you're here and I'm able to take the measure of you, I sense your loyalties are not to your service or even to your homeland, but are solely to yourself and your own survival. I gather this ingeniously incredible operation was your idea. Perhaps you were looking for a safe haven for yourself, or perhaps you thought you might really be able to serve your masters. The fact that they went along with it confirms my sense that a mood of desperation now prevails at Tirpitzufer.[8] None of that matters to me. The only thing that does matter is the quality of your information and the degree to which you're willing to reveal it. For purposes of this discussion I'll address you now as Foigel. And if you cooperate,' he smiled cunningly, 'Foigel you shall remain.'

I listened carefully as he laid out my alternatives. If after further questioning I refused to concede I was an Abwehr agent, I would be subjected to harsh interrogation, and then, after I confessed, as inevitably I would, I would be executed as a spy. If on the other hand I owned up to my true role, I would, after divulging to him every single fact I knew regarding the Nazi leadership, be relocated to Washington, DC where I would act as a double agent under OSS control. There I would ostensibly fulfill my role as an Abwehr operative. I would receive agents in my consulting room, accept their reports, turn them over to my control officer for alteration, and then relay them on for transmission back to Germany. If my work was exemplary I would, after the German surrender, be released from OSS supervision. After that I could continue to reside in the US under the name of Foigel, or return to Germany as a private citizen under any name of my choosing.

---

[7] I learned years later that it was probably the diplomatic courier, Fritz Kolbe, who informed on my operation. Kolbe, operating under the code name 'George Wood,' was later described by Dulles as 'undoubtedly one of the best secret agents any intelligence service has ever had.'

[8] 76/78 Tirpitzufer, HQ of the Abwehr, adjacent to the building that housed the offices of the OKW (Armed Forces High Command.)

'So it's either play the tough guy and take the nasty consequences or cooperate and be well rewarded for your assistance.'
Dulles' eyes sparkled as he gazed deeply into mine. 'You
strike me as an intelligent fellow. You have an interesting if
checkered past. I've offered you an excellent deal. Take an
hour to think it over. I'm sure you'll make the proper choice.'

He rang for an assistant who showed me to a small windowless room in the cellar of the mansion. There I quickly made
my decision. Dulles had shown great perception. I was, as he
said, interested solely in my survival.

Let me say here that I greatly enjoyed psychoanalytic work
and believed I performed it well. Though I hadn't earned my
diplomas the proper way, I believed I could offer therapeutic
analysis on a par with any practitioner I'd met. I was a kind
and sympathetic listener, my interpretations were creative,
often deep, I was good at pointing out connections, and female
patients of a certain age and class seemed to like me very
much. I had a way with them. I knew how to draw out their
most intimate fantasies and thoughts. Thinking ahead, I had
no trouble imagining a useful life for myself as Dr Samuel
Foigel, psychoanalyst – a life of contentment, respect, and
affluence. I had been a private matrimonial investigator, a party
hack and fixer, and then, thanks to a brief fortuitous encounter
with Frau Lou Salomé, had discovered my vocation as an
analyst. In short, there was no question as to my response.

Dulles was pleased. 'You will play an important role in our
effort,' he told me, laying his hands on my shoulders. 'If you
feel squeamish now, in time you'll be proud of what you've
done. You will become a player in a Great Cause. You will
meet and work with outstanding people. I don't mind telling
you I envy the fun you're going to have leading a double life.
But then, that has always been your life, hasn't it? Yes, I feel
I know you, Foigel. You are one of us, the cadre of the
duplicitous.'

He paused, then asked sharply: 'Now tell me everything
you know about Martin Bormann.'

TWENTY-TWO

I meet Eva Foigel in the lobby of her midtown Manhattan hotel. In person she looks older than in her website photos – a stocky woman with age-appropriate facial lines and short silver swept-back hair. I figure her for around fifty-five. She sports small silver earrings, wears elegant flats, and is simply yet expensively dressed in a dark gray Jil Sander pants suit over a light gray silk blouse. She strikes me as serenely self-assured. Despite a friendly smile, she projects the allure of a woman used to getting her way.

'They have a little bar here,' she says, guiding me toward an alcove off the lobby. 'Let's get ourselves a table, order drinks, and chat.'

She speaks, I note, like an American. 'I expected you'd have a German accent,' I tell her.

'I was born in Cleveland, brought up in the States until I was twelve. After my father died, my mother took me to her parents' hometown, Vienna. Been there ever since.'

After we order beers she gazes at me. I'm struck by the intensity of her blue-flecked eyes. 'You have many questions. First off you want to know how I met Chantal.'

'I do,' I tell her, surprised by the speed at which she's moving the conversation.

'It's not a long story. We met by chance. It was in Vienna at a public lecture about the early days of psychoanalysis, the so-called heroic period . . . a special interest of mine. Chantal wandered in, sat down a few seats away. I was impressed by the way she carried herself and I liked the way she looked. Later, she confessed, she liked my looks too. Our eyes met, we exchanged smiles. After the lecture I asked if she'd join me at a coffee house. She agreed, we went to one nearby, sat and talked until two a.m.'

Eva sips from her beer. She smiles as she recalls that first encounter.

'She told me she'd come to Vienna on leave from college to improve her German and because of her interest in Freud. As we talked we discovered we shared a Jewish heritage. When she asked me about myself, I told her exactly what I did – that I was a professional dominatrix catering to male fantasies of female power, a role I regarded as akin to that of a psychotherapist . . . and often a lot more effective. She was immediately intrigued. When I described the kinds of scenes I created, she said I sounded like a director of an intimate form of theater . . . which, of course, I am. She asked if she could observe me at work. I told her she could, but by the very act of observing she would also become a participant. She understood. "I will be The Voyeur," she said. "My presence as witness will intensify the effect."'

Eva shakes her head. 'She was amazing . . . so smart, intuitive. Turned out she had a natural gift for erotic domination. A born actress, she thrived in my theatrical dungeon. I'd had apprentices before, but never one so talented or astute.'

'So she became your apprentice?'

'The next day. She stayed with me for three years. I taught her everything I knew. We worked together. We also fell in love. You know that, of course.'

'Yes, from the letters. A friend translated them for me. When I realized how intimate they were I was surprised she stored them inside a book.'

'Which one, do you remember?'

'A book of old photographs of traditional Viennese coffee houses.'

'Of course!' Eva's delighted. 'An excellent hiding place since we spent so much time in them. *Kaffehauskultur* is among the great joys of Viennese life.'

'Still I wonder why, when she sold her books, she didn't pull your letters out.'

'Perhaps she was so busy getting rid of stuff she forgot they were there.'

'Why do you think she was in such a rush?'

'She was scared.'

'Do you know why?' I ask holding my breath, hoping I'll finally learn the reason.

'She called me on Skype a few days after she abandoned the loft, told me she was staying in a hotel. I could tell she was upset. She muttered something about not wanting to sound paranoid.'

Eva exhales. 'It takes courage to do our kind of work, dealing with the eccentric fantasies of strangers. Occasionally our kind of treatment will release something in a client and he'll explode. I taught her how to handle these situations, and she took the usual precautions. My guess is she must have felt severely threatened by something she didn't think she could handle. When I asked her again what was going on, she said it had to do with the photograph. "The Luzern?" I asked. "In a way," she said. She promised she'd tell me the details when she saw me. She mentioned she had a few things to settle before she came to Vienna to cool off. She asked if she could stay with me. I told her she knew she didn't have to ask. She was grateful. "I want to spend a few weeks with you," she told me, "walking the streets as we used to do. I need some time to figure out the rest of my life."

'She said she was thinking of returning to school, getting her degree, then finding a new career. She loved black-and-white photography and had always admired the work of Helmut Newton. "I'd like to apprentice to a good art photographer," she told me, "learn how it's done and see how I might fit in."'

Eva lowers her eyes. When she speaks again it's with sorrow. 'After that I didn't hear from her. She didn't answer my emails or calls. Worried, I phoned Lynx. She didn't know anything more than that Chantal had seemed upset then disappeared. I was frantic. Then two weeks later Lynx emailed me that Chantal had been killed. At first I refused to believe it. I thought maybe she'd faked her death and was walking around someplace free of whatever had frightened her. Then her brother confirmed it. When he told me he had her ashes I was devastated. I knew my dear Chantal was truly gone.'

She turns to me, brightens. 'It's a lovely evening. Let's stretch our legs. I love New York this time of year.'

We exit the hotel. A cool breeze has replaced the summer humidity that hung over the city when I arrived. The rush hour has passed, the sidewalks aren't crowded. It's possible to speak in normal tones as we make our way toward Fifth Avenue.

'I love the tempo here,' Eva tells me, 'so different from the measured pace of old Vienna. It's good to come for a few days and drink up the energy. But I could never live here.'

Reaching Fifth, we turn and start uptown, passing store windows, banks, office towers. Feeling strangely comfortable walking beside Eva, I ask her about Chantal's interests as reflected in her library: Lou Andreas-Salomé; Freud and psychoanalysis; Hitler and the Third Reich.

'Those are all *my* interests,' she tells me. 'Dear Chantal, madly in love with me, soon took them up as her own. You know they call Vienna "City of Dreams". I think it's impossible to take up residence there and not become interested in Freud. She was already interested in him, which was why she happened to attend the lecture. As for Hitler and Salomé, those have long been special interests of mine. Once I told Chantal about Lou, she fixated on her. Most people concentrate on the relationship with Nietzsche or the years with Rilke, but for personal reasons I'm more interested in her time with Freud. After I shared my reasons, Chantal took them up with even more fervor than myself.'

Eager as I am to hear about these personal reasons, I'm relieved when she asks me about myself. She perks up when I mention I'm in therapy with a neo-Freudian analyst whom I see weekly for sessions that revolve around unresolved issues with my father.

'Interesting . . . I also have daddy issues.' She pronounces 'issues' as if the word can barely describe them. But when I recount Dad's criminal history, his stint in prison, and the destruction he wreaked on our family by his toxic combination of charm and lies, I can tell by her reaction she understands that for me the word 'issues' is also an understatement.

When she asks about my performance work, I describe *Recital*, *Black Mirrors*, and my Weimar piece. She seems especially impressed when I recount my recent femme-fatale gig in Rex's Vertigo.

'I sense you enjoyed doing that one,' she says. 'Perhaps more than you like to admit.'

Surprised by her insight, I ask how I betrayed myself.

'There was no betrayal. I heard it in your voice, saw it in your eyes.'

Meeting her gaze, I feel that I can safely confide in her, that like Dr Maude she won't judge or disparage me no matter what I say.

She suggests we have dinner at a nearby restaurant. Then she stops to gaze at me again. 'I think now I understand, without you telling me, why you're so intrigued by Chantal. You have much in common – beauty, brains, a love of performance, and a fascination with decadence. But have no fear . . . I won't come on to you. You've signaled many things, but not that.' She chuckles. 'Unless . . . well, that would be up to you. Personally I prefer to court rather than be courted. But if you're so inclined, I'd happily make an exception.'

Amused, I shake my head. I also decide not to disclose my erotic dreams about Chantal. Settling the matter with a quick clasp of hands, we turn east on 62nd Street.

En route to the restaurant, I ask if she made the same exception in regard to Chantal.

She laughs. 'In her case I was definitely the seducer. I could tell she was ripe for it, but shy and inexperienced. It took me about a week to bed her. Then there was no turning back. It was, as the Viennese say – *Wunderbar!* Really, the best time in my life. I think of Chantal as my greatest love. Even after we parted I held her close in my heart.'

To hear such an admission from such a powerful woman brings home how closely bound they'd been.

Waiting for the light to change, I turn to her. 'May I ask a personal question?'

'You want to know what caused the break-up? It was a gentle drifting apart, not a dramatic rupture. Certainly the age difference was a factor. Also the intensity of our relationship and of our joint practice as dominatrices. A passion as powerful as ours could not but burn out after a time. I think in the end the cause was mutual exhaustion. We both realized quite sadly the time had come to separate.'

She leads me to a small Italian restaurant she's fond of on account of the food and because the proprietor allows diners to linger on after coffee and dessert. Over dinner she explains the source of the fascinations later adopted by Chantal.

'Earlier you mentioned having daddy issues. I had major ones. My father was an extraordinary man. I don't necessarily say that in praise. I've yet to come to grips with who he was and many of the things he did. To this day I'm haunted by him.'

Her dad, she tells me, was sixty when she was born, so she only knew him in his final years. He had an amazing life story, or rather two life stories, although she only learned about the first after her mother died and she inherited three things: a book, a drawing, and a manuscript.

The book was a signed first edition copy of Freud's *Die Traumdeutung*, 'The Interpretation of Dreams,' warmly inscribed by Freud to Lou Salomé. Eva tells me she recently put it up for auction in Vienna, where it fetched over a hundred thousand euros. She donated the entire sum to the Vienna Psychoanalytic Society.

When I gasp and interrupt to ask how on earth her father acquired such a treasure, she politely suggests I hold my questions until she's finished.

The second item, an erotic drawing, was alleged to have been made by Adolf Hitler when, prior to World War I, he was trying to eke out a living as a young artist in Vienna. Supposedly, Eva tells me, he presented it as a gift to Lou Salomé, which, if true, occurred under circumstances that remain obscure. What's interesting about this drawing, she says, is that it reprises the famous Luzern photograph of Lou, Nietzsche, and Paul Rée that enraptured Chantal.

Eva pulls out her cell phone, shows me the drawing on the screen. I stare at it dumbfounded.

'No Hitler scholar will authenticate it,' she says. 'Though it bears his initials on the back and a short dedication to Lou in what looks to be his handwriting, experts claim it's psychologically impossible for Hitler to have drawn it and that it bears no resemblance to any other drawing he ever made. Everyone I've consulted assures me it's a worthless forgery.'

The third item, she tells me, the manuscript, was a memoir written by her father in his final years. In it he described his strange double life: first, as a man named Ernst Fleckstein, a private investigator in Munich specializing in matrimonial work; later a 'fixer' for the Nazi leader, Martin Bormann; and, finally, a major in the German intelligence service. And then a totally different second identity acquired in the early nineteen-forties when he decided to flee Germany: a Jewish doctor/psychoanalyst named Samuel Foigel, which was the name by which Eva's mother knew him and the name Eva continues to use as her own.

She summarizes her father's memoir in broad strokes. Listening I'm most intrigued by his description of his encounter with Lou Salomé on a mission, assigned to him by Bormann, to reclaim the scandalous erotic drawing.

'I think now,' she says, 'you may understand why I'm so fascinated by Frau Lou, as much as or perhaps even more than my father was. If I'm to believe what he wrote, it was the few minutes he spent trying to persuade her to hand over the drawing that later made him decide to become an analyst. I'm not sure what really motivated him. There're hints in the memoir and many things left unstated. To hear my mother tell it, he helped a great many people. She herself had been one of his patients. Dad was what they call a natural, gifted in the art if not the science of psychotherapy. It gave him great pleasure to interpret his patients' dreams, help them work through the origins of their erotic fantasies, unravel the truth and underlying meanings of their childhood traumas. Yes, he took advantage of some of his female patients. By his own account he bedded a few . . . including my mom. In those days such misbehavior was not all that uncommon. In the end, despite his many ethical shortcomings, I believe my father did his patients much good. Yet it's still hard for me to believe that this man, so ruthless in his early life, would later become so empathetic. It's as if the very act of taking on Foigel's identity totally changed his character.'

'Was he a Nazi?' I ask, fascinated by what she's telling me.

'He was a party member, but not a believer. In those days many played that game. He played it well to further his ambitions. He was by his own admission an opportunist. Some might describe him as a psychopath . . . which, I gather, is how you view your dad.'

'Compared to yours mine was an amateur. Isn't it strange your father took on the identity of a Jew?'

'He was never, far as I can tell, anti-Semitic. I believe the only reason he made that choice was because he thought it would make for a great disguise.'

'And this all goes back to a single brief meeting with Lou Salomé?'

'So he claims. According to his memoir their meeting was a turning point.'

'Chantal knew this?'

'All of it! She helped me work it through. In a way it became the focus of our lives together – trying to solve the mystery of my father's past.'

I mention the map folded inside Chantal's Baedeker Guide bearing highlighted markings defining buildings and routes.

Eva smiles. 'I remember that map. Chantal liked to mark the places we visited and the routes we walked. We loved retracing the footsteps of the writers, artists, and thinkers who lived there before World War I. We also traveled beyond Vienna. We went to Göttingen, where Lou lived and conducted her analytic practice, saw the very house where my father confronted her. We found the place outside Munich where the blackmailing Father Stempfle was murdered, an act for which my father claims he felt remorse. We visited his old office suite in Berlin, where he practiced as a fake analyst, and the suburban villa where he played an unwitting role in the suicide of a movie star who'd been traumatized by a bizarre encounter with Hitler. The point wasn't just to retrace his footsteps, but to get a feeling for the various places where he lived and worked. I'm not sure all these walks and visits helped. What did help was making them with Chantal. I'm still haunted by my father's double life, but, thanks to her, with less anguish than before.'

So many things I've puzzled over are now coming clear: Chantal calling her loft 'The Eagle's Nest'; the many notes in books about Hitler regarding his sexuality; the speculative notes in the margins of all the biographies of Lou Salomé . . . and more.

After dinner, we linger over coffee. It's then that I broach the subject of Chantal's fixation on the Luzern photograph.

Eva nods. 'It looks almost innocent today, doesn't it? Chantal and I spent hours mulling over it. She saw things in it I hadn't seen, and when she saw how it connected to the Hitler drawing she became obsessed with it. What did it *mean*? What was the backstory? And what was the backstory *behind* the backstory, the unconscious forces at work within the three protagonists revealed by their odd mismatched postures and expressions? It's a fascinating picture, and perhaps indecipherable. Also great fun to speculate about.'

Eva listens closely as I share Dr Maude's interpretation.

'I think you have an excellent shrink,' she says when I'm finished. 'That's as good a take on it as I've heard. We must remember that this photo was taken long before Freud revealed the role of the unconscious. When they posed in Luzern I doubt any of them fully grasped the undercurrents.'

'Did you know Chantal set up her own version of it?'

'She sent it to me. She wrote that she loved making it. When I saw it I took it as an act of homage. By placing herself in Lou's position in the chariot, I believe she was declaring something important about who she was.' Eva's eyes turn moist. 'I thought she looked exceptionally glamorous. I viewed it as a superb modern-day reinterpretation of the original. I also thought it showed great talent. I believe if she'd lived she'd have been successful as a fine art photographer. Her take on the Luzern picture suggests a direction she could have taken – reinterpreting famous photographs from the past. It hurts me to think of all the wonderful things she might have accomplished.'

As we walk back toward the hotel, I tell her I keep a reproduction of the Luzern photo beside my computer as I write.

At this she stops walking, turns and peers at me intently. 'In your email you mentioned doing a piece about Chantal. Do I understand you've already started?'

I nod. 'Writing it in the place where Chantal used to live . . . maybe this'll strike you as crazy but sometimes I feel her spirit with me when I work. My shrink thinks I may be overly obsessed with Chantal and overly committed to this project.

I've told her becoming obsessed is the only way I'm able to create.'

'I don't think you're crazy, Tess. And I don't think there's anything wrong with being obsessed.'

As we walk on I tell her honestly I feel I must understand Chantal better than I do. 'You've clarified many things,' I tell her, 'but still I find her mysterious. I don't mean her everyday life, but her feelings, her mind. When I try to get a fix on her I feel like I'm peering into a kaleidoscope. Every time I rotate the shaft I see a different pattern. I have so many questions. What did she really feel when she sessioned with clients? Besides her love relationship with you and her friendships with Lynx and Josh, what other people played significant roles in her life? Who were her other lovers? Were they men, women, or both? Was her reenactment of the Luzern photograph intended solely as a work of art, or did she make it in order to revel in some sort of personal psychodrama? And finally, of course, who killed her and why?'

I pause. 'There's something else I'll be putting into this piece – my obsession with her and with her obsessions. I even imagine a possible opening line: "Let me tell you how I took up residence in a loft previously occupied by a professional dominatrix . . ."'

'Oh, I like that!' Eva says. 'I'd definitely pay to see *that* performance!'

I decide then to confide what I know about Scarpaci's investigation, but without mentioning he and I are now involved.

'He's a good detective,' I assure her, 'absolutely committed to finding out who killed Chantal. He thinks her killer was probably one of her clients. He has a couple suspects.'

'I hope he finds out who it was.' She speaks solemnly. 'I hate the notion that her killer might get away with it.'

We continue walking in silence back to her hotel. In the lobby Eva turns to me.

'How long will you be in New York?'

'Through tomorrow night.'

'So you're free in the morning?' I nod. 'I have an early appointment. I think it would be interesting for you to tag

along. The person I'm going to see is notoriously difficult.
Please wait in the bar while I give him a call. I'll join you in
a few minutes and let you know if he agrees.'

The bar's deserted. I take a seat, order a cognac, sit back,
and review the extraordinary hours I've spent with Eva and
her many startling revelations. She revealed many things I
didn't know, keys to Chantal's character and obsessions, more
than enough, I think, to enhance my play.

A thought hits me then, a possible theme: that the more I
find out about Chantal the less I understand her. And that my
real subject is the story of my quest.

The play could be staged, I decide, as a labyrinthine quest,
through which I, the seeker, would lead the audience. It could
start and finish with the Luzern photograph. In between secrets
would be revealed and questions would be posed. At the end
there would still be mystery, the mystery of a woman's life.
The dramatic conflict would not end with a revelation, but
would reside in the experience of the quest.

Eva returns to the bar. She's smiling.

'We're on! Meet me here at nine. I've ordered a car. I'll tell
you more tomorrow.'

We're in a rented limo, heading, Eva informs me, for a house
in Woodside, Queens.

'We're going to meet a man named Quentin Soames, a
person I'd normally avoid. He's the reason I came to New
York. Heard of him?'

I shake my head.

'He's a self-styled Freud-debunker. There're a number of
them. He's the most prominent. Basically they think Freud
was a fraud and they're obsessive about proving it. They scour
old hotel registers, look up people whose family members
were in treatment with him, pride themselves on digging up
little bits of dirt that everyone already knows . . . such as proof
he was having an affair with his sister-in-law or was involved
in a youthful homosexual liaison with Wilhelm Fleiss. But
Soames, who publishes a blog, is after bigger fish. Lately he's
become obsessed with the notion that there was some sort of
contact between Freud and Hitler. He's not the only one.

There's an absurd story going around that Freud had one of Hitler's cheesy watercolors hanging in his house. I saw a documentary at a psychoanalytic conference that raised the possibility they may have regularly exchanged greetings when Hitler walked daily down a particular street and Freud walked to an intersecting street to purchase his morning paper.'

'Sounds like the intersecting routes Chantal drew on the map.'

She nods. 'We tried to track their walks. We had good reason. If we were to believe my father's memoir, Hitler somehow met Salomé during the year she was in Vienna studying with Freud and came to know her well enough that he felt comfortable giving her that erotic drawing. It's hard to think of a more unlikely pair – the famous, elegant fifty-one-year-old intellectual and the scruffy twenty-three-year-old failed watercolorist! Assuming they did meet, where did the young still-unformed Hitler find the nerve to present such a formidable lady with such a drawing? It seems so implausible, and yet years later, according to the memoir, my father is sent to Lou by Bormann to try and buy the drawing back.'

She tells me some of her father's story: how when Lou refused to admit she knew what he was talking about, he concluded she was lying. And then how after her death he found the drawing hidden beneath the cushions of her analytic couch.

Eva reminds me of what we do know: Lou never spoke publically about the Nazi regime, never uttered a word of disapproval. Even more tantalizing, the day after she died a contingent of elite Gestapo assault troops went to her house, took away all the books and documents, then sealed the place up.

'What were they looking for? You've read the biographies, you know the theories – books by Jewish authors, letters from Nietzsche . . . or, as my father writes, a certain drawing.'

It starts to rain when we emerge from the Midtown Tunnel, then cut through Long Island City to Northern Boulevard. Our driver maneuvers through a series of drab rain-slick streets into Woodside, a multi-ethnic neighborhood of mosques, syna-gogues, churches, Irish sports pubs, and Thai, Filipino, and Latin-American restaurants.

Eva shakes her head. 'I told you all the Hitler scholars scoffed when I showed them the drawing. One of them must have mentioned it to Soames. He contacted me, wrote that there'd long been rumors about such a drawing . . . rumors he'd traced back to Marie Bonaparte, one of the few women beside Lou admitted to Freud's inner circle. According to Soames, Bonaparte told several people about what she took to be a throwaway comment by Freud, that years before Lou had shown him a highly charged erotic drawing Hitler had presented to her.'

I've read about Marie Bonaparte in several of Chantal's books. Immensely wealthy, she'd been one of Freud's patients then became an analyst herself. She helped Freud get to Britain with his family, books, and collections by paying the huge taxes demanded by the Nazis in return for an exit permit.

Eva continues: 'When Soames contacted me I blew him off. I didn't like his debunking game. But then a month ago he wrote me again saying he'd acquired copies of letters that confirmed a connection between Hitler, Salomé, and Freud. He said he'd share them with me only if I came to New York and showed him my drawing. That's why I'm seeing him. Today is show-and-tell.'

We wind our way through residential side streets lined with three-story brick apartment buildings, finally stopping in front of a narrow two-story wooden house fronted by a minuscule fenced-in dog run. The color of the siding is a drab pea-soup green. The interior, I note, is concealed by drawn shades.

As we step out of the limo and open our umbrellas, I hear a dog growling inside. The front door opens just as we reach it. A short balding middle-aged man with a lined face and poorly groomed goatee greets us with a frozen smile.

'Frau Eva Foigel I presume,' he says, bowing old-world style as if in respect. 'Or should I properly address you as "Gräfin"?' Before Eva can answer, he turns to me. 'And you, my dear, must be Performance Artist Berenson.' He bows again, informs us we have nothing to fear from his dog, a large black Doberman watching us intently from the bottom of the stairs. 'Charley can be quite the menace if he believes an unwelcome stranger has entered the premises. But seeing

how warmly I've welcomed you, he'll be sweet as a pussy cat
. . . won't you, Charley Boy?'

The dog lets out with a grunt, slobbers saliva onto the floor,
then turns and retires up the stairs. The house interior, I note,
is uncommonly gloomy due to the drawn shades and a bare
low-wattage bulb hanging from the front hall ceiling.

My first impression of Soames, after his arch welcome, is
that there may be more to fear from him than from his dog.
Something about him reeks of single-minded intensity, a harsh
narrow world-view.

Glancing at Eva, I observe the withering manner with which
she peers at him. Turning to him I find him peering back at
her the same way.

'Not to be rude,' Soames says, 'but there are house rules.
No photography and no recording devices. Kindly leave your
phones on the hall table, then follow me to the study.'

Eva and I exchange a glance, then shrug and place our
phones on the table. We follow Soames into a small room off
the hall crammed with filing cabinets secured with combination locks. A desk beneath the shaded windows supports two
large computer screens. Soames motions us to a triangular
arrangement of chairs set up in the center of the room. He
waits for us to sit then takes the chair opposite.

'I know what they say about me,' he begins. 'That I'm a
crazed old man set upon an obsessive mission. And yet,' he
adds with a tight little grin, 'there are some who would do
most anything to stop me. The Freud Cult People, of course,
the true-blue acolytes, who take every word their master wrote
as scripture and denounce anyone who holds a contrary view.
They mock my research and heap ridicule upon me . . . for
which I care not a damn. Just as Samson brought down the
Temple of Dagon, so I shall topple the Myth of Freud.'

He grins at us again. 'Do you find me grandiose? Such passion
over such small stakes! But, dear ladies, make no mistake, the
stakes are huge. If a man of Freud's undeniable intellectual gifts
is allowed to perpetrate a fraud under the guise of science then
"science" has no meaning.'

Eva peers at him. 'I read all this on your blog. Seems the
Freudians aren't the only ones attacking you.'

'Oh, there are others! Mossad has tapped my phone and tried to crack my encryption codes. Why do they bother, you ask? Because they fear that if I can show that Freud *did* know Hitler, was aware of him years before he came to power and did *nothing* to stop him, then, in a metaphysical sense, that great Jewish intellectual must bear some guilt for the Shoah. Such a proposition from a "goy scholar" cannot be tolerated.'

Soames laughs. It's clear he relishes being regarded as crazed.

'And then,' he continues, 'we have the Hitlerians . . .'

Just as Eva warned me, he raves on for a while about them, ending with: '. . . so, you see, I am under attack from three sides. It is good to have enemies. Keeps one on one's toes. So . . . now that we've dispensed with all that, shall we proceed to the matter at hand? You brought the drawing, Gräfin?'

Eva meets his eyes. 'You have the letters?'

'Ah ha! It's "I'll show you mine if you show me yours". I like you, Gräfin! I operate the same way.'

Again he pronounces 'Gräfin' with mock-awe. Glancing at Eva I see she's seething.

Soames, ignoring her glare, informs us that although many boxes of material in the Freud Archive, housed in the Library of Congress, are embargoed ('in many cases until the 2030s, and, in one case, 2102 – can you imagine! Whatever can they be so worried about!') he has, he whispers, gained access to this restricted material. ('Let's just say I have a mole. Librarians don't earn much. I found one in need.') As a result, he tells us, he's been able to obtain photocopies of a revealing exchange between Salomé and Freud.

'Allow me,' he says, 'to read aloud in English translation the following pertinent passage: "In regard to the young man whose drawing we analyzed my last day in Vienna, I marvel daily at the mystery of fate, this great reversal of fortune. Twenty years ago he groveled before me. Now all of Germany grovels before him!"'

Eva stares at him. 'May I see these letters?'

Soames meets her stare. 'Of course! And may I simultaneously see the drawing?'

I watch closely as Eva hesitates. It's clear she's making a decision. If she shows Soames the drawing she'll have nothing more to bargain with. On the other hand, if she can read the letters she may learn how Lou Salomé viewed her father.

'You may see the drawing,' she tells Soames. 'But you may not copy it. Clear?'

'I set the same condition regarding the letters. You may read them, but you may not take notes.'

She nods, reaches into her purse, extracts two pages.

'These are copies front and back. I did not bring the original.'

'Understood,' Soames says reaching for her pages with one hand while handing over his photocopies with the other.

He's the first to react, or perhaps, I should say, to make sounds, joyful murmurings to which he adds a succession of 'Oh my *God*!'s followed by a loud 'Is this not the Holy Grail!' and an even louder 'Oh, Lord, I think I'm going to faint!'

But Eva isn't listening. Her face is transfixed. She turns to me. 'It fits perfectly,' she whispers. 'It confirms Dad *was* sent to retrieve the drawing. This letter corroborates his memoir.'

Soames doesn't hear her. He's too wrapped up in his ecstasy. He's still muttering greedy little exclamations ('This is dynamite. It'll blow the Freud myth sky-high! Freud *knew*, he'd *seen* the pathology with his own eyes, and yet never said a word!'), when Eva rises from her chair.

'This has been interesting,' she says. 'Time now for us to leave.'

'Oh, please, not yet!' Soames pleads. 'We must negotiate!'

'There's nothing to negotiate,' she tells him. 'I always believed my drawing was authentic. Now that that's confirmed, my business with you is finished.'

He stares at her uncertain how to react. Suddenly she reaches down and grasps the drawing out of his hand.

'Give it back!' he cries. 'I know people who'll pay you a fortune for it!'

Eva tosses the photocopied letters at him, then regards him with contempt. 'Lou Salomé wouldn't sell the drawing to this Fleckstein character she mentions, and I won't sell it to you.' She turns to me. 'Come, Tess. Our driver's waiting.'

Soames rises too. For the first time since we entered his house he looks rattled.

'Really, Gräfin,' he pleads. 'This is not the time to leave. We've only just begun.'

'Perhaps *you've* only begun, but I'm finished.'

'You can't sit on this, Gräfin! It changes everything we know about Hitler and shows up Freud as a hypocrite. It's a double bombshell. It's what a scholar lives for!'

'But you're not a scholar,' she tells him calmly. 'You're a zealot.'

In the car, driving back to Manhattan, Eva shows me she kept back a page from Soames's photocopied Salomé–Freud letters. She translates the passage that set her off:

'Lou wrote: ". . . do you remember my describing the visit of a rather oily young man named Fleckstein who claimed he was prepared to offer me an enormous sum in return for the drawing just mentioned? Now I learn that Fleckstein has been making regular inquiries about my health. They are, you see, eagerly awaiting my death, after which I believe they intend to descend upon my little fortress here to retrieve that precious item! I do not believe that they will find it as I have secreted it well."'

She looks at me. 'Do you understand what this means to me, Tess? It totally validates Dad's account, that in the end, miraculously, he *did* find the drawing hidden inside her couch!'

She shakes her head. 'Soames is a scary little man, unbalanced and also foolish. He raves about a double bombshell but he misses the significance of what he saw. He has no idea that Hitler's drawing was based on the Luzern photograph. That explains why Hitler gave it to Lou and why she kept it. Soames is so blinded by his delusions he couldn't see that, and even if he could, he wouldn't comprehend it.'

Back at the hotel, saying goodbye, Eva embraces me, then stands back and fixes me with her blue-flecked eyes.

'I can see how strongly you feel about your project, Tess. For that reason alone I encourage you. And if you complete it and mount a production, I'd certainly love to see it. But in the end it's your project, your idea, your theme. You must do it your own way.'

Before I can respond, she presents me with the photocopy of Hitler's drawing, the one she snatched out of Soames's hand. 'A parting gift,' she says softly. 'Something to think about, maybe even use in your play. As for understanding Chantal, I suggest you think of her as a healer. There was something she'd often say, something that may strike you as self-serving or even corny, but which she meant with all her heart. "In everything I do," she'd say, "in my small way I want to help make the world a better place." That, I think, makes her an exceptional person worthy of your best effort.'

On the red-eye back to San Francisco, I think over the extra-ordinary hours I spent with Eva and our bizarre visit to see Quentin Soames. I learned many things from her, but one in particular stands out – that the reason Chantal panicked and suddenly left the Buckley had something to do with the Luzern photograph.

In the middle of the flight, somewhere over the Great Plains, I stare out the airplane window. It's night. I can make out occasional lights on the prairie far below. I'm filled with excitement for I now see a way to fit the many puzzle pieces together. The Luzern photograph is what binds them. And now I also know my theme: that in the end we are all unknowable.

TWENTY-THREE

Extract from the Unpublished Memoirs of Major Ernst
Fleckstein

(AKA Dr Samuel Foigel)

From the time I arrived in the US things went well for
me.

I enjoyed my work in Washington, my only regret
being that my role as a double agent was quickly curtailed. I
betrayed the Abwehr agents who came to me and felt no
remorse for having done so. There were only three of them,
plus the courier who took their reports, and the radioman in
Baltimore who transmitted them. As it turned out, two of the
three were fabricators, their reports simply elaborated versions
of articles appearing in the press. The third was a misguided
young German-American enlisted man working as a translator
in the Pentagon. In short it was a pathetic apparatus which
my OSS handler, Jim Landon, decided wasn't worth exploiting.

'We'll roll them all up, agents, courier, and transmission
guy,' he told me, 'then put you to work on something useful.'

I was sorry not to have served longer as a double agent as
I had expected to find it a role well suited to my temperament.
And there was something, I admit, a bit glamorous about it
too. But Landon, a forensic psychiatrist, soon placed me on
a team preparing psychological profiles of the Nazi leadership
(Hitler, Bormann, Heydrich, Himmler, Göring, Goebbels, Hess,
Kaltenbrunner, and Rosenberg) with two principal issues in
mind: descriptions of each man's vulnerabilities and informed
speculation as to how each would react to the prospect of
German defeat.

I enjoyed this work, adding what details I knew or had
picked up during my time in Berlin, sometimes even inventing
vignettes when I believed they would be revealing of
character.

Jim and I became friends. He was the only OSS officer, aside from Dulles, who knew my former identity. At first he questioned my ability to practice authentic psychoanalysis, but in time he showed a grudging respect. 'I believe you're good at it . . . whatever *it* is,' he told me, expressing a view then held by many American psychiatrists that Freud's discoveries were speculative and his methods ineffective.

I should add that during this period I enjoyed playing the refugee Jew. In fact I reveled in the role. There was something cleansing about it, I'd almost say cathartic, considering the anti-Semitic venom to which I and all Germans of my generation had been subjected for so many years. I also realized that my story, that of a Jewish psychoanalyst who'd hidden and worked in plain sight in Berlin, caused many of my OSS colleagues to regard me as heroic. In time I was able to do just what my Abwehr handlers had instructed: internalize my legend so deeply that it occurred to me one day, peering at myself in the shaving mirror, that I was no longer *pretending* to be Foigel, that in fact I had *become* him!

In 1947, having attained American citizenship and an impressive ribboned medal for my wartime service, I decided to start my life anew in Cleveland, Ohio. This may seem an odd choice, but several considerations entered in.

Foremost was the encouragement of Jim Landon. Cleveland was his hometown, to which he'd returned after the war. If I also moved there he promised to help me set up my practice by referring patients and encouraging his medical colleagues to do the same. At the time there were very few practicing analysts in the city to meet a relatively high demand by a segment of the educated upper-middle class. This would enable me to quickly build the kind of specialist practice I wanted, catering to the needs of well-to-do neurotic female patients, who, despondent over their roles as suburban mothers and wives, were desperate to find meaning and satisfaction in their lives.

In addition Cleveland was regarded as a friendly city where a newly arrived European Jew would be warmly welcomed. Lastly, I felt it important to choose a locale where I was unlikely to be recognized by anyone who knew me in my past life. Recognition, I knew, was the great danger I might someday face, and for which I was at all times prepared. Thus my task was to reduce the possibility. To achieve this I made a point of keeping a low profile, that of the shy but highly proficient Jewish refugee analyst with the subtle seductive manner and beguiling German accent.

On Jim's advice I rented a suite in an upscale medical building on Carnegie Avenue and fitted it out with modernist Bauhaus-style furniture. My single extravagance was the purchase of a luxurious black leather Mies van der Rohe-designed chaise longue to serve as my analytic couch. I hung my forged diplomas on the wall, placed my name on the lobby roster, and opened for business. Through Jim's referrals and those of his friends I was soon on my way to achieving the American Dream.

In 1958 I married a former patient, Rachel Shapiro. She had come to me six years earlier, a pretty and deeply troubled young grad student at Western Reserve University. She was the daughter of refugee Jewish-Austrian parents who had departed Vienna just prior to the Anschluss. I worked with her intensely over three years, seeing her in session four times a week. Nearly all her relatives had been killed in the Holocaust. She suffered recurring nightmares about a fiery death as well as a generalized debilitating anxiety. Her father, a violin teacher, and her mother, a potter, lived in an unpretentious middle-class house on Cleveland's East Side.

Although we yearned for one another while Rachel was my patient and in fact consummated our relationship many times during those years on my butter-soft black-leather analytic couch, we waited a full year after termination of treatment before going public with our romance.

In June 1960, our only child was born. We named her Eva after Rachel's grandmother. I was then sixty years old.

The same year I purchased a fine Tudor-style house on a quiet street in the upscale suburb of Shaker Heights. Rachel, having attained her graduate degree in microbiology, started work as a researcher in the nephritis lab at Western Reserve

Medical School. We enrolled Eva in the exclusive private Ashley-Burnett school just walking distance from our house. In short all was going well for us. Life was good.

In late July 1966, as I was showing out my last patient of the day, I discovered a not-very-well-dressed gentleman sitting in my waiting room.

I did not recognize him at first but he seemed to know me, coming toward me with a broad ingratiating leer and addressing me by name in German.

'Herr Doktor Foigel?'

Immediately I went on guard.

'I'm sorry,' I said, 'do we know one another?'

'I know you as Dr Ernst Fleckstein. Or are you actually this Foigel person whose nameplate is affixed to the door?'

'Excuse me!'

'You look frightened, dear doctor. As well you should. Your worst nightmare has just arrived.'

At first I thought he might be an Israeli agent or perhaps one of Simon Wiesenthal's boys. But if he were I couldn't imagine what interest he would have in Fleckstein. Although I'd been a party member, I played no role in the Holocaust nor had I ever served in an official capacity in the Third Reich. Except for my regrettable role in the Stempfle assassination (known only to Bormann and Hess) and the intelligence I'd provided concerning the Solf Circle, my hands were relatively clean.

My visitor, as it turned out, was a smalltime blackmailer who had not smoked me out by intellect or detection, but had simply spotted me by coincidence as I, Rachel, and Eva were leaving a movie theater. His name was Karl Gangloff. He'd been the elevator man at 29 Wielandstrasse, the building where Dr Ernst Fleckstein, acting as an Abwehr agent, had practiced psychoanalysis from 1940 to 1943.

I'm certain that in my previous life I would have reacted violently to Gangloff's appearance. Fleckstein the fixer would immediately have begun to calculate how best to kill this smirking little peasant, then devise an efficient way to dispose of his body. But I was Foigel then, and Foigel was a far cooler type, not aggressive or quick to anger, rather a cerebral gentleman in his late sixties with an agreeable low-key manner and a deep understanding of human psychology.

'Come in, Karl,' I told him, beckoning him into my consulting room. 'Make yourself comfortable. Care for a cup of tea?'

As I prepared his libation and engaged him in small talk, I observed him growing increasingly nervous. This was not the reception he'd expected. I was supposed to cower before him, fearful of the damage he could do me, eager to pay whatever outrageous sum he demanded to keep silent about my past.

Finally he interrupted. 'I'm here for money, Herr Fleckstein.' He tried to sound authoritative, but I detected strain in his voice.

'Oh, you're in need of funds?' I asked lightly. 'Well, aren't we all these days?'

Peering around my consulting room, he noted that I seemed to have done quite well for myself. Meantime, he told me, he was totally dependent on relatives, his sister's kids, who'd sponsored his immigration, found a job for him as a janitor in a machine-tools plant, and had taken him into their home. He added that he didn't much like them and they made it clear they felt pretty much the same way.

I told him how sorry I was to hear of his predicament, but that I hadn't a clue why he thought I'd be inclined to help him out.

At this he exploded. 'Don't play games with me!' he shouted. 'Here you are, pretending to be a Jew of all things. I doubt you'll want your patients, friends, wife, daughter, and in-laws to find out who you really are.'

In response I peered at him with great curiosity. 'Who *do* you think I am?'

Oh, he was certain he knew the answer to that! I was Dr Ernst Fleckstein. He'd interacted with me several times a day for four years. We would greet one another when I arrived every morning, and wish one another goodnight every evening when I left for home. There were many important people among my patients – noblewomen and generals' wives. And then suddenly, too suddenly, I closed my practice. People said

I'd been transferred to the Eastern Front. Karl didn't believe it. He'd heard whispers I was a spy. And now here I was, in Cleveland, Ohio, USA, carrying on life as a Jew! Such a transformation! So ingenious! But then he'd always suspected I was a clever fellow.

I let him rant like this for some time. When finally he ran out of gas, I asked if I'd ever treated him poorly.

He was quick to acknowledge I'd always been gracious and polite. 'A damn good tipper too!' He added, 'Unlike some who worked in that building who held their noses in the air like they thought they were better than ordinary folk.'

I gazed at him then, a sad expression on my face. 'You say all that, Karl, and yet here you are trying to extort money from me.'

He hung his head. He was sorry I'd put it that way. Clearly I was rich and he was in need, and he was only suggesting that I share a little of my new-found wealth.

'I gather you want a loan?' I asked.

He snickered. 'If that's how you want to view it.'

I opened my desk drawer, pulled out my checkbook, uncapped my pen prepared to write. I asked him if five hundred dollars would tide him over, mentioning that of course he'd have to repay me when his lot improved.

Again he turned angry, warning me of serious consequences if I failed to pay him a proper sum.

I studied him. 'Why do I feel you're threatening me, Karl? Do you really expect that will get you anywhere?'

'Call it a threat if you like,' he said. 'Meantime you can write me a check for five thousand to start things off.'

I gave him a pitying look, told him I found him pathetic and assured him he'd not get a solitary cent out of me. He glared back as I calmly shut my checkbook.

'And by the way,' I asked, 'why do you keep calling me Fleckstein?'

'Because you *are* Fleckstein!'

I shook my head.

He was insistent. 'You're Fleckstein! I'd know you anywhere.'

I shook my head again. 'You have it all wrong, Karl. I was always Foigel, even back when I *pretended* to be Fleckstein.'

He stared at me in amazement as I explained:

'I was always Samuel Foigel, a Jewish psychoanalyst practicing under the false name of Ernst Fleckstein. That was how I hid myself from little men like you who pranced the streets despising and disparaging Jews, calling us names, beating us up, in many cases killing us. You didn't just greet me when I walked into the building, Karl. You didn't just say, "*Guten Morgen, Herr Doktor.*" No, you clicked your heels and shouted, "*Heil Hitler!*" in my face . . . and despite my disgust, I had to respond in kind to maintain my disguise.'

I smiled at him, explaining that everyone in Cleveland knew my past, that I was even regarded as something of a hero – the Jewish doctor who hid in plain sight in the center of Berlin, the one who treated the wives of some of the highest officials of the Third Reich and then revealed all he could squeeze out of them to Allied Intelligence.

'So, you see,' I told him, 'you have nothing on me . . . but now *I* have something on *you*, a nasty little Nazi who somehow lied his way to America, and is now trying to blackmail one of the few surviving members of the German-Jewish resistance.'

I told him I was recording our conversation, and, depending on his attitude, might turn the tape over to the authorities. On the other hand, I told him, employing a more compassionate tone, *if* I helped him out with the five hundred dollars he'd spat upon a few minutes before, and *if* he humbly thanked me for my generosity and then left my office never to show his piggish little Nazi face to me again, then, maybe, *just maybe*, I might choose to be merciful and recall him as the convivial elevator operator with whom I'd exchanged those thousands of friendly greetings, and not the sniveling little turd of a blackmailer he had today shown himself to be.

Karl stared at me speechless, deflated, confused, all swagger drained away. His eyes shifted in panic as he struggled to rethink his position. He was also to my delight no longer questioning whether I was Fleckstein or Foigel, rather desperately trying to figure out how best to beat a hasty retreat.

I waited him out. Finally he spoke.

'I sincerely apologize, Dr Foigel. I had no idea. None! A

Jew named Foigel pretending to be a Nazi named Fleckstein
– I can hardly believe it.' He turned obsequious. 'It turns out,
sir, you were even more clever than I thought.'

'And the five hundred – I'm still happy to loan it to you,'
I told him, 'providing you give me a proper receipt.'

I could see him recalculating. 'No, sir,' he said, 'I'm going
to pass on that.'

'Really? I thought you were in dire need.'

'I believe I'll be safer if there's no record I approached
you.'

'Seems you're clever too, Karl. You've made a good
decision.'

'I think I'll go now, sir.'

'Excellent idea.'

'You won't be seeing me again.'

'No,' I confirmed, 'I expect not.'

When he reached out his hand to shake mine, I regarded it
as one might regard the paw of a repulsive creature. Then I
turned my back while he slunk his way out my office.

That evening I arrived home triumphant at having finessed
the very situation I'd been dreading so many years. Rachel,
noting my buoyant mood, greeted me with a loving embrace
while little Eva ran to me and threw her arms about my waist.

'You look cheerful,' Rachel said. 'Had a good day?'

'Excellent in every respect,' I assured her.

'Well,' she said, 'better wash up. Dinner will be on the table
in fifteen minutes.'

It's been a year since I last added to this memoir. Every day
since I have counted my good fortune: beautiful loving wife,
charming loving daughter, rewarding professional life helping
others in pain. And even though my doctors now tell me things
look bleak, I thank the gods of destiny (such as they are!) for
these last calm fruitful years.

Three months ago I closed my practice, referring my patients
to several fine local practitioners. Since then I have turned my
attention to literature. I've long wanted to catch up on works
written in my native language by the authors Frau Lou
mentioned during my 1934 visit: Heinrich Mann, Bertolt

Brecht, Robert Musil, Erich Maria Remarque, Arthur Schnitzler, Ernst Toller, Franz Werfel, as well as others with whom she had both loving, angry, and casual relationships: Rainer Maria Rilke, Frank Wedekind, August Strindberg, Hugo von Hofmannsthal, Gerhart Hauptmann, Stefan Zweig . . . and of course the great philosopher/poet/psychologist Friedrich Nietzsche.

Nietzsche wrote: 'To see others suffer does one good, to make others suffer even more. This is a hard saying but an ancient, mighty, all-too-human principle. Without cruelty there is no festival.'

This from a man who fell madly for Lou Salomé, and who, upon being rejected by her, created an aesthetic of human cruelty.

I have lived in a violent cruel age. I believe my experiences as a matrimonial investigator and later as Bormann's fixer gave me insights into the dark side of human nature, insights that have served me well in my career as an autodidactic psycho-analyst. From looking into the hard eyes of Bormann, the cold cruel eyes of Hitler, and then the knowing vulnerable eyes of Lou Salomé, I was able to shift my life from one dominated by selfish and amoral narcissism to one touched by kindness and compassion.

I have set down these memories of my life in an attempt to clarify my experiences and put them into perspective. As the reader can tell, many of the events described herein are entangled with what is now regarded as the great nightmare of the twentieth century. This memoir is not an apologia. I make no pleas for forgiveness for past actions, nor do I claim to feel great remorse for anything I have done. My life has been what it has been, it has now mostly passed, and today suffering a grave illness and with the end of life in sight, I have chosen to set these memories down in writing for the benefit of my soon-to-be widowed wife, my beloved daughter, and whatever progeny may come after.

With these words I end my chronicle.

TWENTY-FOUR

The day after my return from New York I set up the three versions of the Luzern photo side by side on my desk: the original showing Lou Salomé with Nietzsche and Rée; the copy Eva gave me of the supplicatory version drawn by Hitler; and Chantal's amazing glamorous reenactment photograph. Now sitting at my computer working on my Chantal project I often turn to this trio and try to puzzle them out.

It's essential to find out what frightened Chantal so much she felt she had to flee the building. To find an ending for my play I must know who killed Chantal and why.

When I'm not at my desk I take runs around Lake Merritt, wander downtown Oakland thinking up scenes, and enjoy evening trysts with Scarpaci at his apartment in Temescal. On Wednesday, the three 'Luzern images' in hand, I take the bus to Berkeley to see Dr Maude.

I lay out the three pictures in turn on the small table between our chairs. I can see she's fascinated as she picks up each one and examines it.

'Want to hear what I think?' she asks.

I tell her of course I do, that her brilliant Freudian interpretation of the original Luzern image is the prism through which I now view it.

She nods. 'Nietzsche set up the Luzern photo as a kind of memorandum of their chastity/study arrangement. It was his vision of what he hoped would be Lou's role in his and Paul Rée's lives. As for the young Hitler, since you tell me the photo was widely known we can safely assume he saw it, and, based on this drawing, fetishized it. He used it as a matrix for a drawing he presented to Lou to express his desire for subjugation. As for Chantal's version, you use the word reenactment, but I see it more as an *hommage*. Like Hitler, she uses the

Luzern photograph as a source of inspiration, creating an image by which she claims for herself the role of dominatrix.

'Each artist was telling a story and each had a particular audience in mind. For Nietzsche it was the other two actors in his drama . . . and probably no one else. He couldn't have anticipated that the image would become famous. For Hitler the intended audience could only have been Lou. He was communicating something so personal and shameful he couldn't bring himself to put it into words. Years later, having become the all-powerful Führer, he couldn't bear the thought that there existed a drawing documenting this youthful masochistic fantasy. That's why he had Bormann send Eva's father to try to buy it back.'

'What about Chantal – what was her story, her audience?'

'You say she put it on her website for all to see, but I think her real audience was herself. Her photo was a way to identify with Lou, whom she greatly admired, and at the same time assert her own identity. It's very controlled and beautifully done. She certainly had talent.'

Later in session, after I describe more of what Eva shared with me, Dr Maude expresses disgust regarding the motives and methods of Quentin Soames.

'Freud had his faults,' she tells me. 'He could be controlling and dogmatic. He played his followers against one another and he harbored a substantial amount of anger. All this is well known. But I'm offended that someone as mediocre as Soames dares to think he can topple one of the giants of the twentieth century.'

She tells me how, when she visited the Freud Museum in Hampstead, she was moved to tears. It wasn't just the ambience of Freud's study, she says, but her knowledge that the process, which she'd made her life's work, had been developed in that room set up exactly as in Vienna.

'It was there,' she tells me, 'that feelings and urges that mystified people since the dawn of history were finally uncovered and explained.'

I ask her what she thinks really went on between Freud and Lou.

'Based on their letters, they regarded one another with great respect. There was never a question of becoming lovers. Still it was Lou's late-in-life association and friendship with Freud, in addition to her youthful liaisons with Nietzsche and Rilke, that place her at the center of the intellectual and literary culture of her time. This plus her own achievements makes her a commanding figure.' She peers at me. 'We've talked a lot about Chantal's obsession with Lou. What are your feelings about her?'

'Admiration, respect, fascination,' I tell her, 'though perhaps not so much as was felt by Chantal.' I also admit I've considered what it would be like to be the lover of a succession of great men. 'I don't think I'd be a happy muse. The Great Man sees his brilliance reflected in her eyes. Not my kind of role. I don't want to be anyone's accessory.'

'And your erotic dreams about Chantal – what do you think they mean?'

I tell her that since I'm having really good sex with Scarpaci, I don't think of them so much as lesbian fantasies as attempts to seal a connection with my subject.

Dr Maude likes that. Her last words at end of session: 'I felt we were drifting, Tess, but based on what you just said, I think we're back on track. This obsession with Chantal – at first I was worried for you. It seemed too intense. But now I think it's helping you work through your issues. And because of that I think this play you're working on may be the most powerful thing you'll have done.'

Tonight over dinner Scarpaci tells me he feels stymied on the investigation. He hasn't ruled out Josh Garske or Carl Hughes despite an inability to develop evidence against either of them.

'I blew it with Josh,' he tells me. 'He knows I suspect him. Now he's paranoid and won't talk to me. Meantime Hughes has hired a lawyer who won't allow him to submit to more interviews.' He shakes his head. 'I've eliminated Kurt and the killer of the domme in East San Jose. Which leaves me wondering about Chantal's other clients. Like if she flipped the script on some guy, and he couldn't take it.'

Later we're lying in his bed. We've finished making love. He's cupping me and gently stroking my breasts. It's cold outside, the kind of chill that settles upon the East Bay in August. Scarpaci gets up and walks naked to the window. His body looks good from the back, lean and well shaped. He shuts the window, turns, stands facing me against the glass. Ambient light from outside limns his form.

'There's a stack of open case files on my desk,' he says. 'Maybe I want to solve this one too much. Could be that's blinding me to something obvious.' He shakes his head then makes me a promise: 'I won't give up on this. Sooner or later we'll get a break. Or maybe I'll suddenly see the light.'

Tonight, sitting at my computer, my eyes stray to my inkblots, then to Queen of Swords resting against Chantal's St. Andrew's Cross, then to the trio of images on my desk.

Each one tells a story. And they're all coded images, I think.

Eleven this morning: I've been up for hours, have taken a run, am now working at my computer.

The buzzer breaks my concentration. It's Clarence. Seems there's water seeping into the unit below. He wants to come up and check my pipes. I tell him I'm working but of course he can come up and do whatever needs to be done. I go back to my computer. I'm working on a scene between Chantal and Lou, a dream sequence in which they meet and make love. It's based, on my erotic dreams about Chantal. I'm just at the point where Lou draws Chantal to her and kisses her, when Clarence knocks at the door.

I open it to find him wearing a pair of bibbed coveralls and hauling a bag of plumber's tools. Motioning him in I tell him I've been meaning to thank him for tipping me off about the green hoodie guy.

'Yeah, him . . . haven't seen him around lately.'

'That's because I took care of him.'

Clarence raises his eyebrows to show he's impressed. 'Chantal's chariot looks right at home here,' he says, pointing. 'Actually she had it angled a little different. May I?'

He goes to it, moves it slightly.

'It was more like this. When she wanted to use it in a scene, she'd have the guy pull it out to the center of the room then play horsey with him. What she called equestrian games.'

'You seem to know a lot about her scenes, Clarence.'

'She liked telling me stuff.' He giggles. 'Maybe she thought it would turn me on. Anyway, I'm here about the leak. I'll check out the kitchen and bath.'

He goes to the galley kitchen then kneels before the cupboard beneath the sink. I go back to work. Later I hear him go into the bathroom. After a few minutes he returns to the main loft.

'Nothing serious,' he says. 'Needed tightening, that's all.' He peers over my shoulder. At first I'm annoyed, thinking he's looking at my screen. I save and clear, then turn to discover he's gazing at my trio of Luzern images.

'Interesting picture,' he says, pointing at Chantal's *hommage* photo. 'She looks so great there, beautiful and commanding. Any chance you could make me a copy? I'd like to have something to remember her by.'

When I run into Josh in the lobby, we nod politely, ask one another how things are going, but avoid any real exchange.

Today, ascending together in the elevator, he suddenly turns to me.

'I loved Chantal,' he says. 'I never told her, but I'm sure she knew.'

'Wow, Josh! That's a big thing to share. What brings this on?'

'Scarpaci suspects me, but, see, I could never harm her. She meant too much to me. And now that she's gone I feel empty whenever I come into the building. I'm thinking of moving. I know I won't find as good a deal anywhere else, but every time I pass through the lobby I feel the darkness.' He looks down. The elevator has reached his floor. 'Sorry to burden you. Guess I oughta see a shrink.'

I'm moved, but the elevator door rolls closed before I can tell him so.

Later, thinking about what he said, I phone him to ask if I can come down and talk.

'Sure,' he says. 'I'm just sitting here sketching.'

He leaves his door open for me. I find him lying on his couch, sketchbook by his side.

I tell him I hope he doesn't move out. 'You'll probably feel haunted no matter where you go.'

'I know it's not the building. But sometimes it feels like it.'

'What made you decide to tell me that in the elevator?'

'The elevator reminds me of her. I don't know how many times we rode it together giggling at the weird way the lights dim between floors and the quirky way it jerks to a stop. Since you're writing about her I wanted you to know how I felt.' He peers at me. 'Are you writing in a little part for me?'

'Want me to?'

He nods. I don't commit myself but tell him it's a possibility. Then I ask if he'd mind if I worked his Queen of Swords portrait into my script.

'Not at all,' he says. 'Consider it on semi-permanent loan. If you get a production use it as a prop. Maybe someone'll see it and be impressed.' He sits up. 'Something I've been meaning to tell you, Tess. What I do, working in other artists' styles – there are serious people who consider that a legitimate art form. There've been a number of great art forgers – van Meegeren, David Stein, and lately a Chinese guy, Pei-Shen Qian, who did great Pollocks, Rothkos, and Klines. I'm good but not in their league. Stein could knock out a Picasso, a Chagall, or a Miro in an hour. When a gallery gave him a show, "Forgeries by Stein", the New York State Attorney General brought suit to have it closed. The judge ruled for Stein. In his decision he wrote: "His work in perfecting the style of the masters may properly be ascribed to that special talent with which true artists are uniquely endowed." In other words Stein deserved respect for his ability to work in other artists' styles. He'd only be guilty of a crime if he forged their signatures on his paintings.'

I find it sad that Josh sees himself as a B-level art forger and finds it necessary to quote a judge to validate his work. I'm thinking of some way to reassure him, tell him how good his tarot queens are and how he should do more work like that, when, out of thin air, he brings up something that totally surprises me: Chantal's request that he forge a suite of erotic drawings by Hitler.

'She showed me what she said was a photocopy of a Hitler

drawing. She told me it belonged to a friend. She assured me it was genuine, but, because of the erotic content, no expert would authenticate it. She wanted me to produce others in the same style so that it would seem like a trove of them had surfaced. I was struck by how close it was to the photograph she took of me and the other guy yoked to her chariot.'

'Did you make the drawings for her?'

He shakes his head. 'Couldn't. Told her there was nothing in her friend's drawing I could copy, no defining style I could fasten on to. She was disappointed. She even muttered something to the effect that she'd thought she was lucky to know a real live art forger, and how sad that I couldn't come through for her. This was just before I went down to LA to see my kids. I was upset. I didn't expect her to react this way. So on my way out I left a note under her door telling her I'd try to make the drawings when I got back. But then when I came back . . .' He shakes his head. 'Well . . . she was gone.' I see tears forming in his eyes. 'If I'd drawn them for her maybe she'd still be alive.'

Back upstairs I immediately phone Scarpaci. He's less moved by Josh's feelings of guilt than annoyed by the way he oozes out info when it suits him.

'Sounds like Chantal decided he was useless,' he says.

I disagree. 'Based on everything I've learned about her she wasn't a user. Plus they were friends. But suppose she had a buyer lined up, someone she was trying to persuade to purchase Eva's drawing?'

'Seems like a long shot,' Scarpaci says. 'Why don't you check with Eva, see if she knows anything about a buyer.'

Early this morning I Skype Eva in Vienna, our first contact since we parted in New York.

She shakes her head when I tell her what Chantal asked Josh to do.

'Yeah,' she says, 'I knew about that. Chantal, bless her, had this crazy notion that my father's Hitler drawing would be more credible if it were part of a series. I reminded her Dad's drawing could well be a forgery, that there's plenty in his memoir that defies belief. But if it *did* turn out to be real (as I now know from Lou's letter to Freud it is) it wouldn't be helpful to surround it with forgeries. She saw my point, admitted it was a harebrained scheme, and promised to drop it.'

Eva rolls her eyes. 'Maybe she decided to try it anyway. Since she was friends with a forger . . . why not. I met Josh when I visited last year. Nice man. I liked his Queen of Swords portrait a lot. I'm sorry he's feeling guilty, but he was right to turn her down. Like she said, it wasn't one of her better ideas . . .'

Hearing this I decide not to tell her Josh is Scarpaci's prime suspect. But I do ask if she thinks Chantal was seeking a buyer for the drawing.

Again Eva shakes her head. 'She never said anything about that, and I'm sure she would if she had someone in mind.'

I'm running every day now, my only exercise since I quit San Pablo Martial Arts. And though I've set aside for now my desire to learn to fight, I miss the cardio workouts, shadow-boxing, jump-roping, and slugging the bags.

Until I find a new gym, I decide to continue my kickboxing workouts at home. I go to a sporting goods store on College Avenue, buy a forty-pound heavy bag, then summon Josh to install it.

He hangs in my bedroom then, amused at the notion of me taking out my aggressions on a dummy, refuses to leave till I put on a little boxing exhibition.

'I love to watch warrior women,' he says, then suddenly his eyes turn sad. 'I'm sorry, Tess. Gotta go.'

'Hey, what's the matter?'

'This kind of joshing reminds me of Chantal, the way we used to kid around.'

This morning, studying the three pictures on my desk, I recall what Dr Maude said: that each of the images tells a story. Each, I believe, also contains a secret embedded consciously or unconsciously by its maker. Nietzsche's secret is complex. Hitler's is transparent. Chantal's is mysterious. I believe the painter René Magritte put it well: 'Everything we see hides another thing. We always want to see what is hidden.'

Dr Maude wants me to concentrate on resolving my anger toward my father.

'He died before you came to terms with him. He left you with just that one decent message. Urging you to live an honest life – that was out of character for him, but my guess is he was sincere. He was a psychopath, the sort of toxic person who can't manage life unless he lies. But even psychopaths have moments of clarity. He looked at you, had an insight, and, that single time, shared it with you. That's the heritage he left you, and that, I think, is what you must hold on to. Recall his lies and scams and you'll be left with bitterness.'

I'm writing scenes I've imagined between Lou and young Hitler, leading up to his presentation of his drawing. I've decided to set them at the kind of coffeehouse depicted in the book in which Chantal filed Eva's love letters. The phone rings. It's Scarpaci.

'Free for an early dinner?'

'I'm working, but sure. What's going on?'

'Something could be about to break. Meet me at six at Tribune Tavern and I'll fill you in.' He pauses. 'By the way, how much rent do you pay?'

'There's a non sequitur. Seventeen-fifty including utilities.'

'Terrific deal! You got about fifteen hundred square feet. Market rate for a live/work loft top floor of a historical downtown building should run close to four grand. I'm thinking why so low? I'm also thinking why was Chantal in such a hurry to give up her business there and move out? Was she afraid of someone who knew where she lived? She could have put in a top-of-the-line security system. But what if it had to do with someone in the building? That points back to Josh. But again I ask myself – why's the rent so low? What's going on in the Buckley I don't know about?'

'Talk to Clarence. His aunt owns the place. He manages it for her.'

'I'll do that. What about the other tenants?'

I tell him the little I know. Josh is the only one I've gotten close to. I've seen the others, nodded to them in the lobby, exchanged niceties with a few. I tell him there're a number of surly Chinese businessmen who have offices on the lower floors, several of whom might be sleazy. There're also lawyers and accountants, a Vietnamese woman who imports ceramic elephants, and several artists and craftspeople in the residential lofts, types Clarence claims he likes because, as he puts it, 'they class up the joint.'

'I wonder what sort of rent those arty types pay.'

'*Arty!* Please, Scarpaci! That's what people say when they want to put someone down because they think she undeservedly regards herself as an artist.'

'Sorry. I should have said artists and craftspeople.'

'You're forgiven. As for rent, Clarence claims he sets the amount on how much he wants a prospective tenant in the building.'

'Strange way to do business. On the other hand, if I were a building manager and a very attractive young woman wanted to rent a loft, I might be inclined to give her a break.'

'You're thinking of Chantal?'

'I'm thinking of both of you.'

'Is this what you meant when you said you were on to something?'

'There could be a connection.'

'Why so mysterious?'

'We know Chantal was scared, but she wouldn't say why. We also know she was in a big hurry to get out of there. So I ask myself: was there something going on in the building that drove her out?'

I get to Tribune Tavern early. It's a ground-floor restaurant in the old Oakland Tribune Tower, always busy, filled with judges, politicians, journalists, and city administrators greeting one another as they come and go. I grab a corner table then wait for Scarpaci. I feel a little thrill when I see him come through the door then make his way gracefully across the room. When he's seated and looks at me, I notice a sparkle in his eyes.

'You look pretty pleased with yourself,' I tell him.

He admits he is. 'Ramos picked up a perp who claims he knows something about quote that-whip-lady-murder-thing unquote. This perp's a wanna-be gangsta rap artist. He wants to exchange his info for a pass on a manslaughter charge.'

'Can he really get off in return for info?'

'That's what his lawyer and the ADA are negotiating. If the info's good the ADA might reduce the charge, but he's reluctant because most of the time the "info" turns out to be bogus. It's a nasty world out there.'

I find this upsetting, but Scarpaci, I note, is still smiling.

'I still don't get why you're so cheerful.'

'Don't know about cheerful. Hopeful maybe. This is the first time we've heard anything about Chantal from the street.' He pauses. 'Remember Nadia, my *fortochnitsa*?'

'Your electronic wizard – how could I forget her?'

'I'm sending her out to do a little black-bag job for me tonight. If she finds what I'm hoping I may be able to get a warrant and wrap this thing up.'

He refuses to say more. 'Call me superstitious, but I'd rather wait till everything falls into place.'

I'm back at work writing my Lou/Hitler scenes, when I decide to take a break. I go into my bedroom, put on gloves, and go to work on my new heavy bag. After a fifteen-minute workout I return to the main room to continue writing. As always before I start, I peer at the three pictures on my desk.

Looking at them I ask myself: *What could Chantal have meant when she told Eva she was scared because of something having to do with the Luzern photograph? What's in it? What's not in it? Think like Dr Maude*, I urge myself. *Think psychoanalytically!*

There's nothing in the Luzern photograph that could have scared her. It was taken over a hundred thirty years ago. Yet Eva remembered asking her 'The Luzern?' to which Chantal responded 'In a way.'

It's then that I get an idea for the final scene in my play – I'll step forward, address the audience, tie the three rendi-

tions of the Luzern photograph together. I'll describe the way
they're linked, how the bizarre late nineteenth-century photograph, appropriated and twisted by Hitler in 1913, came to
obsess a twenty-first-century dominatrix to the extent she
decided to reinterpret it.

Suddenly another idea snaps into place: *What if Chantal
didn't mean the original Luzern picture? What if she was
referring to her own hommage photo?*

As I ponder that I'm hit by a third idea, one so powerful I
immediately pick up the phone and call Carl Hughes.

He's annoyed to hear from me. 'My lawyer doesn't want
me to talk to you guys.'

'I'm not a cop, Carl. I need to talk to you about those
blackmail pictures. This could be important.'

'Important to you maybe. Why to me?'

'Because it could hold the answer to why Chantal was
killed.'

'I didn't appreciate the way you set me up, Tess. You know
the saying – fooled once, shame on you, fooled twice . . .'

Before I can tell him I'm sorry he feels I fooled him, he
starts telling me how the pressure from Scarpaci has turned
his life upside-down.

'My wife made me go into therapy. Now she's put me out
of the house. I'm living at a hotel. I'm distracted at work. My
lawyer's costing me a fortune. Everything's fucked up because
I was stupid. I should never have gotten involved with a woman
like that . . .'

'I don't think you were stupid, Carl. You had desires. You
acted on them. I think that's brave.' I pause. 'I really need to
talk to you about those pictures. Name a place and I'll jump
in a cab. I can be in San Francisco in twenty minutes.' Silence.
'Hey, come on, meet with me.'

Finally he relents. He tells me to meet him at a bar near
his hotel.

'I'm sitting here now,' he tells me, 'guzzling bourbon and
feeling sorry for myself.'

I spot him soon as I walk in, slouched at a small table in a
corner, unshaven, wearing a faded gray T-shirt, looking less the

confident besuited museum curator I met in Oakland than a scruffy inebriated loser reveling in loneliness and rejection.

Making my way to him, I scan the place. It's a shabby bar with barely any customers. A middle-aged guy perched on a bar stool is talking to the dyke bartender. She wears a cowboy hat and fringed leather vest. There's a poster for an old John Wayne film on the wall.

'Hi, Carl.' I sit down opposite. 'Thanks for meeting me.'

'Yeah . . . sure . . . So what's on your mind, Tess? What's so damn important?'

It takes me a while to get him talking about the photo session he did with Chantal and Josh. He tells the same story as Josh about the first set not working out because of Chantal's annoyance with the see-through hoods, and how she then buckled them into black-leather fetish helmets.

'Those photos you got in the mail – they were from the first set, right?'

'Had to be,' he says. 'The images were fuzzy but I recognized myself.'

'Fuzzy?'

'They seemed like blow-ups.' He pauses. 'There was something off about them too. The angle – it didn't seem right. Chantal's camera was on a tripod at waist level. But those pictures looked like they were taken from higher up.'

Thinking immediately of Chantal's ceiling cameras, I ask: 'How much higher?'

'Like maybe she was standing above us. I figure she must have taken them with a cellphone, snapped them off when we weren't looking. When I saw them I thought it was part of the blackmail game I wanted her to play with me. But when I called her she denied she'd sent them. When I described them to her, she got really upset, claimed she hadn't taken any such pictures then hung up. Never heard from her again.' He stares at me. 'If she didn't send them who did? The other guy? Why?' He seems to have sobered up. 'What would anyone have to gain? There were never any blackmail demands.'

'Don't know, Carl. Maybe someone just wanted to fuck with you. She had security cameras in the ceiling. I think that's how they were taken. The way I reconstruct it, soon as you described those pictures she realized someone was using her own security cameras to spy on her. I think that must be what freaked her out, caused her to sell off her stuff in a hurry and move out of the building.'

He looks stunned. 'So when she said she didn't send them to me she was telling me the truth?'

'Sure looks that way . . .'

I take the BART back to the East Bay. I feel terrible about what I've discovered. Everything now points to Josh, Scarpaci's main suspect, the guy I've been defending all along. It still seems implausible. Josh told me he loved Chantal . . . but he's told me many fibs along the way. I don't know what to believe. I do know I have to phone Scarpaci, tell him Carl's so-called blackmail shots were likely taken from one of Chantal's security cameras. Let him figure out the rest. It's possible, I know, that someone else had access to Chantal's feed. And even if Josh did send Carl those pictures that doesn't necessarily mean he killed her. He was, I remind myself, down in LA when she disappeared.

I walk from the BART station back to the Buckley. Tonight the heat feels oppressive. I notice black herons moving restlessly in the yucca trees. Hearing cawing I look up, spot seagulls circling over downtown like giant black bats.

The lobby at the Buckley is deserted. The Art Deco décor – yellow and black tile floor, interlocking brass-work on the elevator surround – glows in the dim light cast by the geometric sconces and reverse pyramid chandelier. Everything's lustrous. The lobby as always projects an aura of faded luxury.

I glance at the concierge's podium where Clarence stands in the morning exchanging greetings with arriving office tenants.

I ring for the elevator. It arrives with a jerk. The door rolls open. The ornate interior is brightly lit. I push the button for the penthouse. The elevator gives a little shake then starts its ascent. I lean against the back wall anticipating the weird way the lights will dim then brighten as it passes every floor.

I get off at the penthouse, peer around to make sure no

one's lingering in the hall, unlock my door, enter, close it, and double lock it from inside.

I pause in the foyer, scan the books that once belonged to Chantal, glance up at the Lou Salomé quote over the archway, step into the main loft, and switch on the lights.

It's then I see Clarence sitting still as a mannequin in the middle of my couch.

At that moment everything comes clear. Clarence somehow got access to Chantal's camera feed. When Carl described the so-called blackmail pictures to her, Chantal understood this. *Of course that scared her! How could it not? Of course she had to move!*

This revelation frightens me. Looking at Clarence sitting there I start to shake.

'Hey, Tess.' His tone lacks any trace of deference.

I warn myself to stay cool, hide my fear. He's the building manager. He has keys. *But what the hell is he doing in here at midnight?*

'I understand you and the detective are seeing a lot of each other,' he says.

'You understand that? Really?' I add a little edge to my voice. 'Tell you what I don't understand, Clarence – what the fuck are you doing sitting here in my living room in the dark?'

He raises his eyebrows. 'I came up to do more work on your pipes then decided to take a breather. That's when I noticed the manuscript on your desk. Read through it.' He gestures toward my printout beside him. 'Interesting project. Chantal was an interesting woman. Only problem, Tess – you got her all wrong.'

'All right, Clarence, that's enough,' I tell him, gathering up my courage. 'You had no right to look through my manuscript and you've no right to be in here. I want you to go.' I pull out my cellphone. 'I'm calling 911.'

'Don't do that, Tess.' The formerly over-accommodating building manager now addresses me like a drill sergeant. 'Put down the phone and sit,' he orders with a strong undercurrent of threat. Fearing what he might do, I put my phone in my pocket and take a seat.

'Chantal wasn't at all like the woman in your play,' he says, pushing my pages contemptuously aside. 'I knew her, watched her, saw everything she did, spent hours monitoring her sessions. It wasn't hard. I came in here one day when she was out, played around with her computer, discovered the software that controlled her security cameras. A few key strokes and I fixed things so I received the feed whether she thought she was streaming it or not. Her fault, if you think about – she's the one had those cameras installed. What'd she expect me to do when I found out about them? Of course I watched her. I watched her for hours at a time.'

'She didn't know?' I ask, trying to keep my voice steady.

'Oh, she *knew*. She sensed it just like you did. That's why you taped over the lenses – to taunt me, right?' He giggles. 'You caught me watching you through the skylight too. You *knew* it was me. Who the hell else could it have been?'

His tone is mocking. I'm seriously frightened now. I know it's unlikely he'd tell me these things then just walk away. He also knows I'm allied with Scarpaci. There's a steely menace in his manner, the kind of intensity you see in the chilly eyes of a snake preparing to strike. My only hope, I know, is to stay cool and keep him talking until I can find a way to change the dynamic.

You're an actress! Turn the tables! Improvise!

'You should be careful what you say to me,' I warn him. 'I wouldn't want to see you mess up your life. If you tell me anything that implicates you in Chantal's death that could put you in a very bad light.'

He appears to be listening, but doesn't react. There's a distant look in his eyes as if he's thinking about something else. Then he starts speaking in a strange otherworldly voice, the kind of rhapsodic monotone an actor might use to deliver a soliloquy.

'She was amazing, you know? So powerful . . . yet touched by grace. We talked a lot. She told me things about her clients, intimate things, their quirks and fantasies. She liked feeling their need. "That's the best part," she told me, "feeling how desperately they need me and knowing how well I can sate their desires, toy with them, tantalize them, show them who they really are. Then afterwards look into their eyes and see their gratitude for everything I've given them . . .'"

He continues like this, speaking dreamily about Chantal and the secrets she shared with him, the things he saw her do, the vulnerability he sensed in her when she thought she was alone. But *he* was watching. He saw *everything*. He knew *everything* about her, the hard dominant side she showed her clients and the soft needy side she kept concealed.

'. . . she talked to herself, paced the room, mumbling like I've seen you do when you're rehearsing . . .'

Seen me! Fuck!

'. . . her power thing – most of that was an act. Good one too. She knew what she was doing, knew exactly what buttons to push to bring a client to his knees. It was thrilling to watch her take control, bend those guys to her will. I considered asking her for a session. I thought I might enjoy being in her power. Temporarily, just for an hour or two. But I knew if I did everything would change. She had plenty of slaves. She needed me as a friend. She knew I cared for her, watched out for her, protected her. Josh thought he played that role, but I was her *real* protector. Then I got bored, decided to play a little game with her, mix things up a bit. I'd heard that guy, Carl, beg her to blackmail him, and the scornful way she refused. So I thought, OK, that's what he wants, let's give him a taste of it, shake him up, put a little scare into the guy and see how they both react. Big mistake! Didn't think it through. Soon as he described those pictures to her she knew they'd been taken by her cameras even when she thought she'd turned them off. I watched her as she went straight to her laptop and trashed the monitoring software. That must be when she decided to move. I understood I was going to lose her. I knew too there was nothing I could do about it . . . and, the worst part, that it was all my fault.'

He stares at me. 'I know you figured some of this out. I've heard you and the detective talking . . .'

Heard us! Did he come up here after Nadia swept the place and bug it again? If so then he knows everything we know, including our conversations about why Chantal was in such a rush to leave.

He seems to be in a trance state now, lost in a reverie. Observing him closely, I think about escape. Can I make a run for it? Since I double-locked the door, he'll be on me before I can unlatch it. He's not a big man, but he's strong. I remember the way his muscles bulged when he delivered the chariot.

I peer around the loft looking for something to hit him with, something that will stun him long enough for me to get away. Smash the glass top of my coffee table then stab him with a shard? Make a dash for the kitchen, grab a chef's knife, then lunge at him if he tries to stop me leaving?

I feel my heart pounding. Suddenly I get an idea. What if I *become* Chantal, *become* the dominatrix he watched, the one he longed for from a distance because he was too cowardly to ask her for a session?

Try it! Act it out!

'Stand, Clarence!' I order, standing up myself. I give him a menacing look. 'You've been nasty. You know how I treat nasty boys. I punish them.'

He stares at me, startled. For a moment I'm afraid he's going to laugh. But to my surprise he obeys, stands, hangs his head. Without knowing whether he's faking, merely humoring me, I decide to take my domination act as far as I can.

'Nasty boys who spy on ladies always get found out. You've been in here when I've been out, haven't you, Clarence?' He nods. 'You've probably sniffed around in my lingerie drawer.' He grins. 'I'm going to punish you for that. Go to the cell.' He hesitates. I raise my voice. 'You heard me! Move!' He shakes his head. 'You dare to defy me, Clarence!' And then, before he can answer, 'Know what I think? I think you *want* to be punished, but you're too chickenshit to admit it.'

I grab hold of his arm, pull him forward, then get behind him and shove him roughly toward the jail alcove.

'You're going into the cell. I'm going to lock you up in there so you can think about all the nasty things you've done and how sorry you are for having done them. Before I let you out you're going to apologize for your transgressions.'

I push him hard again, get him almost to the cell door. I pull it open then push him forward.

Just two more steps and I'll have him caged!

The intercom sounds. The buzz jolts Clarence. He turns. His trance is broken. He peers at me, eyes cold and menacing.

'Who's that?' he demands.

'Scarpaci.'

'Don't answer!'

'He knows I'm here. He's got a key.'

Clarence grabs hold of me. I feel his strength as he shoves me backward.

'Go to the intercom. Tell him you're working. Tell him to come back later.' He puts me in a chokehold. 'Do it or I'll snap your neck.'

I nod, feign weakness, go slack, pretend to stumble.

I start whimpering. 'My ankle gave out.'

Then, just as he slightly loosens his grip, I smash my elbow hard into his stomach and break loose. He stumbles back into the cell doorway. We're facing one another. I assume a Muay Thai stance. As he's about to lunge toward me, I kick out violently, catch him hard in the groin with the tip of my shoe. As he starts to crumble, I clobber him with a knuckle punch to the face. Then as blood spurts from his nose, I twirl, jab my elbow hard into the side of his head, step out of the cell, slam the door, lock it, and pull the key.

Bleeding, screaming with pain, he rolls on the cell floor.

Suddenly calm, I turn my back, go to the front door and open it.

Nadia's standing there. I look at her and start to shake.

'You didn't answer so I came up,' she says. 'Detective Scarpaci sent me to change the locks.'

I'm still trembling when Scarpaci shows up. The last few minutes have been wild. A herd of cops came in, cuffed Clarence, and dragged him off. Now that they're gone Scarpaci holds me tight, working to calm me as I quiver in his arms. After I settle down, he listens carefully as I repeat everything Clarence said.

I tell him too that I don't know where I found the nerve to go on attack.

'My kickboxing skills are pretty meager,' I tell him.

'Maybe not so meager,' he says. 'You messed him up pretty good. You have fighting spirit, Tess. Fight-or-flight – your systems get elevated and you become a fighting animal. Now you're coming down from it. It takes a while.'

He insists I lie back. He warns it may take hours for my pulse and blood pressure to return to normal, and that I'll likely experience headaches and fatigue.

'It'll pass,' he promises. 'You've got a good shrink. She'll know how to treat it.'

He leans down, kisses me, then tells me about his arrangement with Nadia.

'I had her do something illegal tonight – slip into the building, locate the Wi-Fi router, hack into it and then into Clarence's computer. I began to wonder about him when I asked myself why Chantal felt she had to flee the building. If Clarence was spying on her and she found out, that would be a very good reason. Nadia called me an hour ago. She discovered a huge amount of video of Chantal doing sessions. That's when I told her to come up here and change your locks.'

He shakes his head. 'Once I made a deal with the ADA and the perp's attorney, the perp squawked. He'd heard on the street that a pair of Chinese gang boys were boasting that a couple months ago they got a call to go over to the Buckley, pick up a body, and dump it. Ramos is out looking for them. When he finds them I'm pretty sure they'll rat Clarence out.'

All this was happening while I was talking to Carl Hughes! When I tell Scarpaci how it hit me the so-called blackmail photographs sent to Carl could be the key, we marvel that we were each closing in on Clarence from different angles at the same time.

'Actually,' I tell him, 'Carl's description of the blackmail photos pretty much convinced me they'd been sent by Josh. The moment I saw Clarence sitting here in the dark I knew it had to be him.'

Scarpaci congratulates me for coaxing Carl into describing the photos in detail.

'I should've done that,' he says. 'Chantal was smart. Soon as Carl described those pictures she realized someone had access to her cameras. Clarence had keys to her loft so he was the obvious suspect.'

Looking at him I sense there's more. When he hesitates, I insist he tell me everything. He peers at me, then shakes his head.

'Clarence had video of you from your early days in the loft. Good thing Lynx told you about those cameras and you taped them off.'

Hearing this I start to shake again.

'Hey, we caught the guy.' He comforts me. 'It's over now.'

It's been four days since I found Clarence on my couch. Scarpaci tells me how yesterday, with his lawyer present, Clarence calmly told his story.

'He'd been snooping on Chantal, she found out, moved out of the building, then came back two nights later because she forgot something, maybe her strongbox. She found Clarence sitting in the dark in the loft the way you found him when you came back from meeting Carl. She confronted him, accused him of spying on her and sending the blackmail photos to Carl. When he claimed he didn't know what she was talking about, she took a swing at him, he deflected it, they fought, and during the struggle he strangled her.

'Clear case of self-defense according to his lawyer. But then Clarence panicked, called a Chinese drug dealer he knew, who sent over a pair of goons to haul off Chantal's body. Meantime Clarence, on his own fight-or-flight high, found her motorcycle parked outside, drove it to the bay, dumped it, then using a room key he'd found in her pocket, went to her hotel, cleaned out her room, and brought everything, including her laptop, back to the Buckley and stashed it in a closet behind his office.

'That's his story,' Scarpaci tells me. 'Maybe true, maybe not. He strikes me as more of a psycho-voyeur than a stone-cold killer. But once he got his hands on her neck, he couldn't stop. We found all Chantal's stuff in that closet plus hundreds of stills of her pinned to the walls. I felt like I was in one of those TV cop shows where the detectives break into the room behind the false wall where the weird killer's set up a shrine. You've seen the scene a dozen times. The detective partners stare in wonder, then the young one turns to the older and says something like, "Gee, this guy was really *obsessed*!" I've been waiting for years to find an actual little room like that. Never thought it'd happen.'

He pauses, looks into my eyes. 'I know what's disturbing you, Tess.'

'He strangled her in here. I've been living for weeks in the very place where she was killed. I'm having trouble getting my head around that.'

'Think you can handle it?'

'Not sure,' I tell him.

TWENTY-FIVE

It's March now, eight months since Clarence's arrest, four since he pled guilty to voluntary manslaughter and was sentenced to eleven years in Corcoran. In that time I've completed my play, *The Luzern Photograph.*

I'm still living in the Buckley. It took me a while to come to terms with the fact that Chantal was murdered in my loft. Dr Maude helped me deal with it. She says she's not one for paranormal interpretations, but thinks the sense I had that Chantal was guiding my hand as I wrote may have been based on some sort of vibe. I don't know whether she's right about that, but it's true I spent a good amount time trying to imagine what went on in the loft before I moved in. Also Chantal's hidden strongbox never felt right to me. It was as if she'd left it for me to find, examine the contents, puzzle over them, then put them together to tell her story.

I've changed things in the loft, had the cell door and St. Andrews Cross removed, and the whole place repainted. The landlady, Mrs Chen, has appointed a new building manager. Occasionally when he runs into me he mutters vague threats about raising my rent to market rate. Then we both smile, mutual acknowledgement I'm grandfathered in.

I've signed up at a new gym, Oakland Kickboxing, just off Jack London Square. My coach there, an ex-Marine named Deb Dawson, specializes in training female fighters. She's a lot more open than Kurt but no less rigorous. 'We'll figure out together how far you want to go with this,' she tells me, 'then I'll help get you there.'

Josh has moved to LA to be near his kids. There he continues to create paintings in the styles of famous modernist artists for restaurants and cafés. Sometimes when I'm alone in the elevator I miss the guy in the black watch cap and overalls with FUCK BAD ART stenciled on the back, wincing as the apparatus goes through its weird lighting changes.

Because of cutbacks at OPD, Scarpaci's workload is even heavier than before. And since I've been so immersed in writing, we've restricted our time together to three nights a week. I believe this has made us especially ardent lovers.

After we make love we rest, then talk, laugh, and share tales from our lives.

Tonight, in a mellow post-coital mood, I confide my anxiety.

'Remember,' I ask, 'how you used to worry that you wanted to solve Chantal's murder too much?'

'I was haunted. I tried not to let on, but it drove me crazy.'

I tell him that's the way I now feel about my play.

'It's like I'm in a high-stakes game, I've gone all in and now everything in my life is riding on the next turn. It could take months or even years to raise production money. Can I bring this project to life or will it end up as just an interesting script?'

Scarpaci tells me he's wary of my poker imagery. 'All in, high stakes – I hear desperation in your voice. You've been on a creative high. May be time to take a break.'

He suggests we take off for a week, fly to Hawaii. He knows a guy who rents basic beach huts near Kaanapali. We could unwind there, he says, laze around, grill fish, swim and snorkel. It sounds idyllic, but I tell him I'm afraid if I take time off I'll lose momentum.

'I need to fix the play, make it better. The characters have taken on fictional lives of their own. I've written scenes as I imagined they took place, made others up. I've reconceived it as drama, not the docudrama I set out to write. Now I wonder if it'll work.'

'I'm sure it will,' he tells me. He leans over to kiss me. 'Your friends believe in you and so do I. Now all you have to do is believe in yourself.'

Rex meets me for coffee at his favorite hangout, Tartine Bakery & Cafe on Guerrero. We grab a corner table, place our orders, then look at one another with very serious expressions until I break down and start to giggle.

'It's brilliant, Tess,' he says. 'And, yeah, it needs work. Never read a play that didn't. It's complex and ambitious and it'll cost a bundle to stage. All those rooms with different things happening at once, the banks of TV monitors, the audience wandering through, you leading them, then disappearing, then reappearing in another scene on another floor. You've done what you set out to do, written an immersive theater piece.'

'What'll it cost?'

'My guess – three hundred thou. With sets, costumes, cast, it could easily come to more. And that's just to open. To break even with payroll and rental you'd have to gross seventy-five a week. The show would have to run two to three years before investors got their money back.' He pauses, takes a breath. 'Not saying you can't do that. You could go on Kickstarter and try to raise money there. Or try and line up a production partner, maybe a single wealthy investor like Grace Wei. I could go on.'

'Please,' I urge, trying not to sink into a funk.

'You know all this and you know the odds. Say you find a deserted warehouse and spend six months transforming it into something resembling the labyrinth in your script. Then you'd have all the worries that come with managing a big production. 'Til now all your pieces have been one-woman. This is different. For this you'd need a staff.'

I peer at him. 'Got another idea?' He nods. 'I came here to hear what you think. Whatever it is . . . I can take it.'

Rex draws himself up. He looks at me closely, then lets loose.

'Forget the total-work-of-art concept. Think of *Luzern* another way. Cut back on production values. Give up your notion of immersive promenade theater. Instead go minimal. You and maybe five other actors. Simple wardrobe. A few key props. Brilliant lighting design. Fabulous sound plot supplemented by Luis and his cello. The original Luzern photograph and its reenactments projected onto a section of wall. I imagine a black box production, the audience seated on three sides. No sets, just a few tables, chairs, a platform or two.'

He pulls out a drawing to show me his plan.

'You won't have to rewrite much. Just take out all your production ideas and pare the script down to bare-bones scenes. If you're willing to go that route, we could start soon as we find space. It wouldn't cost much. I could cast it in a week. Rehearse it for four. If we luck into the right venue we could open in two months. If we do it well, as I know we can, word'll get around and people'll fly in to see it. From LA, Chicago, New York. Maybe someone'll approach you and say: "Hey, this is great, let's sex it up and go immersive." Then you can go back to your original idea or blow them off because you like it just fine the way we're doing it.'

My head is reeling. *Why didn't I think of this? Was I so taken by the fad for immersive theater I forgot the kind of theater I like best?*

'Think it'd work pared down?'

'It'd be stronger. I love what I think of as your *Citizen Kane* concept: the more you learn about Chantal the less you know. I also like that you start with the Luzern photograph then keep circling back to it. The three versions and the way they connect up suggests a three-act structure – the original 1882 picture, Hitler's drawing, and Chantal's reinterpretation. It's all about obsession. Your final scene pulls it all together. I love the way you step forward to address the audience, recounting the circuitous route by which a photograph taken over a hundred thirty years ago led to the murder of an Oakland dominatrix. The first time I read it I thought you'd structured it as a circle, but after rereading I see it more like a variation on a Möbius strip, a story that twists several times as it circles back upon itself. I think a big production would detract. I think we should put our energy and commitment into creating a series of short powerful scenes that will accumulate and become an avalanche. You know my work, Tess, and I know yours. At heart we're minimalists. Let's do what we do best . . .'

I nod as he talks on, all the while rethinking my play.

'. . . for Chantal's studio all we need is the cross, cell, and chariot. But no walls, no alcove. Build a four-sided cage and erect a free-standing cross.'

'Yeah! And for the Lou/Young Man scenes, just a café table and a couple bentwood chairs set up in a pool of light.'

'Lots of shadows. The actors walk from one light pool to another.'

'Sharply honed blackout sketches. Lights snap on, the characters walk into a lit area from opposite sides, perform the scene, then blackout. They walk away, a pause . . . then—'

'—the lights bathe another area. Actors emerge again. No wardrobe changes.'

'Maybe a few for the women.'

'OK. Then . . .'

In an hour, excited, we've talked it through.

'I'm sold,' I tell him. 'We're going minimalist.'

Dr Maude likes my script.

'You pulled it together and best of all made it your own. You're more relaxed today. Last week I was worried. You seemed edgy.'

I tell her I was until I talked things through with Rex.

'I was trying too hard to go big. He convinced me there's more power in stripping it down to the core story.'

'What I like best about your script,' she says at end of session, 'is the way you worked your material through. Successful psychotherapy is story-telling. We take a lot of mixed-up material – feelings, dreams, events from the past – then weave it all together into a coherent story the patient can live with. You've been through some rough patches. This latest adventure of yours – I know at times it's been tough. Now you've structured it into a play.' Her eyes glow as she meets mine. 'I find that very admirable!'

It's been six weeks since we leased our venue: the same San Francisco warehouse where Scarpaci took me for Pretty Boys' Beat-Down Night. The fight club's been closed. Scarpaci, who knows the landlord, helped us negotiate our lease.

We're deep into rehearsals now, working twelve-hour days. I've never seen Rex work so hard. We quarrel about script changes, and, occasionally, I give in. So far we've had only two screaming fights. I imagine we'll have a few more before we open.

This afternoon we break early from rehearsal to prepare for the arrival of Antonio DaCosta, the famous transgendered fetish photographer known for his images of rock and movie stars in bondage. Rex describes DaCosta's vision: 'Helmut Newton meets Annie Leibovitz.' Since his pictures have graced

the covers of *Rolling Stone* and *Vanity Fair*, it's a coup for
Rex to have lured him to San Francisco.

Emerging from my dressing room, wearing my red Weimar/
Vertigo dress, hair down so it flows around my shoulders, I
find everyone in our troupe assembled on our stage: cast,
stagehands, electricians, even our accountant and volunteer
ticket takers. Two of DaCosta's drop-dead gorgeous female
assistants are setting up lights, illuminating my chariot, while
a third is fitting out two hunky young men, naked but for
loincloths, with gold papier-mâché comedy and tragedy masks,
the smile and the grimace, symbols of theater.

Rex brings DaCosta over to meet me. I'm surprised by his
appearance. I expected a gaunt haunted artist type, not the
courtly guy with flowing white hair who bends to kiss my
hand.

'A pleasure, señora,' he says. He speaks with a charming
Spanish accent. 'I have come a long way to take your picture.'

Before I can thank him he tells me he's read *The Luzern
Photograph*, liked it very much and conversed about it at
length with Rex.

'It's kinky and *I* am kinky,' he says. 'I think we make a
good match.'

I glance at Rex, who nods to assure me DaCosta's not being
ironic. I don't know much about him, only that he's famously
mysterious about his private life and has a hissy fit if anyone
tries to take *his* picture. There're rumors he's asexual and lives
with his mother in a villa outside Marrakech where he hosts
sex parties attended by the rich and famous. The one thing
everyone agrees on is that he has an uncanny ability to convince
well-known people to strip off their clothes then allow themselves to be tied up, often into awkward stress positions. His
pictures are instantly recognizable on account of the pained
expressions on his subjects' faces. He's been quoted as saying:
'I like to apply duress. My aim is always to photograph struggle.'

'My conception for you is simple,' DaCosta tells me. 'We will
put you in the chariot, harness up the boys,' he gestures toward
the masked young men, 'put some wind in your hair,' he gestures
toward a pair of enormous fans, 'then let you loose upon the
world.' He smiles. 'I have brought you a beautiful whip.'

He snaps his fingers, says something in Spanish. One of the assistants hurries over with a tan cloth bag. DaCosta opens it and withdraws a long black single-tail leather whip that bears a strong resemblance to the one Chantal named 'Blackspur.'

'For you, señora, to use on the boys as you see fit.' I stare at him, appalled. 'I jest. The threat is always more powerful than the punishment. You agree?'

'Oh, I do. Certainly,' I tell him.

He smiles coyly. 'Just allow the lash to hang loose, much as Frau Salomé does in the famous Luzern picture.'

When he excuses himself to see to the lighting, Rex nudges me.

'What'd you think?'

'I like the idea of the dramatist transported by the theater muses. But I don't get it about the muscle boys. The muses were goddesses. Thalia for comedy, Melpomene for tragedy.'

'I know, but he's into boys and he wants it kinky. Also boys'll make it more like the Luzern picture.'

The boys are pretty and they sport lovely abs. I suppose I should be grateful DaCosta doesn't want to tie me up. And I realize that his photo will not only make a great publicity shot, but will also look terrific on the home page of my website.

DaCosta announces he's ready. I step into Chantal's chariot. One of the assistants harnesses up the guys while another hands me the reins and whip. The third assistant turns on a big electric fan. Suddenly I feel my hair blown from behind.

'This picture will be a metaphor,' DaCosta tells me, assuming a director's tone. 'You're standing straight and confident in the chariot, face forward, eyes clear. You're riding to the theater across the plains of ancient Greece. Your muses are taking you there. Along the road you come upon an itinerant photographer. Anachronism, yes, but never mind. At heart I'm a surrealist. Adoring this vision that has come out of nowhere, I step forward to beg you to stop and pose.' DaCosta takes a step then assumes a mock-supplicant's stance. 'Theater Goddess, kindly pull at your reins to halt your charging chariot.' His tone changes back to that of director. 'Now turn. Look at me. Muses too. I want all eyes on my lens.'

I turn as he instructs. The whole company, assembled behind DaCosta, is gazing at me, eager to see my expression.

I look out at them and nod. I know how to do this.

You belong in this chariot. It's a warrior's chariot and you're a warrior-actress. Theater can be a cruel art. You've fought hard at it and sometimes prevailed. You take chaos, form it, put pieces together, tell stories. The theater muses guide you but in the end it's you who have control. Show them that! Show them your power! Show them your triumph!

DaCosta raises his camera and starts to shoot. *Click!Click!Click!Click . . .!*

You're neither Lou Andreas-Salomé nor Chantal Desforges. You're Tess Berenson, you've written a play and soon you'll perform it. Show them that!

An assistant hands DaCosta another camera. This one makes a different sound:

Whap!Whap!Whap!Whap . . .!

You're an actor, player, performer. You're a beguiler, deceiver, diseuse. You're a monologuist, dramatist, storyteller. Show them! Show them that!

DaCosta moves forward and backward as he takes shot after shot. *Click!Click!Click!Click! Whap!Whap! Whap!Whap! Whoosh!Whoosh!Whoosh!Whoosh!*

He circles me, but no matter where he goes I lock my eyes to his lens.

Show them . . . show them . . . show them who you are!

His assistants hand him different cameras. He works the scene, works it some more. Finally, after what seems an eternity, he stops, hands off his cameras, peers at me, beams.

'Got it! *Gracias!*' He turns to his assistants. 'Cut!' The fans stop turning. The lights go off. The shoot is finished.

I blink, smile, hand off the whip, step out of the chariot. The boy muses and crew crowd around to congratulate me.

Rex takes me in his arms. '*That*,' he whispers in my ear, 'was a performance!'

'Yes, it was,' I whisper back. 'And now *my* Luzern photograph has been taken.'

AUTHOR'S AFTERWORD

Ever since, decades ago, I learned about the extraordinary life of Lou Andreas-Salomé, I wanted to find a way to put her into a novel. It was only after I focused on the Luzern photograph of 1882 that I discovered my point of departure.

For those interested in learning more about this fascinating woman, I recommend the three major English language biographies, *My Sister, My Spouse* by H. F. Peters, *Salomé* by Angela Livingstone, and *Frau Lou* by Rudolph Binion.

For interesting takes on the Luzern photograph, I would also mention the essays 'Reading Lou von Salomé's Triangles' by Babette Babich, 'Nietzsche and Lou Salomé: a Biographical Reading of the Coincidences of Life and Work in 1882' by William Beatty Warner, and the books *Nietzsche's Women: Beyond the Whip* by Carol Diethe and *Nietzsche and Rée* by Robin Small.

As research I delved deeply into Lou's own writings. For this novel I have especially drawn on *The Freud Journal of Lou Andreas-Salomé*, *Sigmund Freud and Lou Andreas-Salomé Letters*, as well as Lou's books *Nietzsche* and *Looking Back, Memoirs*.

I want to thank the following friends for guidance, research ideas and comments on early drafts: Elatia Harris, Gabriele Hoff, M. Violet Leonard, and Eugenia Martino; my very supportive agent, George Lucas; and my wife, Paula Wolfert, without whose belief and support I would not have been able to see this project through.

WB